Praise for Harlan Coben

'It is always satisfying to discover a new crime writer – and this is the business . . . this book will keep you up until 2 a.m.' *The Times*

'Harlan Coben. He's smart, he's funny, and he has something to say' Michael Connelly

'An increasingly frightening conspiracy with an unguessable ending . . . hard to put down' *Sunday Telegraph*

'At last a British publisher has given British readers the chance to discover something every US mystery fan already knows – that Harlan Coben is one of the most entertaining and intriguing crime writers around'
Val McDermid, *Manchester Evening Guardian*

'What sets Harlan Coben above the crowd are wit and . . . an entertaining plot' *Los Angeles Times Book Review*

'Fast action, snappy dialogue and plenty of insider hoops material make this a fast, enjoyable read' *Toronto Star*

'Coben . . . scores a hole in one! The characters are deftly etched and the details keenly observed'
Publishers Weekly

'Coben is still one of America's masters of the hook, the twist and the surprise ending' *Literary Review*

By Harlan Coben

Play Dead
Deal Breaker
Drop Shot
Fade Away
Back Spin
One False Move
The Final Detail
Darkest Fear
Tell No One
Gone for Good
No Second Chance
Just One Look
The Innocent
Promise Me
The Woods
Hold Tight
Long Lost
Caught
Live Wire
Shelter
Stay Close
Seconds Away
Six Years
Found
The Stranger

Back Spin

HARLAN COBEN

An Orion paperback

First published in Great Britain in 2002
by Orion Books
This paperback edition published in 2002
by Orion Books Ltd,
Orion House, 5 Upper St Martin's Lane,
London WC2H 9EA

An Hachette UK company

Reissued 2011

Published by arrangement with Dell Publishing,
an imprint of The Bantam Dell Publishing Group,
a division of Random House, Inc.

A CIP catalogue record for this book
is available from the British Library.

Printed and bound by Clays Ltd, Elcograf S.p.A.

The Orion Publishing Group's policy is to use papers
that are natural, renewable and recyclable products and
made from wood grown in sustainable forests. The logging
and manufacturing processes are expected to conform to
the environmental regulations of the country of origin.

www.orionbooks.co.uk

Acknowledgements

When an author is writing about an activity he enjoys about as much as sticking his tongue in a fan (golf), he needs help and lots of it. With that in mind the author wishes to thank the following: James Bradbeer, Jr, Peter Roisman, Maggie Griffin, Craig Coben, Larry Coben, Jacob Hoye, Lisa Erbach Vance, Frank Snyder, the rec.sports.golf board, Knitwit, Sparkle Hayter, Anita Meyer, the many golfers who regaled me with their scintillating tales (snore), and of course, Dave Bolt. While the US Open is a real golf tournament and Merion is a real golf club, this book is a work of fiction. I took some liberties, combined locales and tournaments, that kind of thing. As always, any errors – factual or otherwise – are totally the fault of these people. The author is not to blame.

Myron and I tried. But we're still not sure we get it.

For the Armstrongs,
The World's Greatest In-Laws,
Jack and Nancy
Molly, Jane, Eliza, Sara, John and Kate
Thank you all for Anne

Chapter 1

Myron Bolitar used a cardboard periscope to look over the suffocating throngs of ridiculously clad spectators. He tried to recall the last time he'd actually used a toy periscope, and an image of sending in proof-of-purchase seals from a box of Cap'n Crunch cereal flickered in front him like headache-inducing sunspots.

Through the mirrored reflection, Myron watched a man dressed in knickers – knickers, for crying out loud – stand over a tiny white sphere. The ridiculously clad spectators mumbled excitedly. Myron stifled a yawn. The knickered man crouched. The ridiculously clad spectators jostled and then settled into an eerie silence. Sheer stillness followed, as if even the trees and shrubs and well-coiffed blades of grass were holding their collective breath.

Then the knickered man whacked the white sphere with a stick.

The crowd began to murmur in the indistinguishable

syllables of backstage banter. As the ball ascended, so did the volume of the murmurs. Words could be made out. Then phrases. 'Lovely golf stroke.' 'Super golf shot.' 'Beautiful golf shot.' 'Truly fine golf stroke.' They always said *golf* stroke, like someone might mistake it for a *swim* stroke, or – as Myron was currently contemplating in this blazing heat – a *sun*stroke.

'Mr Bolitar?'

Myron took the periscope away from his eyes. He was tempted to yell 'Up periscope,' but feared some at stately, snooty Merion Golf Club would view the act as immature. Especially during the US Open. He looked down at a ruddy-faced man of about seventy.

'Your pants,' Myron said.

'Pardon me?'

'You're afraid of getting hit by a golf cart, right?'

They were orange and yellow in a hue slightly more luminous than a bursting supernova. To be fair, the man's clothing hardly stood out. Most in the crowd seemed to have woken up wondering what apparel they possessed that would clash with, say, the free world. Orange and green tints found exclusively in several of your tackiest neon signs adorned many. Yellow and some strange shades of purple were also quite big – usually together – like a color scheme rejected by a Midwest high school cheerleading squad. It was as if being surrounded by all this God-given natural beauty made one want to do all in his power to offset it. Or maybe there was something else at work here. Maybe the ugly clothes had a more functional origin. Maybe in the old days, when animals roamed free, golfers dressed this way to ward off dangerous wildlife.

Good theory.

'I need to speak with you,' the elderly man whispered. 'It's urgent.'

The rounded, jovial cheeks belied his pleading eyes. He suddenly gripped Myron's forearm. 'Please,' he added.

'What's this about?' Myron asked.

The man made a movement with his neck, like his collar was on too tight. 'You're a sports agent, right?'

'Yes.'

'You're here to find clients?'

Myron narrowed his eyes. 'How do you know I'm not here to witness the enthralling spectacle of grown men taking a walk?'

The old man did not smile, but then again, golfers were not known for their sense of humor. He craned his neck again and moved closer. His whisper was hoarse. 'Do you know the name Jack Coldren?' he asked.

'Sure,' Myron said.

If the old man had asked the same question yesterday, Myron wouldn't have had a clue. He didn't follow golf that closely (or at all), and Jack Coldren had been little more than a journeyman over the past twenty years or so. But Coldren had been the surprise leader after the US Open's first day, and now, with just a few holes remaining in the second round, Coldren was up by a commanding eight strokes. 'What about him?'

'And Linda Coldren?' the man asked. 'Do you know who she is?'

This one was easier. Linda Coldren was Jack's wife and far and away the top female golfer of the past decade. 'Yeah, I know who she is,' Myron said.

The man leaned in closer and did the neck thing again. Seriously annoying – not to mention contagious. Myron found himself fighting off the desire to mimic the

3

movement. 'They're in deep trouble,' the old man whispered. 'If you help them, you'll have two new clients.'

'What sort of trouble?'

The old man looked around. 'Please,' he said. 'There are too many people. Come with me.'

Myron shrugged. No reason not to go. The old man was the only lead he'd unearthed since his friend and business associate Windsor Horne Lockwood III – Win, for short – had dragged his sorry butt down here. Being that the US Open was at Merion – home course of the Lockwood family for something like a billion years – Win had felt it would be a great opportunity for Myron to land a few choice clients. Myron wasn't quite so sure. As near as he could tell, the major component separating him from the hordes of other locust-like agents swarming the green meadows of Merion Golf Club was his naked aversion for golf. Probably not a key selling point to the faithful.

Myron Bolitar ran MB SportsReps, a sports representation firm located on Park Avenue in New York City. He rented the space from his former college roommate, Win, a Waspy, old-money, big-time investment banker whose family owned Lock-Horne Securities on the same Park Avenue in New York. Myron handled the negotiations while Win, one of the country's most respected brokers, handled the investments and finances. The other member of the MB team, Esperanza Diaz, handled everything else. Three branches with checks and balances. Just like the American government. Very patriotic.

Slogan: *MB SportsReps – the other guys are commie pinkos*.

As the old man ushered Myron through the crowd,

several men in green blazers – another look sported mostly at golf courses, perhaps to camouflage oneself against the grass – greeted him with whispered, 'How do, Bucky,' or 'Looking good, Buckster,' or 'Fine day for golf, Buckaroo.' They all had the accent of the rich and preppy, the kind of inflection where *mommy* is pronounced 'mummy' and summer and winter are verbs. Myron was about to comment on a grown man being called Bucky, but when your name is Myron, well, glass houses and stones and all that.

Like every other sporting event in the free world, the actual playing area looked more like a giant billboard than a field of competition. The leader board was sponsored by IBM. Canon handed out the periscopes. American Airlines employees worked the food stands (an airline handling food – what think tank came up with that one?). Corporate Row was jam-packed with companies who shelled out over one hundred grand a pop to set up a tent for a few days, mostly so that company executives had an excuse to go. Travelers Group, Mass Mutual, Aetna (golfers must like insurance), Canon, Heublein. Heublein. What the hell was a Heublein? They looked like a nice company. Myron would probably buy a Heublein if he knew what one was.

The funny thing was, the US Open was actually less commercialized than most tourneys. At least they hadn't sold their name yet. Other tournaments were named for sponsors and the names had gotten a little silly. Who could get up for winning the JC Penney Open or the Michelob Open or even the Wendy's Three-Tour Challenge?

The old man led him to a primo parking lot. Mercedeses, Caddies, limos. Myron spotted Win's Jaguar.

The USGA had recently put up a sign that read MEMBERS PARKING ONLY.

Myron said, 'You're a member of Merion.' Dr Deduction.

The old man twisted the neck thing into something approaching a nod. 'My family dates back to Merion's inception,' he said, the snooty accent now more pronounced. 'Just like your friend Win.'

Myron stopped and looked at the man. 'You know Win?'

The old man sort of smiled and shrugged. No commitment.

'You haven't told me your name yet,' Myron said.

'Stone Buckwell,' he said, hand extended. 'Everyone calls me Bucky.'

Myron shook the hand.

'I'm also Linda Coldren's father,' he added.

Bucky unlocked a sky-blue Cadillac and they slid inside. He put the key in the ignition. The radio played Muzak – worse, the Muzak version of 'Raindrops Keep Falling on My Head.' Myron quickly opened the window for air, not to mention noise.

Only members were allowed to park on the Merion grounds, so it wasn't too much of a hassle getting out. They made a right at the end of the driveway and then another right. Bucky mercifully flipped off the radio. Myron stuck his head back in the car.

'What do you know about my daughter and her husband?' Bucky asked.

'Not much.'

'You are not a golf fan, are you, Mr Bolitar?'

'Not really.'

'Golf is truly a magnificent sport,' he said. Then he

6

added, 'Though the word *sport* does not begin to do it justice.'

'Uh-huh,' Myron said.

'It's the game of princes.' Buckwell's ruddy face glowed a bit now, the eyes wide with the same type of rapture one saw in the very religious. His voice was low and awed. 'There is nothing quite like it, you know. You alone against the course. No excuses. No teammate. No bad calls. It's the purest of activities.'

'Uh-huh,' Myron said again. 'Look, I don't want to appear rude, Mr Buckwell, but what's this all about?'

'Please call me Bucky.'

'Okay. Bucky.'

He nodded his approval. 'I understand that you and Windsor Lockwood are more than business associates,' he said.

'Meaning?'

'I understand you two go back a long way. College roommates, am I correct?'

'Why do you keep asking about Win?'

'I actually came to the club to find him,' Bucky said. 'But I think it's better this way.'

'What way?'

'Talking to you first. Maybe after . . . well, we'll see. Shouldn't hope for too much.'

Myron nodded. 'I have no idea what you're talking about.'

Bucky turned onto a road adjacent to the course called Golf House Road. Golfers were so creative.

The course was on the right, imposing mansions on the left. A minute later, Bucky pulled into a circular driveway. The house was fairly big and made of something called river rock. River rock was big in this area, though

Win always referred to it as 'Mainline Stone.' There was a white fence and lots of tulips and two maple trees, one on each side of the front walk. A large porch was enclosed on the right side. The car came to a stop, and for a moment neither of them moved.

'What's this all about, Mr Buckwell?'

'We have a situation here,' he said.

'What kind of situation?'

'I'd rather let my daughter explain it to you.' He grabbed the key out of the ignition and reached for the door.

'Why come to me?' Myron asked.

'We were told you could possibly help.'

'Who told you that?'

Buckwell started rolling his neck with greater fervor. His head looked like it'd been attached by a loose ball socket. When he finally got it under control, he managed to look Myron in the eyes.

'Win's mother,' he said.

Myron stiffened. His heart plummeted down a dark shaft. He opened his mouth, closed it, waited. Buckwell got out of the car and headed for the door. Ten seconds later, Myron followed.

'Win won't help,' Myron said.

Buckwell nodded. 'That's why I came to you first.'

They followed a brick path to a door slightly ajar. Buckwell pushed it open. 'Linda?'

Linda Coldren stood before a television in the den. Her white shorts and sleeveless yellow blouse revealed the lithe, toned limbs of an athlete. She was tall with short spunky black hair and a tan that accentuated the smooth, long muscles. The lines around her eyes and mouth placed her in her late thirties, and he could see instantly why she

8

was a commercial darling. There was a fierce splendor to this woman, a beauty derived from a sense of strength rather than delicacy.

She was watching the tournament on the television. On top of the set were framed family photographs. Big, pillowy couches formed a V in one corner. Tactfully furnished, for a golfer. No putting green, AstroTurf carpet. None of that golf artwork that seemed a step or two below the aesthetic class of, say, paintings of dogs playing poker. No cap with a tee and ball on the brim hanging from a moose head.

Linda Coldren suddenly swung her line of vision toward them, firing a glare past Myron before settling on her father. 'I thought you were going to get Jack,' she snapped.

'He hasn't finished the round yet.'

She motioned to the television. 'He's on eighteen now. I thought you were going to wait for him.'

'I got Mr Bolitar instead.'

'Who?'

Myron stepped forward and smiled. 'I'm Myron Bolitar.'

Linda Coldren flicked her eyes at him, then back to her father. 'Who the hell is he?'

'He's the man Cissy told me about,' Buckwell said.

'Who's Cissy?' Myron asked.

'Win's mother.'

'Oh,' Myron said. 'Right.'

Linda Coldren said, 'I don't want him here. Get rid of him.'

'Linda, listen to me. We need help.'

'Not from him.'

'He and Win have experience with this type of thing.'

9

'Win,' she said slowly, 'is psychotic.'

'Ah,' Myron said. 'Then you know him well?'

Linda Coldren finally turned her attention to Myron. Her eyes, deep and brown, met his. 'I haven't spoken to Win since he was eight years old,' she said. 'But you don't have to leap into a pit of flames to know it's hot.'

Myron nodded. 'Nice analogy.'

She shook her head and looked back at her father. 'I told you before: no police. We do what they say.'

'But he's not police,' her father said.

'And you shouldn't be telling anyone.'

'I only told my sister,' Bucky protested. 'She'd never say anything.'

Myron felt his body stiffen again. 'Wait a second,' he said to Bucky. 'Your sister is Win's mother?'

'Yes.'

'You're Win's uncle.' He looked at Linda Coldren. 'And you're Win's first cousin.'

Linda Coldren looked at him like he'd just peed on the floor. 'With smarts like that,' she said, 'I'm glad you're on our side.'

Everyone's a wiseass.

'If it's still unclear, Mr Bolitar, I could break out some poster board and sketch a family tree for you.'

'Could you use lots of pretty colors?' Myron said. 'I like pretty colors.'

She made a face and turned away. On the television, Jack Coldren lined up a twelve-foot putt. Linda stopped and watched. He tapped it; the ball took off and arched right into the hole. The gallery applauded with modest enthusiasm. Jack picked up the ball with two fingers and then tipped his hat. The IBM leader board flashed on the screen. Jack Coldren was up by a whopping nine strokes.

Linda Coldren shook her head. 'Poor bastard.'

Myron kept still. So did Bucky.

'He's waited twenty-three years for this moment,' she continued. 'And he picks now.'

Myron glanced at Bucky. Bucky glanced back, shaking his head.

Linda Coldren stared at the television until her husband exited to the clubhouse. Then she took a deep breath and looked at Myron. 'You see, Mr Bolitar, Jack has never won a professional tournament. The closest he ever came was in his rookie year twenty-three years ago, when he was only nineteen. It was the last time the US Open was held at Merion. You may remember the headlines.'

They were not altogether unfamiliar. This morning's papers had rehashed it a bit. 'He lost a lead, right?'

Linda Coldren made a scoffing sound. 'That's a bit of an understatement, but yes. Since then, his career has been completely unspectacular. There were years he didn't even make the tour.'

'He picked a hell of a time to snap his streak,' Myron said. 'The US Open.'

She gave him a funny look and folded her arms under her chest. 'Your name rings a bell,' she said. 'You used to play basketball, right?'

'Right.'

'In the ACC. North Carolina?'

'Duke,' he corrected.

'Right, Duke. I remember now. You blew out your knee after the draft.'

Myron nodded slowly.

'That was the end of your career, right?'

Myron nodded again.

'It must have been tough,' she said.

Myron said nothing.

She made a waving motion with her hand. 'What happened to you is nothing compared to what happened to Jack.'

'Why do you say that?'

'You had an injury. It may have been tough, but at least you weren't at fault. Jack had a six-stroke lead at the US Open with only eight holes left. Do you know what that's like? That's like having a ten-point lead with a minute left in the seventh game of the NBA finals. It's like missing a wide-open slam dunk in the final seconds to lose the championship. Jack was never the same man after that. He never recovered. He has spent his whole life since, just waiting for the chance of redemption.' She turned back to the television. The leader board was back up. Jack Coldren was still up by nine strokes.

'If he loses again . . .'

She did not bother finishing the thought. They all stood in silence. Linda staring at the television. Bucky craning his neck, his eyes moist, his face quivering near tears.

'So what's wrong, Linda?' Myron asked.

'Our son,' she said. 'Somebody has kidnapped our son.'

Chapter 2

'I shouldn't be telling you this,' Linda Coldren said. 'He said he'd kill him.'

'Who said?'

Linda Coldren took several deep breaths, like a child atop the high board. Myron waited. It took some time, but she finally took the plunge.

'I got a call this morning,' she said. Her large brown eyes were wide and everywhere now, settling down on no one spot for more than a second. 'A man said he had my son. He said if I called the police, he would kill him.'

'Did he say anything else?'

'Just that he'd call back with instructions.'

'That's it?'

She nodded.

'What time was this?' Myron asked.

'Nine, nine-thirty.'

Myron walked over to the television and picked up one

of the framed photographs. 'Is this a recent photograph of your son?'

'Yes.'

'How old is he?'

'Sixteen. His name is Chad.'

Myron studied the photograph. The smiling adolescent had the fleshy features of his father. He wore a baseball cap with the brim curled the way kids like to nowadays. A golf club rested proudly on his shoulder like a minuteman with a bayonet. His eyes were squinted as though he were looking into the sun. Myron looked over Chad's face, as if it might give him a clue or some rare insight. It didn't.

'When did you first notice that your son was missing?'

Linda Coldren gave her father a quick glance, then straightened up, holding her head high as if she were readying himself for a blow. Her words came slow. 'Chad had been gone for two days.'

'Gone?' Myron Bolitar, Grand Inquisitor.

'Yes.'

'When you say gone—'

'I mean just that,' she interrupted. 'I haven't seen him since Wednesday.'

'But the kidnapper just called today?'

'Yes.'

Myron started to speak, stopped himself, softened his voice. Tread gently, fair Myron. Ever gently. 'Did you have any idea where he was?'

'I assumed he was staying with his friend Matthew,' Linda Coldren replied.

Myron nodded, as if this statement showed brilliant insight. Then nodded again. 'Chad told you that?'

'No.'

'So,' he said, aiming for casual, 'for the past two days, you didn't know where your son was.'

'I just told you: I thought he was staying with Matthew.'

'You didn't call the police.'

'Of course not.'

Myron was about to ask another follow-up question, but her posture made him rethink his words. Linda took advantage of his indecisiveness. She walked to the kitchen with an upright, fluid grace. Myron followed. Bucky seemed to snap out of a trance and trailed.

'Let me make sure I'm following you,' Myron said, approaching from a different angle now. 'Chad vanished before the tournament?'

'Correct,' she said. 'The Open started Thursday.' Linda Coldren pulled the refrigerator handle. The door opened with a sucking pop. 'Why? Is that important?'

'It eliminates a motive,' Myron said.

'What motive?'

'Tampering with the tournament,' Myron said. 'If Chad had vanished today – with your husband holding such a big lead – I might think that someone was out to sabotage his chances of winning the Open. But two days ago, before the tournament had begun . . .'

'No one would have given Jack a snowball's chance in hell,' she finished for him. 'Oddsmakers would have put him at one in five thousand. At best.' She nodded as she spoke, seeing the logic. 'Would you like some lemonade?' she asked.

'No, thanks.'

'Dad?'

Bucky shook his head. Linda Coldren bent down into the refrigerator.

'Okay,' Myron said, clapping his hand together, trying his best to sound casual. 'We've ruled out one possibility. Let's try another.'

Linda Coldren stopped and watched him. A gallon glass pitcher was gripped in her hand, her forearm bunching easily with the weight. Myron debated how to approach this. There was no easy way.

'Could your son be behind this?' Myron asked.

'What?'

'It's an obvious question,' Myron said, 'under the circumstances.'

She put the pitcher down on a wooden center block.

'What the hell are you talking about? You think Chad faked his own kidnapping?'

'I didn't say that. I said I wanted to check out the possibility.'

'Get out.'

'He was gone two days, and you didn't call the police,' Myron said. 'One possible conclusion is that there was some sort of tension here. That Chad had run away before.'

'Or,' Linda Coldren countered, her hands tightening into fists, 'you could conclude that we trusted our son. That we gave him a level of freedom compatible with his level of maturity and responsibility.'

Myron looked over at Bucky. Bucky's head was lowered. 'If that's the case—'

'That's the case.'

'But don't responsible kids tell their parents where they're going? I mean, just to make sure they don't worry.'

Linda Coldren took out a glass with too much care. She set it on the counter and slowly poured herself some

16

lemonade. 'Chad has learned to be very independent,' she said as the glass filled. 'His father and I are both professional golfers. That means, quite frankly, that neither one of us is home very often.'

'Your being away so much,' Myron said. 'Has it led to tension?'

Linda Coldren shook her head. 'This is useless.'

'I'm just trying—'

'Look, Mr Bolitar, Chad did not fake this. Yes, he's a teenager. No, he's not perfect, and neither are his parents. But he did not fake his own kidnapping. And if he did – I know he didn't, but let's just pretend for the sake of argument that he did – then he is safe and we do not need you. If this is some kind of cruel deception, we'll learn it soon enough. But if my son is in danger, then following this line of thought is a waste of time I can ill afford.'

Myron nodded. She had a point. 'I understand,' he said.

'Good.'

'Have you called his friend since you heard from the kidnapper? The one you thought he might've been staying with?'

'Matthew Squires, yes.'

'Did Matthew have any idea where he was?'

'None.'

'They're close friends, right?'

'Yes.'

'Very close?'

She frowned. 'Yes, very.'

'Does Matthew call here a lot?'

'Yes. Or they talk by E-mail.'

'I'll need Matthew's phone number,' Myron said.

'But I just told you I spoke to him already.'

'Humor me,' Myron said. 'Okay, now let's back up a second. When was the last time you saw Chad?'

'The day he disappeared.'

'What happened?'

She frowned again. 'What do you mean, what happened? He left for summer school. I haven't seen him since.'

Myron studied her. She stopped and looked back at him a little too steadily. Something here was not adding up. 'Have you called the school,' he asked, 'to see if he was there that day?'

'I didn't think of it.'

Myron checked his watch. Friday. Five P.M. 'I doubt anyone will still be there, but give it a shot. Do you have more than one phone line?'

'Yes.'

'Don't call on the line the kidnapper called in on. I don't want the line tied up in case he calls back.'

She nodded. 'Okay.'

'Does your son have any credit cards or ATM cards or anything like that?'

'Yes.'

'I'll need a list. And the numbers, if you have them.'

She nodded again.

Myron said, 'I'm going to call a friend, see if I can get an override Caller ID put in on this line. For when he calls back. I assume Chad has a computer?'

'Yes,' she said.

'Where is it?'

'Up in his room.'

'I'm going to download everything on it to my office via his modem. I have an assistant named Esperanza. She'll comb through it and see what she can find.'

'Like what?'

'Frankly I have no idea. E-mails. Correspondence. Bulletin boards he participates in. Anything that might give us a clue. It's not a very scientific process. You check out enough stuff and maybe something will click.'

Linda thought about it for a moment. 'Okay,' she said.

'How about you, Mrs Coldren? Do you have any enemies?'

She sort of smiled. 'I'm the number one-rated woman golfer in the world,' she said. 'That gives me a lot of enemies.'

'Anyone you can imagine doing this?'

'No,' she said. 'No one.'

'How about your husband? Anybody who hates your husband enough?'

'Jack?' She forced out a chuckle. 'Everyone loves Jack.'

'What's that supposed to mean?'

She just shook her head and waved him off.

Myron asked a few more questions, but there was little left for him to excavate. He asked if he could go up to Chad's room and she led him up the stairs.

The first thing Myron saw when he opened Chad's door were the trophies. Lots of them. All golf trophies. The bronze figure on the top was always a man coiled in postswing position, the golf club over his shoulder, his head held high. Sometimes the little man wore a golf cap. Other times he had short, wavy hair like Paul Hornung in old football reels. There were two leather golf bags in the right corner, both jammed past capacity with clubs. Photographs of Jack Nicklaus, Arnold Palmer, Sam Snead, Tom Watson blanketed the walls. Issues of *Golf Digest* littered the floor.

'Does Chad play golf?' Myron asked.

Linda Coldren just looked at him. Myron met her gaze and nodded sagely.

'My powers of deduction,' he said. 'They intimidate some people.'

She almost smiled. Myron the Alleviator, Master Tension-Easer. 'I'll try to still treat you the same,' she said.

Myron stepped toward the trophies. 'Is he any good?'

'Very good.' She turned away suddenly and stood with her back to the room. 'Do you need anything else?'

'Not right now.'

'I'll be downstairs.'

She didn't wait for his blessing.

Myron walked in. He checked the answering machine on Chad's phone. Three messages. Two from a girl named Becky. From the sound of it, she was a pretty good friend. Just calling to say, like, hi, see if he wanted to, like, do anything this weekend, you know? She and Millie and Suze were going to, like, hang out at the Heritage, okay, and if he wanted to come, well, you know, whatever. Myron smiled. Times they might be a-changin', but her words could have come from a girl Myron had gone to high school with or his father or his father's father. Generations cycle in. The music, the movies, the language, the fashion – they change. But that's just outside stimuli. Beneath the baggy pants or the message-cropped hair, the same adolescent fears and needs and feelings of inadequacy remained frighteningly constant.

The last call was from a guy named Glen. He wanted to know if Chad wanted to play golf at 'the Pine' this weekend, being that Merion was off-limits because of the

Open. 'Daddy,' Glen's preppy taped voice assured Chad, 'can get us a tee time, no prob.'

No messages from Chad's close buddy Matthew Squires.

He snapped on the computer. Windows 95. Cool. Myron used it too. Chad Coldren, Myron immediately saw, used America Online to get his E-mail. Perfect. Myron hit FLASHSESSION. The modem hooked on and screeched for a few seconds. A voice said, 'Welcome. You have mail.' Dozens of messages were automatically downloaded. The same voice said, 'Good-bye.' Myron checked Chad's E-mail address book and found Matthew Squires's E-mail address. He skimmed the downloaded messages. None were from Matthew.

Interesting.

It was, of course, entirely possible that Matthew and Chad were not as close as Linda Coldren thought. It was also entirely possible that even if they were, Matthew had not contacted his friend since Wednesday – even though his friend had supposedly vanished without warning. It happens.

Still, it was interesting.

Myron picked up Chad's phone and hit the redial button. Four rings later a taped voice came on. 'You've reached Matthew. Leave a message or don't. Up to you.'

Myron hung up without leaving a message (it was, after all, 'up to him'). Hmm. Chad's last call was to Matthew. That could be significant. Or it could have nothing to do with anything. Either way, Myron was quickly getting nowhere.

He picked up Chad's phone and dialed his office. Esperanza answered on the second ring.

'MB SportsReps.'

'It's me.' He filled her in. She listened without interrupting.

Esperanza Diaz had worked for MB SportReps since its inception. Ten years ago, when Esperanza was only eighteen years old, she was the Queen of Sunday Morning Cable TV. No, she wasn't on any infomercial, though her show ran opposite plenty of them, especially that one with the abdominal exerciser that bore a striking resemblance to a medieval instrument of torture; rather, Esperanza had been a professional wrestler named Little Pocahontas, the Sensual Indian Princess. With her petite, lithe figure bedecked in only a suede bikini, Esperanza had been voted FLOW'S (Fabulous Ladies Of Wrestling) most popular wrestler three years running – or, as the award was officially known, the Babe You'd Most Like to Get in a Full Nelson. Despite this, Esperanza remained humble.

When he finished telling her about the kidnapping, Esperanza's first words were an incredulous, 'Win has a mother?'

'Yep.'

Pause. 'There goes my spawned-from-a-satanic-egg theory.'

'Ha-ha.'

'Or my hatched-in-an-experiment-gone-very-wrong theory.'

'You're not helping.'

'What's to help?' Esperanza replied. 'I like Win, you know that. But the boy is – what's the official psychiatric term again? – cuckoo.'

'That cuckoo saved your life once,' Myron said.

'Yeah, but you remember how,' she countered.

Myron did. A dark alley. Win's doctored bullets. Brain

matter tossed about like parade confetti. Classic Win. Effective but excessive. Like squashing a bug with a wrecking ball.

Esperanza broke the long silence. 'Like I said before,' she began softly, 'cuckoo.'

Myron wanted to change the subject. 'Any messages?'

'About a million. Nothing that can't wait, though.' Then she asked, 'Have you ever met her?'

'Who?'

'Madonna,' she snapped. 'Who do you think? Win's mother.'

'Once,' Myron said, remembering. More than ten years ago. He and Win had been having dinner at Merion, in fact. Win hadn't spoken to her on that occasion. But she had spoken to him. The memory made Myron cringe anew.

'Have you told Win about this yet?' she asked.

'Nope. Any advice?'

Esperanza thought a moment. 'Do it over the phone,' she said. 'At a very safe distance.'

Chapter 3

They got a quick break.

Myron was still sitting in the Coldrens' den with Linda when Esperanza called back. Bucky had gone back to Merion to get Jack.

'The kid's ATM card was accessed yesterday at 6:18 P.M.,' Esperanza said. 'He took out $180. A First Philadelphia branch on Porter Street in South Philly.'

'Thanks.'

Information like that was not difficult to obtain. Anybody with an account number could pretty much do it with a phone by pretending they were the account holder. Even without one, any semi-human who had ever worked in law enforcement had the contacts or the access numbers or at least the wherewithal to pay off the right person. It didn't take much anymore, not with today's overabundance of user-friendly technology. Technology did more than depersonalize; it ripped your life wide open, gutted you, stripped away any pretense of privacy.

A few keystrokes revealed all.

'What is it?' Linda Coldren asked.

He told her.

'It doesn't necessarily mean what you think,' she said. 'The kidnapper could have gotten the PIN number from Chad.'

'Could have,' Myron said.

'But you don't believe it, do you?'

He shrugged. 'Let's just say I'm more than a little skeptical.'

'Why?'

'The amount, for one thing. What was Chad's max?'

'Five hundred dollars a day.'

'So why would a kidnapper only take $180?'

Linda Coldren thought a moment. 'If he took too much, someone might get suspicious.'

Myron sort of frowned. 'But if the kidnapper was that careful,' he began, 'why risk so much for $180? Everyone knows that ATMs are equipped with security cameras. Everyone also knows that even the simplest computer check can yield a location.'

She looked at him evenly. 'You don't think my son is in danger.'

'I didn't say that. This whole thing may look like one thing and be another. You were right before. It's safest to assume that the kidnapping is real.'

'So what's your next step?'

'I'm not sure. The ATM machine was on Porter Street in South Philadelphia. Is that someplace Chad likes to hang out?'

'No,' Linda Coldren said slowly. 'In fact, it's a place I would never imagine him going.'

'Why do you say that?'

'It's a dive. One of the sleaziest parts of the city.'

Myron stood. 'You got a street map?'

'In my glove compartment.'

'Good. I'll need to borrow your car for a little while.'

'Where are you going?'

'I'm going to drive around this ATM.'

She frowned. 'What for?'

'I don't know,' Myron admitted. 'Like I said before, investigating is not very scientific. You do some leg-work and you push some buttons and you hope something happens.'

Linda Coldren reached into a pocket for her keys. 'Maybe the kidnappers grabbed him there,' she said. 'Maybe you'll see his car or something.'

Myron almost slapped himself in the head. A car. He had forgotten something so basic. In his mind, a kid disappearing on his way to or from school conjured up images of yellow buses or strolling sprightly with a book bag. How could he have missed something as obvious as a car trace?

He asked her the make and model. Gray Honda Accord. Hardly a car that stands out in a crowd. Pennsylvania license plate 567-AHJ. He called it in to Esperanza. Then he gave Linda Coldren his cellular phone number.

'Call me if anything happens.'

'Okay.'

'I'll be back soon,' he said.

The ride wasn't far. He traveled, it seemed, from green splendor to concrete crap instantaneously – like on *Star Trek* where they step through one of those time portals.

The ATM was a drive-through located in what would generously be labeled a business district. Tons of cameras. No human tellers. Would a kidnapper really risk this?

Very doubtful. Myron wondered where he could get a copy of the bank's videotape without alerting the police. Win might know somebody. Financial institutions were usually anxious to cooperate with the Lockwood family. The question was, would Win be willing to cooperate?

Abandoned warehouses – or at least, they looked abandoned – lined the road. Eighteen-wheelers hurried by like something out of an old convoy movie. They reminded Myron of the CB craze from his childhood. Like everyone else, his dad had bought one – a man born in the Flatbush section of Brooklyn who grew up to own an undergarment factory in Newark, barking 'breaker one nine' with an accent he had picked up watching the movie *Deliverance*. Dad would be driving on Hobart Gap Road between their house and the Livingston Mall – maybe a one-mile drive – asking his 'good buddies' if there was any sign of 'smokeys.' Myron smiled at the memory. Ah, CBs. He was sure that his father still had his someplace. Probably next to the eight-track player.

On one side of the ATM was a gas station so generic that it didn't even bother having a name. Rusted cars stood upon crumbling cinder blocks. On the other side, a dirt-bag, no-tell motel called the Court Manor Inn greeted customers with green lettering that read: $19.99 PER HOUR.

Myron Bolitar Traveling Tip #83: You may not be dealing with a five-star deluxe property when they prominently advertise hourly rates.

Under the price, in smaller black print, the sign read, MIRRORED CEILINGS AND THEME ROOMS SLIGHTLY EXTRA. Theme rooms. Myron didn't even want to know. The last line, back in the green big print: ASK ABOUT OUR FREQUENT VISITORS CLUB. Jesus.

Myron wondered if it was worth a shot and decided, why not? It probably wouldn't lead to anything, but if Chad was hiding out – or even if he'd been kidnapped – a no-tell was as good a place as any to disappear.

He parked in the lot. The Court Manor was a textbook two-level dump. The outer stairs and walkway terraces were made of rotting wood. The cement walls had that unfinished, swirling look that could cut your hand if you leaned against it wrong. Small chunks of concrete lay on the ground. An unplugged Pepsi machine guarded the door like one of the Queen's guards. Myron passed it and entered.

He'd expected to find the standard no-tell lobby interior – that is, an unshaven Neanderthal in a sleeveless, too-short undershirt chewing on a toothpick while sitting behind bullet-proof glass burping up a beer. Or something like that. But that was not the case. The Court Manor Inn had a high wooden desk with a bronze sign reading CONCIERGE on top of it. Myron tried not to snicker. Behind the desk, a well-groomed, baby-faced man in his late twenties stood at attention. He wore a pressed shirt, starched collar, dark tie tied in a perfect Windsor knot. He smiled at Myron.

'Good afternoon, sir!' he exclaimed. He looked and sounded like a John Tesh substitute on *Entertainment Weekly*. 'Welcome to the Court Manor Inn!'

'Yeah,' Myron said. 'Hi.'

'May I be of some service to you today, sir?'

'I hope so.'

'Great! My name is Stuart Lipwitz. I'm the new manager of the Court Manor Inn.' He looked at Myron expectantly.

Myron said, 'Congrats.'

'Well, thank you, sir, that's very kind. If there are any problems – if anything at the Court Manor does not meet your expectations – please let me know immediately. I will handle it personally.' Big smile, puffed-out chest. 'At the Court Manor, we guarantee your satisfaction.'

Myron just looked at him for a minute, waiting for the full-wattage smile to dim a bit. It didn't. Myron took out the photograph of Chad Coldren.

'Have you seen this young man?'

Stuart Lipwitz did not even look down. Still smiling, he said, 'I'm sorry, sir. But are you with the police?'

'No.'

'Then I'm afraid I can't help you. I'm very sorry.'

'Pardon me?'

'I'm sorry, sir, but here at the Court Manor Inn we pride ourselves on our discretion.'

'He's not in any trouble,' Myron said. 'I'm not a private eye trying to catch a cheating husband or anything like that.'

The smile did not falter or sway. 'I'm sorry, sir, but this is the Court Manor Inn. Our clientele use our services for a variety of activities and often crave anonymity. We at the Court Manor Inn must respect that.'

Myron studied the man's face, searching for some signal that this was a put-on. Nothing. His whole persona glowed like a performer in an *Up with People* halftime show. Myron leaned over the desk and checked out the shoes. Polished like twin mirrors. The hair was slicked back. The sparkle in the eye looked real.

It took Myron some time, but he finally saw where this was leading. He took out his wallet and plucked a twenty from the billfold. He slid it across the counter. Stuart Lipwitz looked at it but made no move.

'What's this for, sir?'

'It's a present,' Myron said.

Stuart Lipwitz did not touch it.

'It's for one piece of information,' Myron continued. He plucked out another and held it in the air. 'I have another, if you'd like.'

'Sir, we have a credo here at the Court Manor Inn: The guest must come first.'

'Isn't that a prostitute's credo?'

'Pardon me, sir?'

'Never mind,' Myron said.

'I am the new manager of the Court Manor Inn, sir.'

'So I've heard.'

'I also own ten percent.'

'Your mom must be the envy of her mah-jongg group.'

Still the smile. 'In other words, sir, I am in it for the long term. That's how I look at this business. Long term. Not just today. Not just tomorrow. But into the future. For the long term. You see?'

'Oh,' Myron said flatly. 'You mean long term?'

Stuart Lipwitz snapped his fingers. 'Precisely. And our motto is this: There are many places you can spend your adultery dollar. We want it to be here.'

Myron waited a moment. Then he said, 'Noble.'

'We at the Court Manor Inn are working hard to earn your trust, and trust has no price. When I wake up in the morning, I have to look at myself in the mirror.'

'Would that mirror be on the ceiling?'

Still smiling. 'Let me explain it another way,' he said. 'If the client knows that the Court Manor Inn is a place he can feel safe to commit an indiscretion, he or she will be more likely to return.' He leaned forward, his eyes wet with excitement. 'Do you see?'

30

Myron nodded. 'Repeat business.'

'Precisely.'

'Referrals too,' Myron added. 'Like, "Hey, Bob, I know a great place to get some ass on the side." '

A nod added to the smile. 'So you understand.'

'That's all very nice, Stuart, but this kid is fifteen years old. Fifteen.' Actually, Chad was sixteen, but what the hey. 'That's against the law.'

The smile stayed, but now it signaled disappointment in the favorite pupil. 'I hate to disagree with you, sir, but the statutory rape law in this state is fourteen. And secondly, there is no law against a fifteen-year-old renting a motel room.'

The guy was dancing too much, Myron thought. No reason to go through this rigmarole if the kid had never been here. Then again, let's face facts. Stuart Lipwitz was probably enjoying this. The guy was several french fries short of a Happy Meal. Either way, Myron thought, it was time to shake the tree a bit.

'It is when he is assaulted in your motel,' Myron said. 'It is when he claims that someone got an extra key from the front desk and used it to break into the room.' Mr Bluff Goes to Philadelphia.

'We don't have extra keys,' Lipwitz said.

'Well, he got in somehow.'

Still the smile. Still the polite tone. 'If that were the case, sir, the police would be here.'

'That's my next stop,' Myron said, 'if you don't cooperate.'

'And you want to know if this young man' – Lipwitz gestured to the photograph of Chad – 'stayed here?'

'Yes.'

The smile actually brightened a bit. Myron almost

shaded his eyes. 'But, sir, if you are telling the truth, then this young man would be able to tell if he was here. You wouldn't need me for that, correct?'

Myron's face remained neutral. Mr Bluff had just been outsmarted by the new manager of the Court Manor Inn. 'That's right,' he said, changing tactics on the fly. 'I already know he was here. It was just an opening question. Like when the police ask you to state your name even though they already know it. Just to get the ball rolling.' Mr Improvision Takes Over for Mr Bluff.

Stuart Lipwitz took out a piece of paper and began to scribble. 'This is the name and telephone number of the Court Manor Inn's attorney. He will be able to help you with any problems you may have.'

'But what about that handling it personally stuff? What about the satisfaction guarantee?'

'Sir.' He leaned forward, maintaining eye contact. Not a hint of impatience had crept into his voice or face. 'May I be bold?'

'Go for it.'

'I don't believe a word you're saying.'

'Thanks for the boldness,' Myron said.

'No, thank you, sir. And do come again.'

'Another prostitution credo.'

'Pardon me?'

'Nothing,' Myron said. 'May I too be bold?'

'Yes.'

'I may punch you in the face very hard if you don't tell me if you've seen this kid.' Mr Improvision Loses His Cool.

The door swung open hard. A couple entwined about one another stumbled in. The woman was openly rubbing the man's crotch. 'We need a room pronto,' the man said.

Myron turned to them and said, 'Do you have your frequent visitor card?'

'What?'

Still the smile from Stuart Lipwitz. 'Good-bye, sir. And have a nice day.' Then he rejuvenated the smile and moved toward the writhing mound. 'Welcome to the Court Manor Inn. My name is Stuart Lipwitz. I'm the new manager.'

Myron headed out to his car. He took a deep breath in the parking lot and looked back behind him. The whole visit already had an unreal feeling, like one of those descriptions of alien abductions *sans* the anal probe. He got in the car and dialed Win's cellular. He just wanted to leave him a message on the machine. But to Myron's surprise, Win answered.

'Articulate,' he drolled.

Myron was momentarily taken aback. 'It's me,' he said.

Silence, Win hated the obvious. 'It's me,' was both questionable grammar (at best) and a complete waste. Win would know who it was by the voice. If he didn't, hearing 'It's me' would undeniably not help.

'I thought you didn't answer the phone on the course,' Myron said.

'I'm driving home to change,' Win said. 'Then I'm dining at Merion.' Mainliners never ate; they dined. 'Care to join me?'

'Sounds good,' Myron said.

'Wait a second.'

'What?'

'Are you properly attired?'

'I don't clash,' Myron said. 'Will they still let me in?'

'My, my, that was very funny, Myron. I must write that one down. As soon as I stop laughing, I plan on locating a pen. However, I am so filled with mirth that I may wrap my precious Jag around an upcoming telephone pole. Alas, at least I will die with jocularity in my heart.'

Win.

'We have a case,' Myron said.

Silence. Win made this so easy.

'I'll tell you about it at dinner.'

'Until then,' Win said, 'it'll be all I can do to douse my mounting excitement and anticipation with a snifter of cognac.'

Click, Gotta love that Win.

Myron hadn't driven a mile when the cellular phone rang. Myron switched it on.

It was Bucky. 'The kidnapper called again.'

Chapter 4

'What did he say?' Myron asked.

'They want money,' Bucky said.

'How much?'

'I don't know.'

Myron was confused. 'What do you mean, you don't know? Didn't they say?'

'I don't think so,' the old man said.

There was noise in the background. 'Where are you?' Myron asked.

'I'm at Merion. Look, Jack answered the phone. He's still in shock.'

'Jack answered?'

'Yes.'

Doubly confused. 'The kidnapper called Jack at Merion?'

'Yes. Please, Myron, can you get back over here? It'll be easier to explain.'

'On my way.'

He drove from the seedy motel to a highway and then into green. Lots of green. The Philadelphia suburbs were lush lawns and high bushes and shady trees. Amazing how close it was – at least in a geographic sense – to the meaner streets of Philly. Like most cities, there was tremendous segregation in Philadelphia. Myron remembered driving with Win to Veterans Stadium for an Eagles game a couple of years back. They'd gone through an Italian block, a Polish block, an African American block; it was as if some powerful, invisible force field – again, like on *Star Trek* – isolated each ethnicity. The City of Brotherly Love could almost be called Little Yugoslavia.

Myron turned down Ardmore Avenue. Merion was about a mile away. His thoughts turned to Win. How, he wondered, would his old friend react to the maternal connection in this case?

Probably not well.

In all the years they had been friends, Myron had heard Win mention his mother on only one occasion.

It had been during their junior year at Duke. They were college roommates, just back from a wild frat party. The beer had flowed. Myron was not what you'd call a good drinker. Two drinks and he'd usually end up trying to French-kiss a toaster. He blamed this on his ancestry – his people had never handled spirits well.

Win, on the other hand, seemed to have been weaned on schnapps. Liquor never really affected him much. But at this particular party, the grain alcohol-laced punch made even his steps wobble a bit. It took Win three tries to unlock their dorm room door.

Myron quickly collapsed on his bed. The ceiling spun counterclockwise at a seemingly death-defying speed. He closed his eyes. His hands gripped the bed and held on in terror. His face had no color. Nausea clamped down painfully on his stomach. Myron wondered when he would vomit and prayed it would be soon.

Ah, the glamour of college drinking.

For a while neither of them said anything. Myron wondered if Win had fallen asleep. Or maybe Win was gone. Vanished into the night. Maybe he hadn't held on to his spinning bed tightly enough and the centrifugal force had hurled him out the window and into the great beyond.

Then Win's voice cut through the darkness. 'Take a look at this.'

A hand reached out and dropped something on Myron's chest. Myron risked letting go of the bed with one hand. So far, so good. He fumbled for whatever it was, found it, lifted it into view. A streetlight from outside – campuses are lit up like Christmas trees – cast enough illumination to make out a photograph. The color was grainy and faded, but Myron could still make out what looked to be an expensive car.

'Is that a Rolls-Royce?' Myron asked. He knew nothing about cars.

'A Bentley S Three Continental Flying Spur,' Win corrected, '1962. A classic.'

'Is it yours?'

'Yes.'

The bed spun silently.

'How did you get it?' Myron asked.

'A man who was fucking my mother gave it to me.'

The end. Win had shut down after that. The wall he put up was not only impenetrable but unapproachable, filled with land mines and a moat and lots of high-voltage electric wires. Over the ensuing decade and a half, Win had never again mentioned his mother. Not when the packages came to the dorm room every semester. Not when the packages came to Win's office on his birthday even now. Not even when they saw her in person ten years ago.

The plain dark wood sign merely read MERION GOLF CLUB. Nothing else. No 'For Members Only.' No 'We're Elitist and We Don't Want You.' No 'Ethnics Use Service Entrance.' No need. It was just a given.

The last US Open threesome had finished a while back and the crowd was mostly gone now. Merion could hold only seventeen thousand for a tournament – less than half the capacity of most courses – but parking was still a chore. Most spectators were forced to park at nearby Haverford College. Shuttle buses ran constantly.

At the top of the driveway a guard signaled him to stop.

'I'm here to meet Windsor Lockwood,' Myron said.

Instant recognition. Instant wave-through.

Bucky ran over to him before he had the car in park. The rounded face was more jowly now, as if he were packing wet sand in his cheeks.

'Where is Jack?' Myron asked.

'The western course.'

'The what?'

'Merion has two courses,' the older man explained, stretching his neck again. 'The east, which is the more famous one, and the west. During the Open, the western course is used as a driving range.'

'And your son-in-law is there?'

'Yes.'

'Driving balls?'

'Of course.' Bucky looked at him, surprised. 'You always do that after a round. Every golfer on the tour knows that. You played basketball. Didn't you used to practice your shot after a game?'

'No.'

'Well, as I told you earlier, golf is very special. Players need to review their play immediately after a round. Even if they've played well. They focus in on their good strokes, see if they can figure out what went wrong with the bad strokes. They recap the day.'

'Uh-huh,' Myron said. 'So tell me about the kidnapper's call.'

'I'll take you to Jack,' he said. 'This way.'

They walked across the eighteen fairway and then down sixteen. The air smelled of freshly cut grass and pollen. It'd been a big year for pollen on the East Coast; nearby allergists swooned with greedy delight.

Bucky shook his head. 'Look at these roughs,' he said. 'Impossible.'

He pointed to long grass. Myron had no idea what he was talking about so he nodded and kept walking.

'Damn USGA wants this course to bring the golfers to their knees,' Bucky ranted on. 'So they grow the rough way out. Like playing in a rice paddy, for chrissake. Then they cut the greens so close, the golfers might as well be putting on a hockey rink.'

Myron remained silent. They two men kept walking.

'This is one of the famed stone-quarry holes,' Bucky said, calmer now.

'Uh-huh.' The man was babbling. People do that when they're nervous.

'When the original builders reached sixteen, seventeen,

and eighteen,' Bucky continued, sounding not unlike a tour guide in the Sistine Chapel, 'they ran across a stone quarry. Rather than giving up then and there, they plowed ahead, incorporating the quarry into the hole.'

'Gosh,' Myron said softly, 'they were so brave back then.'

Some babble when nervous. Some grow sarcastic.

They reached the tee and made a right, walking along Golf House Road. Though the last group had finished playing more than an hour ago, there were still at least a dozen golfers hitting balls. The driving range. Yes, professional golfers hit balls here – practicing with a wide array of woods and irons and big clubs, nay, warheads, they called Bertha and Cathy and the like – but that was only part of what went on. Most touring pros used the range to work out strategies with their caddies, check on equipment with their sponsors, network, socialize with fellow golfers, smoke a cigarette (a surprising amount of pros chain-smoke), even talk to agents.

In golf circles, the driving range was called the office.

Myron recognized Greg Norman and Nick Faldo. He also spotted Tad Crispin, the new kid on the block, the latest next Jack Nicklaus – in a phrase, the dream client. The kid was twenty-three, good-looking, quiet, engaged to an equally attractive, happy-just-to-be-here woman. He also did not yet have an agent. Myron tried not to salivate. Hey, he was as human as the next guy. He was, after all, a sports agent. Cut him some slack.

'Where is Jack?' Myron asked.

'Down this way,' Bucky said. 'He wanted to hit alone.'

'How did the kidnapper reach him?'

'He called the Merion switchboard and said it was an emergency.'

'And that worked?'

'Yes,' Bucky said slowly. 'Actually, it was Chad on the phone. He identified himself as Jack's son.'

Curious? 'What time did the call come in?'

'Maybe ten minutes before I called you.' Bucky stopped, gestured with his chin. 'There.'

Jack Coldren was a touch pudgy and soft in the middle, but he had forearms like Popeye's. His flyaway hair did just that in the breeze, revealing bald spots that had started off the day better covered. He whacked the ball with a wood club and an uncommon fury. To some this might all seem very strange. You have just learned your son is missing and you go out and hit golf balls. But Myron understood. Hitting balls was comfort food. The more stress Myron was under, the more he wanted to go in his driveway and shoot baskets. We all have something. Some drink. Some do drugs. Some like to take a long drive or play a computer game. When Win needed to unwind, he often watched videotapes of his own sexual exploits. But that was Win.

'Who's that with him?' Myron asked.

'Diane Hoffman,' Bucky said. 'Jack's caddie.'

Myron knew that female caddies were not uncommon on the men's pro tour. Some players even hired their wives. Saves money. 'Does she know what's going on?'

'Yes. Diane was there when the call came in. They're pretty close.'

'Have you told Linda?'

Bucky nodded. 'I called her right away. Do you mind

41

introducing yourself? I'd like to go back to the house and check up on her.'

'No problem.'

'How will I reach you if something comes up?'

'Call my cellular.'

Bucky nearly gasped. 'Cellular phones are forbidden at Merion.' Like it was a papal command.

'I walk on the wild side,' Myron said. 'Just call.'

Myron approached them. Diane Hoffman stood with her feet shoulder-width apart, her arms folded, her face intent on Coldren's backswing. A cigarette dangled from her lips almost vertically. She didn't even glance at Myron. Jack Coldren coiled his body and then let go, snapping like a released spring. The ball rocketed over the distant hills.

Jack Coldren turned, looked at Myron, smiled tightly, nodded a hello. 'You're Myron Bolitar, right?'

'Right.'

He shook Myron's hand. Diane Hoffman continued to study her player's every move, frowning as if she'd spotted a flaw in his hand-shaking technique. 'I appreciate your helping us out,' he said.

Face-to-face now – no more than a few feet away – Myron could see the devastation on the man's face. The jubilant glow after nailing the putt on eighteen had been snuffed out by something more pasty and sickly. His eyes had the surprised, uncomprehending look of a man who'd just been sucker punched in the stomach.

'You tried making a comeback recently,' Jack said. 'With New Jersey.'

Myron nodded.

'I saw you on the news. Gutsy move, after all these years.'

Stalling. Not sure how to begin. Myron decided to help. 'Tell me about the call.'

Jack Coldren's eyes swerved over the expanse of green. 'Are you sure it's safe?' he asked. 'The guy on the phone told me no police. To just act normal.'

'I'm an agent seeking clients,' Myron said. 'Talking to me is about as normal as it gets.'

Coldren thought about that for a moment then nodded. He still hadn't introduced Diane Hoffman. Hoffman didn't seem to mind. She remained about ten feet away, rock-still. Her eyes remained narrow and suspicious, her face weathered and pinched. The cigarette ash was incredibly long now, almost defying gravity. She wore a cap and one of those caddie vests that looked like a jogger's night reflector.

'The club president came up to me and whispered that there was an emergency call from my son. So I went inside the clubhouse and picked it up.'

He stopped suddenly and blinked several times. His breathing became heavier. He was wearing a tad-too-tight, yellow V-necked golf shirt. You could see his body expand against the cotton blend with each inhale. Myron waited.

'It was Chad,' he finally spat out. 'All he could say was "Dad," before someone grabbed the phone away from him. Then a man with a deep voice came on the line.'

'How deep?' Myron asked.

'Pardon?'

'How deep was the voice?'

'Very.'

'Did it sound funny to you? A little robotic?'

'Now that you mention it, yes, it did.'

Electronic altering, Myron guessed. Those machines

43

could make Barry White sound like a four-year-old girl. Or vice versa. They weren't hard to get. Even Radio Shack sold them now. The kidnapper or kidnappers could be any sex. Linda and Jack Coldren's description of a 'male voice' was irrelevant. 'What did he say?'

'That he had my son. He told me that if I called the police or anybody like that, Chad would pay. He told me that someone would be watching me all the time.' Jack Coldren accentuated the point by looking around again. No one suspicious lurked about, though Greg Norman waved and gave them a smiling thumbs-up. G'day, mate.

'What else?' Myron asked.

'He said he wanted money,' Coldren said.

'How much?'

'He just said a lot. He wasn't sure yet how much, but he wanted me to get it ready. He said he'd call back.'

Myron made a face. 'But he didn't tell you how much?'

'No. Just that it would be a lot.'

'And that you should get it ready.'

'Right.'

This made no sense. A kidnapper who wasn't sure how much ransom to extort? 'May I be blunt, Jack?'

Coldren stood a little taller, tucked in his shirt. He was what some would call boyishly and disarmingly handsome. His face was big and unthreatening with cottony, malleable features. 'Don't sugarcoat anything for me,' he said. 'I want the truth.'

'Could this be a hoax?'

Jack shot a quick glance at Diane Hoffman. She moved slightly. Might have been a nod. He turned back to Myron. 'What do you mean?'

'Could Chad be behind this?'

44

The longer flyaway hairs got caught up in a cross-breeze and fell down into his eyes. He pushed them away with his fingers. Something came across his face. Rumination, maybe? Unlike Linda Coldren, the idea had not snapped him into a defensive stance. He was pondering the possibility, or perhaps merely grasping at an option that meant safety for his son.

'There were two different voices,' Coldren said. 'On the phone.'

'It could be a voice changer.' Myron explained what that was.

More rumination. Coldren's face scrunched up. 'I really don't know.'

'Is it something you can imagine Chad doing?'

'No,' Coldren replied. 'But who can imagine anyone's kid doing something like this? I'm trying to remain objective here, hard as that is. Do I think my boy could do something like this? Of course not. But then again, I wouldn't be the first parent to be wrong about my kid; now, would I?'

Fair enough, Myron thought. 'Has Chad ever run away?'

'No.'

'Any trouble in the family? Anything that might make him want to do something like this?'

'Something like fake his own kidnapping?'

'It doesn't have to be that extreme,' Myron said. 'Maybe something you or your wife did that got him upset.'

'No,' he said, his voice suddenly faraway. 'I can't think of anything.' He looked up. The sun was low and not very strong anymore, but he still sort of squinted up at Myron, the side of his hand resting on his forehead in an

45

eye-shading salute. The posture reminded Myron of the photograph of Chad he'd seen at the house.

Jack said, 'You have a thought, Myron, don't you?'

'Barely.'

'I'd still like to hear it,' Coldren said.

'How badly do you want to win this tournament, Jack?'

Coldren gave a half-smile. 'You were an athlete, Myron. You know how badly.'

'Yes,' Myron said, 'I do.'

'So what's your point?'

'Your son is an athlete. He probably knows too.'

'Yes,' Coldren said. Then: 'I'm still waiting for the point.'

'If someone wanted to hurt you,' Myron said, 'what better way than to mess up your chance of winning the Open?'

Jack Coldren's eyes had that sucker punched look again. He took a step back.

'I'm only theorizing,' Myron added quickly. 'I'm not saying your son is doing that . . .'

'But you need to explore every avenue,' Jack Coldren finished for him.

'Yes.'

Coldren recovered, but it took him a little time. 'Even if what you're saying is true, it doesn't have to be Chad. Someone else could have done this to get at me.' Again he glanced over at his caddie. Still looking at her, he said, 'Wouldn't be the first time.'

'What do you mean?'

Jack Coldren didn't answer right away. He turned away from both of them and squinted out toward where he'd been hitting balls. There was nothing to see. His back was to Myron. 'You probably know I lost the Open a long time ago.'

'Yes.'

He didn't elaborate.

'Did something happen back then?' Myron asked.

'Maybe,' Jack Coldren said slowly. 'I don't know anymore. The point is, someone else might be out to get me. It doesn't have to be my son.'

'Maybe,' Myron agreed. He didn't go into the fact that he'd pretty much dismissed this possibility because Chad had vanished before Coldren had his lead. No reason to go into it now.

Coldren turned back to Myron. 'Bucky mentioned something about an ATM card,' he said.

'Your son's ATM card was accessed last night. At Porter Street.'

Something crossed his face. Not for long. Not for more than a second. A flash and then it was gone. 'On Porter Street?' he repeated.

'Yep. A First Philadelphia Bank on Porter Street in South Philadelphia.'

Silence.

'Are you familiar with that part of town?'

'No,' Coldren said. He looked over at his caddie. Diane Hoffman remained the statue. Arms still folded. Feet still shoulder-width apart. Ash finally gone.

'Are you sure?'

'Of course I am.'

'I visited there today,' Myron said.

His face remained steady. 'Did you learn anything?'

'No.'

Silence.

47

Jack Coldren gestured behind him. 'You mind if I take a few more swings while we talk?'

'Not at all.'

He put on his glove. 'Do you think I should play tomorrow?'

'That's up to you,' Myron said. 'The kidnapper said to act normal. Your not playing would certainly draw suspicion.'

Coldren bent down to put a ball on the tee. 'Can I ask you something, Myron?'

'Sure.'

'When you played basketball, how important was winning to you?'

Odd question. 'Very.'

Jack nodded like he'd been expecting that. 'You won the NCAA championship one year, right?'

'Yes.'

Coldren shook his head. 'Must have been something.'

Myron did not reply.

Jack Coldren picked up a club and flexed his fingers around the grip. He lined up next to the ball. Again the smooth coil-and-release movement. Myron watched the ball sail away. For a moment no one spoke. They just looked off into the distance and watched the final streaks of sun color the sky purple.

When Coldren finally spoke, his voice was thick. 'You want to hear something awful?'

Myron moved closer to him. Coldren's eyes were wet.

'I still care about winning this thing,' Coldren said. He looked at Myron. The pain on his face was so naked, Myron almost reached out and hugged him. He imagined that he could see the reflection of the man's past in his eyes, the years of torment, of thinking of what might have

48

been, of finally having the chance at redemption, of having that chance suddenly snatched away.

'What kind of man still thinks about winning at a time like this?' Coldren asked.

Myron didn't say anything. He didn't know the answer. Or maybe he feared that he did.

Chapter 5

Merion's clubhouse was an expanded white farmhouse with black shutters. The only splash of color came from the green awnings shading the famed back porch and even that was muted by the surrounding green of the golf course. You expected something more awe-inspiring or intimidating at one of the country's most exclusive clubs, and yet the simplicity seemed to say, 'We're Merion. We don't need more.'

Myron walked past the pro shop. Golf bags were lined up on a metal stand. The men's locker room door was on his right. A bronze sign read that Merion had been designated a historic landmark. A bulletin board listed members' handicaps. Myron skimmed the names for Win's. Three handicap. Myron didn't know much about golfing, but he knew that was pretty damn good.

The outside porch had a stone floor and about two dozen tables. The legendary dining area did more than overlook the first tee – it actually seemed perched right over it. From here, members watched golfers tee off with the practiced glares of Roman senators at the Colosseum. Powerful businessmen and community leaders often crumbled under such century-old scrutiny. Even professionals were not immune – the porch's dining facility was kept open during the Open. Jack Nicklaus and Arnold Palmer and Ben Hogan and Bobby Jones and Sam Snead had all been subjected to the small restaurant noises, the grating tinkling of glass and silverware blending most disharmoniously with golf's hushed crowds and distant cheers.

The porch was packed with members. Most were men – elderly and red-faced and well fed. They wore blue or green blazers with different crests on them. Their ties were loud and usually striped. Many had floppy white or yellow hats on their heads. Floppy hats. And Win had been worried about Myron's 'attire.'

Myron spotted Win at a corner table with six chairs. He sat alone. His expression was both glacial and serene, his body completely at ease. A mountain lion patiently waiting for prey. One would think that the blond hair and patrician good looks would be life assets for Win. In many ways, they were; in many more ways, they branded him. His entire appearance reeked of arrogance, old money, and elitism. Most people did not respond well to that. A specific, seething hostility frothed and boiled over when people looked at Win. To look at such a person was to hate him. Win was used to it. People who judged purely on looks did not concern him. People who judged purely on looks were oft surprised.

Myron greeted his old friend and sat down.

'Would you care for a drink?' Win said.

'Sure.'

'If you ask for a Yoo-Hoo,' Win said, 'I'll shoot you in the right eye.'

'Right eye,' Myron repeated with a nod. 'Very specific.'

A waiter who must have been a hundred years old materialized. He wore a green jacket and pants – green, Myron surmised, so that even the help would blend into the famed milieu. Didn't work, though. The old waiter looked like the Riddler's grandfather. 'Henry,' Win said, 'I'll have an iced tea.'

Myron was tempted to ask for a 'Colt 45, like Billy Dee,' but decided against it. 'I'll have the same.'

'Very good, Mr Lockwood.'

Henry left. Win looked over at Myron. 'So tell me.'

'It's a kidnapping,' Myron said.

Win arched an eyebrow.

'One of the players' sons is missing. The parents have gotten two calls.' Myron quickly told him about them. Win listened in silence.

When Myron finished, Win said, 'You left something out.'

'What?'

'The name of the player.'

Myron kept his voice steady. 'Jack Coldren.'

Win's face betrayed nothing, but Myron still felt a cold gust blow across his heart.

Win said, 'And you've met Linda.'

'Yes.'

'And you know that she is related to me.'

'Yes.'

'Then you must have realized that I will not help.'

'No.'

Win sat back, steepled his fingers. 'Then you realize it now.'

'A boy might be in real danger,' Myron said. 'We have to help.'

'No,' Win said. 'I do not.'

'You want me to drop it?'

'What you do is your affair,' Win said.

'Do you want me to drop it?' Myron repeated.

The iced teas came. Win took a gentle sip. He looked off and tapped his chin with his index finger. His signal to end the topic. Myron knew better than to push it.

'So who are the other seats for?' Myron asked.

'I am mining a major lead.'

'A new client?'

'For me, almost definitely. For you, a barely remote possibility.'

'Who?'

'Tad Crispin.'

Myron's chin dropped. 'We're having dinner with Tad Crispin?'

'As well as our old friend Norman Zuckerman and his latest rather attractive ingenue.'

Norm Zuckerman was the owner of Zoom, one of the largest sneaker and sporting apparel companies in the country. He was also one of Myron's favorite people. 'How did you get to Crispin? I heard he was agenting himself.'

'He is,' Win said, 'but he still wants a financial adviser.' Barely in his mid-thirties, Win was already something of a Wall Street legend. Reaching out to Win made sense. 'Crispin is quite a shrewd young man, actually,' he went on. 'Unfortunately, he believes that all agents are thieves. That they have the morals of a prostitute practicing politics.'

'He said that? A prostitute practicing politics?'

'No, I came up with that one myself.' Win smiled. 'Pretty good, no?'

Myron nodded. 'No.'

'Anyway, the Zoom folks here are tailing him like a lapdog. They're introducing a whole new line of men's clubs and clothing on the back of young Mr Crispin.'

Tad Crispin was in second place, a goodly distance behind Jack Coldren. Myron wondered how happy Zoom was about Coldren possibly stealing their thunder. Not very, he supposed.

'So what do you make of Jack Coldren's good showing?' Myron asked. 'You surprised?'

Win shrugged. 'Winning was always very important to Jack.'

'Have you known him long?'

Flat eyes. 'Yes.'

'Did you know him when he lost here as a rookie?'

'Yes.'

Myron calculated the years. Win would have been in elementary school. 'Jack Coldren hinted that he thought someone tried to sabotage his chances back then.'

Win made a noise. 'Guff,' he said.

'Guff?'

'You don't recall what happened?'

'No.'

'Coldren claims his caddie gave him the wrong club on sixteen,' Win said. 'He asked for a six iron and supposedly his caddie handed him an eight. His shot landed short. More specifically, in one of the rock quarry bunkers. He never recovered.'

'Did the caddie admit the error?'

'He never commented, as far as I know.'

'What did Jack do?'

'He fired him.'

Myron chewed on that tidbit. 'Where is the caddie now?'

'I do not have the slightest idea,' Win said. 'He wasn't a young man at the time and this was more than twenty years ago.'

'Do you remember his name?'

'No. And this conversation is officially terminated.'

Before Myron could ask why, a pair of hands covered his eyes. 'Guess who?' came a familiar sing-song. 'I'll give you a couple of hints: I'm smart, good-looking, and loaded with talent.'

'Gee,' Myron said, 'before that hint, I would have thought you were Norm Zuckerman.'

'And with the hint?'

Myron shrugged. 'If you add "adored by women of all ages," I'd think it was me.'

Norman Zuckerman laughed heartily. He bent down and gave Myron a big, loud smack on the cheek. 'How are you, meshuggener?'

'Good, Norm. You?'

'I'm cooler than Superfly in a new Coupe de Ville.'

Zuckerman greeted Win with a loud hello and an enthusiastic handshake. Diners stared in distaste. The stares did not quiet Norman Zuckerman. An elephant gun could not quiet Norman Zuckerman. Myron liked the man. Sure, a lot of it was an act. But it was a genuine act. Norm's zest for everything around him was contagious. He was pure energy; the kind of person who made you examine yourself and left you feeling just a little wanting.

Norm brought forward a young woman who'd been standing behind him. 'Let me introduce you to Esme

Fong,' he said. 'She's one of my marketing vee-pees. In charge of the new golf line. Brilliant. The woman is absolutely brilliant.'

The attractive ingenue. Early-to-mid twenties, Myron guessed. Esme Fong was Asian with perhaps a hint of Caucasian. She was petite with almond eyes. Her hair was long and silky, a black fan with an earthy auburn tinge. She wore a beige business suit and white stockings. Esme nodded a hello and stepped closer. She wore the serious face of an attractive young woman who was afraid of not being taken seriously because she was an attractive young woman.

She stuck out her hand. 'A pleasure to meet you, Mr Bolitar,' she said crisply. 'Mr Lockwood.'

'Doesn't she have a firm handshake?' Zuckerman asked. Then turning to her: 'What's with all the *mister*s? This is Myron and Win. They're practically family, for crying out loud. Okay, Win's a little goyish to be in my family. I mean, his people came over on the *Mayflower*, while most of mine fled a czar pogrom in a cargo ship. But we're still family, right, Win?'

'As rain,' Win said.

'Sit down already, Esme. You're making me nervous with all the seriousness. Try a smile, okay?' Zuckerman demonstrated, pointing at his teeth. Then he turned to Myron, spread his hands. 'The truth, Myron. How do I look?'

Norman was over sixty. His customary loud clothing, matching the man's personality, hardly stood out after what Myron had seen today. His skin was dark and rough; his eyes dropped inside black circles; his features jutted out in classical Semitism; his beard and hair were too long and somewhat unkempt.

'You look like Jerry Rubin at the Chicago Seven trial,' Myron said.

'Just the look I wanted,' Norm said. 'Retro. Hip. Attitude. That's what's in nowadays.'

'Hardly Tad Crispin's look,' Myron said.

'I'm talking about the real world, not golf. Golfers don't know from hip or attitude. Hasidim are more open to change than golfers, you know what I'm saying? I'll give you an example: Dennis Rodman is not a golfer. You know what golfers want? The same thing they've wanted since the dawn of sports marketing: Arnold Palmer. That's what they want. They wanted Palmer, then Nicklaus, then Watson – always good ol' boys.' He pointed a thumb at Esme Fong. 'Esme is the one who signed Crispin. He's her boy.'

Myron looked at her. 'Quite a coup,' he said.

'Thank you,' she said.

'We'll see how big a coup it is,' Zuckerman said. 'Zoom is moving into golf in a very big way. Huge. Humongous. Gigantic.'

'Enormous,' Myron said.

'Mammoth,' Win added.

'Colossal.'

'Titantic.'

'Bunyanesque.'

Win smiled. 'Brobdingnagian,' he said.

'Oooo,' Myron said. 'Good one.'

Zuckerman shook his head. 'You guys are funnier than the Three Stooges without Curly. Anyway, it's a helluva campaign. Esme is running it for me. Male and female lines. Not only have we got Crispin, but Esme's landed the numero uno female golfer in the world.'

'Linda Coldren?' Myron asked.

'Whoa!' Norm clapped his hands once. 'The Hebrew hoopster knows his golf! By the way, Myron, what kind of name is *Bolitar* for a member of the tribe?'

'It's a long story,' Myron said.

'Good, I wasn't interested anyway. I was just being polite. Where was I?' Zuckerman threw one leg over the other, leaned back, smiled, looked about. A ruddy-faced man at a neighboring table glared. 'Hi, there,' Norm said with a little wave. 'Looking good.'

The man made a huffing noise and looked away.

Norm shrugged. 'You'd think he never saw a Jew before.'

'He probably hasn't,' Win said.

Norm looked back over at the ruddy-faced man. 'Look!' Zuckerman said, pointing to his head. 'No horns!'

Even Win smiled.

Zuckerman turned his attention back to Myron. 'So tell me, you trying to sign Crispin?'

'I haven't even met him yet,' Myron said.

Zuckerman put his hand to his chest, feigning surprise. 'Well then, Myron, this is some eerie coincidence. You being here when we're about to break bread with him – what are the odds? Wait.' Norm stopped, put his hand to his ear. 'I think I hear *Twilight Zone* music.'

'Ha-ha,' Myron said.

'Oh, relax, Myron. I'm teasing you. Lighten up, for crying out loud. But let me be honest for a second, okay? I don't think Cripsin needs you, Myron. Nothing personal, but the kid signed the deal with me himself. No agent. No lawyer. Handled it all on his own.'

'And got robbed,' Win added.

Zuckerman put a hand to his chest. 'You wound me, Win.'

'Crispin told me the numbers,' Win said. 'Myron would have gotten him a far better deal.'

'With all due respect to your centuries of upper-crust inbreeding, you don't know what the hell you're talking about. The kid left a little money in the till for me, that's all. Is that a crime nowadays – for a man to make a profit? Myron's a shark, for crying out loud. He rips off my clothes when we talk. He leaves my office, I don't even have undies left. I don't even have furniture. I don't even have an office. I start out with this beautiful office and Myron comes in and I end up naked in some soup kitchen someplace.'

Myron looked at Win. 'Touching.'

'He's breaking my heart,' Win said.

Myron turned his attention to Esme Fong. 'Are you happy with how Crispin's been playing?'

'Of course,' she said quickly. 'This is his first major, and he's in second place.'

Norm Zuckerman put a hand on her arm. 'Save the spinning for those morons in the media. These two guys are family.'

Esme Fong shifted in her seat. She cleared her throat. 'Linda Coldren won the US Open a few weeks ago,' she said. 'We're running dual television, radio, and print ads – they'll both be in every spot. It's a new line, completely unknown to golf enthusiasts. Naturally, if we could introduce Zoom's new line with two US Open winners, it would be helpful.'

Norm pointed his thumb again. 'Ain't she something? *Helpful*. Nice word. Vague. Look, Myron, you read the sports section, am I right?'

'As rain.'

'How many articles did you see on Crispin before the tournament began?'

'A lot.'

'How much coverage has he gotten in the past two days?'

'Not much.'

'Try none. All anybody is talking about is Jack Coldren. In two days that poor son of a bitch is either going to be a miracle man of messianic proportions or the most pitiful loser in the history of the world. Think about it for a second. A man's entire life – both his past and his future – will be shaped by a few swings of a stick. Nuts, when you think about it. And you know what the worst part is?'

Myron shook his head.

'I hope like hell he messes up! I feel like a major son of a bitch, but that's the truth. My guy comes back and wins, you wait and see the way Esme spins it. The brilliant play of newcomer Tad Crispin forces a veteran to crack. The new kid stares down the pressure like Palmer and Nicklaus combined. You know what it'll mean to the launch of the new line?' Zuckerman looked over at Win and pointed. 'God, I wish I looked like you. Look at him, for crying out loud. He's beautiful.'

Win, in spite of himself, laughed. Several ruddy-faced men turned and stared. Norman waved at them, friendly-like. 'Next time I come,' Norm said to Win, 'I'm wearing a yarmulke.'

Win laughed harder. Myron tried to remember the last time he'd seen his friend laugh so openly. It'd been a while. Norm had that effect on people.

Esme Fong glanced at her watch and rose. 'I only

stopped by to say hello,' she explained. 'I really must be going.'

All three men stood. Norm bussed her cheek. 'Take care, Esme, okay? I'll see you tomorrow morning.'

'Yes, Norm.' She gave Myron and Win demure smiles accompanied by a shy lowering of the head. 'Nice meeting you, Myron. Win.'

She left. The three men sat. Win steepled his fingers. 'How old is she?' Win asked.

'Twenty-five. Phi Beta Kappa from Yale.'

'Impressive.'

Norm said, 'Don't even think it, Win.'

Win shook his head. He wouldn't. She was in the business. Harder to disentangle. When it came to the opposite sex, Win liked quick and absolute closure.

'I stole her from those sons of bitches at Nike,' Norm said. 'She was a bigwig in their basketball department. Don't get me wrong. She was making a ton of dough, but she smartened up. Hey, it's like I told her: There's more to life than money. You know what I'm saying?'

Myron refrained from rolling his eyes.

'Anyway, she works like a dog. Always checking and rechecking. In fact, she's on her way to Linda Coldren's right now. They're going to have a late-night tea party or something girly-girl.'

Myron and Win exchanged a glance. 'She's going to Linda Coldren's house?'

'Yeah, why?'

'When did she call her?'

'What do you mean?'

'Was this appointment made a long time ago?'

'What, now, I look like a receptionist?'

'Forget it.'

'Forgotten.'

'Excuse me a second,' Myron said. 'Do you mind if I go make a call?'

'Am I your mother?' Zuckerman made a shooing motion. 'Go already.'

Myron debated using his cellular phone but decided not to piss off the Merion gods. He found a phone booth in the men's locker room foyer and dialed the Coldrens' house. He used Chad's line. Linda Coldren answered.

'Hello?'

'Just checking in,' Myron said. 'Anything new?'

'No,' Linda said.

'Are you aware that Esme Fong is coming over?'

'I didn't want to cancel,' Linda Coldren explained. 'I didn't want to do anything that would draw attention.'

'You'll be okay, then?'

'Yes,' she said.

Myron watched Tad Crispin walk by in the direction of Win's table. 'Were you able to reach the school?'

'No; nobody was there,' she said. 'So what do we do next?'

'I don't know,' Myron said. 'I have the override Caller ID on your phone. If he calls again, we should be able to get the number.'

'What else?'

'I'll try to speak to Matthew Squires. See what he can tell me.'

'I already spoke to Matthew,' Linda said impatiently. 'He doesn't know anything. What else?'

'I could get the police involved. Discreetly. There's not much else I can do on my own.'

'No,' she said firmly. 'No police. Jack and I are both adamant on that point.'

62

'I have friends in the FBI—'

'No.'

He thought about his conversation with Win. 'When Jack lost at Merion, who was his caddie?'

She hesitated. 'Why would you want to know that?'

'I understand Jack blamed his caddie for the loss.'

'In part, yes.'

'And that he fired him.'

'So?'

'So I asked about enemies. How did the caddie feel about what happened?'

'You're talking about something that happened over twenty years ago,' Linda Coldren said. 'Even if he did harbor a deep hatred for Jack, why would he wait so long?'

'This is the first time the Open has been at Merion since then. Maybe that's reawakened dormant anger. I don't know. Chances are there's nothing to this, but it might be worth checking out.'

He could hear talking on the other end of the line. Jack's voice. She asked Myron to hold on a moment.

A few moments later, Jack Coldren came on the line. Without preamble, he said, 'You think there's a connection between what happened to me twenty-three years ago and Chad's disappearance?'

'I don't know,' Myron said.

His tone was insistent. 'But you think—'

'I don't know what I think,' he interrupted. 'I'm just checking out every angle.'

There was a stony silence. Then: 'His name was Lloyd Rennart,' Jack Coldren said.

'Do you know where he lives?'

'No. I haven't seen him since the day the Open ended.'

'The day you fired him.'

'Yes.'

'You never bumped into him again? At the club or a tournament or something?'

'No,' Jack Coldren said slowly. 'Never.'

'Where did Rennart live back then?'

'In Wayne. It's the neighboring town.'

'How old would he be now?'

'Sixty-eight.' No hesitation.

'Before this happened, were you two close?'

Jack Coldren's voice, when he finally spoke, was very soft. 'I thought so,' he said. 'Not on a personal level. We didn't socialize. I never met his family or visited his home or anything like that. But on the golf course' – he paused – 'I thought we were very close.'

Silence.

'Why would he do it?' Myron asked. 'Why would he purposely ruin your chances of winning?'

Myron could hear him breathing. When he spoke again, his voice was hoarse and scratchy. 'I've wanted to know the answer to that for twenty-three years.'

Chapter 6

Myron called in Lloyd Rennart's name to Esperanza. It probably wouldn't take much. Again modern technology would simplify the feat. Anyone with a modem could type in the address www.switchboard.com – a website that was virtually a telephone directory of the entire country. If that site didn't work, there were others. It probably wouldn't take long, if Lloyd Rennart was still among the living. If not, well, there were sites for that too.

'Did you tell Win?' Esperanza asked.

'Yes.'

'How did he react?'

'He won't help.'

'Not surprising,' she said.

'No,' he agreed.

Esperanza said, 'You don't work well alone, Myron.'

'I'll be fine,' he said 'You looking forward to graduation?'

Esperanza had been going to NYU Law School at night for the past six years. She graduated on Monday.

'I probably won't go.'

'Why not?'

'I'm not big on ceremony,' she said.

Esperanza's only close relative, her mother, had died a few months back. Myron suspected that her death had more to do with Esperanza's decision than not being big on ceremony.

'Well, I'm going,' Myron said. 'Sitting front row center. I want to see it all.'

Silence.

Esperanza broke it. 'Is this the part where I choke back tears because someone cares?'

Myron shook his head. 'Forget I said anything.'

'No, really, I want to get it right. Should I break down in loud sobs or just sniffle a little? Or better yet, I could get a little teary, like Michael Landon on *Little House on the Prairie*.'

'You're such a wiseass.'

'Only when you're being patronizing.'

'I'm not being patronizing. I care. Sue me.'

'Whatever,' she said.

'Any messages?'

'About a million, but nothing that I can't handle until Monday,' she said. 'Oh, one thing.'

'What?'

'The bitch asked me out to lunch.'

'The bitch' was Jessica, the love of Myron's life. Putting it kindly, Esperanza did not like Jessica. Many assumed that this had something to do with jealousy, with some sort of latent attraction between Esperanza and Myron. Nope. For one thing, Esperanza liked, er, flexibility in her love life. For a while she had dated a guy named Max, then a woman named Lucy, and now another woman named Hester. 'How many times have I asked you not to call her that?' Myron said.

'About a million.'

'So are you going?'

'Probably,' she said. 'I mean, it's a free meal. Even if I do have to look at her face.'

They hung up. Myron smiled. He was a bit surprised. While Jessica did not reciprocate Esperanza's animosity, a lunch date to thaw out their personal cold war was not something Myron would have anticipated. Perhaps now that they were living together, Jess figured it was time to offer an olive branch. What the hell. Myron dialed Jessica.

The machine picked up. He heard her voice. When the beep came on, he said, 'Jess? Pick up.'

She did. 'God, I wish you were here right now.' Jessica had a way with openings.

'Oh?' He could see her lying on the couch, the phone cord twisted in her fingers. 'Why's that?'

'I'm about to take a ten-minute break.'

'A full ten minutes?'

'Yup.'

'Then you'd be expecting extended foreplay?'

She laughed. 'Up for it, big guy?'

'I will be,' he said, 'if you don't stop talking about it.'

'Maybe we should change the subject,' she said.

Myron had moved into Jessica's Soho loft a few months ago. For most people, this would be a somewhat dramatic change – moving from a suburb in New Jersey to a trendy section of New York, moving in with a woman you love, etc. – but for Myron, the change rivaled puberty. He had spent his entire life living with his mom and dad in the classic suburban town of Livingston, New Jersey. Entire life. Age zero to six in the upstairs bedroom on the right. Age six to thirteen in the upstairs bedroom on the left. Age thirteen to thirty-something in the basement.

After that long, the apron strings become steel bands.

'I hear you're taking Esperanza out for lunch,' he said.

'Yup.'

'How come?'

'No reason.'

'No reason?'

'I think she's cool. I want to go to lunch. Stop being so nosy.'

'You realize, of course, that she hates you.'

'I can handle it,' Jessica said. 'So how's the golf tournament?'

'Very strange,' he said.

'How so?'

'Too long a story to tell now, sweetcakes. Can I call you later?'

'Sure.' Then: 'Did you say "sweetcakes"?'

When they hung up, Myron frowned. Something was amiss. He and Jessica had never been closer, their relationship never stronger. Moving in together had been the right move, and a lot of their past demons had been exorcised away of late. They were loving toward each other, considerate of each other's feelings and needs, and almost never fought.

So why did Myron feel like they were standing on the cusp of some deep abyss?

He shook it off. All of this was just the by-product of an overstimulated imagination. Just because a ship is sailing

68

upon smooth waters, he surmised, does not mean it is heading for an iceberg.

Wow, that was deep.

By the time he got back to the table, Tad Crispin was sipping an iced tea too. Win made the introductions. Crispin was dressed in yellows, lots of yellows, kind of like the man with the yellow hat from the Curious George books. Everything was yellow. Even his golf shoes. Myron tried not to make a face.

As if reading his mind, Norm Zuckerman said, 'This isn't our line.'

'Good to hear,' Myron said.

Tad Crispin stood. 'Nice to meet you, sir.'

Myron offered up a great big smile. 'It's a true honor to meet you, Tad.' His voice reeked with the sincerity of, say, a chain-store appliance salesman. The two men shook hands. Myron kept on smiling. Crispin began to look wary.

Zuckerman pointed a thumb at Myron and leaned toward Win. 'Is he always this smooth?'

Win nodded. 'You should see him with the ladies.'

Everyone sat.

'I can't stay long,' Crispin said.

'We understand, Tad,' Zuckerman said, doing the shooing thing again with both hands. 'You're tired, you need to concentrate on tomorrow. Go already, get some sleep.'

Crispin sort of smiled a little and looked at Win. 'I want you to have my account,' he said.

'I don't "have" accounts,' Win corrected. 'I advise on them.'

'There's a difference?'

'Most definitely,' Win said. 'You are in control of your

money at all times. I will make recommendations. I will make them to you directly. No one else. We will discuss them. You will then make a final decision. I will not buy or sell or trade anything without you being fully aware of what is going on.'

Crispin nodded. 'That sounds good.'

'I thought it might,' Win said. 'From what I see, you plan on watching your money carefully.'

'Yes.'

'Savvy,' Win said with a nod. 'You've read about too many athletes retiring broke. Of being taken advantage of by unscrupulous money managers and the like.'

'Yes.'

'And it will be my job to help you maximize your return, correct?'

Crispin leaned forward a bit. 'Correct.'

'Very well, then. It will be my task to help maximize your investment opportunities *after* you earn it. But I would not be serving your best interests if I did not also tell you how to make more.'

Crispin's eyes narrowed. 'I'm not sure I follow.'

Zuckerman said, 'Win.'

Win ignored him. 'As your financial consultant, I would be remiss if I did not make the following recommendation: You need a good agent.'

Crispin's line of vision slid toward Myron. Myron remained still, looking back at him steadily. He turned back to Win. 'I know you work with Mr Bolitar,' Crispin said.

'Yes and no,' Win said. 'If you decide to use his services I do not make one penny more. Well, that's not exactly true. If you choose to use Myron's services, you will make more money and subsequently I will have more of your money to invest. So in that way, I will make more.'

'Thanks,' Crispin said, 'but I'm not interested.'

'That's up to you,' Win said, 'but let me just explain a little further what I meant by yes and no. I manage assets worth approximately four hundred million dollars. Myron's clients represent less than three percent of that total. I am not employed by MB SportsReps. Myron Bolitar is not employed by Lock-Horne Securities. We do not have a partnership. I have not invested in his enterprise and he is not invested in mine. Myron has never looked at, asked about, or in any way discussed the financial situation of any of my clients. We are totally separate. Except for one thing.'

All eyes were on Win. Myron, not famous for knowing when to keep his mouth shut, knew now.

'I am the financial consultant for every one of his clients,' Win said. 'Do you know why?'

Crispin shook his head.

'Because Myron insists upon it.'

Crispin looked confused. 'I don't understand. If he gets nothing out of it—'

'I didn't say that. He gets plenty out of it.'

'But you said—'

'He, too, was an athlete; did you know that?'

'I heard something about it.'

'He knows what happens to athletes. How they get cheated. How they squander their earnings, never fully accepting the fact that their careers can be over in a heartbeat. So he insists – insists, mind you – that he does not handle their finances. I've seen him refuse clients because of this. He further insists that I handle them. Why? For the same reason you sought me out. He knows

I am the best. Immodest but true. Myron further insists that they see me in person at least once every quarter. Not just phone calls. Not just faxes or E-mails or letters. He insists that I go over every item in the account personally with them.'

Win leaned farther back and steepled his fingers. The man loved to steeple his fingers. It looked good on him. Gave him an air of wisdom. 'Myron Bolitar is my best friend. I know he'd give his life for me and I for him. But if he ever thought that I was not doing what was in a client's best interest, he would take away their portfolios without a second thought.'

Norm said, 'Beautiful speech, Win. Got me right there.' He pointed to his stomach.

Win gave him the look. Norm stopped smiling.

'I made the deal with Mr Zuckerman on my own,' Crispin said. 'I could make others.'

'I won't comment on the Zoom deal,' Win said. 'But I will tell you this. You are a bright young man. A bright man knows not only his strengths but equally important, he knows his weaknesses. I do not, for example, know how to negotiate an endorsement contract. I may know the basics, but it is not my business. I'm not a plumber. If a pipe in my house broke, I would not be able to fix it. You are a golfer. You are one of the greatest talents I have ever seen. You should concentrate on that.'

Tad Crispin took a sip of iced tea. He crossed his ankle on his knee. Even his socks were yellow. 'You are making a hard sale for your friend,' he said.

'Wrong,' Win said. 'I would kill for my friend, but financially I owe him nothing. You, on the other hand, are my client, and thus I have a very serious fiscal responsibility with regard to you. Stripping it bare, you have asked me to increase your portfolio. I will suggest several investment sources to you. But this is the best recommendation I can make.'

Crispin turned to Myron. He looked him up and down, studying him hard. Myron almost brayed so he could examine his teeth. 'He makes you sound awfully good,' Crispin said to Myron.

'I am good,' Myron said. 'But I don't want him to give you the wrong impression. I'm not quite as altruistic as Win might have made me sound. I don't insist clients use him because I'm a swell guy. I know that having him handle my clients is a major plus. He improves the value of my services. He helps keep my clients happy. That's what I get out of it. Yes, I insist on having clients heavily involved in the decision-making on money matters, but that's as much to protect me as them.'

'How so?'

'Obviously you know something about managers or agents robbing athletes.'

'Yes.'

'Do you know why so much of that occurs?'

Crispin shrugged. 'Greed, I suppose.'

Myron tilted his head in a yes-and-no gesture. 'The main culprit is apathy. An athlete's lack of involvement. They get lazy. They decide it's easier to fully trust their agent, and that's bad. Let the agent pay the bills, they say. Let the agent invest the money. That kind of thing. But that won't ever happen at MB SportsReps. Not because I'm watching. Not because Win's watching. But because you are watching.'

'I'm watching now,' Crispin said.

'You're watching your money, true. I doubt you're watching everything else.'

Crispin considered that for a moment. 'I appreciate the talk,' he said, 'but I think I'm okay on my own.'

Myron pointed at Tad Crispin's head. 'How much are you getting for that hat?' he asked.

'Excuse me?'

'You're wearing a hat with no company logo on it,' Myron explained. 'For a player of your ilk, that's a loss of at least a quarter of a million dollars.'

Silence.

'But I'm going to be working with Zoom,' Crispin said.

'Did they purchase hat rights from you?'

He thought about it. 'I don't think so.'

'The front of the hat is a quarter million. We can also sell the sides if you want. They'll go for less. Maybe we'll total four hundred grand. Your shirt is another matter.'

'Now just wait one minute here,' Zuckerman interjected. 'He's going to be wearing Zoom shirts.'

'Fine, Norm,' Myron said. 'But he's allowed to wear logos. One on the chest, one on either sleeve.'

'Logos?'

'Anything. Coca-Cola maybe. IBM. Even Home Depot.'

'Logos on my shirt?'

'Yep. And what do you drink out there?'

'Drink? When I play?'

'Sure. I can probably get you a deal with Powerade or one of the soda companies. How about Poland Spring water? They might be good. And your golf bag. You have to negotiate a deal for your golf bag.'

'I don't understand.'

'You're a billboard, Tad. You're on television. Lots of fans see you. Your hat, your shirt, your golf bag – those are all places to post ads.'

Zuckerman said, 'Now hold on a second. He can't just—'

A cell phone began to sound, but it never made it past the first ring. Myron's finger reached the ringer and turned it off with a speed that would have made Wyatt Earp retire. Fast reflexes. They came in handy every once in a while.

Still, the brief sound had drawn the ire of nearby club members. Myron looked around. He was on the receiving end of several dagger-glares, including one from Win.

'Hurry around behind the clubhouse,' Win said pointedly. 'Let no one see you.'

Myron gave a flippant salute and rushed out like a man with a suddenly collapsing bladder. When he reached a safe area near the parking lot, he answered the call.

'Hello.'

'Oh, God . . .' It was Linda Coldren. Her tone struck the marrow of his bone.

'What's wrong?'

'He called again,' she said.

'Do you have it on tape?'

'Yes.'

'I'll be right ov—'

'No!' she shouted. 'He's watching the house.'

'You saw him?'

'No. But . . . Don't come here. Please.'

'Where are you calling from?'

'The fax line in the basement. Oh God, Myron, you should have heard him.'

'Did the number come up on the Caller ID?'

'Yes.'

'Give it to me.'

She did, Myron took out a pen from his wallet and wrote the number down on an old Visa receipt.

'Are you alone?'

'Jack is right here with me.'

'Anybody else? What about Esme Fong?'

'She's upstairs in the living room.'

'Okay,' Myron said. 'I'll need to hear the call.'

'Hold on. Jack is plugging the machine in now. I'll put you on the speaker so you can hear.'

Chapter 7

The tape player was snapped on. Myron heard the phone ringing first. The sound was surprisingly clear. Then he heard Jack Coldren: 'Hello?'

'Who's the chink bitch?'

The voice was very deep, very menacing, and definitely machine-altered. Male or female, young or old, it was anyone's guess.

'I don't know what—'

'You trying to fuck with me, you dumb son of a bitch? I'll start sending you the fucking brat in little pieces.'

Jack Coldren said, 'Please—'

'I told you not to contact anyone.'

'We haven't.'

'Then tell me who that chink bitch is who just walked into your house.'

Silence.

'You think we're stupid, Jack?'

'Of course not.'

'So who the fuck is she?'

'Her name is Esme Fong,' Coldren said quickly. 'She works for a clothing company. She's just here to set up an endorsement deal with my wife, that's all.'

'Bullshit.'

'It's the truth, I swear.'

'I don't know, Jack . . .'

'I wouldn't lie to you.'

'Well, Jack, we'll just see about that. This is gonna cost you.'

'What do you mean?'

'One hundred grand. Call it a penalty price.'

'For what?'

'Never you fucking mind. You want the kid alive? It's gonna cost you one hundred grand now. That's in—'

'Now hold on a second.' Coldren cleared his throat. Trying to gain some footing, some degree of control.

'Jack?'

'Yes?'

'You interrupt me again and I'm going to stick your kid's dick in a vise.'

Silence.

'You get the money ready, Jack. One hundred grand. I'll call you back and let you know what to do. Do you understand?'

'Yes.'

'Don't fuck up, Jack. I enjoy hurting people.'

The brief silence was shattered by a sharp, sudden scream, a scream that jangled nerve endings and raised hackles. Myron's hand tightened on the receiver.

The phone disconnected. Then a dial tone. Then nothing.

Linda Coldren took him off the speaker. 'What are we going to do?'

'Call the FBI,' Myron said.

'Are you out of your mind?'

'I think it's your best move.'

Jack Coldren said something in the background. Linda came back on the line. 'Absolutely not. We just want to pay the ransom and get our son back.'

No point in arguing with them. 'Sit tight. I'll call you back as soon as I can.'

Myron disconnected the call and dialed another number. Lisa at New York Bell. She'd been a contact of theirs since the days he and Win had worked for the government.

'A Caller ID came up with a number in Philadelphia,' he said. 'Can you find an address for me?'

'No problem,' Lisa said.

He gave her the number. People who watch too much television think this sort of thing takes a long time. Not anymore. Traces are instantaneous now. No 'keep him on a little longer' or any of that stuff. The same is true when it comes to finding the location of a phone number. Any operator almost anywhere can plug the number into her computer or use one of those reverse directories, and whammo. Heck, you don't even need an operator. Computer programs on CD-ROM and websites did the same thing.

'It's a pay phone,' she said.

Not good news, but not unexpected either. 'Do you know where?'

'The Grand Mercado Mall in Bala-Cynwyd.'

'A mall?'

'Yes.'

'You're sure?'

'That's what it says.'

'Where in the mall?'

'I have no idea. You think they list it "between Sears and Victoria's Secret"?'

This made no sense. A mall? The kidnapper had dragged Chad Coldren to a mall and made him scream into a phone?

'Thanks, Lisa.'

He hung up and turned back toward the porch. Win was standing directly behind him. His arms were folded, his body, as always, completely relaxed.

'The kidnapper called,' Myron said.

'So I overheard.'

'I could use your help tracking this down.'

'No,' Win said.

'This isn't about your mother, Win.'

Win's face did not change, but something happened to his eyes. 'Careful,' was all he said.

Myron shook his head. 'I have to go. Please make my excuses.'

'You came here to recruit clients,' Win said. 'You claimed earlier that you agreed to help the Coldrens in the hopes of representing them.'

'So?'

'So you are excruciatingly close to landing the world's top golf protégé. Reason dictates that you stay.'

'I can't.'

Win unfolded his arms, shook his head.

'Will you do one thing for me? To let me know if I'm wasting time or not?'

Win remained still.

'You know how I told you about Chad using his ATM card?'

'Yes.'

'Get me the security videotape of the transaction,' he said. 'It may tell me if this whole thing is just a hoax on Chad's part.'

Win turned back to the porch. 'I'll see you at the house tonight.'

Chapter 8

Myron parked at the mall and checked his watch. Seven forty-five. It had been a very long day and it was still relatively early. He entered through a Macy's and immediately located one of those big table blueprints of the mall. Public telephones were marked with blue locators. Eleven altogether. Two at the south entrance downstairs. Two at the north entrance upstairs. Seven at the food court.

Malls were the great American geographical equalizer. Between shiny anchor stores and beneath excessively floodlit ceilings, Kansas equaled California, New Jersey equaled Nevada. No place was truly more Americana. Some of the stores inside might be different, but not by much. Athlete's Foot or Foot Locker, Rite Aid or CVS, Williams-Sonoma or Pottery Barn, the Gap or Banana Republic or Old Navy (all, coincidentally, owned by the same people), Waldenbooks or B. Dalton, several anonymous shoe stores, a Radio Shack, a Victoria's Secret, an art gallery with Gorman, McKnight, and Behrens, a museum store of some kind, two record stores – all wrapped up in some Orwellian, sleek-chrome neo-Roman Forum with chintzy fountains and overstated marble and dentist-office sculptures and unmanned information booths and fake ferns.

In front of a store selling electric organs and pianos sat an employee dressed in an ill-fitting navy suit and a sailor's cap. He played 'Muskrat Love' on an organ. Myron was tempted to ask him where Tenille was, but he refrained. Too obvious. Organ stores in malls. Who goes to the mall to buy an organ?

He hurried past the Limited or the Unlimited or the Severely Challenged or something like that. Then Jeans Plus or Jeans Minus or Shirts Only or Pants Only or Tank Top City or something like that. They all looked pretty much the same. They all employed lots of skinny, bored teenagers who stocked shelves with the enthusiasm of a eunuch at an orgy.

There were lots of high school kids draped about – just hanging, man – and looking very, er, rad. At the risk of sounding like a reverse racist, all the white boys looked the same to him. Baggie shorts. White T-shirts. Unlaced black hundred-dollar high-top sneakers. Baseball cap pulled low with the brim worked into a nifty curve, covering a summer buzzcut. Thin. Lanky. Long-limbed. Pale as a Goya portrait, even in the summer. Poor posture. Eyes that never looked directly at another human being. Uncomfortable eyes. Slightly scared eyes.

He passed a hair salon called Snip Away, which sounded more like a vasectomy clinic than a beauty parlor. The Snip Away beauticians were either reformed mall girls or guys named Mario whose fathers were named Sal. Two patrons sat in a window – one getting a perm, the other a bleach job. Who wanted that? Who wanted to sit in a window and have the whole world watch you get your hair done?

He took an escalator up past a plastic garden complete with plastic vines to the crowned jewel of the mall: the food court. It was fairly empty now, the dinner crowd long since gone. Food courts were the final outpost of the great American melting pot. Italian, Chinese, Japanese, Mexican, Middle Eastern (or Greek), a deli, a chicken place, one fast food chain like McDonald's (which had the biggest crowd), a frozen yogurt place, and then a few strange offshoots – the ones started by people who dream of franchising themselves into becoming the next Ray Kroc. Ethiopian Ecstasy. Sven's Swedish Meatballs. Curry Up and Eat.

Myron checked for numbers on the seven phones. All had been whited out. Not surprising, the way people abused them nowadays. No problemo either. He took out his cellular phone and punched in the number from the Caller ID. A phone starting ringing immediately.

Bingo.

The one on the far right. Myron picked it up to make sure. 'Hello?' he said. He heard the hello in his cellular phone. Then he said to himself through the cellular, 'Hello, Myron, nice to hear from you.' He decided to stop talking to himself, too early in the evening to be this goofy.

He hung up the phone and looked around. A group of mall girls inhabited a table not far away. They sat in a closed circle with the protectiveness of coyotes during mating season.

Of the food stands, Sven's Swedish Meatballs had the

best view of the phone. Myron approached. Two men worked the booth. They both had dark hair and dark skin and Saddam Hussein mustaches. One's name tag read Mustafa. The other Achmed.

'Which one of you is Sven?' he asked.

No smiles.

Myron asked about the phone. Mustafa and Achmed were less than helpful. Mustafa snapped that he worked for a living, and didn't watch phones. Achmed gestured and cursed him in a foreign tongue.

'I'm not much of a linguist,' Myron said, 'but that didn't sound like Swedish.'

Death glares.

'Bye now. I'll be sure to tell all my friends.'

Myron turned toward the table of mall girls. They all quickly looked down, like rats scurrying in the glare of a flashlight. He stepped toward them. Their eyes darted to and fro with what they must have thought were surreptitious glances. He heard a low cacophony of 'ohmygod! Ohmygod! Ohmygod! he'scomingover!'

Myron stopped directly at their table. There were four girls. Or maybe five or even six. Hard to say. They all seemed to blend into one another, into one hazy, indistinct mesh of hair and black lipstick and Fu Manchu-length fingernails and earrings and nose rings and cigarette smoke and too-tight halter tops and bare midriffs and popping gum.

The one sitting in the middle looked up first. She had hair like Elsa Lancaster in *The Bride of Frankenstein* and what looked like a studded dog collar around her neck. The other faces followed suit.

'Like, hi,' Elsa said.

Myron tried his most gentle, crooked smile. Harrison

Ford in *Regarding Henry*. 'Do you mind if I ask you a few questions?'

The girls all looked at one another. A few giggles escaped. Myron felt his face redden, though he wasn't sure why. They elbowed one another. No one answered. Myron proceeded.

'How long have you been sitting here?' he asked.

'Is this, like, one of those mall surveys?'

'No,' Myron said.

'Good. Those are, like, so lame, you know?'

'Uh-huh.'

'It's like, get away from me already, Mr Polyester Pants, you know?'

Myron said 'uh-huh' again. 'Do you remember how long you've been sitting here?'

'Nah. Amber, you know?'

'Like, we went to the Gap at four.'

'Right, the Gap. Fab sale.'

'Ultra sale. Love that blouse you bought, Trish.'

'Isn't it, like, the total package, Mindy?'

'Totally. Ultra.'

Myron said, 'It's almost eight now. Have you been here for the past hour?'

'Like, hello, anybody home? At least.'

'This is, like, our spot, you know?'

'No one else, like, sits here.'

'Except that one time when those gross lame-os tried to move in.'

'But, like, whoa, don't even go there, 'kay?'

They stopped and looked at Myron. He figured the answer to his prior question was yes, so he plowed ahead. 'Have you seen anybody use that pay phone?'

'Are you, like, a cop or something?'

86

'As if.'

'No way.'

'Way.'

'He's too cute to be a cop.'

'Oh, right, like Jimmy Smits isn't cute.'

'That's, like, TV, dumb wad. This is real life. Cops aren't cute in real life.'

'Oh, right, like Brad isn't totally cute? You, like, love him, remember?'

'As if. And he's not a cop. He's, like, some rent-a-uniform at Florsheim.'

'But he's so hot.'

'Totally.'

'Ultra buff.'

'He likes Shari.'

'Eeeuw. Shari?'

'I, like, hate her, you know?'

'Me too. Like, does she only shop at Sluts "R" Us, or what?'

'Totally.'

'It's, like, "Hello, Dial-a-Disease, this is Shari speaking."'

Giggles.

Myron looked for an interpreter. 'I'm not a cop,' he said.

'Told you.'

'As if.'

'But,' Myron said, 'I am dealing with something very important. Life-and-death. I need to know if you remember anyone using that phone – the one on the far right – forty-five minutes ago.'

'Whoa!' The one called Amber pushed her chair back.

'Clear out, because I'm, like, gonna barf for days, you know?'

'Like, Crusty the Clown.'

'He was, like, so gross!'

'Totally gross.'

'Totally.'

'He, like, winked at Amber!'

'As if!'

'Totally eeeuw!'

'Gag city.'

'Bet that slut Shari would have Frenched him.'

'At least.'

Giggles.

Myron said, 'You saw somebody?'

'Serious groatie.'

'Totally crusty.'

'He was, like, hello, ever wash your hair?'

'Like, hello, buy your cologne at the local Gas-N-Go?'

More giggles.

Myron said, 'Can you describe him to me?'

'Blue jeans from, like, "Attention, Kmart shoppers." '

'Work boots. Definitely not Timberland.'

'He was, like, so skinhead wanna-be, you know?'

Myron said, 'Skinhead wanna-be?'

'Like, a shaved head. Skanky beard. Tattoo of that thing on his arm.'

'That thing?' Myron tried.

'You know, that tattoo.' She kind of drew something in the air with her finger. 'It kinda looks like a funny cross from, like, the old days.'

Myron said, 'You mean a swastika?'

'Like, whatever. Do I look like a history major?'

'Like, how old was he?' Like. He'd said *like*. If he

stayed here much longer, he'd end up getting some part of him pierced. Way.

'Old.'

'Grampa-ville.'

'Like, at least twenty.'

'Height?' Myron asked. 'Weight?'

'Six feet.'

'Yeah, like six feet.'

'Bony.'

'Very.'

'Like, no ass at all.'

'None.'

'Was anybody with him?' Myron asked.

'As if.'

'Him?'

'No way.'

'Who would be with a skank like that?'

'Just him by that phone for like half an hour.'

'He wanted Mindy.'

'Did not!'

'Wait a second,' Myron said. 'He was there for half an hour?'

'Not that long.'

'Seemed a long time.'

'Maybe like fifteen minutes. Amber, like, always exaggerates.'

'Like, fuck you, Irish, all right? Just fuck you.'

'Anything else?' Myron asked.

'Beeper.'

'Right, beeper. Like anybody would ever call that skank.'

'Held it right up to the phone, too.'

Probably not a beeper. Probably a microcassette player.

That would explain the scream. Or a voice changer. They also came in a small box.

He thanked the girls and handed out business cards that listed his cellular phone number. One of the girls actually read it. She made a face.

'Like, your name is really Myron?'

'Yes.'

They all just stopped and looked at him.

'I know,' Myron said. 'Like, ultra lame-o.'

He was heading back to his car when a nagging thought suddenly resurfaced. The kidnapper on the phone had mentioned a 'chink bitch.' Somehow he had known about Esme Fong arriving at the house. The question was, how?

There were two possibilities. One, they had a bug in the house.

Not likely. If the Coldren residence was bugged or under some kind of electronic surveillance, the kidnapper would also have known about Myron's involvement.

Two, one of them was watching the house.

That seemed most logical. Myron thought a moment. If someone had been watching the house only an hour or so ago, it was fair to assume that they were still there, still hiding behind a bush or up a tree or something. If Myron could locate the person surreptitiously, he might be able to follow them back to Chad Coldren.

Was it worth the risk?

Like, totally.

Chapter 9

Ten o'clock.

Myron used Win's name again and parked in Merion's lot. He checked for Win's Jaguar, but it was nowhere to be seen. He parked and checked for guards. No one. They'd all been stationed at the front entrance. Made things easier.

He quickly stepped over the white rope used to hold back the galley and started crossing the golf course. It was dark now, but the lights from the houses across the way provided enough illumination to cross. For all its fame, Merion was a tiny course. From the parking lot to Golf House Road, across two fairways, was less than a hundred yards.

Myron trudged forward. Humidity hung in the air in a heavy blanket of beads. Myron's shirt began to feel sticky. The crickets were incessant and plenteous, their swarming tune as monotonous as a Mariah Carey CD, though not quite as grating. The grass tickled Myron's sockless ankles.

Despite his natural aversion to golf, Myron still felt the appropriate sense of awe, as if he were trespassing over sacred ground. Ghosts breathed in the night, the same way they breathed at any sight that had borne legends. Myron remembered once standing on the parquet floor at Boston Garden when no one else was there. It was a week after he had been picked by the Celtics in the first round of the NBA draft. Clip Arnstein, the Celtics' fabled general manager, had introduced him to the press earlier that day. It had been enormous fun. Everybody had been laughing and smiling and calling Myron the next Larry Bird. That night, as he stood alone in the famed halls of the Garden, the championship flags hanging from the rafters actually seemed to sway in the still air, beckoning him forward and whispering tales of the past and promises of what was to come.

Myron never played a game on that parquet floor.

He slowed as he reached Golf House Road and stepped over the white rope. Then he ducked behind a tree. This would not be easy. Then again, it would not be easy for his quarry either. Neighborhoods like this noted anything suspicious. Like a parked car where it didn't belong. That had been why Myron had parked in the Merion lot. Had the kidnapper done likewise? Or was his car out on the street? Or had someone dropped him off?

He kept low and darted to another tree. He looked, he assumed, rather doofy – a guy six-feet four inches tall and comfortably over two hundred pounds darting between bushes like something left on the cutting room floor of *The Dirty Dozen*.

But what choice did he have?

He couldn't just casually walk down the street. The kidnapper might spot him. His whole plan relied on the fact that he could spot the kidnapper before the kidnapper spotted him. How to do this? He really did not have a clue. The best he could come up with was to keep circling closer and closer to the Coldren house, looking out for, er, uh, something.

He scanned the surroundings – for what, he wasn't sure. Someplace for a kidnapper to use as a lookout spot, he guessed. A safe place to hide, maybe, or a perch where a man with binoculars could survey the scene. Nothing. The night was absolutely windless and still.

He circled the block, dashing haphazardly from one bush to another, feeling now very much like John Belushi breaking into Dean Wormer's office in *Animal House*.

Animal House and *The Dirty Dozen*. Myron watched too many movies.

As he continued to spiral closer to the Coldrens' residence, Myron realized that there was probably a good chance that he'd be the 'spottee' rather than the 'spotter.' He tried to hide himself better, to concentrate on making himself become part of the night, to blend in to the background and become invisible.

Myron Bolitar, Mutant Ninja Warrior.

Lights twinkled from spacious homes of stone and black shutters. They were all imposing and rather beautiful with a tutelary, stay-away coziness about them. Solid homes. The third-little-piggie homes. Settled and staying and proud homes.

He was getting very close to the Coldren house now. Still nothing – not even a single car parked on the roads. Sweat coated him like syrup on a stack of pancakes. God, he wanted to take a shower. He hunched down and watched the house.

Now what?

Wait. Be on the lookout for movement of some kind. Surveillance and the like was not Myron's forte. Win usually handled that kind of stuff. He had the body control and the patience. Myron was already getting fidgety. He wished he'd brought a magazine or something to read.

The three minutes of monotony was broken when the front door opened. Myron sat up. Esme Fong and Linda Coldren appeared in the door frame. They said their good-byes. Esme gave Linda the firm handshake and headed to her car. Linda Coldren shut the front door. Esme Fong started her car and left.

A thrill a second, this surveillance stuff.

Myron settled back behind a shrub. There were lots of shrubs around here. Everywhere one looked, there were shrubs of various sizes and shapes and purposes. Rich blue bloods must really like shrubs, Myron decided. He wondered if they had had any on the *Mayflower*.

His legs were beginning to cramp from all this crouching. He straightened them out one at a time. His bad knee, the one that ended his basketball career, began to throb. Enough. He was hot and sticky and in pain. Time to get out of here.

Then he heard a sound.

It seemed to be coming from the back door. He sighed, creaked to his feet, and circled. He found yet another comfy shrub and hid behind it. He peered out.

Jack Coldren was in the backyard with his caddie, Diane Hoffman. Jack held a golf club in his hands, but he wasn't hitting. He was talking with Diane Hoffman.

Animatedly. Diane Hoffman was talking back. Equally animated. Neither one of them seemed very pleased. Myron could not hear them, but they were both gesturing like mad.

An argument. A rather heated argument.

Hmm.

Of course, there probably was an innocent explanation. Caddies and players argue all the time, Myron guessed. He remembered reading how Seve Ballesteros, the Spanish former wunderkind, was always fighting with his caddie. Bound to happen. Routine stuff, a caddie and a pro having a little tiff, especially during such a pressure-filled tournament as the US Open.

But the timing was curious.

Think about it a second. A man gets a terrifying call from a kidnapper. He hears his son scream in apparent fright or pain. Then, a couple of hours later, he is in his backyard arguing about his backswing with his caddie.

Did that make sense?

Myron decided to move closer, but there was no straight path. Shrubs again, like tackle dummies at a football practice. He'd have to move to the side of the house and circle in behind them. He made a quick bolt to his left and risked another glance. The heated argument continued. Diane Hoffman took a step closer to Jack.

Then she slapped him in the face.

The sound sliced through the night like a scythe. Myron froze. Diane Hoffman shouted something. Myron heard the word *bastard*, but nothing else. Diane flicked her cigarette at Jack's feet and stormed off. Jack looked down, shook his head slowly, and went back inside.

Well, well, Myron thought. Must have been some trouble with that backswing.

Myron stayed behind the shrub. He heard a car start in the driveway. Diane Hoffman's, he assumed. For a moment, he wondered if she had a role in this. Obviously she had been in the house. Could she be the mysterious lookout? He leaned back and considered the possibility. The idea was just starting to soak in and settle when Myron spotted the man.

Or at least he assumed it was a man. It was hard to tell from where he was crouched. Myron could not believe what he was seeing. He had been wrong. Dead wrong. The perpetrator hadn't been hiding in the bushes or anything like that. Myron watched now in silence as someone dressed completely in black climbed out an upper-floor window. More specifically – if memory didn't fail him – Chad Coldren's bedroom window.

Hello there.

Myron ducked down. Now what? He needed a plan. Yes, a plan. Good thinking. But what plan? Did he grab the perp now? No. Better to follow him. Maybe he'd lead him back to Chad Coldren. That would be nice.

He took another peek out. The black-clad figure had scaled down a white lattice fence with entwined ivy. He jumped the last few feet. As soon as he hit the ground, he sprinted away.

Great.

Myron followed, trying to stay as far behind the figure as possible. The figure, however, was running. This made following silently rather difficult. But Myron kept back. Didn't want to risk being seen. Besides, chances were good that the perpetrator had brought a car or was getting picked up by someone. These streets barely had any traffic. Myron would be bound to hear an engine.

But then what?

What would Myron do when the perp got to the car? Run back to get his own? No, that wouldn't work. Follow a car on foot? Er, not likely. So what exactly was he going to do?

Good question.

He wished Win were here.

The perp kept running. And running. Myron was starting to suck air. Jesus, who the hell was he chasing anyway, Frank Shorter? Another quarter mile passed before the perp abruptly veered to the right and out of view. The turn was so sudden that for a moment Myron wondered if he'd been spotted. Impossible. He was too far back and his quarry had not so much as glanced over his shoulder.

Myron tried to hurry a bit, but the road was gravelly. Running silently would be impossible. Still, he had to make up ground. He ran high atop his tiptoes, looking not unlike Baryshnikov with dysentery. He prayed nobody would see him.

He reached the turn. The name of the street was Green Acres Road. Green Acres. The old TV show theme song started in his head, like someone had pressed buttons on a jukebox. He couldn't stop it. Eddie Albert rode a tractor. Eva Gabor opened boxes in a Manhattan penthouse. Sam Drucker waved from behind the counter of his general store. Mr Haney pulled his suspenders with both thumbs. Arnold the pig snorted.

Man, the humidity was definitely getting to him.

Myron wheeled to the right and looked ahead.

Nothing.

Green Acres was a short cul-de-sac with maybe five homes. Fabulous homes, or so Myron assumed. Towering shrub walls – again with the shrubs – lined either side of the street. Locked gates were on the driveways, the kind that worked by remote control or by pushing a combination in a keypad. Myron stopped and looked down the road.

So where was our boy?

He felt his pulse quicken. No sign of him. The only escape route was through the woods between two houses in the cul-de-sac. He must have gone in there, Myron surmised – if, that is, he was trying to escape and not, say, hide in the bushes. He might, after all, have spotted Myron. He might have decided to duck down somewhere and hide. Hide and then pounce when Myron walked by.

These were not comforting thoughts.

Now what?

He licked the sweat off his upper lip. His mouth felt terribly dry. He could almost hear himself sweat.

Suck it up, Myron, he told himself. He was six-four and two hundred and twenty pounds. A big guy. He was also a black belt in tae kwon do and a well-trained fighter. He could fend off any attack.

Unless the guy was armed.

True. Let's face it. Fight training and experience were helpful, but they did not make one bullet-proof. Not even Win. Of course, Win wouldn't have been stupid enough to get himself into this mess. Myron carried a weapon only when he thought it was absolutely necessary. Win, on the other hand, carried at least two guns and one bladed instrument at all times. Third world countries should be as well armed as Win.

So what to do?

He looked left and right, but there was no place much for anybody to hide. The shrub walls were thick and fully impenetrable. That left only the woods at the end of the road. But there were no lights down that way and the woods looked dense and forbidding.

Should he go in?

No. That would be pointless at best. He had no idea how big the woods were, what direction to head in, nothing. The odds of finding the perpetrator were frighteningly remote. Myron's best hope was that the perp was just hiding for a while, waiting for Myron to clear out.

Clear out. That sounded like a plan.

Myron moved back to the end of Green Acres. He turned left, traveled a couple of hundred yards, and settled behind yet another shrub. He and shrubs were on a first-name basis by now. This one he named Frank.

He waited an hour. No one appeared.

Great.

He finally stood up, said good-bye to Frank, and headed back to the car. The perpetrator must have escaped through the woods. That meant that he had planned an escape route or, more probably, he knew the area well. Could mean that it was Chad Coldren. Or it could mean that the kidnappers knew what they were doing. And if that was so, it meant there was a good chance that they now knew about Myron's involvement and the fact that the Coldrens had disobeyed them.

Myron hoped like hell it was just a hoax. But if it wasn't, if this was indeed a real kidnapping, he wondered about repercussions. He wondered how the kidnappers would react to what he had done. And as he continued on his way, Myron remembered their previous phone call and the harrowing, flesh-creeping sound of Chad Coldren's scream.

Chapter 10

'Meanwhile, back at stately Wayne Manor . . .'

That voice-over from the TV *Batman* always came to Myron when he reached the steely gates of the Lockwood estate. In reality, Win's family home looked very little like Bruce Wayne's house, though it did offer up the same aura. A tremendous serpentine driveway wound to an imposing stone mansion on the hill. There was grass, lots of it, all the blades kept at a consistently ideal length, like a politician's hair in an election year. There were also lush gardens and hills and a swimming pool, a pond, a tennis court, horse stables, and a horse obstacle course of some kind.

All in all, the Lockwood estate was very 'stately' and worthy of the term 'manor,' whatever that meant.

Myron and Win were staying at the guest house – or as Win's father liked to call it, 'the cottage.' Exposed beams, hardwood floors, fireplace, new kitchen with a big island in the middle, pool room – not to mention five bedrooms, four and half baths. Some cottage.

Myron tried to sort through what was happening, but all he came up with was a series of paradoxes, a whole lot of 'which came first, the chicken or the egg?' Motive, for example. On the one hand, it might make sense to kidnap Chad Coldren to throw off Jack Coldren. But Chad had been missing since *before* the tournament, which meant the kidnapper was either very cautious or very prophetic. On the other hand, the kidnapper had asked for one hundred grand, which pointed to a simple case of kidnapping for money. A hundred grand was a nice, tidy sum – a little low for a kidnapping, but not bad for a few days' work.

But if this was merely a kidnapping to extort mucho dinero, the timing was curious. Why now? Why during the one time a year the US Open was played? More than that, why kidnap Chad during the one time in the last twenty-three years the Open was being played at Merion – the one time in almost a quarter of a century that Jack Coldren had a chance to revisit and redeem his greatest failing?

Seemed like a hell of a coincidence.

That brought it back to a hoax and a scenario that went something like this: Chad Coldren disappears before the tournament to screw around with his dad's mind. When that doesn't work – when, to the contrary, Dad starts winning – he ups the ante and fakes his own kidnapping. Taking it a step farther, one could assume that it had been Chad Coldren who had been climbing out of his own window. Who better? Chad Coldren knew the area. Chad Coldren probably knew how to go through those woods.

Or maybe he was hiding out at a friend's house who lived on Green Acres Road. Whatever.

It added up. It made sense.

All of this assumed, of course, that Chad truly disliked his father. Was there evidence of that? Myron thought so. Start off with the fact that Chad was sixteen years old. Not an easy age. Weak evidence for sure, but worth keeping in mind. Second – and far, far more important – Jack Coldren was an absent father. No athlete is away from home as much as a golfer. Not basketball players or football players or baseball players or hockey players. The only ones who come close are tennis players. In both tennis and golf, tournaments are taking place almost all year – there is little so-called off season – and there is no such thing as a home game. If you were lucky, you hit your home course once a year.

Lastly – and perhaps most crucial of all – Chad had been gone for *two* days without raising eyebrows. Forget Linda Coldren's discourse on responsible children and open child-raising. The only rational explanation for their nonchalance was that this had happened before, or at the very least, was not unexpected.

But there were problems with the hoax scenario too.

For example, how did Mr Total Grunge from the mall fit in?

There was indeed the rub. What role was the Crusty Nazi playing in all this? Did Chad Coldren have an accomplice? Possibly, but that really didn't fit in well with a revenge scenario. If Chad was indeed behind all this, Myron doubted that the preppy golfer would join forces with a 'skinhead wanna-be,' complete with a swastika tattoo.

So where did that leave Myron?

Baffled.

As Myron pulled up to the guest house, he felt his heart constrict. Win's Jag was there. But so was a green Chevy Nova.

Oh, Christ.

Myron got out of the car slowly. He checked the license plate on the Nova. Unfamiliar. As he expected. He swallowed and moved away.

He opened the cottage's front door and welcomed the sudden onslaught of air-conditioning. The lights were out. For a moment he just stood in the foyer, eyes closed, the cool air tingling his skin. An enormous grandfather clock ticked.

Myron opened his eyes and flicked on a light.

'Good evening.'

He pivoted to his right. Win was seated in a high-back leather chair by the fireplace. He cupped a brandy snifter in his hand.

'You were sitting in the dark?' Myron asked.

'Yes.'

Myron frowned. 'A bit theatrical, don't you think?'

Win switched on a nearby lamp. His face was a tad rosy from the brandy. 'Care to join me?'

'Sure. I'll be right back.'

Myron grabbed a cold Yoo-Hoo from the refrigerator and sat on the couch across from his friend. He shook the can and popped it open. They drank in silence for several minutes. The clock ticked. Long shadows snaked across the floor in thin, almost smoky tendrils. Too bad it was summertime. This was the kind of setting that begged for a roaring fire and maybe some howling wind. An air conditioner just didn't cut it.

Myron was just getting comfortable when he heard a toilet flush. He looked a question at Win.

'I am not alone,' Win said.

'Oh.' Myron adjusted himself on the couch. 'A woman?'

'Your gifts,' Win said. 'They never cease to amaze.'

'Anybody I know?' Myron asked.

Win shook his head. 'Not even somebody I know.'

The norm. Myron looked steadily at his friend. 'You want to talk about this?'

'No.'

'I'm here if you do.'

'Yes, I see that.' Win swished around the drink in the snifter. He finished it in one gulp and reached for the crystal decanter. There was a slight slur in his speech. Myron tried to remember the last time he had seen Win the vegetarian, the master of several martial arts, the transcendental meditator, the man so at ease and in focus with his surroundings, have too much to drink.

It had been a very long time.

'I have a golf question for you,' Myron said.

Win nodded for him to proceed.

'Do you think Jack Coldren can hang on to this lead?'

Win poured the brandy. 'Jack will win,' he said.

'You sound pretty sure.'

'I am sure.'

'Why?'

Win raised the glass to his mouth and looked over the rim. 'I saw his eyes.'

Myron made a face. 'What's that supposed to mean?'

'He has it back. The look in the eyes.'

'You're kidding, right?'

'Perhaps I am. But let me ask you something.'

'Go ahead.'

'What separates the great athletes from the very good? The legend from the journeyman? Simply put, what makes winners?'

'Talent,' Myron said. 'Practice. Skill.'

Win gave a slight shake of the head. 'You know better than that.'

'I do?'

'Yes. Many have talent. Many practice. There is more to the art of creating a true winner.'

'This look-in-the-eye thing?'

'Yes.'

Myron winced. 'You're not going to start singing "Eye of the Tiger," are you?'

Win cocked his head. 'Who sang that song?'

The continuing trivia game. Win knew the answer, of course. 'It was in *Rocky II*, right?'

'*Rocky III*,' Win corrected.

'That the one with Mr T?'

Win nodded. 'Who played . . . ?' he prompted.

'Clubber Lange.'

'Very good. Now who sang the song?'

'I don't remember.'

'The name of the group was Survivor,' Win said. 'Ironic name when you think of how quickly they vanished, no?'

'Uh-huh,' Myron said. 'So what is this great divider, Win? What makes a winner?'

Win took another swish and sip. 'Wanting,' he said.

'Wanting?'

'Hunger.'

'Uh-huh.'

'The answer isn't surprising,' Win said. 'Look in Joe DiMaggio's eyes. Or Larry Bird's. Or Michael Jordan's.

Look at pictures of John McEnroe in his prime, or Chris Evert. Look at Linda Coldren.' He stopped. 'Look in the mirror.'

'The mirror? I have this?'

'When you were on the court,' Win said slowly, 'your eyes were barely sane.'

They fell into silence. Myron took a swig of Yoo-Hoo. The cold aluminum felt good in his hand. 'You make the whole "wanting" thing sound like it's all foreign to you,' Myron said.

'It is.'

'Bull.'

'I am a good golfer,' Win said. 'Correction: I am a very good golfer. I practiced quite a bit in my youth. I have even won my share of tournaments. But I never wanted it bad enough to move up to that next level.'

'I've seen you in the ring,' Myron countered. 'In martial arts tournaments. You seemed plenty "wanting" to me.'

'That is very different,' Win said.

'How so?'

'I do not view a martial arts tournaments as a sporting contest, whereby the winner brings home a chintzy trophy and brags to colleagues and friends – nor do I view it as a competition that will lead to some sort of empty emotion that the insecure among us perceive as glory. Fighting is not a sport to me. It's about survival. If I could lose in there' – he motioned to an imaginary ring – 'I could lose in the real world.' Win looked up in the air. 'But . . .' His voice drifted off.

'But?' Myron repeated.

'But you may be on to something.'

'Oh?'

Win steepled his fingers. 'You see, fighting is life-and-death to me. That's how I treat it. But the athletes we've been talking about take it a step further. Every competition, even the most banal, is viewed by them as life-and-death – and losing is death.'

Myron nodded. He didn't buy it, but what the hell. Keep him talking. 'I don't get something,' he said. 'If Jack has this special "wanting," why hasn't he ever won a professional tournament?'

'He lost it.'

'The wanting?'

'Yes.'

'When?'

'Twenty-three years ago.'

'During the Open?'

'Yes,' Win said again. 'Most athletes lose it in a slow burnout. They grow weary or they win enough to quench whatever inferno rages in their bellies. But that was not the case with Jack. His fire was extinguished in one crisp, cold gust. You could almost see it. Twenty-three years ago. The sixteenth hole. The ball landing in the stone quarry. His eyes have never been the same.'

'Until now,' Myron added.

'Until now,' Win agreed. 'It took him twenty-three years, but he stoked the flames back to life.'

They both drank. Win sipped. Myron guzzled. The chocolaty coldness felt wonderful sliding down his throat. 'How long have you known Jack?' Myron asked.

'I met him when I was six years old. He was fifteen.'

'Did he have the "wanting" back then?'

Win smiled at the ceiling. 'He would sooner carve out his own kidney with a grapefruit spoon than lose to someone on the golf course.' He lowered his gaze to

Myron. 'Did Jack Coldren have the "wanting"? He was the pure definition.'

'Sounds like you admired him.'

'I did.'

'You don't anymore?'

'No.'

'What made you change?'

'I grew up.'

'Wow.' Myron took another swig of Yoo-Hoo. 'That's heavy.'

Win chuckled. 'You wouldn't understand.'

'Try me.'

Win put down the brandy snifter. He leaned forward very slowly. 'What is so great about winning?'

'Pardon?'

'People love a winner. They look up to him. They admire – nay, revere – him. They use terms like *hero* and *courage* and *perseverance* to describe him. They want to be near him and touch him. They want to be like him.'

Win spread his hands. 'But why? What about the winner do we want to emulate? His ability to blind himself to anything but the pursuit of empty aggrandizement? His ego-inflating obsession with wearing a hunk of metal around his neck? His willingness to sacrifice anything, including people, in order to best another human being on a lump of AstroTurf for a cheesy statuette?' He looked up at Myron, his always serene face suddenly lost. 'Why do we applaud this selfishness, this self-love?'

'Competitive drive isn't a bad thing, Win. You're talking about extremes.'

'But it is the extremists we admire most. By its nature, what you call "competitive drive" leads to extremism and destroys all in its path.'

'You're being simplistic, Win.'

'It is simple, my friend.'

They both settled back. Myron stared up at the exposed beams. After some time, he said, 'You have it wrong.'

'How so?'

Myron wondered how to explain it. 'When I played basketball,' he began, 'I mean, when I really got into it and reached these levels you're talking about – I barely thought about the score. I barely thought about my opponent or about beating somebody. I was alone. I was in the zone. This is going to sound stupid, but playing at the top of my game was almost Zen-like.'

Win nodded. 'And when did you feel this way?'

'Pardon?'

'When did you feel your most – to use your word – *Zen*?'

'I don't follow.'

'Was it at practice? No. Was it during an unimportant game or when your team was up by thirty points? No. What brought you to this sweat-drenched state of Nirvana, my friend, was competition. The desire – the naked need – to defeat a top-level opponent.'

Myron opened his mouth to counter. Then he stopped. Exhaustion was starting to take over. 'I'm not sure I have an answer to that,' he said. 'At the end of the day, I like to win. I don't know why. I like ice cream too. I don't know why either.'

Win frowned. 'Impressive simile,' he said flatly.

'Hey, it's late.'

Myron heard a car pull up front. A young blond entered the room and smiled. Win smiled back. She bent down and kissed him. Win had no problem with that. Win was never outwardly rude to his dates. He was not the type to rush them out. He had no problem with them staying the night, if it made them happier. Some might mistake this for kindness or a tender spot in the soul. They'd be wrong. Win let them stay because they meant so little to him. They could never reach him. They could never touch him. So why not let them stay?

'That's my taxi,' the blonde said.

Win's smile was blank.

'I had fun,' she said.

Not even a blink.

'You can reach me through Amanda if you want' – she looked at Myron, then back at Win – 'well, you know.'

'Yes,' Win said. 'I know.'

The young woman offered up an uncomfortable smile and left.

Myron watched, trying to keep his face from registering shock. A prostitute! Christ, she was a prostitute! He knew that Win had used them in the past – in the mid-eighties, he used to order in Chinese food from Hunan Grill and Asian prostitutes from the Noble House bordello for what he called 'Chinese Night' – but to still partake, in this day and age?

Then Myron remembered the Chevy Nova and his whole body went cold.

He turned to his friend. They looked at each other. Neither one of them said anything.

'Moralizing,' Win said. 'How nice.'

'I didn't say anything.'

'Indeed.' Win stood.

'Where are you going?'

'Out.'

Myron felt his heart pound. 'Mind if I go with you?'

'Yes.'

'What car are you taking?'

Win did not bother responding, 'Good night, Myron.'

Myron's mind raced for solutions, but he knew it was hopeless. Win was going. There was no way to stop him.

Win stopped at the door and turned back to him. 'One question, if I may.'

Myron nodded, unable to speak.

'Was Linda Coldren the one who first contacted you?' Win asked.

'No,' Myron said.

'Then who?'

'Your uncle Bucky.'

Win arched an eyebrow. 'And who suggested us to Bucky?'

Myron looked back at Win steadily, but he couldn't stop shaking. Win nodded and turned back to the door.

'Win?'

'Go to sleep, Myron.'

Chapter 11

Myron did not go to sleep. He didn't even bother trying.

He sat in Win's chair and tried to read, but the words never registered. He was exhausted. He leaned back against the rich leather and waited. Hours passed. Disjointed images of Win's potential handiwork wrested free in a heavy spray of dark crimson. Myron closed his eyes and tried to ride it out.

At 3:30 A.M., Myron heard a car pull up. The ignition died. A key clicked in the door and then it swung open. Win stepped inside and looked at Myron with nary a trace of emotion.

'Good night,' Win said.

He walked away. Myron heard the bedroom door close and let loose a held breath. Fine, he thought. He lifted himself into a standing position and made his way to his bedroom. He crawled under the sheets, but sleep still would not come. Black, opaque fear fluttered in his stomach. He had just begun to slide into true REM sleep when the bedroom door flew open.

'You're still asleep?' a familiar voice asked.

Myron managed to tear his eyes open. He was used to Esperanza Diaz barging into his office without knocking; he wasn't used to her doing it where he slept.

'What time is it?' he croaked.

'Six-thirty.'

'In the morning?'

Esperanza gave him one of her patented glares, the one road crews tried to hire out to raze large rock formations. With one finger she tucked a few spare strands of her raven locks behind her ear. Her shimmering dark skin made you think of a Mediterranean cruise by moonlight, of clear waters and puffy-sleeved peasant blouses and olive groves.

'How did you get here?' he asked.

'Amtrak red-eye,' she said.

Myron was still groggy. 'Then what did you do? Catch a cab?'

'What are you, a travel agent? Yes, I took a cab.'

'Just asking.'

'The idiot driver asked me for the address three times. Guess he's not used to taking Hispanics into this neighborhood.'

Myron shrugged. 'Probably thought you were a domestic,' he said.

'In *these* shoes?' She lifted her foot so he could see.

'Very nice.' Myron adjusted himself in the bed, his body still craving sleep. 'Not to belabor the point, but what exactly are you doing here?'

'I got some information on the old caddie.'

'Lloyd Rennart?'

Esperanza nodded. 'He's dead.'

'Oh.' Dead. As in dead end. Not that it had been much of a beginning. 'You could have just called.'

'There's more.'

'Oh?'

'The circumstances surrounding his death are' – she stopped, bit her lower lip – 'fuzzy.'

Myron sat up a bit. 'Fuzzy?'

'Lloyd Rennart apparently committed suicide eight months ago.'

'How?'

'That's the fuzzy part. He and his wife were on vacation in a mountain range in Peru. He woke up one morning, wrote a brief note, then he jumped off a cliff of some kind.'

'You're kidding.'

'Nope. I haven't been able to get too many details yet. The *Philadelphia Daily News* just had a brief story on it.' There was a hint of a smile. 'But according to the article, the body had not yet been located.'

Myron was starting to wake up in a big hurry. 'What?'

'Apparently Lloyd Rennart took the plunge in a remote crevasse with no access. They may have located the body by now, but I couldn't find a follow-up article. None of the local papers carried an obituary.'

Myron shook his head. No body. The questions that sprang to mind were obvious: could Lloyd Rennart still be alive? Did he fake his own death in order to plot out his revenge? Seemed a tad out there, but you never know. If he had, why would he have waited twenty-three years? True, the US Open was back at Merion. True, that could make old wounds resurface. But still. 'Weird,' he said. He looked up at her. 'You could have told me all this on the phone. You didn't have to come all the way down here.'

'What the hell is the big deal?' Esperanza snapped. 'I wanted to get out of the city for the weekend. I thought seeing the Open would be fun. You mind?'

'I was just asking.'

'You're so nosy sometimes.'

'Okay, okay.' He held up his hands in mock surrender. 'Forget I asked.'

'Forgotten,' she said. 'You want to fill me in on what's going on?'

He told her about the Crusty Nazi at the mall and about losing the black-clad perpetrator.

When he finished, Esperanza shook her head. 'Jesus,' she said. 'Without Win, you're hopeless.'

Ms Morale Booster.

'Speaking of Win,' Myron said, 'don't talk to him about the case.'

'Why?'

'He's reacting badly.'

She watched him closely. 'How badly?'

'He went night visiting.'

Silence.

'I thought he stopped doing that,' she said.

'I thought so too.'

'Are you sure?'

'There was a Chevy parked in the driveway,' Myron said. 'He took it out of here last night and didn't get back till three-thirty.'

Silence. Win stored a bunch of old, unregistered Chevys. Disposable cars, he called them. Completely untraceable.

Esperanza's voice was soft. 'You can't have it both ways, Myron.'

'What are you talking about?'

'You can't ask Win to do it when it suits you, then get pissed off when he does it on his own.'

'I never ask him to play vigilante.'

'Yeah, you do. You involve him in violence. When it suits your needs, you unleash him. Like he's a weapon of some kind.'

'It's not like that.'

'It is like that,' she said. 'It is exactly like that. When Win goes out on these night errands, he doesn't hurt the innocent, does he?'

Myron considered the question. 'No,' he said.

'So what's the problem? He is just attacking a different type of guilty. He picks out the guilty instead of you.'

Myron shook his head. 'It's not the same thing.'

'Because you judge?'

'I don't send him out to hurt people. I send him out to watch people or to back me up.'

'I'm not sure I see the difference.'

'Do you know what he does when he night visits, Esperanza? He walks through the worst neighborhoods he can find in the middle of the night. Old FBI buddies tell him where drug dealers or child pornographers or street gangs hang out – alleyways, abandoned buildings, what-ever – and he goes strolling through those hellholes no cop would dare tread.'

'Sounds like Batman,' Esperanza countered.

'You don't think it's wrong?'

'Oh, I think it's wrong,' she replied steadily. 'But I'm not sure you do.'

'What the hell is that supposed to mean?'

'Think about it,' she said. 'About why you're really upset.'

Footsteps approached. Win stuck his head in the doorway. He was smiling like a guest star on the opening credits of the *Love Boat*. 'Good morning, all,' he said with far too much cheer. He bussed Esperanza's cheek. He was decked out in classic, though fairly understated, golf clothes. Ashworth shirt. Plain golf cap. Sky-blue pants with pleats.

'Will you be staying with us, Esperanza?' he asked in his most solicitous tone.

Esperanza looked at him, looked at Myron. Nodded.

'Wonderful, You can use the bedroom down the hall on the left.' Win turned to Myron. 'Guess what?'

'I'm all ears, Mr Happy Face,' Myron said.

'Crispin still wants to meet with you. It appears that your walking out last night actually made something of an impression on him.' Big smile, spread hands. 'The reluctant suitor approach. I must try it sometime.'

Esperanza said, 'Tad Crispin? *The* Tad Crispin?'

'The very,' Win replied.

She gave Myron an approving look. 'Wow.'

'Indeed,' Win said. 'Well, I must be going. I'll see you at Merion. I'll be at the Lock-Horne tent most of the day.' Renewing the smile. 'Ta-ta.'

Win started to leave, stopped, snapped his fingers. 'I almost forgot.' He tossed Myron a videotape. 'Maybe this will save you some time.'

The videotape landed on the bed. 'Is this . . . ?'

'The bank security tape from First Philadelphia,' Win said. 'Six-eighteen on Thursday afternoon. As per your request.' One more smile, one more wave. 'Have a great day.'

Esperanza watched him go. ' "Have a great day"?' she repeated.

Myron shrugged.

'Who the hell was that guy?' she asked.

'Wink Martindale,' Myron said. 'Come on. Let's go downstairs and watch this.'

Chapter 12

Linda Coldren opened the door before Myron knocked.

'What is it?' she asked.

Linda's face was drawn, accentuating the already high cheekbones. Her eyes had a lost and hollow look. She hadn't slept. The pressure was growing unbearable. The worrying. The not knowing. She was strong. She was trying to stand up to it. But her son's disappearance was beginning to gnaw away at her core.

Myron held up the videotape. 'Do you have a VCR?' he asked.

In something of a daze, Linda Coldren led him to the same television he had seen her watching yesterday when they first met. Jack Coldren appeared from a back room, his golf bag on his shoulder. He, too, looked worn. There were sacks under his eyes, fleshy pouches like soft cocoons. Jack tried to toss up a welcoming smile, but it sputtered up like a lighter low on fluid.

'Hey, Myron.'

'Hey, Jack.'

'What's going on?'

Myron slid the tape into the opening. 'Do you know anybody who lives on Green Acres Road?' he asked.

Jack and Linda looked each other.

'Why do you want to know that?' Linda asked.

'Because last night I watched your house. I saw somebody crawl out a window.'

'A window?' It was Jack. He lowered his eyebrows. 'What window?'

'Your son's.'

Silence.

Then Linda asked, 'What does that have to do with Green Acres Road?'

'I followed whoever it was. He turned down Green Acres Road and disappeared – either into a house or into the woods.'

Linda lowered her head. Jack stepped forward and spoke. 'The Squires live on Green Acres Road,' he said. 'Chad's best friend Matthew.'

Myron nodded. He was not surprised. He flicked on the television. 'This is a bank security tape from First Philadelphia.'

'How did you get it?' Jack asked.

'It's not important.'

The front door opened and Bucky entered. The older man, dressed today in checked pants with a yellow-and-green top, stepped into the den doing his customary neck craning bit. 'What's going on here?' he demanded.

Nobody replied.

'I said—'

'Just watch the screen, Dad,' Linda interrupted.

'Oh,' Bucky said softly, moving in closer.

Myron turned the channel to Three and hit the PLAY button. All eyes were on the screen. Myron had already seen the tape. He studied their faces instead, watching for reactions.

On the television, a black-and-white image appeared. The bank's driveway. The view was from up high and a bit distorted, a concave fish-eye effect to capture as much space as possible. There was no sound. Myron had the tape all cued up on the right spot. Almost immediately a car pulled into view. The camera was on the driver's side.

'It's Chad's car,' Jack Coldren announced.

They watched in rapt silence as the car window lowered. The angle was a bit odd – above the car and from the machine's point of view – but there was no doubt. Chad Coldren was the driver. He leaned out the window and put his card in the ATM machine slot. His fingers tripped across the buttons like an experienced stenographer's.

Young Chad Coldren's smile was bright and happy.

When his fingers finished their little rumba, Chad settled back into the car to wait. He turned away from the camera for a moment. To the passenger seat. Someone was sitting next to Chad. Again Myron watched for a reaction. Linda, Jack, and Bucky all squinted, all trying to make out a face, but it was impossible. When Chad finally turned back to the camera, he was laughing. He pulled the money out, grabbed his card, leaned back into the car, closed the window, and drove off.

Myron switched off the VCR and waited. Silence flooded the room. Linda Coldren slowly lifted her head. She kept her expression steady, but her jaw trembled from being so set.

'There was another person in the car,' Linda offered. 'He could have had a gun on Chad or—'

'Stop it!' Jack shouted. 'Look at his face, Linda! For crying out loud, just look at his goddamn smirking face!'

'I know my son. He wouldn't do this.'

'You don't know him,' Jack countered. 'Face it, Linda. Neither one of us knows him.'

'It's not what it looks like,' Linda insisted, speaking more to herself than anyone in the room.

'No?' Jack gestured at the television, his face reddening. 'Then how the hell do you explain what we just saw? Huh? He was laughing, Linda. He's having the time of his life at our expense.' He stopped, struggled with something. 'At my expense,' he corrected himself.

Linda gave him a long look. 'Go play, Jack.'

'That's exactly what I am going to do.'

He lifted his bag. His eyes met Bucky's. Bucky remained silent. A tear slid down the older man's cheek. Jack tore his gaze away and started for the door.

Myron called out, 'Jack?'

Coldren stopped.

'It still might not be what it looks like,' Myron said.

Again with the eyebrows. 'What do you mean?'

'I traced the call you got last night,' Myron explained. 'It was made from a mall pay phone.' He briefly filled them in on his visit to the Grand Mercado Mall and the Crusty Nazi. Linda's face kept slipping from hope to heartbreak and mostly confusion. Myron understood. She wanted her son to be safe. But at the same time, she did not want this to be some cruel joke. Tough mix.

'He is in trouble,' Linda said as soon as he'd finished. 'That proves it.'

'That proves nothing,' Jack replied in tired exasperation. 'Rich kids hang out at malls and dress like punks too. He's probably a friend of Chad's.'

Again Linda looked at her husband hard. Again she said in a measured tone, 'Go play, Jack.'

Jack opened his mouth to say something, then stopped. He shook his head, adjusted the bag on his shoulder, and left. Bucky crossed the room. He tried to hold his daughter, but she stiffened at his touch. She moved away, studying Myron's face.

'You think he's faking too,' she said.

'Jack's explanation makes sense.'

'So you're going to stop looking?'

'I don't know,' Myron said.

She straightened her back. 'Stay with it,' she began, 'and I promise to sign with you.'

'Linda . . .'

'That's why you're here in the first place, right? You want my business. Well, here's the deal. You stay with me and I'll sign whatever you want. Hoax or no hoax. It'll be quite a coup, no? Signing the number one-ranked female golfer in the world?'

'Yes,' Myron admitted. 'It would be.'

'So there you go.' She stuck out her hand. 'Do we have a deal?'

Myron kept his hands by his side. 'Let me ask you something.'

'What?'

'Why are you so sure it's not a hoax, Linda?'

'You think I'm being naive?'

'Not really,' he said. 'I just want to know what makes you so certain.'

She lowered her hand and turned away from him. 'Dad?'

Bucky seemed to snap out of a daze. 'Hmm?'

'Would you mind leaving us alone for a minute?'

'Oh,' Bucky said. Neck crane. Then another. Two of them back-to-back. Good thing he wasn't a giraffe. 'Yes, well, I wanted to get to Merion anyway.'

'You go ahead, Dad. I'll meet you there.'

When they were alone, Linda Coldren began to pace the room. Myron was again awed by her looks – the paradoxical combination of beauty, strength and now delicacy. The strong, toned arms, yet the long, slender neck. The harsh, pointed features, yet the soft indigo eyes. Myron had heard beauty described as 'seamless'; hers was quite the opposite.

'I'm not big on' – Linda Coldren made quote marks in the air with her fingers – 'woman's intuition or any of that mother-knows-her-boy-best crap. But I know that my son is in danger. He wouldn't just disappear like this. No matter how it looks, that's not what happened.'

Myron remained silent.

'I don't like asking for help. It's not my way – to depend on someone else. But this is a situation . . . I'm scared. I've never felt fear like this in all of my life. It's all-consuming. It's suffocating. My son is in trouble and I can't do anything to help him. You want proof that this is not a hoax. I can't provide that. I just know. And I'm asking you to please help me.'

Myron wasn't sure how to respond. Her argument came straight from the heart, *sans* facts or evidence. But that didn't make her suffering any less real. 'I'll check out Matthew's house,' he said finally. 'Let's see what happens after that.'

Chapter 13

In the light of day, Green Acres Road was even more imposing. Both sides of the street were lined with ten-foot-high shrubs so thick that Myron couldn't tell how thick. He parked his car outside a wrought iron gate and approached an intercom. He pressed a button and waited. There were several surveillance cameras. Some remained steady. Some whirred slowly from side to side. Myron spotted motion detectors, barbed wire, Dobermans.

A rather elaborate fortress, he thought.

A voice as impenetrable as the shrubs came through the speaker. 'May I help you?'

'Good morning,' Myron said, offering up a friendly-but-not-a-salesman smile to the nearest camera. Talking to a camera. He felt like he was on *Nightline*. 'I'm looking for Matthew Squires.'

Pause. 'Your name, sir?'

'Myron Bolitar.'

'Is Master Squires expecting you?'

'No.' *Master* Squires?

'Then you do not have an appointment?'

An appointment to see a sixteen-year-old? Who is this kid, Doogie Howser? 'No, I'm afraid I don't.'

'May I ask the purpose of your visit?'

'To speak to Matthew Squires.' Mr Vague.

'I am afraid that will not be possible at this time,' the voice said.

'Will you tell him it involves Chad Coldren?'

Another pause. Cameras pirouetted. Myron looked around. All the lenses were aiming down from up high, glaring at him like hostile space aliens or lunchroom monitors.

'In what way does it involve Master Coldren?' the voice asked.

Myron squinted into a camera. 'May I ask with whom I am speaking?'

No reply.

Myron waited a beat, then said, 'You're supposed to say, "I am the great and powerful Oz."'

'I am sorry, sir. No one is admitted without an appointment. Please have a nice day.'

'Wait a second. Hello? Hello?' Myron pressed the button again. No reply. He leaned on it for several seconds. Still nothing. He looked up into the camera and gave his best caring-homespun-family-guy smile. Very Tom Brokaw. He tried a small wave. Nothing. He took a small step backward and gave a great big Jack Kemp fake-throwing-a-football wave. Nada.

He stood there for another minute. This was indeed odd. A sixteen-year-old with this kind of security? Something was not quite kosher. He pressed the button one more time. When no one responded he looked into the camera, put a thumb in either ear, wiggled his fingers and stuck out his tongue.

When in doubt, be mature.

Back at his car, Myron picked up the car phone and dialed his friend Sheriff Jake Courter.

'Sheriff's office.'

'Hey, Jake. It's Myron.'

'Fuck. I knew I shouldn't have come in on Saturday.'

'Ooo, I'm wounded. Seriously, Jake, do they still call you the Henny Youngman of law enforcement?'

Heavy sigh. 'What the fuck do you want, Myron? I just came in to get a little paperwork done.'

'No rest for those vigilantly pursuing peace and justice for the common man.'

'Right,' Jake said. 'This week, I went out on a whole twelve calls. Guess how many of them were for false burglar alarms?'

'Thirteen.'

'Pretty close.'

For more man twenty years, Jake Courier had been a cop in several of the country's meanest cities. He'd hated it and craved a quieter life. So Jake, a rather large black man, resigned from the force and moved to the picturesque (read: lily-white) town of Reston, New Jersey. Looking for a cushy job, he ran for sheriff. Reston was a college (read: liberal) town, and thus Jake played up his – as he put it – 'blackness' and won easily. The white man's guilt, Jake had told Myron. The best vote-getter this side of Willie Horton.

'Miss the excitement of the big city?' Myron asked.

'Like a case of herpes,' Jake countered. 'Okay, Myron, you've done the charm thing on me. I'm like Play-Doh in your paws now. What do you want?'

'I'm in Philly for the US Open.'

'That's golf, right?'

'Yeah, golf. And I wanted to know if you've heard of a guy name Squires.'

Pause. Then: 'Oh, shit.'

'What?'

'What the fuck are you involved in now?'

'Nothing. It's just that he's got all this weird security around his house—'

'What the fuck are you doing by his house?'

'Nothing.'

'Right,' Jake said. 'Guess you were just strolling by.'

'Something like that.'

'Nothing like that.' Jake sighed. Then: 'Ah what the hell, it ain't on my beat anymore. Squires. Reginald Squires aka Big Blue.'

Myron made a face. 'Big Blue?'

'Hey, all gangsters need a nickname. Squires is known as Big Blue. Blue, as in blue blood.'

'Those gangsters,' Myron said. 'Pity they don't channel their creativity into honest marketing.'

' "Honest marketing," ' Jake repeated. 'Talk about your basic oxymoron. Anyway Squires got a kiloton of family dough and all this blue-blood breeding and schooling and shit.'

'So what's he doing keeping such bad company?'

'You want the simple answer? The son of a bitch is a serious wacko. Gets his jollies hurting people. Kinda like Win.'

'Win doesn't get his jollies hurting people.'

'If you say so.'

'If Win hurts someone, there's a reason. To prevent them from doing it again or to punish or something.'

129

'Sure, whatever,' Jake said. 'Kinda touchy though, aren't we, Myron?'

'It's been a long day.'

'It's only nine in the morning.'

Myron said, 'For what breeds time but two hands on a clock?'

'Who said that?'

'No one. I just made it up.'

'You should consider writing greeting cards.'

'So what is Squires into, Jake?'

'Want to hear something funny? I'm not sure. Nobody is. Drugs and prostitution. Shit like that. But very upscale. Nothing very well organized or anything. It's more like he plays at it, you know? Like he gets involved in whatever he thinks will give him a thrill, then dumps it.'

'How about kidnapping?'

Brief pause. 'Oh shit, you are involved in something again, aren't you?'

'I just asked you if Squires was into kidnapping.'

'Oh. Right. Like it's a hypothetical question. Kinda like, "If a bear shits in the forest and no one is around, does it still reek"?'

'Precisely. Does kidnapping reek like his kind of thing?'

'Hell if I know. The guy is a major league loon, no question. He blends right into all that snobbish bullshit – the boring parties, the shitty food, the laughing at jokes that aren't remotely funny, the talking with the same boring people about the same boring worthless bullshit—'

'It sounds like you really admire them.'

'Just my point, my friend. They got it all, right? On the outside. Money, big homes, fancy clubs. But they're all so fucking boring – shit, I'd kill myself. Makes me wonder if maybe Squires feels that way too, you know?'

'Uh-huh,' Myron said. 'And Win is the scary one here, right?'

Jake laughed. 'Touché. But to answer your question, I don't know if Squires would be into kidnapping. Wouldn't surprise me though.'

Myron thanked him and hung up. He looked up. At least a dozen security cameras lined the top of the shrubs like tiny sentinels.

What now?

For all he knew, Chad Coldren was laughing his ass off, watching him on one of those security cameras. This whole thing could be an exercise in pure futility. Of course, Linda Coldren had promised to be a client. Much as he didn't want to admit it to himself, the idea was not wholly unpleasant. He considered the possibility and started to smile. If he could also somehow land Tad Crispin . . .

Yo, Myron, a kid may be in serious trouble.

Or, more likely, a spoiled brat or neglected adolescent – take your pick – is playing hooky and having some fun at his parents' expense.

So the question remained: What now?

He thought again about the videotape of Chad at the ATM machine. He didn't go into details with the Coldrens, but it bothered him. Why there? Why that particular ATM machine? If the kid was running away or hiding out, he might have to pick up money. Fine and dandy, that made sense.

But why would he do it at Porter Street?

Why not do it at a bank closer to home? And equally important, what was Chad Coldren doing in that area in the first place? There was nothing there. It wasn't a stop between highways or anything like that. The only thing in that neighborhood that would require cash was the Court Manor Inn. Myron again remembered *motelier extra-ordinaire* Stuart Lipwitz's attitude and wondered.

He started the car. It might be something. Worth looking into, at any rate.

Of course, Stuart Lipwitz had made it abundantly clear that he would not talk. But Myron thought he had just the tool to make him change his mind.

Chapter 14

'Smile!'

The man did not smile. He quickly shifted the car in reverse and backed out. Myron shrugged and lowered the camera. It was on a neck strap and bounced lightly against his chest. Another car approached. Myron lifted the camera again.

'Smile!' Myron repeated.

Another man. Another no smile. This guy managed to duck down before shifting his car into reverse.

'Camera shy,' Myron called out to him. 'Nice to see in this age of paparazzi overkill.'

It didn't take long. Myron had been on the sidewalk in front of the Court Manor Inn for less than five minutes when he spotted Stuart Lipwitz sprinting toward him. Big Stu was in full custom – gray tails, wide tie, a concierge key pin in the suit's lapel. Gray tails at a no-tell motel. Like a maître d' at Burger King. Watching Stu move closer, a Pink Floyd song came to mind: *Hello, hello,*

hello, is there anybody out there? David Bowie joined in: *Ground control to Major Tom.*

Ah, the seventies.

'You there,' he called out.

'Hi, Stu.'

No smile this time. 'This is private property,' Stuart Lipwitz said, a little out of breath. 'I must ask you to remove yourself immediately.'

'I hate to disagree with you, Stu, but I am on a public sidewalk. I got every right to be here.'

Stuart Lipwitz stammered, then flapped his arms in frustration. With the tails, the movement kind of reminded Myron of a bat. 'But you can't just stand there and take pictures of my clientele,' he semi-whined.

' "Clientele," ' Myron repeated. 'Is that a new euphemism for *john*?'

'I'll call the police.'

'Ooooo. Stop scaring me like that.'

'You are interfering with my business.'

'And you are interfering with mine.'

Stuart Lipwitz put his hands on his hips and tried to look threatening. 'This is the last time I'll ask you nicely. Leave the premises.'

'That wasn't nice.'

'Excuse me?'

'You said it was the last time you'd ask me nicely,' Myron explained. 'Then you said, "Leave the premises." You didn't say *please*. You didn't say, "Kindly leave the premises." Where's the nice in that?'

'I see,' Lipwitz said. Beads of sweat dotted his face. It was hot and the man was, after all, in tails. 'Please kindly leave the premises.'

'Nope. But now, at least, you're a man of your word.'

Stuart Lipwitz took several deep breaths. 'You want to know about the boy, don't you? The one in the picture.'

'You bet.'

'And if I tell you if he was here, will you leave?'

'Much as it would pain me to leave this quaint locale, I would somehow tear myself away.'

'That, sir, is blackmail.'

Myron looked at him. 'I would say "*blackmail* is such an ugly word," but that would be too cliché. So instead I'll just say "Yup." '

'But' – Lipwitz started stammering – 'that's against the law!'

'As opposed to, say, prostitution and drug dealing and whatever other sleazy activity goes on in this fleabag?'

Stuart Lipwitz's eyes widened. 'Fleabag? This is the Court Manor Inn, sir. We are a respectable—'

'Stuff it, Stu. I got pictures to take.' Another car pulled up. Gray Volvo station wagon. Nice family car. A man about fifty years old was neatly attired in a business suit. The young girl in the passenger seat must have shopped – as the mall girls had recently taught him – at Sluts 'R' Us.

Myron smiled and leaned toward the window. 'Whoa, sir, vacationing with your daughter?'

The man splashed on a classic deer-caught-in-the-headlights look. The young prostitute whooped with laughter. 'Hey, Mel, he thinks I'm your daughter!' She whooped again.

Myron raised the camera. Stuart Lipwitz tried to step in his way, but Myron swept him away with his free hand. 'It's Souvenir Day at the Court Manor,' Myron said. 'I can put the picture on a coffee mug if you'd like. Or maybe a decorative plate?'

The man in the business suit reversed the car. They were gone several seconds later.

Stuart Lipwitz's face reddened. He made two fists. Myron looked at him. 'Now Stuart . . .'

'I have powerful friends,' he said.

'Ooooo. I'm getting scared again.'

'Fine. Be that way.' Stuart turned away and stormed up the drive. Myron smiled. The kid was a tougher nut to crack than he'd anticipated, and he really didn't want to do this all day. But let's face it: There were no other leads and besides, playing with Big Stu was fun.

Myron waited for more customers. He wondered what Stu was up to. Something frantic, no doubt. Ten minutes later, a canary yellow Audi pulled up and a large black man slid out. The black man was maybe an inch shorter than Myron, but he was built. His chest could double as a jai alai wall and his legs resembled the trunks of redwoods. He glided when he moved – not the bulky moves one usually associated with the overmuscled.

Myron did not like that.

The black man had sunglasses on and wore a red Hawaiian shirt with blue jean shorts. His most noticeable feature was his hair. The kinks had been slicked straight and parted on the side, like old photographs of Nat King Cole.

Myron pointed at the top of the man's head. 'Is that hard to do?' he asked.

'What?' the black man said. 'You mean the hair?'

Myron nodded. 'Keeping it straight like that.'

'Nah, not really. Once a week I go to a guy named Ray. In an old-fashioned barbershop, as a matter of fact. The kind with the pole in front and everything.' His smile was almost wistful. 'Ray takes care of it for me. Also gives me a great shave. With hot towels and everything.' The man stroked his face for emphasis.

'Looks smooth,' Myron said.

'Hey, thanks. Nice of you to say. I find it relaxing, you know? Doing something just for me. I think it's important. To relieve the stress.'

Myron nodded. 'I hear you.'

'Maybe I'll give you Ray's number. You could stop by and check it out.'

'Ray,' Myron repeated. 'I'd like that.'

The black man stepped closer. 'Seems we have a little situation here, Mr Bolitar.'

'How did you know my name?'

He shrugged. Behind the sunglasses, Myron sensed that he was being sized up. Myron was doing the same. Both were trying to be subtle. Both knew exactly what the other was doing.

'I'd really appreciate it if you would leave,' he said very politely.

'I'm afraid I can't do that,' Myron said. 'Even though you did ask nicely.'

The black man nodded. He kept his distance. 'Let's see if we can work something out here, okay?'

'Okeydokey.'

'I got a job to do here, Myron. You can appreciate that, can't you?'

'Sure can,' Myron said.

'And so do you.'

'That's right.'

The black man took off his sunglasses and put them in his shirt pocket. 'Look, I know you won't be easy. And you know I won't be easy. If push comes to shove, I don't know which one of us will win.'

'I will,' Myron said. 'Good always triumphs over evil.'

The man smiled. 'Not in this neighborhood.'

'Good point.'

'I'm also not sure it's worth it to either one of us to find out. I think we're both probably past the proving-himself, macho-bullshit stage.'

Myron nodded. 'We're too mature.'

'Right.'

'It seems then,' Myron continued, 'that we've hit an impasse.'

'Guess so,' the black man agreed. 'Of course, I could always take out a gun and shoot you.'

Myron shook his head. 'Not over something this small. Too many repercussions involved.'

'Yeah. I didn't think you'd go for it, but I had to give it a whirl. You never know.'

'You're a pro,' Myron agreed. 'You'd feel remiss if you didn't at least try. Hell, I'd have felt cheated.'

'Glad you understand.'

'Speaking of which,' Myron said, 'aren't you a tad high-level to be dealing with this situation?'

'Can't say I disagree.' The black man walked closer to Myron. Myron felt his muscles tighten; a not-unpleasant anticipatory chill steeled him.

'You look like a guy who can keep his mouth shut,' the man said.

Myron said nothing. Proving the point.

'The kid you had in that picture, the one that got Leona Helmsley's panties in a bunch? He was here.'

'When?'

The black man shook his head. 'That's all you get. I'm being very generous. You wanted to know if the kid was here. The answer is yes.'

'Nice of you,' Myron said.

'I'm just trying to make it simple. Look, we both know that Lipwitz is a dumb kid. Acts like this urinal is the Beverly Wilshire. But the people who come here, they don't want that. They want to be invisible. They don't even want to look at themselves, you know what I'm saying?'

Myron nodded.

'So I gave you a freebie. The kid in the picture was here.'

'Is he still here?'

'You're pushing me, Myron.'

'Just tell me that.'

'No. He only stayed that one night.' He spread his hands. 'Now you tell me, Myron. Am I being fair with you?'

'Very.'

He nodded. 'Your turn.'

'I guess there's no way you'll tell me who you're working for.'

The black man made a face. 'Nice meeting you, Myron.'

'Same here.'

They shook hands. Myron got into his car and drove away.

He had almost reached Merion when the cellular rang. He picked up and said hello.

'Is this, like, Myron?'

Mall girl. 'Hi, yes. Actually this is Myron, not just like him.'

'Huh?'

'Never mind. What's up?'

'That skank you were, like, looking for last night?'

'Right.'

'He's, like, back at the mall.'

'Where at the mall?'

'The food court. He's on line at the McDonald's.'

Myron spun the car around and hit the gas pedal.

Chapter 15

The Crusty Nazi was still there.

He sat at a corner table by himself, downing a burger of some sort like it had personally offended him. The girls were right. *Skank* was the only word to describe him, even though Myron didn't know what the word meant or if it even existed. The punk's face was aiming for tough-guy-unshaven, but a lack of testosterone made it land far closer to upkempt-adolescent-Hasid. He wore a black baseball cap with a skull and crossbones decal. His ripped white T-shirt was rolled all the way up to reveal milky, reedy arms, one with a swastika tattoo. Myron shook his head. Swastika. The kid was too old to be so utterly clueless.

The Crusty Nazi took another vicious bite, clearly furious with his burger now. The mall girls were there, pointing toward Crusty like Myron might not know which guy they'd been talking about. Myron signaled them to stop with a shushing finger at his lips. They obeyed, overcompensating by engaging in a too-loud, too-casual conversation, sliding furtive-to-the-point-of-totally-obvious glances in his direction. Myron looked away.

The Crusty Nazi finished his burger and stood. Good timing. As advertised, Crusty was very skinny. The girls were, right – the boy had no ass. None at all. Myron couldn't tell if the kid was going for that too-big-jeans look or if it was because he lacked a true backside, but every few steps, Crusty paused to hitch up the pants. Myron suspected a bit of both.

He followed him outside into the blazing sun. Hot. Damn hot. Myron felt almost a nostalgic longing for the omnipresent mall air-conditioning. Crusty strutted cool-like into the lot. Going to his car, no doubt. Myron veered to the right so as to get ready to follow. He slid into his Ford Taurus (read: Chick Trawler) and started up the engine.

He slowly cruised the lot and spotted Crusty heading way out to the last row of cars. Only two vehicles were parked out there. One was a silver Cadillac Seville. The other was a pickup truck with those semi-monster wheels, a Confederate flag decal, and the words BAD TO THE BONE painted on the side. Using his years of investigative know-how, Myron deduced that the pickup truck was probably Crusty's vehicle. Sure enough, Crusty opened the door and hopped up and in. Amazing. Sometimes Myron's powers of deduction bordered on the psychic. Maybe he should get a 900 line like Jackie Stallone.

Tailing the pickup truck was hardly a challenge. The vehicle stuck out like a golfer's clothing in a monastery, and El Crust-ola wasn't heavy on the gas pedal. They drove for about half an hour. Myron had no idea where they were going, but up ahead he recognized Veterans Stadium. He'd gone with Win to several Eagles games there. Win always had seats on the fifty-yard line, lower tier. Being an old stadium, the 'luxury' skyboxes at the Vet were too high up; Win did not care for them. So he chose instead to sit with the masses. Big of him.

About three blocks before the stadium, Crusty pulled down a side road. He threw his pickup into park and got out running. Myron once again debated calling Win for backup, but it was pointless. Win was at Merion. His phone would be off. He wondered again about last night and about Esperanza's accusations this morning. Maybe she was right. Maybe he was, at least partially, responsible for what Win did. But that wasn't the point. He knew that now. The truth, the one that scared Esperanza too, was far clearer:

Maybe Myron didn't care so much.

You read the papers and you watch the news and you see what Myron has seen and your humanity, your basic faith in human beings, begins to look frighteningly Pollyanna. That was what was really eating away at him – not that he was repulsed by what Win did, but that it really didn't bother him that much.

Win had an eerie way of seeing the world in black and white; lately, Myron had found his own gray areas blackening. He didn't like that. He did not like the change that experience – seeing the cruelty man inflicts on man – was forcing upon him. He tried to hold on to his old values, but the rope was getting awfully slick. And why was he holding on, anyway? Was it because he truly believed in these values, or because he liked himself more as a person who believed?

He didn't know anymore.

He should have brought a gun. Stupid. Still he was only following some grunge-ball. Of course, even a grunge-ball could fire a gun and kill him. But what choice did he have? Should he call the police? Well, that would appear a bit extreme based on what he had. Come back later with a firearm of some sort? By that time, Crusty could be gone – along with Chad Coldren maybe.

Nope, he had to follow. He'd just be careful.

Myron was not sure what to do. He stopped the car at the end of the block and got out. The street was crowded with low-rise brick dwellings that all looked the same. At one time, this might have been a nice area, but now the neighborhood looked like a man who'd lost his job and stopped bathing. There was an overgrown, faded quality to it, like a garden that no one bothered to tend anymore.

Crusty turned down an alleyway. Myron followed. Lots of plastic garbage bags. Lots of rusted fire escapes. Four legs stuck out of a refrigerator box. Myron heard snoring. At the end of the alley, Crusty turned right. Myron trailed slowly. Crusty had gone into what looked like an abandoned building through a fire door. There was no knob or anything, but the door was slightly ajar. Myron reached in with his fingers and pried it open.

As soon as he crossed the musty threshold, Myron heard a primal scream. Crusty. Right in front of him. Something swung toward Myron's face. Fast reflexes paid off. Myron managed to duck enough so that the iron bar only clipped his shoulder blade. A quick flash of pain bolted down his arm. Myron dropped to the ground. He rolled across the cement floor and stood back up.

There were three of them now. All armed with crowbars or tire irons. All with shaved heads and tattooed swastikas. They were like sequels to the same awful

144

movie. The Crusty Nazi was the original. Beneath the Planet of Crusty Nazi – the one on his left – was smiling with idiotic glee. The one on his right – Escape from the Planet of Crusty Nazi – looked a bit more frightened. The weak link, Myron thought.

'Changing a tire?' Myron asked.

The Crusty Nazi slapped the tire iron against his palm for emphasis. 'Gonna flatten yours.'

Myron raised his hand in front of him with the palm facing down. He shook it back and forth and said, 'Eh.'

'Why the fuck you following me, asshole?'

'Me?'

'Yeah, you. Why the fuck you following me?'

'Who says I'm following you?'

There was momentary confusion on Crusty's face. Then: 'You think I'm fucking stupid or something?'

'No, I think you're Mr Mensa.'

'Mister what?'

Beneath the Planet of Crusty Nazi said, 'He's just fucking with you, man.'

'Yeah,' Escape chimed in. 'Fucking with you.'

Crusty's wet eyes bulged out. 'Yeah? Is that what you're doing, asshole? You fucking with me, huh? Is that what you're doing? Fucking with me?'

Myron looked at him. 'Can we move on please?'

Beneath said, 'Let's fuck him up a little. Soften his ass up.'

Myron knew that three of them were probably not experienced fighters, but he also knew that three armed men beat one good man on almost any given day. They were also a bit too jittery, their eyes as glazed as morning doughnuts. They were constantly sniffing and rubbing their noses.

Two words: Coked up. Or Nose Candy. Or Toot Sweet. Take your pick.

Myron's best chance was to confuse and strike. Risky. You wanted to piss them off, to upset their already-tipsy equilibrium. But at the same time, you wanted to control it, to know when to back off a bit. A delicate balance requiring Myron Bolitar, darling of the high wire, to perform high above the crowd without the benefit of a safety net.

Once again Crusty asked, 'Why the fuck you following me, asshole?'

'Maybe I'm just attracted to you,' Myron said. 'Even if you don't have an ass.'

Beneath started cackling. 'Oh man, oh man, let's fuck him up. Let's fuck him up good.'

Myron tried to give them the tough-guy look. Some mistook this for constipation, but he was getting better at it. Practice. 'I wouldn't do that if I were you.'

'Oh no?' It was Crusty. 'Give me one good reason why we don't just fuck you up. Give me one good reason why I don't break every fucking rib in your body with this.' He raised the tire iron. In case Myron thought he was being too subtle.

'You asked before if I thought you were stupid,' Myron said.

'Yeah, so?'

'So do you think I'm stupid? Do you think somebody who meant you harm would be dumb enough to follow you in here – knowing what was about to go down?'

That made all three of them pause.

'I followed you,' Myron continued, 'as a test.'

'What the fuck you talking about?'

'I work for certain people. We won't mention names.'

146

Mostly, Myron thought, because he didn't know what the hell he was talking about. 'Let's just say they are in a business you guys frequent.'

'Frequent?' More nose rubbing. Toot, sweet, toot, sweet.

'Frequent,' Myron repeated. 'As in occurring or appearing quite often or at close intervals. Frequent.'

'What?'

Jesus. 'My employer,' Myron said, 'he needs someone to handle certain territory. Somebody new. Somebody who wants to make ten percent on sales and get all the free blow they can.'

Eyes went buggy.

Beneath turned to Crusty. 'You hear that, man?'

'Yeah, I hear him.'

'Shit, we don't get no commission from Eddie,' Beneath went on. 'The fucker is so small-time.' He gestured at Myron with the tire iron. 'This guy, man, look how fucking old he is. He's gotta be working for somebody with juice.'

'Got to be,' Escape added.

The Crusty One hesitated, squinted suspicion. 'How did you find out about us?'

Myron shrugged. 'Word gets around.' Shovel, shovel.

'So you was just following me for some kinda fucking test?'

'Right.'

'Just came to the mall and decided to follow me?'

'Something like that.'

Crusty smiled. He looked at Escape and at Beneath. His grip on the tire iron tightened. Uh-oh. 'Then how the fuck come you were asking about me last night, huh? How come you want to know about a call I made?'

Uh-oh.

Crusty stepped closer, eyes aglow.

Myron raised his hand. 'The answer is simple.' They all hesitated. Myron took advantage. His foot moved like a piston, shooting out and landing squarely on the knee of the unprepared Escape. Escape fell. Myron was already running.

'Get the fucker!'

They chased, but Myron had already slammed his shoulder into the fire door. The 'macho-bullshit' part of him, as his friend at the Court Manor Inn had described it, wanted to try to take them on, but he knew that would be foolhardy. They were armed. He wasn't.

By the time Myron reached the end of the alley, his lead was only about ten yards. He wondered if he'd have enough time to open his car door and get in. No choice. He'd have to try.

He grabbed the handle and swung the door open. He was sliding in when a tire iron whacked his shoulder. Pain erupted. He kept rolling, closing the door. A hand grabbed it, offered resistance. Myron used his weight and leaned into the pull.

His window exploded.

Glass tinkled down into his face. Myron kicked his heel through the open window and hit face. The grip on the door released. He already had the key out and in the ignition. He turned it as the other car window exploded. Crusty leaned into the car, his eyes blazing with fury.

'Motherfucker, you're gonna die!'

The tire iron was heading toward his face again. Myron blocked it. From behind him, he felt a sharp blow connect with his lower neck. Numbness ensued. Myron shifted into reverse and flew out of the spot, tires squealing.

Crusty tried to leap into the car through the broken window. Myron elbowed him in the nose and Crusty's grip eased. He fell hard to the pavement, but then he jumped right back up. That was the problem with fighting cokeheads. Pain often does not register.

All three men ran for the pickup, but Myron already had too big a lead. The battle was over. For now.

Chapter 16

Myron called in the pickup truck's license plate number, but that was a dead end. The plate had expired four years ago. Crusty must have taken it off a car in a dump or something. Not uncommon. Even petty crooks knew enough not to use their real plates when committing a traceable crime.

He circled back and checked the inside of the building for clues. Bent syringes and broken vials and empty bags of Doritos lay scattered about the cement. There was also an empty garbage can. Myron shook his head. Bad enough being a drug dealer. But a litterbug?

He looked around a bit more. The building was abandoned and half-burned out. There was no one inside. And no clues.

Okay, so what did this all mean? Were the three coke-heads the kidnappers? Myron had a hard time picturing it. Cokeheads break into houses. Cokeheads jump people in alleyways. Cokeheads attack with tire irons. Coke-heads, by and large, do not plan elaborate kidnappings.

But on the other hand, how elaborate was this kidnap-ping? The first two times the kidnapper called, he didn't even know how much money to extort. Wasn't that a little odd? Could it be that all this was merely the work of some out-of-their-league crusty cokeheads?

Myron got into his car and headed toward Win's house. Win had plenty of vehicles. He'd switch for a car without smashed windows. The residual damage to his body seemed to be clearing up. A bruise or two but noth-ing broken. None of the blows had landed flush, except the ones to his car windows.

He ran several possibilities through his head and even-tually managed to come up with a pretty decent scenario. Let's say that for some reason Chad Coldren decided to check into the Court Manor Inn. Maybe to spend some time with a girl. Maybe to buy some drugs. Maybe because he enjoyed the friendly service. Whatever. As per the bank surveillance camera, Chad grabbed some dough at a local ATM. Then he checked in for the night. Or the hour. Or whatever.

Once at the Court Manor Inn, something went awry. Stu Lipwitz's denials notwithstanding, the Court Manor is a sleazy joint patronized by sleazy people. It wouldn't be hard to get in trouble there. Maybe Chad Coldren tried to buy drugs from Crusty. Maybe he witnessed a crime. Maybe the kid just talked too much and some nasty people realized that he came from money. Whatever. The life orbits of Chad Coldren and the Crusty Nazi's crew dovetailed. The end result was a kidnapping.

It kinda fit.

The key word here: *kinda*.

On the road toward Merion, Myron helped deflate his own scenario with several well-placed puncture holes. First of all, the timing. Myron had been convinced that the kidnapping had something to do with Jack's return to playing the US Open at Merion. But in his Crusty-orbit scenario, the nagging timing question had to be written off as mere coincidence. Okay, maybe Myron could live with that. But then how, for example, had the Crusty Nazi – stationed at a mall pay phone – known that Esme Fong was in the Coldren house? How did the man who climbed out the window and disappeared on Green Acres Road – a person Myron had been sure was either Matthew Squires or Chad Coldren – fit into all this? Was the well-shielded Matthew Squires in cahoots with the Crusties? Or was it just a coincidence that the window man disappeared down Green Acres Road?

The scenario balloon was going *sssss* in a very big way.

By the time Myron got to Merion, Jack Coldren was on the fourteenth hole. His partner for today's round was none other than Tad Crispin. No surprise there. First place and second place were normally the final twosome of the day.

Jack was still playing well, though not spectacularly. He'd lost only one stroke off his lead, remaining a very comfortable eight strokes ahead of Tad Crispin. Myron trudged toward the fourteenth green. Green – that word again. Everything was so dang green. The grass and trees, naturally, but also tents, overhangs, scoreboards, the many television towers and scaffolds – everything was lush green to blend in with the picturesque natural sur-roundings, except, of course, for the sponsors' boards, which drew the eye with all the subtlety of Vegas hotel signs. But hey, the sponsors paid Myron's salary. Be kinda hypocritical to complain.

'Myron, sweetheart, get your wiggly ass over here.'

Norm Zuckerman beckoned Myron forward with a big wave. Esme Fong stood next to him. 'Over here,' he said.

'Hey, Norm,' Myron said. 'Hi, Esme.'

'Hi, Myron,' Esme said. She was dressed a bit more casual today, but she still clutched at her briefcase like it was a favorite stuffed animal.

Norm threw his arm around Myron's back, draping the hand over the sore shoulder. 'Myron, tell me the truth here. The absolute truth. I want the truth, okay?'

'The truth?'

'Very funny. Just tell me this. Nothing more, just this. Am I not a fair man? The truth, now. Am I a fair man?'

'Fair,' Myron said.

'Very fair, am I right? I am a very fair man.'

'Let's not push it, Norm.'

Norm put up both hands, palms out. 'Fine, be that way. I'm fair. Good enough, I'll take it,' He looked over toward Esme Fong. 'Keep in mind, Myron is my adversary. My worst enemy. We're always on opposite sides. Yet he is willing to admit that I'm a fair man. We straight on that?'

Esme rolled her eyes. 'Yes, Norm, but you're preaching to the converted. I already told you that I agreed with you on this—'

'Whoa,' Norm said, as though reining in a frisky pony. 'Just hold the phone a sec, because I want Myron's opinion too. Myron, here's the deal. I bought a golf bag. Just one. I wanted to test it out. Cost me fifteen grand for the year.'

Buying a golf bag meant pretty much what it said.

Norm Zuckerman had bought the rights to advertise on a golf bag. In other words, he put a Zoom logo on it. Most of the golf bags were bought by the big golf companies – Ping, Titleist, Golden Bear, that kind of thing. But more and more often, companies that had nothing to do with golf advertised on the bags. McDonald's, for example. Spring-Air mattresses. Even Pennzoil oil. Pennzoil. Like someone goes to a golf tournament, sees the Pennzoil logo, and buys a can of oil.

'So?' Myron said.

'So, look at it!' Norm pointed at a caddie. 'I mean, just look at it!'

'Okay, I'm looking.'

'Tell me, Myron, do you see a Zoom logo?'

The caddie held the golf bag. Like on every golf bag, there were towels draped over the top in order to clean off the clubs.

Norm Zuckerman spoke in a first-grade-teacher singsong. 'You can answer orally, Myron, by uttering the syllable "no." Or if that's too taxing on your limited vocabulary, you can merely shake your head from side to side like this.' Norm demonstrated.

'It's under the towel,' Myron said.

Norm dramatically put his hand to his ear. 'Pardon?'

'The logo is under the towel.'

'No shit it's under the towel!' Norm railed. Spectators turned and glared at the crazy man with the long hair and heavy beard. 'What good does that do me, huh? When I film an advertisement for TV, what good would it do me if they stick a towel in front of the camera? When I pay all those schmucks a zillion dollars to wear my sneakers, what good would it do me if they wrapped their feet in towels? If every billboard I had was covered with a great big towel—'

'I get the picture, Norm.'

'Good. I'm not paying fifteen grand for some idiot caddie to cover my logo. So I go over to the idiot caddie and I kindly tell him to move the towel away from my logo and the son of a bitch gives me this look. This look, Myron. Like I'm some brown stain he couldn't rinse out of the toilet. Like I'm this little ghetto Jew who's gonna take his goy crap.'

Myron looked over at Esme. Esme smiled and shrugged.

'Nice talking to you, Norm,' Myron said.

'What? You don't think I'm right?'

'I see your point.'

'So if it was your client, what would you do?'

'Make sure the caddie kept the logo in plain view.'

'Exactamundo.' He swung his arm back around Myron's shoulder and lowered his head conspiratorially. 'So what's going on with you and golf, Myron?' he whispered.

'What do you mean?'

'You're not a golfer. You don't have any golf clients. All of a sudden I see you with my very own eyes closing in on Tad Crispin – and now I hear you're hanging out with the Coldrens.'

'Who told you that?'

'Word gets around. I'm a man with tremendous sources. So what's the deal? Why the sudden interest in golf?'

'I'm a sports agent, Norm. I try to represent athletes. Golfers are athletes. Sort of.'

'Okay, but what's up with the Coldrens?'

'What do you mean?'

'Look, Jack and Linda are lovely people. Connected, if you know what I mean.'

'I don't know what you mean.'

'LBA represents Linda Coldren. Nobody leaves LBA. You know that. They're too big. Jack, well, Jack hasn't done anything in so long, he hasn't even bothered with an agent. So what I'm trying to figure out is, why are the Coldrens suddenly hot to trot with you?'

'Why do you want to figure that out?'

Norm put his hand on his chest. 'Why?'

'Yeah, why would you care?'

'Why?' Norm repeated, incredulous now. 'I'll tell you why. Because of you, Myron. I love you, you know that. We're brothers. Tribe members. I want nothing but the best for you. Hand to God, I mean that. You ever need a recommendation, I'll give it to you, you know that.'

'Uh-huh.' Myron was less than convinced. 'So what's the problem?'

Norm threw up both hands. 'Who said there's a problem? Did I say there was a problem? Did I even use the word *problem*? I'm just curious, that's all. It's part of my nature. I'm a curious guy. A modern-day *yenta*. I ask a lot of questions. I stick my nose in where it doesn't belong. It's part of my makeup.'

'Uh-huh,' Myron said again. He looked over at Esme Fong, who was now comfortably out of earshot. She shrugged at him. Working for Norm Zuckerman probably meant you did a lot of shrugging. But that was part of Norm's technique, his own version of good-cop, bad-cop. He came across as erratic, if not totally irrational, while his assistant – always young, bright, attractive –

156

was the calming influence you grabbed on to like a life preserver.

Norm elbowed him and nodded toward Esme. 'She's a looker, huh? Especially for a broad from Yale. You ever see what that school matriculates? No wonder they're known as the Bulldogs.'

'You're so progressive, Norm.'

'Ah, screw progressive. I'm an old man, Myron. I'm allowed to be insensitive. On an old man, insensitive is cute. A cute curmudgeon, that's what they call it. By the way, I think Esme is only half.'

'Half?'

'Chinese,' Norm said. 'Or Japanese. Or whatever. I think she's half white too. What do you think?'

'Good-bye, Norm.'

'Fine, be that way. See if I care. So tell me, Myron, how did you hook up with the Coldrens? Win introduce you?'

'Good-bye, Norm.'

Myron walked off a bit, stopping for a moment to watch a golfer hit a drive. He tried to follow the ball's route. No go. He lost sight of it almost immediately. This shouldn't be a surprise really – it is, after all, a tiny white sphere traveling at a rate of over one hundred miles per hour for a distance of several hundred yards – except that Myron was the only person in attendance who couldn't achieve this ophthalmic feat of hawklike proportions. Golfers. Most of them can't read an exit sign on an interstate, but they can follow the trajectory of a golf ball through several solar systems.

No question about it. Golf is a weird sport.

The course was packed with silent fans, though *fan* didn't exactly feel like the right word to Myron. *Parishioners* was a hell of a lot closer. There was a constant reverie on a golf course, a hushed, wide-eyed respect. Every time the ball was hit, the crowd release was nearly orgasmic. People cried sweet bliss and urged the ball with the ardor of *Price Is Right* contestants: Run! Sit! Bite! Grab! Grow teeth! Roll! Hurry! Get down! Get up! – almost like an aggressive mambo instructor. They lamented over a snap hook and a wicked slice and a babied putt and goofy greens and soft greens and waxed greens and the rub of the green and the pursuit of a snowman and being stymied and when the ball traveled off the fairway and on the fringe and in the rough and deep lies and rough lies and bad lies and good lies. They showed admiration when a player got all of that one or ripped a drive or banged it home and gave dirty looks when someone loudly suggested that a certain tee-shot made a certain player 'da man.' They accused a putter who did not reach the hole of hitting the ball 'with your purse, Alice.' Players were constantly playing shots that were 'unplayable.'

Myron shook his head. All sports have their own lexicons, but speaking golfese was tantamount to mastering Swahili. It was like rich people's rap.

But on a day like today – the sun shining, the blue sky unblemished, the summer air smelling like a lover's hair – Myron felt closer to the chalice of golf. He could imagine the course free of spectators, the peace and tranquillity, the same aura that drew Buddhist monks to mountaintop retreats, the double-cut grass so rich and green that God Himself would want to run barefoot. This did not mean Myron got it – he was still a nonbeliever of heretic proportions – but for a brief moment he could at least envision what it was about this game that ensnared and swallowed so many whole.

When he reached the fourteenth green, Jack Coldren was lining up for a fifteen-foot putt. Diane Hoffman took the pin out of the hole. At almost every course in the world, the 'pin' had a flag on the top. But that would just not do at Merion. Instead, the pole was topped with a wicker basket. No one seemed to know why. Win came up with this story about how the old Scots who invented golf used to carry their lunch in baskets on sticks, which could then double as hole markers, but Myron smelled the pungent odor of lore in Win's rationale rather than fact. Either way, Merion's members made a big fuss over these wicker baskets on the end of a big stick. Golfers.

Myron tried to move in closer to Jack Coldren, looking for Win's 'eye of the tiger.' Despite his protestations, Myron knew very well what Win had meant the previous night, the intangibles that separated raw talent from on-field greatness. Desire. Heart. Perseverance. Win spoke about these things as though they were evil. They were not. Quite the opposite, in fact. Win, of all people, should know better. To paraphrase and completely abuse a famous political quote: Extremism in the pursuit of excellence is no vice.

Jack Coldren's expression was smooth and unworried and distant. Only one explanation for that: the zone. Jack had managed to squeeze his way into the hallowed zone, that tranquil room in which no crowd or big payday or famous course or next hole or knee-bending pressure or hostile opponent or successful wife or kidnapped son may reside. Jack's zone was a small place, comprising only his club, a small dimpled ball, and a hole. All else faded away now like the dream sequence in a movie.

This, Myron knew, was Jack Coldren stripped to his purest state. He was a golfer. A man who wanted to win.

Needed to. Myron understood. He had been there – his zone consisting of a large orange ball and a metallic cylinder – and a part of him would always be enmeshed in that world. It was a fine place to be – in many ways, the best place to be. Win was wrong. Winning was not a worthless goal. It was noble. Jack had taken life's hits. He had striven and battled. He had been battered and bloodied. Yet here he stood, head high, on the road to redemption. How many people are awarded this opportunity? How many people truly get the chance to feel this vibrant, to reside for even a short time on such a plateau, to have their hearts and dreams stirred with such unquenchable inner passion?

Jack Coldren stroked the putt. Myron found himself watching the ball slowly arc toward the hole, lost in that vicarious rush that so fiercely drew spectators to sports. He held his breath and felt something like a tear well up in his eye when the ball dropped in. A birdie. Diane Hoffman made a fist and pumped it. The lead was back up to nine strokes.

Jack looked up at the applauding galley. He acknowledged them with a tip of his hat, but he saw nothing. Still in the zone. Fighting to stay there. For a moment, his eyes locked on Myron's. Myron nodded back, not wanting to nudge him back to reality. Stay in that zone, Myron thought. In that zone, a man can win a tournament. In that zone, a son does not purposely sabotage a father's lifelong dream.

Myron walked past the many portable toilets – they'd been provided by a company with the semiaccurate name Royal Flush – and headed toward Corporate Row. Golf matches had an unprecedented hierarchy for ticket holders. True, at most sporting arenas there was a grading of one sort or another – some had better seats, obviously, while some had access to skyboxes or even courtside seats. But in those cases, you handed a ticket to an usher or ticket collector and took your place. In golf, you displayed your entrance pass all day. The general-admission folk (read: serfs) usually had a sticker plastered on their shirt, not unlike, say, a scarlet letter. Others wore a plastic card that dangled from a metal chain wrapped around their neck. Sponsors (read: feudal lords) wore either red, silver, or gold cards, depending on how much money they spent. There were also different passes for players' family and friends, Merion club members, Merion club officers, even steady sports agents. And the different cards gave you different access to different places. For example, you had to have a colored card to enter Corporate Row. Or you needed a gold card if you wanted to enter one of those exclusive tents – the ones strategically perched on hills like generals' quarters in an old war movie.

Corporate Row was merely a row of tents, each sponsored by one enormous company or another. The theoretical intention of spending at least one hundred grand for a four-day tent rental was to impress corporate clients and gain exposure. The truth, however, was that the tents were a way for the corporate bigwigs to go to the tournament for free. Yes, a few important clients were invited, but Myron also noticed that the company's major officers always managed to show too. And the hundred grand rental fee was just a start. It didn't include the food, the drinks, the employees – not to mention the first-class flights, the deluxe hotel suites, the stretch limos, et cetera, for the bigwigs and their guests.

Boys and girls, can you say, 'Chu-ching goes the cash register'? I thought you could.

Myron gave his name to the pretty young woman at the Lock-Horne tent. Win was not there yet, but Esperanza was sitting at a table in the corner.

'You look like shit,' Esperanza said.

'Maybe. But at least I feel awful.'

'So what happened?'

'Three crackheads adorned with Nazi memorabilia and crowbars jumped me.'

She arched an eyebrow. 'Only three?'

The woman was constant chuckles. He told her about his run-in and narrow escape. When he was finished, Esperanza shook her head and said, 'Hopeless. Absolutely hopeless.'

'Don't get all dewy-eyed on me. I'll be fine.'

'I found Lloyd Rennart's wife. She's an artist of some kind, lives on the Jersey shore.'

'Any word on Lloyd Rennart's body?'

Esperanza shook her head. 'I checked the NVI and Treemaker websites. No death certificate has been issued.'

Myron looked at her. 'You're kidding.'

'Nope. But it might not be on the Web yet. The other offices are closed until Monday. And even if one hasn't been issued, it might not mean anything.'

'Why not?' he asked.

'A body is supposed to be missing for a certain amount of time before the person can be declared dead,' Esperanza explained. 'I don't know – five years or something. But what often happens is that the next of kin files a motion in order to settle insurance claims and the estate. But Lloyd Rennart committed suicide.'

'So there'd be no insurance,' Myron said.

'Right. And assuming everything was held jointly between Rennart and his wife, then there would be no need for her to press it.'

Myron nodded. It made sense. Still it was yet another nagging hangnail that needed to be clipped. 'You want something to drink?' he asked.

She shook her head.

'I'll be right back.' Myron grabbed a Yoo-Hoo. Win had made sure the Lock-Horne tent stocked them. What a pal. A television monitor in the upper corner had a Scoreboard. Jack had just finished the fifteenth hole. Both he and Crispin had parred it. Barring a sudden collapse, Jack was going to take a huge lead into tomorrow's final round.

When Myron got settled again, Esperanza said, 'I want to talk to you about something.'

'Shoot.'

'It's about my graduating law school.'

'Okay,' Myron said, dragging out the word.

'You've been avoiding the subject,' she said.

'What are you talking about? I'm the one who wants to go to your graduation, remember?'

'That's not what I mean.' Her fingers found and began to fiddle with a straw wrapper. 'I'm talking about what happens *after* I graduate. I'm going to be a full-fledged attorney soon. My role in the company should change.'

Myron nodded. 'Agreed.'

'For one thing, I'd like an office.'

'We don't have the space.'

'The conference room is too large,' she countered. 'You can slice a little out of there and a little out of the waiting room. It won't be a huge office, but it'll be good enough.'

Myron nodded slowly. 'We can look into that.'

'It's important to me, Myron.'

'Okay, it sounds possible.'

'Second, I don't want a raise.'

'Don't?'

'That's right.'

'Odd negotiating technique, Esperanza, but you convinced me. Much as I might like to give you a raise, you will not receive one penny more. I surrender.'

'You're doing it again.'

'Doing what?'

'Joking around when I'm serious. You don't like change, Myron. I know that. It's why you lived with your parents until a few months ago. It's why you still keep Jessica around when you should have forgotten about her years ago.'

'Do me a favor,' he said wearily. 'Spare me the amateur analysis, okay?'

'Just stating the facts. You don't like change.'

'Who does? And I love Jessica. You know that.'

'Fine, you love her,' Esperanza said dismissively. 'You're right, I shouldn't have brought it up.'

'Good. Are we done?'

'No.' Esperanza stopped playing with the straw wrapper. She crossed her legs and folded her hands in her lap. 'This isn't easy for me to talk about,' she said.

'Do you want to do it another time?'

She rolled her eyes. 'No, I don't want to do it another time. I want you to listen to me. Really listen.'

Myron stayed silent, leaned forward a little.

'The reason I don't want a raise is because I don't want to work for someone. My father worked his whole life doing menial jobs for a variety of assholes. My mother spent hers cleaning other people's houses.' Esperanza stopped, swallowed, took a breath. 'I don't want to do that. I don't want to spend my life working for anyone.'

'Including me?'

'I said *anyone*, didn't I?' She shook her head. 'Jesus, you just don't listen sometimes.'

Myron opened his mouth, closed it. 'Then I don't see where you're going with this.'

'I want to be a part owner,' she said.

He made a face. 'Of MB SportsReps?'

'No, of AT&T. Of course MB.'

'But the name is MB,' Myron said 'The M is for Myron. B for Bolitar. Your name is Esperanza Diaz. I can't make it MBED. What kind of name is that?'

She just looked at him. 'You're doing it again. I'm trying to have a serious conversation.'

'Now? You pick now when I just got hit over the head with a tire iron—'

'Shoulder.'

'Whatever. Look, you know how much you mean to me—'

'This isn't about our friendship,' she interrupted. 'I don't care what I mean to you right now. I care about what I mean to MB SportsReps.'

'You mean a lot to MB. A hell of a lot.' He stopped. 'But?'

'But nothing. You just caught me a little off balance, that's all. I was just jumped by a group of neo-Nazis. That does funny things to the psyche of people of my persuasion. I'm also trying to solve a possible kidnapping. I know things have to change. I planned on giving you more to do, letting you handle more negotiations, hiring someone new. But a partnership . . . that's a different kettle of gefilte.'

Her voice was unyielding. 'Meaning?'

'Meaning I'd like to think about it, okay? How do you plan on becoming a partner? What percentage do you want? Do you want to buy in or work your way in or what? These are things we'll have to go over, and I don't think now is the time.'

'Fine.' She stood up. 'I'm going to hang around the players' lounge. See if I can strike up a conversation with one of the wives.'

'Good idea.'

'I'll see you later.' She turned to leave.

'Esperanza?'

She looked at him.

'You're not mad, right?'

'Not mad,' she repeated.

'We'll work something out,' he said.

She nodded. 'Right.'

'Don't forget. We're meeting with Tad Crispin an hour after they finish. By the pro shop.'

'You want me there?'

'Yes.'

She shrugged. 'Okay.' Then she left.

Myron leaned back and watched her go. Great. Just what he needed. His best friend in the world as a business partner. It never worked. Money screwed up relationships; it was simply one of life's givens. His father and his uncle – two closer brothers you never saw – had tried it. The outcome had been disastrous. Dad finally bought Uncle Morris out, but the two men didn't speak to each other for four years. Myron and Win had labored painstakingly to keep their businesses separate while maintaining the same interests and goals. It worked because there was no cross-interference or money to divide up. With Esperanza things had been great, but that was because the relationship had always been boss and employee. Their roles were well defined. But at the same time, he understood. Esperanza deserved this chance. She had earned it. She was more than an important employee to MB. She was a part of it.

So what to do?

He sat back and chugged the Yoo-Hoo, waiting for an idea. Fortunately, his thoughts were waylaid when someone tapped his shoulder.

Chapter 17

'Hello.'

Myron turned around. It was Linda Coldren. Her head was wrapped in a semi-babushka and she wore dark sunglasses. Greta Garbo circa 1984. She opened her purse. 'I forwarded the home phone here,' she whispered, pointing to a cellular phone in the purse. 'Mind if I sit down?'

'Please do,' Myron said.

She sat facing him. The sunglasses were big, but Myron could still see a hint of redness around the rims of her eyes. Her nose, too, looked like it had been rubbed raw by a Kleenex overdose. 'Anything new?' she asked.

He told her about the Crusty Nazis jumping him. Linda asked several follow-up questions. Again the internal paradox tore at her: she wanted her son to be safe, yet she did not want it all to be a hoax. Myron finished by saying, 'I still think we should get in touch with the feds. I can do it quietly.'

She shook her head. 'Too risky.'

'So is going on like this.'

Linda Coldren shook her head again and leaned back. For several moments they sat in silence. Her gaze was cast somewhere over his shoulder. Then she said, 'When Chad was born, I took off nearly two years. Did you know that?'

'No,' Myron said.

'Women's golf,' she muttered, 'I was at the height of my game, the top female golfer in the world, and yet you never read about it.'

'I don't follow golf much,' Myron said.

'Yeah, right,' she snorted. 'If Jack Nicklaus took two years off, you would have heard about it.'

Myron nodded. She had a point. 'Was it tough coming back?' he asked.

'You mean in terms of playing or leaving my son?'

'Both.'

She took a breath and considered the question. 'I missed playing,' she said. 'You have no idea how much. I regained the number one spot in a couple of months. As for Chad, well, he was still an infant. I hired a nanny to travel with us.'

'How long did that last?'

'Until Chad was three. That's when I realized that I couldn't drag him around anymore. It wasn't fair to him. A child needs some sort of stability. So I had to make a choice.'

They fell into silence.

'Don't get me wrong,' she said. 'I'm not into the self-pity thing and I'm glad women are given choices. But what they don't tell you is that when you have choices, you have guilt.'

'What kind of guilt?'

'A mother's guilt, the worst kind there is. The pangs are constant and ceaseless. They haunt your sleep. They point accusatory ringers. Every joyous swing of the golf club made me feel like I was forsaking my own child. I flew home as often as I could. I missed some tournaments that I really wanted to play in. I tried damn hard to balance career and motherhood. And every step of the way, I felt like a selfish louse.' She looked at him. 'Do you understand that?'

'Yes, I think so.'

'But you don't really sympathize,' she added.

'Of course I do.'

Linda Coldren gave him a skeptical glance. 'If I had been a stay-at-home mother, would you have been so quick to suspect that Chad was behind this? Didn't the fact that I was an absent mother sway your thinking?'

'Not an absent mother,' Myron corrected. 'Absent parents.'

'Same thing.'

'No. You were making more money. You were by far the more successful parent business-wise. If anyone should have stayed home, it was Jack.'

She smiled. 'Aren't we politically correct?'

'Nope. Just practical.'

'But it's not that simple, Myron. Jack loves his son. And during the years he didn't qualify for the tour, he did stay home with him. But let's face facts: Like it or not, it's the mother who bears that burden.'

'Doesn't make it right.'

'Nor does it let me off the hook. Like I said, I made my choices. If I had to do it all over again, I still would have toured.'

'And you still would have felt guilty.'

She nodded. 'With choice comes guilt. No escaping it.'

Myron took a sip of his Yoo-Hoo. 'You said that Jack stayed home some of the time.'

'Yes,' she said. 'When he failed Q school.'

'Q school?'

'Qualifying school,' she said. 'Every year the top 125 moneymakers get their PGA Tour card automatically. A couple of other players get sponsor exemptions. The rest are forced to go to Q school. Qualifying school. If you don't do well there, you don't play for the year.'

'One tournament decides all that?'

She tilted the glass at him as though making a toast. 'That's right.'

Talk about pressure. 'So when Jack failed Q school, he'd stay home for the year?'

She nodded.

'How did Jack and Chad get along?'

'Chad used to worship his father,' Linda said.

'And now?'

She looked off, her face vaguely pained. 'Now Chad is old enough to wonder why his father keeps losing. I don't know what he thinks anymore. But Jack is a good man. He tries very hard. You have to understand what happened to him. Losing the Open that way – it might sound overly melodramatic, but it killed something inside him. Not even having a son could make him whole.'

'It shouldn't matter so much,' Myron said, hearing the echo of Win in his words. 'It was just one tournament.'

'You were involved in a lot of big games,' she said. 'Ever choke away a victory like Jack did?'

'No.'

'Neither have I.'

Two gray-haired men sporting matching green ascots made their way down the buffet table. They leaned over each food selection and frowned like it had ants. Their plates were still piled high enough to cause the occasional avalanche.

'There's something else,' Linda said.

Myron waited.

She adjusted the sunglasses and put her hands on the table palms down. 'Jack and I are not close. We've haven't been close in many years.'

When she didn't continue, Myron said, 'But you've stayed married.'

'Yes.'

He wanted to ask why, but the question was so obvious, just hanging out there within easy view, that to voice it would be redundant.

'I am a constant reminder of his failures,' she continued. 'It's not easy for a man to live with that. We're supposed to be life partners, but I have what Jack longs for most.' Linda tilted her head. 'It's funny.'

'What?'

'I never allow mediocrity on the golf course. Yet I allowed it to dominate my personal life. Don't you find that odd?'

Myron made a noncommittal motion with his head. He could feel Linda's unhappiness radiating off her like a breaking fever. She looked up now and smiled at him. The smile was intoxicating, nearly breaking his heart. He found himself wanting to lean over and hold Linda Coldren. He felt this almost uncontrollable urge to press her against him and feel the sheen of her hair in his face. He tried to remember the last time he had held such thought for any woman but Jessica; no answer came to him.

'Tell me about you,' Linda suddenly said.

The change of subject caught him off guard. He sort of shook his head. 'Boring stuff.'

'Oh, I doubt that,' she said, almost playfully. 'Come on now. It'll distract me.'

Myron shook his head again.

'I know you almost played pro basketball. I know you hurt your knee. I know you went to law school at Harvard. And I know you tried to make a comeback a few months ago. Want to fill in the blanks?'

'That's pretty much it.'

'No, I don't think so, Myron. Aunt Cissy didn't say that you could help us because you were good at basketball.'

'I worked a bit for the government.'

'With Win?'

'Yes.'

'Doing what?'

Again he shook his head.

'Top secret, huh?'

'Something like that.'

'And you date Jessica Culver?'

'Yes.'

'I like her books.'

He nodded.

'Do you love her?'

'Very much.'

'So what do you want?'

'Want?'

'Out of life. What are your dreams?'

He smiled. 'You're kidding, right?'

'Just getting to the heart of the matter,' Linda said. 'Humor me. What do you want, Myron?' She looked at him with keen interest. Myron felt flushed.

'I want to marry Jessica. I want to move to the suburbs. I want to raise a family.'

She leaned back as though satisfied. 'For real?'

'Yes.'

'Like your parents?'

'Yes.'

She smiled. 'I think that's nice.'

'It's simple,' he said.

'Not all of us are built for the simple life,' she said, 'even if it's what we want.'

Myron nodded. 'Deep, Linda. I don't know what it means, but it sounded deep.'

'Me neither.' She laughed. It was deep and throaty and Myron liked the sound of it. 'Tell me where you met Win.'

'At college,' Myron said. 'Freshman year.'

'I haven't seen him since he was eight years old.' Linda Coldren took a swallow of her seltzer. 'I was fifteen then. Jack and I had already been dating a year, believe it or not. Win loved Jack, by the way. Did you know that?'

'No,' Myron said.

'It's true. He followed Jack everywhere. And Jack could be such a prick back then. He bullied other kids. He was mischievous as all hell. At times he was downright cruel.'

'But you fell for him?'

'I was fifteen,' she said, as if that explained everything. And maybe it did.

'What was Win like as a kid?' Myron asked.

She smiled again, the lines in the corners of her eyes and lips deepening. 'Trying to figure him out, eh?'

'Just curious,' Myron said, but the truth in her words stung. He suddenly wanted to withdraw the question, but it was too late.

'Win was never a happy kid. He was always' – Linda stopped, searching for the word – 'off. I don't know how else to put it. He wasn't crazy or flaky or aggressive or anything like that. But something was not right with him. Always. Even as a child, he had this strange ability to detach.'

Myron nodded. He knew what she meant.

'Aunt Cissy is like that too.'

'Win's mother?'

Linda nodded.' 'The woman can be pure ice when she wants to be. Even when it comes to Win. She acts as though he doesn't exist.'

'She must talk about him,' Myron said. 'To your father, at least.'

Linda shook her head. 'When Aunt Cissy told my father to contact Win, it was the first time she'd mentioned his name to him in years.'

Myron said nothing. Again the obvious question hung in the air unasked: What had happened between Win and his mother? But Myron would never voice it. This conversation had already gone too far. Asking would be an unforgivable betrayal; if Win wanted him to know, he'd tell him.

Time passed, but neither one of them noticed. They talked, mostly about Chad and the kind of son he was. Jack had held on and still led by eight strokes. A gigantic lead. If he blew it this time, it would be worse than twenty-three years ago.

The tent began to empty out, but Myron and Linda stayed and talked some more. A feeling of intimacy began to warm him; he found it hard to breathe when he looked at her. For a moment he closed his eyes. Nothing, he realized, was really going on here. If there was an attraction of some sort, it was simply a classic case of damsel-in-distress syndrome – and there was nothing less politically correct (not to mention Neanderthal) than that.

The crowd was gone now. For a long time nobody came into view. At one point, Win stuck his head into the tent. Seeing them together, he arched an eyebrow and then slipped back out.

Myron checked his watch. 'I have to go. I have an appointment.'

'With whom?'

'Tad Crispin.'

'Here at Merion?'

'Yes.'

'Do you think you'll be long?'

'No.'

She started fiddling with her engagement ring, studying it as though making an appraisal. 'Do you mind if I wait?' she asked. 'We can catch dinner together.' She took off her glasses. The eyes were puffy, but they were also strong and focused.

'Okay.'

He met up with Esperanza at the clubhouse. She made a face at him.

'What?' he said.

'You thinking about Jessica?' Esperanza asked suspiciously.

'No, why?'

'Because you're making your nauseating, lovesick-puppy face. You know. The one that makes me want to throw up on your shoes.'

'Come on,' he said. 'Tad Crispin is waiting.'

*

The meeting ended with no deal. But they were getting close.

'That contract he signed with Zoom,' Esperanza said. 'A major turkey.'

'I know.'

'Crispin likes you.'

'We'll see what happens,' Myron said.

He excused himself and walked quickly back to the tent. Linda Coldren was in the same seat, her back to him, her posture still queenlike.

'Linda?'

'It's dark now,' she said softly. 'Chad doesn't like the dark. I know he's sixteen, but I still leave the hall light on. Just in case.'

Myron remained still. When she turned toward him – when he first saw her smile – it was like something corkscrewed into his heart. 'When Chad was little,' she began, 'he always carried around this red plastic golf club and Wiffle ball. It's funny. When I think about him now, that's how I see him. With that little red club. For a long time I hadn't been able to picture him like that. He's so much like a man now. But since he's been gone, all I see is that little, happy kid in the backyard hitting golf balls.'

Myron nodded. He stretched out his hand toward hers. 'Let's go, Linda,' he said gently.

She stood. They walked together in silence. The night sky was so bright it looked wet. Myron wanted to reach out and hold her hand. But he didn't. When they got to her car, Linda unlocked it with a remote control. Then she opened the door as Myron began circling for the passenger side. He stopped suddenly.

The envelope was on her seat.

For several seconds, neither of them moved. The

envelope was manila, big enough for an eight-by-ten photograph. It was flat except for an area in the middle that puffed up a bit.

Linda Coldren looked up at Myron. Myron reached down, and using his palms, he picked up the envelope by the edges. There was writing on the back. Block letters:

I WARNED YOU NOT SEEK HELP
NOW CHAD PAYS THE PRICE
CROSS US AGAIN AND IT WILL GET MUCH WORSE.

Dread wrapped Myron's chest in tight steel bands. He slowly reached out and tentatively touched the puffy part with just a knuckle. It felt claylike. Carefully, Myron slit the seal open. He turned the envelope upside down and let the contents fall to the car seat.

The severed finger bounced once and then settled onto the leather.

Chapter 18

Myron stared, unable to speak.

Ohmygodohmygodohmygodohmygod . . .

Raw terror engulfed him. He started shivering, and his body went numb. He looked down at the note in his hand. A voice inside his head said, *Your fault, Myron. Your fault.*

He turned to Linda Coldren. Her hand fluttered near her mouth, her eyes wide.

Myron tried to step toward her, but he staggered like a boxer who didn't take advantage of a standing eight count. 'We have to call someone,' he managed, his voice sounding distant even to him. 'The FBI. I have friends—'

'No.' Her tone was strong.

'Linda, listen to me . . .'

'Read the note,' she said.

'But—'

'Read the note,' she repeated. She lowered her head grimly. 'You're out of this now, Myron.'

'You don't know what you're dealing with.'

'Oh no?' Her head snapped up. Her hands tightened into fists. 'I'm dealing with a sick monster,' she said. 'The kind of monster who maims at the slightest provocation.' She stepped closer to the car. 'He cut off my son's finger just because I talked to you. What do you think he'd do if I went directly against his orders?'

Myron's head swirled. 'Linda, paying off the ransom doesn't guarantee—'

'I know that,' she interrupted.

'But . . .' His mind flailed about helplessly and then said something exceedingly dumb. 'You don't even know if it's his finger.'

She looked down now. With one hand, she held back a sob. With the other, she caressed the finger lovingly, without a trace of repulsion on her face. 'Yes,' Linda said softly. 'I do.'

'He may already be dead.'

'Then it makes no difference what I do, does it?'

Myron stopped himself from saying any more. He had sounded asinine enough. He just needed a moment or two to gather himself, to figure out what the next step should be.

Your fault, Myron. Your fault.

He shook it off. He had, after all, been in worse scrapes. He had seen dead bodies, taken on some very bad people, caught and brought killers to justice. He just needed—

All with Win's help, Myron. Never on your own.

Linda Coldren lifted the finger into view. Tears streamed down her cheeks, but her face remained a placid pool.

'Good-bye, Myron.'

'Linda . . .'

'I'm not going to disobey him again.'

'We have to think this through—'

She shook her head. 'We should never have contacted you.'

Cupping her son's severed finger like a baby chick, Linda Coldren slid into the car. She put the finger down carefully and started the car. Then she shifted it into gear and drove away.

Myron made his way to his car. For several minutes he sat and took deep breaths, willing himself to calm down. He had studied martial arts since Win had first introduced him to tae kwon do when they were college freshmen. Meditation was a big part of what they'd learned, yet Myron never quite grasped the critical nuances. His mind had a habit of drifting. Now he tried to practice the simple rules. He closed his eyes. He breathed in through the nose slowly, forcing it down low, letting only his stomach, not his chest, expand. He released it through the mouth, even slower, draining his lungs fully.

Okay, he thought, what is your next step?

The first answer to float to the surface was the most basic: Give up. Cut your losses. Realize that you are very much out of your element. You never really worked for the feds. You only accompanied Win. You were way out of your league on this and it cost a sixteen-year-old boy his finger and maybe more. As Esperanza had said, 'Without Win, you're hopeless.' Learn your lesson and walk away.

And then what? Let the Coldrens face this crisis alone?

If he had, maybe Chad Coldren would still have ten fingers.

The thought made something inside of him crumble. He opened his eyes. His heart started trip-hammering again. He couldn't call the Coldrens. He couldn't call the feds. If he pursued this on his own, he would be risking Chad Coldren's life.

He started up the car, still trying to regain his balance. It was time to be analytical. It was time to be cold. He had to look at this latest development as a clue for a moment. Forget the horror. Forget the fact that he might have screwed up. The finger was just a clue.

One: The placement of the envelope was curious – inside Linda Coldren's locked (yes, it had been locked – Linda had used the remote control to open it) car. How had it gotten there? Had the kidnapper simply broken into the vehicle? Good possibility, but would he have had time in Merion's parking lot? Wouldn't someone have reported it? Probably. Did Chad Coldren have a key that the kidnapper could have used? Hmm. Very good possibility, but one he couldn't confirm unless he spoke to Linda, which was out of the question.

Dead end. For now.

Two: More than one person was involved in this kidnapping. This hardly took brilliant detective work. First off, you have the Crusty Nazi. The phone call at the mall proved that he had something to do with this – not to mention his subsequent behavior. But there was no way a guy like Crusty could sneak into Merion and plant the envelope in Linda Coldren's car. Not without drawing suspicion. Not during the US Open. And the note had warned the Coldrens not to 'cross' them again. Cross. Did that sound like a Crusty word?

Okay, good. What else?

Three: The kidnappers were both vicious and dumb.

Vicious was again obvious – the dumb part maybe less so. But look at the facts. For example, making a large ransom demand over a weekend when you know that the banks won't be open until Monday – was that bright? Not knowing how much to ask for the first two times they called – didn't that say ding-a-ling? And lastly, was it really prudent to cut off a kid's finger just because his parents happened to talk to a sports agent? Did that even make sense?

No.

Unless, of course, the kidnappers knew that Myron was more than a sports agent.

But how?

Myron pulled into Win's long driveway. Unfamiliar people were taking horses out of the stable. As he approached the guest house, Win appeared in the doorway. Myron pulled into a spot and got out.

'How did your meeting with Tad Crispin go?' Win asked.

Myron hurried over to him. 'They chopped off his finger,' he managed, breathy to the point of almost hyperventilating. 'The kidnappers. They cut off Chad's finger. Left it in Linda's car.'

Win's expression did not change. 'Did you discover this before or after your meeting with Tad Crispin?'

Myron was puzzled by the question. 'After.'

Win nodded slowly. 'Then my original question remains: How did your meeting go with Tad Crispin?'

Myron stepped back as though slapped. 'Jesus Christ,' he said in an almost reverent tone. 'You can't be serious.'

'What happens to that family does not concern me. What happens to your business dealings with Tad Crispin does.'

Myron shook his head, stunned. 'Not even you could be that cold.'

'Oh please.'

'Please what?'

'There are far greater tragedies in this world than a sixteen-year-old boy losing his finger. People die, Myron. Floods wipe out entire villages. Men do horrible things to children every day.' He paused. 'Did you, for example, read this afternoon's paper?'

'What are you rambling about?'

'I'm just trying to make you understand,' Win continued in too slow, too measured a voice. 'The Coldrens mean nothing to me – no more than any other stranger and perhaps less. The newspaper is filled with tragedies that hit me on a more personal level. For example . . .'

Win stopped and looked at Myron very steadily.

'For example what?' Myron asked.

'There was a new development in the Kevin Morris case,' Win replied. 'Are you familiar with that one?'

Myron shook his head.

'Two seven-year-old boys – Billy Waters and Tyrone Duffy – have been missing for nearly three weeks. They disappeared while riding their bikes home from school. The police questioned one Kevin Morris, a man with a long record of perversion, including molestation, who had been hanging around the school. But Mr Morris had a very sharp attorney. There was no physical evidence and despite a fairly convincing circumstantial case – they found the boys' bikes in a Dumpster not far from his home – Mr Morris was set free.'

Myron felt something cold press against his heart. 'So what was the new development, Win?'

'The police received a tip late last night.'

'How late?'

Again Win looked at him steadily. 'Very late.'

Silence.

'It seems,' Win went on, 'that someone had witnessed Kevin Morris burying the bodies off a road in the woods near Lancaster. The police dug them up last night. Do you know what they found?'

Myron shook his head again, afraid to even open his mouth.

'Billy Waters and Tyrone Duffy were both dead. They'd been sexually molested and mutilated in ways that even the media couldn't report. The police also found enough evidence at the burial site to arrest Kevin Morris. Fingerprints on a medical scalpel. Plastic bags that matched ones in his kitchen. Semen samples that offer a preliminary match in both boys.'

Myron flinched.

'Everyone seems quite confident that Mr Morris will be convicted,' Win finished.

'What about the person who called in the tip? Will he be a witness?'

'Funny thing,' Win said. 'The man called from a pay phone and never gave his name. No one, it seems, knows who he was.'

'But the police captured Kevin Morris?'

'Yes.'

The two men stared at each other.

'I'm surprised you didn't kill him,' Myron said.

'Then you really don't know me.'

A horse whinnied. Win turned and looked at the magnificent animal. Something strange came across his face, a look of loss.

'What did she do to you, Win?'

Win kept staring. They both knew whom Myron was talking about.

'What did she do to make you hate so much?'

'Don't engage in too much hyperbole, Myron. I am not that simple. My mother is not solely responsible for shaping me. A man is not made up of one incident, and I am a far cry from crazy, as you suggested earlier. Like any other human being, I choose my battles. I battle quite a bit – more than most – and usually on the right side. I battled for Billy Waters and Tyrone Duffy. But I do not wish to battle for the Coldrens. That is my choice. You, as my closest friend, should respect that. You should not try to prod or guilt me into a battle I do not wish to fight.'

Myron was not sure what to say. It was scary when he could understand Win's cold logic. 'Win?'

Win wrested his gaze from the horse. He looked at Myron.

'I'm in trouble,' Myron said, hearing the desperation in his tone. 'I need your help.'

Win's voice was suddenly soft, his face almost pained. 'If that were true, I'd be there. You know that. But you are not in any trouble from which you cannot easily disentangle. Just back away, Myron. You have the option of ending your involvement. To draw me into this against my will – using our friendship in that way – is wrong. Walk away this time.'

'You know I can't do that.'

Win nodded and headed toward his car. 'Like I said, we all choose our battles.'

When he entered the guest house, Esperanza was screaming, 'Bankrupt! Lose a turn! Bankrupt!'

186

Myron came up behind her. She was watching *Wheel of Fortune*.

'This woman is so greedy,' Esperanza said, gesturing at the screen. 'She's got over six thousand dollars and she keeps spinning. I hate that.'

The wheel stopped, landing on the glittery $1,000. The woman asked for a *B*. There were two of them. Esperanza groaned. 'You're back early,' she said. 'I thought you were going out to dinner with Linda Coldren.'

'It didn't work out.'

Esperanza finally turned around and looked at his face. 'What happened?'

He told her. Her dark complexion lost a bit of color along the way. When he finished, Esperanza said, 'You need Win.'

'He won't help.'

'Time to swallow your macho pride and ask him. Beg him if you have to.'

'Been there, done that. He's out.' On the television, the greedy woman bought a vowel. This always baffled Myron. Why do contestants who clearly know the puzzle's solution still buy vowels? To waste money? To make sure their opponents know the answer too?

'But,' he said, 'you're here.'

Esperanza looked at him. 'So?'

It was, he knew, the real reason she had come down in the first place. On the phone she had told him that he didn't work well alone. The words spoke volumes about her true motivation for fleeing the Big Apple.

'Do you want to help?' he asked.

The greedy woman leaned forward, spun the wheel, and then started clapping and shouting, 'Come on, a thousand!' Her opponents clapped too. Like they wanted her to do well. Right.

'What do you want me to do?' Esperanza asked.

'I'll explain on the way. If you want to come.'

They both watched the wheel decelerate. The camera moved in for a close-up. The arrow slowed and slowed before settling on the word BANKRUPT. The audience groaned. The greedy woman kept the smile, but now she looked like someone had just punched her hard in the stomach.

'That's an omen,' Esperanza said.

'Good or bad?' Myron asked.

'Yes.'

Chapter 19

The girls were still at the mall. Still at the food court. Still at the same table. It was amazing, when you thought about it. The long summer days beckoned with sunny skies and chirping birds. School was out, and yet so many teenagers spent all their time inside a glorified school cafeteria, probably lamenting the day they would have to return to school.

Myron shook his head. He was complaining about teenagers. A sure sign of lost youth. Soon he'd be screaming at someone for turning up the thermostat.

As soon as he entered the food court, the girls all turned in his direction. It was like they had people-we-know detectors at every entrance. Myron did not hesitate. Making his expression as stern as possible, he rushed toward them. He studied each face as he approached. These were, after all, just teenagers. The guilty one, Myron was sure, would show it.

And she did. Almost instantly.

She was the one that had been teased yesterday, the one they taunted for being the recipient of a Crusty smile. Missy or Messy or something. It all made sense now. Crusty hadn't spotted Myron's tail. He'd been tipped off. In fact, the whole thing had been arranged. That was how Crusty had known that Myron had been asking questions about him. That explained the seemingly fortuitous timing – that is, Crusty hanging around the food court just long enough for Myron to arrive.

It had all been a big setup.

The one with Elsa Lancaster hair screwed up her face and said, 'Like, what's the matter?'

'That guy tried to kill me,' Myron said.

Lots of gasps. Faces lit up with excitement. To most of them, this was like a television show come to life. Only Missy or Messy or some name with an *M* remained rock-still.

'Not to worry though,' Myron continued. 'We've just about got him. In an hour or two, he'll be under arrest. The police are on their way to find him right now. I just wanted to thank you all for your cooperation.'

The *M* girl spoke: 'I thought you weren't a cop.'

A sentence without the word *like*. Hmm. 'I'm undercover,' Myron said.

'Oh. My. God.'

'Get out!'

'Whoa!'

'You mean like on *New York Undercover*?'

Myron, no stranger to TV, had no idea what she was talking about. 'Exactly,' he said.

'This is *so* cool.'

'Are we, like, going to be on TV?'

'The six o'clock news?'

'That guy on Channel Four is *so* cute, you know?'

'My hair totally sucks.'

'No way, Amber. But mine is like a total rat nest.'

Myron cleared his throat. 'We have this pretty much all wrapped up. Except for one thing. The accomplice.'

Myron waited for one of them to say, 'Accomplice?' No one did. Myron elaborated. 'Someone in this very mall helped that creep set me up.'

'In, like, here?

'In *our* mall?'

'Not *our* mall. No way.'

They said the word *mall* like some people said the word *synagogue*.

'Someone helped that skank?'

'*Our* mall?'

'Eeeuw.'

'I can't, like, believe it.'

'Believe it,' Myron said. 'In fact, he or she is probably here right now. Watching us.'

Heads swirled about. Even *M* managed to get into the act, though it was an uninspired display.

Myron had shown the stick. Now the carrot. 'Look, I want you ladies to keep your eyes and ears open. We'll catch the accomplice. No question about it. Guys like that always talk. But if the accomplice was just a hapless dupe . . .'

Blank faces.

'If she, like, didn't really know the score' – not exactly hip-hop lingo, but they nodded now – 'and she came to me right away, before the cops nail her, well, then I'd probably be able to help her out. Otherwise, she could be charged with attempted murder.'

Nothing. Myron had expected that. *M* would never

admit this in front of her friends. Jail was a great fear-inducer, but it was little more than a wet match next to the bonfire that was teenage peer pressure.

'Good-bye, ladies.'

Myron moved to the other side of the food court. He leaned against a pillar, putting himself in the path between the girls' table and the bathroom. He waited, hoping she'd make an excuse and come over. After about five minutes, M stood up and began walking toward Myron. Just as he planned. Myron almost smiled. Maybe he should have been a high school guidance counselor. Mold young minds, change lives for the better.

The M girl veered away from him and toward the exit. Damn.

Myron quickly trotted over, the smile on full blast. 'Mindy?' He had suddenly remembered her name.

She turned to him but said nothing.

He put on the soft voice and the understanding eyes. A male Oprah. A kinder, gentler Regis. 'Whatever you say to me is confidential,' he said. 'If you're involved in this—'

'Just stay away from me, okay? I'm not, like, involved in anything.'

She pushed past him and hurried past Foot Locker and the Athlete's Foot – two stores Myron had always assumed were the same, alter egos if you will, like you never saw Batman and Bruce Wayne in the same room.

Myron watched her go. She hadn't cracked, which was a bit of a surprise. He nodded and his backup plan went into action. Mindy kept hurrying away, glancing behind her every few steps to make sure Myron wasn't following her. He wasn't.

Mindy, however, did not notice the attractive, jean-clad Hispanic woman just a few feet to her left.

Mindy found a pay phone by the record store that looked exactly like every other mall record store. She glanced about, put a quarter into the slot, and dialed a number. Her finger had just pressed the seventh digit when a small hand reached over her shoulder and hung up the phone.

She spun toward Esperanza. 'Hey!'

Esperanza said, 'Put down the phone.'

'Hey!'

'Right, hey. Now put down the phone.'

'Like, who the fuck are you?'

'Put down the phone,' Esperanza repeated, 'or I'll shove it up a nostril.'

Wide-eyed with confusion, Mindy obeyed. Several seconds later, Myron appeared. He looked at Esperanza. 'Up a nostril?'

She shrugged.

Mindy shouted, 'You can't, like, do that.'

'Do what?' Myron said.

'Like' – Mindy stopped, struggled with the thought – 'like, make me hang up a phone?'

'No law against that,' Myron said. He turned to Esperanza. 'You know any law against that?'

'Against hanging up a phone?' Esperanza emphatically shook her head. 'No, señor.'

'See, no law against it. On the other hand, there is a law against aiding and abetting a criminal. It's called a felony. It means jail time.'

'I didn't aid nothing. And I don't bet.'

Myron turned to Esperanza. 'You get the number?'

She nodded and gave it to him.

'Let's trace it.'

Again, the cyber-age made this task frightening easy. Anybody can buy a computer program at their local software store or hop on certain websites like Biz, type in the number, and voilà, you have a name and address.

Esperanza used a cellular phone to dial the home number of MB SportsReps' new receptionist. Her name was, fittingly, Big Cyndi. Six-five and over three hundred pounds, Big Cyndi had wrestled professionally under the moniker Big Chief Mama, tag-team partner of Esperanza 'Little Pocahontas' Diaz. In the ring, Big Cyndi wore makeup like Tammy Faye on steroids; spiked hair that would have been the envy of Sid and Nancy; ripped muscle-displaying T-shirts; and an awful, sneering glare complete with a ready growl. In real life, well, she was exactly the same.

Speaking Spanish, Esperanza gave Cyndi the number.

Mindy said, 'Hey, I'm, like, outta here.'

Myron grabbed her arm. ' 'Fraid not.'

'Hey! You can't, like, hold me here.'

Myron maintained his grip.

'I'll scream rape.'

Myron rolled his eyes. 'At a mall pay phone. In broad fluorescent light. When I'm standing here with my girlfriend.'

Mindy looked at Esperanza. 'She's your girlfriend?'

'Yes.'

Esperanza began whistling 'Dream Weaver.'

'But you can't, like, make me stay with you.'

'I don't get it, Mindy. You look like a nice girl.' Actually, she was wearing black leggings, too-high pumps, a red halter top, and what looked like a dog choker around her neck. 'Are you trying to tell me that this guy is worth going to jail over? He deals drugs, Mindy. He tried to kill me.'

Esperanza hung up. 'It's a bar called the Parker Inn.'

'You know where it is?' he asked Mindy.

'Yeah.'

'Come on.'

Mindy pulled away. 'Let go,' she said, stretching out the last word.

'Mindy, this isn't fun and games here. You helped someone try to kill me.'

'So you say.'

'What?'

Mindy put her hands on her hips, chewed gum. 'So, like, how do I know that you're not the bad one, huh?'

'Excuse me?'

'You, like, come up to us yesterday, right, all mysterious and stuff, right? You don't, like, have a badge or nothing. How do I know that you aren't, like, after Tito? How do I know that you aren't another drug dealer trying to take over his turf?'

'"Tito?"' Myron repeated, looking at Esperanza. 'A neo-Nazi named Tito?'

Esperanza shrugged.

'None of his friends, like, call him Tito,' Mindy went on. 'It's way too long, you know? So they call him Tit.'

Myron and Esperanza exchanged a glance, shook their heads. Too easy.

'Mindy,' Myron said slowly, 'I wasn't kidding back there. Tito is not a nice fellow. He may, in fact, be involved in kidnapping and maiming a boy about your age. Somebody cut off the boy's finger and sent it to his mother.'

Her face pinched up. 'Oh, that's, like, so gross.'

'Help me, Mindy.'

'You a cop?'

'No,' Myron said. 'I'm just trying to save a boy.'

She waved her hands dismissively. 'Then, like, go. You don't need me.'

'I'd like you to come with us.'

'Why?'

'So you don't try to warn Tito.'

'I won't.'

Myron shook his head. 'You also know how to get to Parker Inn. It'll save us time.'

'Uh-uh, no way. I'm not going with you.'

'If you don't,' Myron said, 'I'll tell Amber and Trish and the gang all about your new boyfriend.'

That snared her attention. 'He's not my boyfriend,' she insisted. 'We just, like, hung out a couple of times.'

Myron smiled. 'So I'll lie,' he said. 'I'll tell them you slept with him.'

'I did not!' she screamed. 'That's, like, so unfair.'

Myron shrugged helplessly.

She crossed her arms and chewed her gum. Her version of defiance. It didn't last long. 'Okay, okay, I'll go.' She pointed a finger at Myron. 'But I don't want Tit to see me, okay? I stay in the car.'

'Deal,' Myron said. He shook his head. Now they were after a man named Tit. What next?

The Parker Inn was a total redneck, biker, skeezer bar. The parking lot was packed with pickup trucks and motorcycles. Country music blared from the constantly opening door. Several men in John Deere baseball caps were using the side of the building as a urinal. Every once in a while one would turn and piss on another. Curses and laughter spewed forward. Fun city.

From his car parked across the street, Myron looked at Mindy and said, 'You used to hang out here?'

She shrugged. 'I, like, came here a couple of times,' she said. 'For excitement, you know?'

Myron nodded. 'Why didn't you just douse yourself with gasoline and light matches?'

'Fuck you, all right? You my father now?'

He held his hands up. She was right. None of his business. 'Do you see Tito's truck?' Myron just couldn't call him Tit. Maybe if he got to know him better.

Mindy scanned the lot. 'No.'

Neither did Myron. 'Do you know where he lives?'

'No.'

Myron shook his head. 'He deals drugs. He wears a swastika tattoo. And he has no ass. But don't tell me . . . underneath all that, Tito is really sweet.'

Mindy shouted, 'Fuck you, all right? Just fuck you.'

'Myron,' Esperanza said by way of warning.

Again Myron put his hands up. They all sat back and watched. Nothing happened.

Mindy sighed as audibly as possible. 'So, like, can I go home now?'

Esperanza said, 'I have a thought.'

'What?' Myron asked.

Esperanza pulled the tail of her blouse out of her jeans. She tied it up, making a knot under her rib cage and revealing plenty of flat, dark stomach. Then she unbuttoned her top to a daring low. A black bra was now visible, Myron noticed, trained detective that he was. She pulled down the visor mirror and began to apply makeup. Lots of makeup. Far too much makeup. She mussed up

197

her hair a bit and rolled up her jeans cuffs. When she finished she smiled at Myron.

'How do I look?' she asked.

Even Myron felt a little weak at the knees. 'You're going to walk in there looking like that?'

'That's how everyone in there dresses.'

'But everyone doesn't look like you,' he said.

'Oh, my, my,' Esperanza said. 'A compliment.'

'I meant, like a chorus dancer in *West Side Story*.'

' "A boy like that," ' Esperanza sang, ' "he keel your brother, forget that boy, go find another—" '

'If I do make you a partner,' Myron said, 'don't dress like this at board meetings.'

'Deal,' Esperanza said. 'Can I go now?'

'First call me on the cellular now. I want to make sure I can hear everything that goes on.'

She nodded, dialed the phone. He picked it up. They tested the connection.

'Don't go playing hero,' he said. 'Just find out if he's there. Something gets out of hand, you get out of there pronto.'

'Okay.'

'And we should have a code word. Something you say if you need me.'

Esperanza nodded, feigning seriousness. 'If I say the words premature ejaculation, it means I want you to come.'

'So to speak.'

Esperanza and even Mindy groaned.

Myron reached into his glove compartment. He snapped it open and pulled out a gun. He was not going to be caught unprepared again. 'Go,' he said.

Esperanza hopped out of the car and crossed the street.

A black Corvette with flame decals on the hood and an extra-*vrooming* engine pulled up. A gold-chain-enmeshed primate raced the engine and leaned his head out the window. He smiled greasily at Esperanza. He hit the gas again, giving off a few more deep *vrooms*. Esperanza looked at the car, then at the driver. 'Sorry to hear about your penis,' she deadpanned.

The car drove off. Esperanza shrugged and waved at Myron. It wasn't an original line, but it never failed her.

'God, I love that woman,' Myron said.

'She's, like, totally hot,' Mindy agreed. 'I wish I looked like her.'

'You should wish to be like her,' he corrected.

'What's the difference? She must, like, really work out, right?'

Esperanza entered the Parker Inn. The first thing that hit her was the smell – a pungent combination of dried vomit and body odor, only less olfactorily pleasing. She wrinkled her nose and continued inside. The floor was hardwood with lots of sawdust. The light was dingy, coming off the pool table ceiling fixtures that were supposed to look like imitation Tiffany lamps. The crowd was probably two-to-one men over women. Everyone was dressed – in a word – cheesy.

Esperanza looked around the room. Then she spoke out loud so that Myron would hear her through the phone. 'About a hundred guys in here fit your description,' she said. 'It's like asking me to find an implant in a strip club.'

Myron's phone was on mute, but she'd bet he was laughing. An implant at a strip club. Not bad, she thought. Not bad at all.

So now what?

People were staring at her, but she was used to that. Three seconds passed before a man approached her. He had a long, kinky beard; bits of coagulated food were lodged in it. He smiled toothlessly, looked her up and down unapologetically.

'I've got a great tongue,' he said to her.

'Now all you need is some teeth.'

She pushed past him and made her way to the bar. Two seconds later, a guy jumped toward her. He wore a cowboy hat. Cowboy hat. Philadelphia. What's wrong with this picture?

'Hey, sweetheart, don't I know you?'

Esperanza nodded. 'Another line that smooth,' she said, 'and I may start to undress.'

The cowboy whooped it up like it was the funniest thing he had ever heard. 'No, little darling, I'm not handing you a line. I'm serious here . . .' His voice sort of drifted off. 'Holy shit!' the man cried. 'It's Little Pocahontas! The Indian Princess! You're Little Pocahontas, right? Don't deny it now, darling. It's you! I can't believe it!'

Myron was probably laughing his ass off right now.

'Nice to see you,' Esperanza said. 'Thank you very much for remembering.'

'Shit, Bobby, take a lookie here. It's Little Pocahontas! Remember? That hot little vixen on FLOW?'

FLOW, of course, stood for the 'Fabulous Ladies Of Wrestling.' The organization's original name had been the 'Beautiful Ladies Of Wrestling,' but once they became popular enough for television, the networks insisted on a new acronym.

'Where?' Another man approached, eyes wide and

drunk and happy. 'Holy shit, you're right! It's her! It's really her!'

'Hey, thanks for the memories, fellas, but—'

'I remember this one time, you were fighting Tatiana the Siberian Husky? Remember that one? Shit, my hard-on nearly poked a hole clean through my bedroom window.'

Esperanza hoped to file that little tidbit under Too Much Information.

An enormous bartender came over. He looked like the pullout centerfold for *Leather Biker Monthly*, Extra big and extra scary. He had long hair, a long scar, and tattoos of snakes slithering up both arms. He shot the two men a glare and – poof – they were gone. Like the glare had evaporated them. Then he turned his eyes toward Esperanza. She met the glare and gave him one back. Neither backed down.

'Lady, what the fuck are you?' he asked.

'Is that a new way of asking what I'm drinking?'

'No.' The mutual glaring continued. He leaned two massive snake-arms on the bar. 'You're too good-looking to be a cop,' he said. 'And you're too good-looking to be hanging out in this toilet.'

'Thanks, I guess,' Esperanza said. 'And you are?'

'Hal,' he said. 'I own this toilet.'

'Hi, Hal.'

'Hi back. Now what the fuck do you want?'

'I'm trying to score some blow,' she said.

'Nah,' Hal said with a shake of his head. 'You'd go to Spic City for that. Buy it from one of your own kind, no offense.' He leaned even closer now. Esperanza couldn't help but wonder if Hal would be a good match for Big

Cyndi. She liked big biker guys. 'Let's cut the crap, sweetheart. What do you want?'

Esperanza decided to try the direct approach. 'I'm looking for a sliver of scum named Tito. People call him Tit. Skinny, shaved head—'

'Yeah, yeah, I *might* know him. How much?'

'Fifty bucks.'

Hal made a scoffing sound. 'You want me to sell out a customer for fifty bucks?'

'A hundred.'

'Hundred and fifty. The deadbeat sack of shit owes me money.'

'Deal,' she said.

'Show me the money.'

Esperanza took the bills out of her wallet. Hal reached it for it, but she pulled back. 'You first,' she said.

'I don't know where he lives,' Hal said. 'He and his goose-stepping faggots come in every night except Wednesdays and Saturdays.'

'Why not Wednesdays and Saturdays?' she asked.

'How the fuck am I supposed to know? Bingo night and Saturday night mass maybe. Or maybe they all do a circle jerk crying "Heil, Hitler" when they shoot off. How the fuck do I know?'

'What's his real name?'

'I don't know.'

She looked around the bar. 'Any of the boys here know?'

'Nah,' Hal said. 'Tit always comes in with the same limp-dicked crew and they leave together. They don't talk to no one else. It's *verboten*.'

'Sounds like you don't like him.'

'He's a stupid punk. They all are. Assholes who blame the fact that they're genetic mutations on other people.'

'So why do you let them hang out here?'

'Because unlike them, I know that this is the US of A. You can do what you want. Anyone is welcome here. Black, white, Spic, Jap, whatever. Even stupid punks.'

Esperanza almost smiled. Sometimes you find tolerance in the strangest places. 'What else?'

'That's all I know. It's Saturday night. They'll be here tomorrow.'

'Fine,' Esperanza said. She ripped the bills in half. 'I'll give you the other half of the bills tomorrow.'

Hal reached out his big hand and closed it over her forearm. His glare grew a little meaner. 'Don't be too smart, hot legs,' he said slowly. 'I can yell *gang bang* and have you on your back on a pool table in five seconds. You give the hundred and fifty now. Then you rip another hundred in half to keep my mouth shut. You got it?'

Her heart was beating wildly in her chest. 'Got it,' she said. She handed him the other half of the bills. Then she took out another hundred, ripped it, and handed it to him.

'Get out, sweet buns. Like now.'

He didn't have to tell her twice.

Chapter 20

There was nothing else they could do tonight. To approach the Squires estate would be foolhardy, at best. He couldn't call or contact the Coldrens. It was too late to try to reach Lloyd Rennart's widow. And lastly – and perhaps most important – Myron was bone-tired.

So he spent the evening at the guest house with his two best friends in the world. Myron, Win, and Esperanza lay sprawled on separate couches like Dalí clocks. They wore T-shirts and shorts and buried themselves deep within puffy pillows. Myron drank too much Yoo-Hoo; Esperanza drank too much diet Coke; Win drank almost enough Brooklyn Lager (Win drank only lager, never beer). There were pretzels and Fritos and Ruffles and freshly delivered pizza. The lights were out. The big-screen television was on. Win had recently taped a whole bunch of *Odd Couple* episodes. They were on the fourth in a row. The best thing about the *Odd Couple*, Myron surmised, was the consistency. They never had a weak episode – how many shows could say that?

Myron bit into a slice of pizza. He needed this. He had barely slept in the millennium since he'd first encountered the Coldrens (in reality, it only had been yesterday). His brain was fried; his nerves were fraying like overused floss. Sitting with Win and Esperanza, their faces blue-lit by the picture tube, Myron felt true contentment.

'It's simply not true,' Win insisted.

'No way,' Esperanza agreed, tossing down a Ring-Ding.

'I'm telling you,' Myron said. 'Jack Klugman is wearing a hairpiece.'

Win's voice was firm. 'Oscar Madison would never wear a rug. Never, I say. Felix, maybe. But Oscar? It simply cannot be.'

'It is,' Myron said. 'That's a hairpiece.'

'You're still thinking of the last episode,' Esperanza said. 'The one with Howard Cosell.'

'Yes, that's it,' Win agreed with a snap of his fingers. 'Howard Cosell. He wore a hairpiece.'

Myron looked up the ceiling, exasperated. 'I'm not thinking of Howard Cosell. I know the difference between Howard Cosell and Jack Klugman. I'm telling you. Klugman is sporting a rug.'

'Where's the line?' Win challenged, pointing at the screen. 'I cannot see a break or a line or a discoloration. And I'm usually quite good at spotting lines.'

'I don't see it either,' Esperanza added, squinting.

'That's two against one,' Win said.

'Fine,' Myron said. 'Don't believe me.'

'He had his own hair on *Quincy*,' Esperanza said.

'No,' Myron said, 'he didn't.'

'Two against one,' Win repeated. 'Majority rules.'

'Fine,' Myron repeated. 'Wallow in ignorance.'

On the screen, Felix fronted for a band called Felix Unger and the Sophisticates. They rambled through an up-tempo number with the repeated phrase 'Stumbling all around.' Kinda catchy.

'What makes you so sure it's a rug?' Esperanza asked.

'*The Twilight Zone*,' Myron said.

'Come again?'

'*The Twilight Zone*. Jack Klugman was in at least two episodes.'

'Ah, yes,' Win said. 'Now, don't tell me, let me see if I remember.' He paused, tapping his lip with his index finger. 'The one with the little boy Pip. Played by . . . ?' Win knew the answer. Life with his friends was an ever-continuing game of Useless Trivia.

'Bill Mumy.' It was Esperanza.

Win nodded. 'Whose most famous role was . . . ?'

'Will Robinson,' Esperanza said. '*Lost in Space*.'

'Remember Judy Robinson?' Win sighed. 'Quite the Earth babe, no?'

'Except,' Esperanza interjected, 'what was up with her clothes? Kmart velour sweaters for space travel? Who came up with that one?'

'And we cannot forget the effervescent Dr Zachery Smith,' Win added. 'The first gay character on series TV.'

'Scheming, conniving, gutless – with a hint of pedophilia,' Esperanza said with a shake of her head. 'He set back the movement twenty years.'

Win grabbed another slice of pizza. The pizza box was white with red-and-green lettering and had the classic caricature of a heavy-set chef twirling a thin mustache with his finger. The box read – and this is absolutely true:

Whether it's a pizza or submarine,
We buy the best,
To prepare the best,
And leave it to you for the rest.

Wordsworth.

'I don't recall Mr Klugman's second *Twilight Zone*,' Win said.

'The one with the pool player,' Myron answered. 'Jonathan Winters was in it too.'

'Ah, yes,' Win said with a serious nod. 'Now I remember. Jonathan Winters's ghost shoots pool against Mr Klugman's character. For bragging rights or some such thing.'

'Correct answer.'

'So what do those two *Twilight Zone* episodes have to do with Mr Klugman's hair?'

'You got them on tape?'

Win paused. 'I believe that I do. I taped the last *Twilight Zone* marathon. One of those episodes is bound to be on it.'

'Let's find it,' Myron said.

It took the three of them almost twenty minutes of sifting through his vast video collection before they finally found the episode with Bill Mumy. Win put it in the VCR and reclaimed his couch. They watched in silence.

Several minutes later, Esperanza said, 'I'll be damned.'

A black-and-white Jack Klugman was calling out 'Pip,' the name of his dead son, his tormented cries chasing a tender apparition from his past. The scene was quite moving, but also very much beside the point. The key factor, of course, was that even though this episode predated the *Odd Couple* by some ten years, Jack Klugman's hairline was in a serious state of retreat.

Win shook his head. 'You are good,' he said in a hushed voice. 'So very good.' He looked at Myron. 'I am truly humbled to be in your presence.'

'Don't feel bad,' Myron said. 'You're special in your own way.'

This was about as heavy as the conversation got.

They laughed. They joked. They made fun of one another. No one talked about a kidnapping or the Coldrens or business or money matters or landing Tad Crispin or the severed finger of a sixteen-year-old boy.

Win dozed off first. Then Esperanza. Myron tried to call Jessica again, but there was no answer. No surprise. Jessica often didn't sleep well. Taking walks, she claimed, inspired her. He heard her voice on the machine and felt something inside him plunge. When the beep came on, he left a message:

'I love you,' he said. 'I will always love you.'

He hung up. He crawled back onto the couch and pulled the cover up to his neck.

Chapter 21

When Myron arrived at Merion Golf Club the next morning, he wondered briefly if Linda Coldren had told Jack about the severed finger. She had. By the third hole, Jack had already dropped three strokes off his lead. His complexion was cartoon Casper. His eyes were as vacant as the Bates Motel, his shoulders slumped like bags of wet peat moss.

Win frowned. 'Guess that finger thing is bothering him.'

Mr Insight.

'That sensitivity workshop,' Myron said, 'it's really starting to pay off.'

'I did not expect Jack's collapse to be so total.'

'Win, his son's finger was chopped off by a kidnapper. That's the kind of thing that could distract someone.'

'I guess.' Win didn't sound convinced. He turned away and started heading up the fairway. 'Did Crispin show you the numbers in his Zoom deal?'

'Yes,' Myron said.

'And?'

'And he got robbed.'

Win nodded. 'Not much you can do about it now.'

'Plenty I can do about it,' Myron said. 'It's called renegotiate.'

'Crispin signed a deal,' Win said.

'So?'

'Please do not tell me that you want him to back out of it.'

'I didn't say I wanted him to back out. I said I wanted to renegotiate.'

' "Renegotiate," ' Win repeated as though the word tasted vinegary. He continued trudging up the fairway. 'How come an athlete who performs poorly never re-negotiates? How come you never see a player who has a terrible season restructure his deal downward?'

'Good point,' Myron said. 'But, you see, I have this job description. It reads something like this: Get the most money I can for a client.'

'And ethics be damned.'

'Whoa, where did that come from? I may search for legal loopholes, but I always play by the rules.'

'You sound like a criminal defense attorney,' Win said.

'Ooo, now that's a low blow,' Myron said.

The crowd was getting caught up in the unfolding drama in an almost disturbing way. The whole experience was like watching a car crash in super slow motion. You were horrified; you stared; and part of you almost cheered the misfortune of a fellow human being. You gaped, wondering about the outcome, almost hoping the crash would be fatal. Jack Coldren was slowly dying. His heart was crumbling like brown leaves caught in a closed fist. You saw it all happening. And you wanted it to continue.

On the fifth hole Myron and Win met up with Norm Zuckerman and Esme Fong. They were both on edge, especially Esme, but then again she had a hell of a lot riding on this round. On the eighth hole they watched Jack miss an easy putt. Stroke by stroke, the lead shrank from insurmountable to comfortable to nail-biting.

On the back nine Jack managed to control the hemorrhaging a bit. He continued to play poorly, but with only three holes left to play, Jack was still hanging on to a two-stroke lead. Tad Crispin was applying pressure, but it would still take a fairly major gaffe on Jack Coldren's part for Tad to win.

Then it happened.

The sixteenth hole. The same hazard that had laid waste to Jack's dream twenty-three years ago. Both men started off fine. They hit good tee-shots to what Win called 'a slightly offset fairway.' Uh-huh. But on Jack's second shot, disaster struck. He came over the top and left the sucker short. Way short.

The ball landed in the stone quarry.

The crowd gasped. Myron watched in horror. Jack had done the unthinkable. Again.

Norm Zuckerman nudged Myron. 'I'm moist,' he said giddily. 'Swear to God, I'm moist in my nether regions. Go ahead, feel for yourself.'

'I'll take your word for it, Norm.'

Myron turned to Esme Fong. Her face lit up. 'Me too,' she said.

A more intriguing proposal but still no sale.

Jack Coldren barely reacted, as if some internal wiring

had shorted out. He was not waving a white flag, but it looked like he should have been.

Tad Crispin took advantage. He hit a fine approach shot and was left with an eight-foot putt that would give him the lead. As young Tad stood over the ball, the silence in the gallery was overwhelming – not just the crowd, but it was as if the nearby traffic and overhead planes and even the grass, the trees, the very course had all aligned themselves against Jack Coldren.

This was big-time pressure. And Tad Crispin responded in a big way.

When the putt dropped into the cup, there was no polite golf clap. The crowd erupted like Vesuvius in the last days. The sound spilled forward in a powerful wave, warming the young newcomer and sweeping aside the dying warhorse. Everyone seemed to want this. Everyone wanted to crown Tad Crispin and behead Jack Coldren. The young handsome man against the ruffled veteran – it was like the golf equivalent of the Nixon-Kennedy debates.

'What a yip master,' someone said.

'A major case of the yips,' another agreed.

Myron looked a question at Win.

'Yip,' Win said. 'The latest euphemism for *choke*.'

Myron nodded. There was nothing worse you could call an athlete. It was okay to be untalented or to screw up or to have an off day – but not to choke. Never to choke. Chokers were gutless. Chokers had their very manhood questioned. Being called a choker was tantamount to standing naked in front of a beautiful woman while she pointed and laughed.

Er, or so Myron imagined.

He spotted Linda Coldren in a private grandstand tent

overlooking the eighteenth hole. She wore sunglasses and a baseball cap pulled low. Myron looked up at her. She did not look back. Her expression was one of mild confusion, like she was working on a math word problem or trying to recall the name behind a familiar face. For some reason, the expression troubled Myron. He stayed in her line of vision, hoping she'd signal to him. She didn't.

Tad Crispin took a one-stroke lead into the final hole. The other golfers were finished for the day, many coming out and standing around the eighteenth green to watch the final act of golf's greatest collapse.

Win started playing Mr Merion. 'The eighteenth hole is a four hundred and sixty-five yard, par four,' he began. 'The tee is in the stone quarry. You need to hit it up the hill – a two-hundred yard carry.'

'I see,' Myron said. Huh?

Tad was up first. He hit what looked like a good, solid drive. The gallery did that polite golf-clap thing. Jack Coldren took his turn. His shot climbed higher, seemingly pulling itself against the elements.

'Very nice golf shot,' Win said. 'Super.'

Myron turned to Esme Fong. 'What happens if it ends in a tie? Sudden death?'

Esme shook her head. 'Other tournaments, yes. But not at the Open. They make both players come back tomorrow and play a whole round.'

'All eighteen holes?'

'Yes.'

Tad's second shot left him just short of the green.

'A solid golf shot,' Win informed him. 'Sets him up nicely for the par.'

Jack took out an iron and approached the ball.

Win smiled at Myron. 'Recognize this?'

213

Myron squinted. Déjà vu swarmed in. He was no golf fan, but from this angle even he recognized the spot. Win kept the picture on his credenza at the office. Almost every golf book or golf pub or golf whatever had the photograph. Ben Hogan had stood exactly where Jack Coldren now stood. In 1950 or thereabouts. Hogan had stroked the famous one-iron that had made him the US Open champion. It was the golf equivalent of 'Havlicek stole the ball!'

As Jack took his practice swing, Myron could not help but wonder about old ghosts and strange possibilities.

'He has an almost impossible task,' Win said.

'Why's that?'

'The pin placement is brutal today. Behind that yawning bunker.'

A yawning bunker? Myron did not bother asking.

Jack fired a long iron at the green. He reached it, but as Win had predicted, he still left himself a good twenty-plus feet away. Tad Crispin took his third shot, a beautiful little chip that came to rest within six inches of the hole. Tad tapped it in for par. That meant that Jack had no chance of winning in regulation. The best he could do was force a tie. If he made this putt.

'A twenty-two-foot putt,' Win said with a grim shake of the head. 'No chance.'

He had said twenty-two feet – not twenty-one feet or twenty-three feet. Twenty-two feet. Win could tell from a quick glance from over fifty yards away. Golfers. Go figure.

Jack Coldren strolled to the green. He bent down, picked up his ball, put down a marker, picked up the marker, put down the ball again in the exact same spot. Myron shook his head. Golfers.

Jack looked very far away, like he was putting from New Jersey. Think about it. He was twenty-two feet away from a hole four-and-a-quarter inches in diameter. Break out a calculator. Do the math.

Myron, Win, Esme, and Norm waited. This was it. The coup de grâce. The part where the matador finally drives the long, thin blade home.

But as Jack studied the break in the green, some sort of transformation seemed to take place. The fleshy features hardened. The eyes became focused and steely and – though it was probably Myron's imagination – a hint of yesterday's 'eye' seemed to flint up in them. Myron looked behind him. Linda Coldren had spotted the change too. For a brief moment she let her attention slip and her eyes sought out Myron's, as if for confirmation. Before Myron could do more than meet her gaze, she looked away.

Jack Coldren took his time. He read the green from several angles. He squatted down, his club pointing in front of him the way golfers do. He talked to Diane Hoffman at some length. But once he addressed the ball, there was no hesitation. The club went back like a metronome and kissed the ball hard on the way down.

The tiny white sphere carrying all of Jack Coldren's dreams circled toward the hole like an eagle seeking its prey. There was no question in Myron's mind. The pull was almost magnetic. Several seemingly infinite seconds later, the tiny white sphere dropped to the bottom of the hole with an audible clink. For a moment there was silence and then another eruption, this one more from surprise than exhilaration. Myron found himself applauding wildly.

Jack had done it. He'd tied the score.

Over the crowd's cacophony, Norm Zuckerman said, 'This is beautiful, Esme. The whole world will be watching tomorrow. The exposure will be incredible.'

Esme looked stunned. 'Only if Tad wins.'

'What do you mean?'

'What if Tad loses?'

'Hey, second place at the US Open?' Norm said, palms up to the sky. 'Not bad, Esme. Not bad at all. That's where we were this morning. Before all this happened. Nothing lost, nothing gained.'

Esme Fong shook her head. 'If Tad loses now, he doesn't come in second place. He's just a loser. He would have gone one-on-one with a famed choke-artist and lost. Outchoked the ultimate choker. It'll be worse than the Buffalo Bills.'

Norm made a scoffing noise. 'You worry too much, Esme,' he said, but his usual bluster had tapered off.

The crowd began to dissipate, but Jack Coldren just stood in the same position, still holding his putter. He did not celebrate. He did not move, even when Diane Hoffman began to pound his back. His features seemed to lose their tone again, his eyes suddenly more glazed than ever. It was as if the effort of that one stroke had drained every ounce of energy, karma, strength, life force right out of him.

Or maybe, Myron wondered, there was something else at work here. Something deeper. Maybe that last moment of magic had given Jack some new insight – some new life clarity – as to the relative, long-term importance of this tournament. Everyone else saw a man who had just sunk the most important putt of his life. But maybe Jack Coldren saw a man standing alone wondering what the big deal was and if his only son was still alive.

Linda Coldren appeared on the fringe of the green. She tried to look enthusiastic as she approached her husband and dutifully kissed him. A television crew followed her. Long-lensed cameras clicked and their flashes strobed. A sportscaster came up to them, microphone at the ready. Linda and Jack both managed to smile.

But behind the smiles, Linda looked almost wary. And Jack looked positively terrified.

Chapter 22

Esperanza had come up with a plan. 'Lloyd Rennart's widow's name is Francine. She's an artist.'

'What kind?'

'I don't know. Painting, sculpture – what's the difference?'

'Just curious. Go ahead.'

'I called her up and said that you were a reporter for the *Coastal Star*. It's a local paper in the Spring Lake area. You are doing a lifestyle piece on several local artists.'

Myron nodded. It was a good plan. People rarely refuse the chance to be interviewed for self-promoting puff pieces.

Win had already gotten Myron's car windows fixed. How, Myron had no idea. The rich. They're different.

The ride took about two hours. It was eight o'clock Sunday night. Tomorrow Linda and Jack Coldren would drop off the ransom money. How would it be done? A meeting in a public place? A go-between? For the ump-teenth time, he wondered how Linda and Jack and Chad were faring. He took out the photograph of Chad. He imagined what Chad's young, carefree face must have looked like when his finger was being severed off. He wondered if the kidnapper had used a sharp knife or a cleaver or an axe or a saw or what.

He wondered what it felt like.

Francine Rennart lived in Spring Lake Heights, not Spring Lake. There was a big difference. Spring Lake was on the Atlantic Ocean and about as beautiful a shore town as you could hope to find. There was plenty of sun, very little crime, and almost no ethnics. It was a problem, actually. The wealthy town was nicknamed the Irish Riviera. That meant no good restaurants. None. The town's idea of *haute cuisine* was food served on a plate rather than in a basket. If you craved exotic, you drove to a Chinese take-out place whose eclectic menu included such rare delicacies as chicken chow mein, and for the especially adventurous, chicken *lo* mein. This was the problem with some of these towns. They needed some Jews or gays or something to spice things up, to add a bit of theater and a couple of interesting bistros.

One man's opinion.

If Spring Lake was an old movie, then Spring Lake Heights would be the other side of the tracks. There weren't slums or anything like that. The area where the Rennarts lived was a sort of tract-house suburbia – the middle ground between a trailer park and circa 1967 split-level colonials. Solid Americana.

Myron knocked on the door. A woman he guessed was Francine Rennart pushed open the screen. Her ready smile was shadowed by a daunting beak of a nose. Her burnt-auburn hair was wavy and undisciplined, like she'd just taken out her curlers but hadn't had time to comb it out.

'Hi,' Myron said.

'You must be from the *Coastal Star*.'

'That's right.' Myron stuck out his hand. 'I'm Bernie Worley.' Scoop Bolitar uses a disguise.

'Your timing is perfect,' Francine said. 'I've just started a new exhibit.'

The living room furniture didn't have plastic on it, but it should have. The couch was off-green. The Barca-Lounger – a real, live BarcaLounger – was maroon with duct tape mending rips. The console television had rabbit ears on top. Collectors plates Myron had seen advertised in *Parade* were neatly hung on a wall.

'My studio's in the back,' she said.

Francine Rennart led him to a big addition off the kitchen. It was a sparsely furnished room with white walls. A couch with a spring sticking out of it sat in the middle of the room. A kitchen chair leaned against it. So did a rolled-up carpet. There was something that looked like a blanket draped over the top in a triangular pattern. Four bathroom wastepaper baskets lined the back wall. Myron guessed that she must have a leak.

Myron waited for Francine Rennart to ask him to sit down. She didn't. She stood with him in the entranceway and said, 'Well?'

He smiled, his brain stuck in a cusp where he was not dumb enough to say, 'Well what?' but not smart enough to know what the hell she was talking about. So Myron froze there with his anchorman-waiting-to-go-to-commercial grin.

'You like it?' Francine Rennart asked.

Still the grin. 'Uh-huh.'

'I know it's not for everybody.'

'Hmm.' Scoop Bolitar engages in sparkling repartee.

She watched his face for a moment. He kept up the idiot grin. 'You don't know anything about installation art, do you?'

He shrugged. 'Got me.' Myron shifted gears on the fly. 'Thing is, I don't do features normally. I'm a sports writer. That's my beat.' Beat. Note the authentic reporter lingo. 'But Tanya – she's my boss – she needed somebody to handle a lifestyle piece. And when Jennifer called in sick, well, the job fell to me. It's a story on a variety of local artists – painters, sculptors . . .' He couldn't think of any other kind of artist, so he stopped. 'Anyway, maybe you could explain a little bit about what it is you do.'

'My art is about space and concepts. It's about creating a mood.'

Myron nodded. 'I see.'

'It's not art, per se, in the classic sense. It goes beyond that. It's the next step in the artistic evolutionary process.'

More nods. 'I see.'

'Everything in this exhibit has a purpose. Where I place the couch. The texture of the carpeting. The color of the walls. The way the sunlight shines in through the windows. The blend creates a specific ambience.'

Oh, boy.

Myron motioned at the, uh, art. 'So how do you sell something like this?'

She frowned. 'You don't sell it.'

'Pardon?'

'Art is not about money, Mr Worley. True artists do

not put a monetary value on their work. Only hacks do that.'

Yeah, like Michelangelo and Da Vinci, those hacks. 'But what do you do with this?' he asked. 'I mean, do you just keep the room like this?'

'No. I change it around. I bring in other pieces. I create something new.'

'And what happens to this?'

She shook her head. 'Art is not about permanence. Life is temporary. Why shouldn't art be the same?'

Oooookay.

'Is there a name for this art?'

'Installation art. But we do not like labels.'

'How long have you been an, uh, installation artist?'

'I've been working on my masters at the New York Art Institute for two years.'

He tried not to look shocked. 'You go to school for this?'

'Yes. It's a very competitive program.'

Yeah, Myron thought, like a TV/VCR repair course advertised by Sally Struthers.

They finally moved back into the living room. Myron sat on the couch. Gently. Might be art. He waited to be offered a cookie. Might be art too.

'You still don't get it, do you?'

Myron shrugged. 'Maybe if you threw in a poker table and some dogs.'

She laughed. Mr Self-Deprecation strikes again. 'Fair enough,' she said.

'Let me shift gears for a moment, if I may,' Myron said. 'How about a little something on Francine Rennart, the person?' Scoop Bolitar mines the personal angle.

She looked a bit wary, but she said, 'Okay, ask away.'

222

'Are you married?'

'No.' Her voice was like a slamming door.

'Divorced?'

'No.'

Scoop Bolitar loves an garrulous interviewee. 'I see,' he said. 'Then I guess you have no children.'

'I have a son.'

'How old is he?'

'Seventeen. His name is Larry.'

A year older than Chad Coldren. Interesting. 'Larry Rennart?'

'Yes.'

'Where does he go to school?'

'Right here at Manasquan High. He's going to be a senior.'

'How nice.' Myron risked it, nibbled on a cookie. 'Maybe I could interview him too.'

'My son?'

'Sure. I'd love a quote from the prodigal son on how proud he is of his mom, of how he supports what she's doing, that kinda thing.' Scoop Bolitar grows pathetic.

'He's not home.'

'Oh?'

He waited for her to elaborate. Nothing.

'Where is Larry?' Myron tried. 'Is he staying with his father?'

'His father is dead.'

Finally. Myron put on the big act. 'Oh, sheesh, I'm sorry. I didn't . . . I mean, you being so young and all. I just didn't consider the possibility that . . .' Scoop Bolitar as Robert DeNiro.

'It's okay,' Francine Rennart said.

'I feel awful.'

'No need to.'

'Have you been widowed long?'

She tilted her head. 'Why do you ask?'

'Background,' he said.

'Background?'

'Yes. I think it's crucial to understanding Francine Rennart the artist. I want to explore how being widowed affected you and your art.' Scoop Bolitar shovels it good.

'I've only been a widow a short time.'

Myron motioned toward the, uh, studio. 'So when you created this work, did your husband's death have any bearing on the outcome? On the color of the wastebaskets maybe. Or the way you rolled up that rug.'

'No, not really.'

'How did your husband die?'

'Why would you—'

'Again, I think it's important for digesting the entire artistic statement. Was it an accident, for example? The kind of death that makes you ponder fickle fate. Was it a long illness? Seeing a loved one suffer—'

'He committed suicide.'

Myron feigned aghast. 'I'm so sorry,' he said.

Her breathing was funny now, her chest giving off short hitches. As Myron watched her, an awful pang struck him deep in the chest. Slow down, he told himself. Stop focusing solely on Chad Coldren and remember that this woman, too, has suffered. She had been married to this man. She had loved him and lived with him and built a life with him and had a child with him.

And after all that, he had chosen to end his life rather than spend it with her.

Myron swallowed. Fiddling with her pathos like this was, at best, unfair. Belittling her artistic expression because he did not understand it was cruel. Myron did not like himself much right now. For a moment he debated just going away – the odds that any of this had anything to do with the case were so remote – but then again, he couldn't simply forget a sixteen-year-old boy with a missing finger, either.

'Were you married long?'

'Almost twenty years,' she said softly.

'I don't mean to intrude, but may I ask you his name?'

'Lloyd,' she said. 'Lloyd Rennart.'

Myron narrowed his eyes as though scanning for a memory. 'Why does that name ring a bell?'

Francine Rennart shrugged. 'He co-owned a tavern in Neptune City. The Rusty Nail.'

'Of course,' Myron said. 'Now I remember. He hung out there a lot, right?'

'Yes.'

'My God, I met the man. Lloyd Rennart. Now I remember. He used to teach golf, right? Was in the big time for a while.'

Francine Rennart's face slid closed like a car window. 'How do you know that?'

'The Rusty Nail. And I'm a huge golf fan. A real duffer, but I follow it like some people follow the Bible.' He was flailing, but maybe he was getting somewhere. 'Your husband caddied Jack Coldren, right? A long time ago. We talked about it a bit.'

She swallowed hard. 'What did he say?'

'Say?'

'About being a caddie.'

'Oh, not much. We mostly talked about some of our favorite golfers. Nicklaus, Trevino, Palmer. Some great courses. Merion mostly.'

'No,' she said.

'Ma'am?'

Her voice was firm. 'Lloyd never talked about golf.'

Scoop Bolitar steps in it in a big way.

Francine Rennart skewered him with her eyes. 'You can't be from the insurance company. I didn't even try to make a claim.' She pondered that for a moment. Then: 'Wait a second. You said you're a sports writer. That's why you're here. Jack Coldren is making a comeback, so you want to do a where-are-they-now story.'

Myron shook his head. Shame flushed his face. Enough, he thought. He took a few deep breaths and said, 'No.'

'Then who are you?'

'My name is Myron Bolitar. I'm a sports agent.'

She was confused now. 'What do you want with me?'

He searched for the words, but they all sounded lame. 'I'm not sure. It's probably nothing, a complete waste of time. You're right. Jack Coldren is making a comeback. But it's like . . . it's like the past is haunting him. Terrible things are happening to him and his family. And I just thought—'

'Thought what?' she snapped. 'That Lloyd came back from the dead to claim vengeance?'

'Did he want vengeance?'

'What happened at Merion,' she said. 'It was a long time ago. Before I met him.'

'Was he over it?'

Francine Rennart thought about that for a while. 'It took a long time,' she said at last. 'Lloyd couldn't get any golf work after what happened. Jack Coldren was still the fair-haired boy and no one wanted to cross him. Lloyd lost all his friends. He started drinking too much.' She hesitated. 'There was an accident.'

Myron stayed still, watching Francine Rennart draw breaths.

'He lost control of his car.' Her voice was robot-like now. 'It slammed into another car. In Narberth. Near where he used to live.' She stopped and then looked at him. 'His first wife died on impact.'

Myron felt a chill rush through him. 'I didn't know,' he said softly.

'It was a long time ago, Mr Bolitar. We met not long after that. We fell in love. He stopped drinking. He bought the tavern right away – I know, I know, it sounds weird. An alcoholic owning a bar. But for him, it worked. We bought this house too. I – I thought everything was okay.'

Myron waited a beat. Then he asked, 'Did your husband give Jack Coldren the wrong club on purpose?'

The question did not seem to surprise her. She plucked at the buttons on her blouse and took her time before answering. 'The truth is, I don't know. He never talked about this incident. Not even with me. But there was something there. It may have been guilt, I don't know.' She smoothed her skirt with both hands. 'But all of this is irrelevant, Mr Bolitar. Even if Lloyd did harbor ill feelings toward Jack, he's dead.'

Myron tried to think of a tactful way of asking, but none came to him. 'Did they find his body, Mrs Rennart?'

His words landed like a heavyweight's hook. 'It-it was a deep crevasse,' Francine Rennart stammered. 'There was no way . . . the police said they couldn't send anyone down there. It was too dangerous. But Lloyd couldn't have survived. He wrote a note. He left his clothes there. I still have his passport . . .' Her voice faded away.

Myron nodded. 'Of course,' he said. 'I understand.'

But as he showed himself out, he was pretty sure that he understood nothing.

Chapter 23

Tito the Crusty Nazi never showed at the Parker Inn.

Myron sat in a car across the street. As usual, he hated surveillance. Boredom didn't set in this time, but the devastated face of Francine Rennart kept haunting him. He wondered about the long-term effects of his visit. The woman had been privately dealing with her grief, locking her private demons in a back closet, and then Myron had gone and blown the hinges off the door. He had tried to comfort her. But in the end what could he say?

Closing time. Still no sign of Tito. His two buddies – Beneath and Escape – were another matter. They'd arrived at ten-thirty. At 1 A.M. they both exited. Escape was on crutches – the aftertaste, Myron was sure, of the nasty side kick to the knee. Myron smiled. It was a small victory, but you take them where you can.

Beneath had his arm slung around a woman's neck. She had a dye job from the planet Bad Bottle and basically looked like the type of woman who might go for a tattoo-infested skinhead – or to say the same thing in a slightly different way, she looked like a regular on *The Jerry Springer Show.*

Both men stopped to urinate on the outside wall. Beneath actually kept his arm around the girl while emptying his bladder. Jesus. So many men peed on that wall that Myron wondered if there was a bathroom inside. The two men broke off. Beneath got into the passenger side of a Ford Mustang. Bad Bleach drove. Escape hobbled onto his own chariot, a motorcycle of some kind. He strapped the crutches onto the side. The two vehicles drove off in separate directions.

Myron decided to follow Escape. When in doubt, tail the one that's lame.

He kept far back and remained extra careful. Better to lose him than risk in the slightest way the possibility of being spotted. But the tail didn't last long. Three blocks down the road, Escape parked and headed into a shabby excuse for a house. The paint was peeling off in flakes the size of manhole covers. One of the support columns on the front porch had completely given way, so the front lip of the roof looked like it'd been ripped in half by some giant. The two upstairs windows were shattered like a drunk's eyes. The only possible reason that this dump hadn't been condemned was that the building inspector had not been able to stop laughing long enough to write up a summons.

Okay, so now what?

He waited an hour for something to happen. Nothing did. He had seen a bedroom light go on and off. That was it. The whole night was fast turning into a complete waste of time.

So what should he do?

He had no answer. So he changed the question around a bit.

What would Win do?

Win would weigh the risks. Win would realize that the situation was desperate, that a sixteen-year-old boy's finger had been chopped off like a bothersome thread. Rescuing him imminently was paramount.

Myron nodded to himself. Time to play Win.

He got out of the car. Making sure he kept out of sight, Myron circled around to the back of the dump. The yard was bathed in darkness. He trampled through grass long enough to hide Viet Cong, occasionally stumbling across a cement block or rake or a garbage can top. His shin got whacked twice; Myron had to bite down expletives.

The back door was boarded up with plywood. The window to its left, however, was open. Myron looked inside. Dark. He carefully climbed into the kitchen.

The smell of spoilage assaulted his nostrils. Flies buzzed about. For a moment, Myron feared that he might find a dead body, but this stink was different, more like the odor of a Dumpster at a 7-Eleven than anything in the rotting flesh family. He checked the other rooms, walking on tiptoes, avoiding the several spots on the floor where there was no floor. No sign of a kidnap victim. No sixteen-year-old boy tied up. No one at all. Myron followed the snoring to the room he had seen the light in earlier. Escape was on his back. Asleep. Without a care.

That was about to change.

Myron leapt into the air and landed hard on Escape's bad knee. Escape's eyes widened. His mouth opened in a scream that Myron cut off with a snap punch in the mouth. He moved quickly, straddling Escape's chest with his knees. He put his gun against the punk's cheek.

'Scream and die,' Myron said.

Escape's eyes stayed wide. Blood trickled out of his mouth. He did not scream. Still, Myron was disappointed in himself. Scream and die ? He couldn't come up with anything better than scream and die?

'Where is Chad Coldren?'

'Who?'

Myron jammed the gun barrel into the bleeding mouth. It hit teeth and nearly gagged the man. 'Wrong answer.'

Escape stayed silent. The punk was brave. Or maybe, just maybe, he couldn't talk because Myron had stuck a gun in his mouth. Smooth move, Bolitar. Keeping his face firm, Myron slowly slid the barrel out.

'Where is Chad Coldren?'

Escape gasped, caught his breath. 'I swear to God, I don't know what you're talking about.'

'Give me your hand.'

'What?'

'Give me your hand.'

Escape lifted his hand into view. Myron grabbed the wrist, turned it, and plucked out the middle finger. He curled it inward and flattened the folded digit against the palm. The kid bucked in pain. 'I don't need a knife,' Myron said. 'I can just grind it into splinters.'

'I don't know what you're talking about,' the kid managed. 'I swear!'

Myron squeezed a little harder. He did not want the bone to snap. Escape bucked some more. Smile a little, Myron thought. That's how Win does it. He has just a hint of a smile. Not much. You want your victim to think you are capable of anything, that you are completely cold, that you might even enjoy it. But you don't want him thinking you are a complete lunatic, out of control, a nut who would hurt you no matter what. Mine that middle ground.

'Please . . .'

'Where is Chad Coldren?'

'Look, I was there, okay? When he jumped you. Tit said he'd give me a hundred bucks. But I don't know no Chad Coldren.'

'Where is Tit?' That name again.

'At his crib, I guess. I don't know.'

Crib? The neo-Nazi was using dated urban street lingo. Life's ironies. 'Doesn't Tito usually hang out with you guys at the Parker Inn?'

'Yeah, but he never showed.'

'Was he supposed to?'

'I guess. It's not like we talk about it.'

Myron nodded. 'Where does he live?'

'Mountainside Drive. Right down the street. Third house on the left after you make the turn.'

'If you're lying to me, I will come back here and slice your eyes out.'

'I ain't lying. Mountainside Drive.'

Myron pointed at the swastika tattoo with the barrel of the gun. 'Why do you have this?'

'What?'

'The swastika, moron.'

'I'm proud of my race, that's why.'

'You want to put all the "kikes" in gas chambers? Kill all the "niggers"?'

'That ain't what we're about,' he said. More confidence in his voice now that he was on well-rehearsed ground. 'We're for the white man. We're tired of being overrun by niggers. We're sick of being trampled on by the Jews.'

Myron nodded. 'Well, by this Jew anyway,' he said. In

life, you take satisfaction where you can. 'You know what duct tape is.'

'Yeah.'

'Gee, and I thought all neo-Nazis were dumb. Where is yours?'

Escape's eyes kinda narrowed. Like he was actually thinking. You could almost hear rusty gears churning. Then: 'I don't have none.'

'Too bad. I was going to use it to tie you up, so you couldn't warn Tito. But if you don't have any, I'll just have to shoot both your kneecaps.'

'Wait!'

Myron used up almost the entire roll.

Tito was in the driver's seat of his pickup truck with the monster wheels.

He was also dead.

Two shots in the head, probably from very close range. Very bloody. There wasn't much of a head left anymore. Poor Tito. No head to match his no ass. Myron didn't laugh. Then again, gallows humor was not his forte.

Myron remained calm, probably because he was still in Win mode. No lights were on in the house. Tito's keys were still in the ignition. Myron took them and unlocked the front door. His search confirmed what he'd already guessed: no one was there.

Now what?

Ignoring the blood and brain matter, Myron went back to the truck and did a thorough search. Talk about not his forte. Myron reclicked the Win icon. Just protoplasm, he told himself. Just hemoglobin and platelets and enzymes and other stuff he'd forgotten since ninth-grade biology. The blocking worked enough to allow him to dig his hands under the seats and into the cushion crevices. His fingers located lots of crud. Old sandwiches. Wrappers from Wendy's. Crumbs of various shapes and sizes.

Fingernail clippings.

Myron looked at the dead body and shook his head. A little late for a scolding, but what the hell.

Then he hit pay dirt.

It was gold. It had a golf insignia on it. The initials *C.B.C.* were engraved lightly on the inside – Chad Buckwell Coldren.

It was a ring.

Myron's first thought was that Chad Coldren had cleverly taken it off and left it behind as a clue. Like in a movie. The young man was sending a message. If Myron was playing his part correctly, he would shake his head, toss the ring in the air, and mutter admiringly, 'Smart kid.'

Myron's second thought, however, was far more sobering.

The severed finger in Linda Coldren's car had been the ring finger.

Chapter 24

What to do?

Should he contact the police? Just leave? Make an anonymous call? What?

Myron had no idea. He had to think first and foremost of Chad Coldren. What risk would calling the police put the kid in?

No idea.

Christ, what a mess. He wasn't even supposed to be involved in this anymore. He was supposed to have – should have – stayed out. But now the proverbial doo-doo was hitting a plethora of proverbial fans. What should he do about finding a dead body? And what about Escape? Myron couldn't just leave him tied and gagged indefinitely. Suppose he vomited into the duct tape, for chrissake?

Okay, Myron, think. First, you should not – repeat, not – call the police. Someone else will discover the body. Or maybe he should make an anonymous call from a pay phone. That might work. But don't the police tape all incoming calls nowadays? They'd have his voice on tape. He could change it maybe. The rhythm and tempo. Make the tone a little deeper. Add an accent or something. Oh, right, like Meryl Streep. Tell the dispatcher to hurry because 'the dingo's got ma baby.'

Wait, hold the phone.

Think about what had just happened. Rewind to about an hour ago and see how it looks. Without provocation, Myron had broken into a man's house. He had physically assaulted the man, threatened him in terrible ways, left him tied and gagged – all in the pursuit of Tito. Not long after this incident, the police get an anonymous call. They find Tito dead in his pickup.

Who is going to be the obvious suspect?

Myron Bolitar, sports agent of the terminally troubled.

Damn.

So now what? No matter what Myron did at this stage – call or not call – he was going to be a suspect. Escape would be questioned. He would tell about Myron, and then Myron would look like the killer. Very simple equation when you thought about it.

So the question remained: What to do?

He couldn't worry about what conclusions the police might leap upon. He also couldn't worry about himself. The focus must be on Chad Coldren. What would be best for him? Hard to say. The safest bet, of course, would be to upset the apple cart as little as possible. Try not to make his presence in all this known.

Okay, good, that made sense.

So the answer was: Don't report it. Let the body lay where it was. Put the ring back in the seat cushion in case the police need it as evidence later. Good, this looked like a plan – a plan that seemed the best way of keeping the kid safe and also obeying the Coldrens' wishes.

Now, what about Escape?

Myron drove back to Escape's shack. He found Escape right where he left him – on his bed, hog-tied and gagged with gray duct tape. He looked half dead. Myron shook him. The punk started to, his face the green of seaweed. Myron ripped off the gag.

Escape retched and did a few dry heaves.

'I have a man outside,' Myron said, removing more duct tape. 'If he sees you move from this window, you will experience an agony very few have been forced to endure. Do you understand?'

Escape nodded quickly.

Experience an agony very few have been forced to endure. Jesus.

There was no phone in the house, so he didn't have to worry about that. With a few more harsh warnings lightly sprinkled with torture clichés – including Myron's personal favorite, 'Before I'm finished, you'll beg me to kill you' – he left the neo-Nazi alone to quake in his goose-stepping black boots.

No one was outside. The proverbial coast was clear. Myron got in the car, wondering yet again about the Coldrens. What was going on with them right now? Had the kidnapper already called? Had he given them instructions? How did Tito's death affect what was happening? Had Chad suffered more bloodshed or had he escaped? Maybe he'd gotten hold of the gun and shot someone.

Maybe. But doubtful. More likely, something had gone awry. Someone had lost control. Someone had gone nuts.

He stopped the car. He had to warn the Coldrens.

Yes, Linda Coldren had clearly instructed him to stay

away. But that was before he'd found a dead body. How could he sit back now and leave them blind? Someone had chopped off their son's finger. Someone had murdered one of the kidnappers. A 'simple' kidnapping – if there is such a thing – had spun off its axis. Blood had been splattered about freely.

He had to warn them. He had to contact the Coldrens and let them know what he had learned.

But how?

He pulled onto Golf House Road. It was very late now, almost two in the morning. Nobody would be up. Myron flicked off his lights and cruised silently. He glided the car into a spot on the property line between two houses – if by some chance one of the occupants was awake and looked out the window, he or she might believe the car belonged to someone visiting a neighbor. He stepped out and slowly made his way on foot toward the Coldren house.

Keeping out of sight, Myron moved closer. He knew, of course, that there was no chance the Coldrens would be asleep. Jack might give it a token effort; Linda wouldn't even sit down. But right now, that didn't much matter.

How was he going to contact them?

He couldn't call on the phone. He couldn't walk up and knock on the door. And he couldn't throw pebbles at the window, like some clumsy suitor in a bad romantic comedy. So where did that leave him?

Lost.

He moved from shrub to shrub. Some of the shrubs were familiar from his last sojourn into these parts. He said hello to them, chatted, offered up his best cocktail-party banter. One shrub gave him a stock tip. Myron ignored it. He circled closer to the Coldren house, slowly, still careful not to be seen. He had no idea what he was going to do, but when he got close enough to see a light on in the den, an idea came to him.

A note.

He would write a note, telling them of his discovery, warning them to be extra careful, offering up his services. How to get the note close to the house? Hmm. He could fold the note into a paper airplane and fly it in. Oh, sure, with Myron's mechanical skills, that would work. Myron Bolitar, the Jewish Wright Brother. What else? Tie the note to a rock maybe? And then what? Smash a window?

As it happened, he didn't have to do any of that.

He heard a noise to his right. Footsteps. On the street. At two in the morning.

Myron quickly dove back down behind a shrub. The footsteps were moving closer. Faster. Someone approaching. Running.

He kept down, his heart beating wildly in his chest. The footsteps grew louder and then suddenly stopped. Myron peeked around the side of the shrub. His view was blocked by still more hedges.

He held his breath. And waited.

The footsteps started up again. Slower this time. Unhurried. Casual. Taking a walk now. Myron craned his neck around the other side of the shrub. Nothing. He moved into a crouch now. Slowly he raised himself, inch by inch, his bad knee protesting. He fought through the pain. His eyes reached the top of the shrub. Myron looked out and finally saw who it was.

Linda Coldren.

She was dressed in a blue sweat suit with running sneakers. Out for a jog? Seemed like a very strange time for it. But you never know. Jack drove golf balls. Myron shot baskets. Maybe Linda was into late-night jogging.

He didn't think so.

She neared the top of the driveway. Myron had to reach her. He clawed a rock out of the dirt and skimmed it toward her. Linda stopped and looked up sharply, like a deer interrupted while drinking. Myron threw another rock. She looked toward the bush. Myron waved a hand. Christ, this was subtle. But if she had felt safe enough to leave the house – if the kidnapper had not minded her taking a little night stroll – then walking toward a bush shouldn't cause a panic either. Bad rationale, but it was getting late.

If not out for a jog, why was Linda out so late?

Unless . . .

Unless she was paying off the ransom.

But no, it was still Sunday night. The banks wouldn't be open. She couldn't raise one hundred grand without going to a bank. She had made that clear, hadn't she?

Linda Coldren slowly approached the bush. Myron was almost tempted to light the bush on fire, deepen his voice, and say, 'Come forward, Moses.' More gallows humor. More not-funny.

When she was about ten feet away, Myron raised his head into view. Linda's eyes nearly leaped out of their sockets.

'Get out of here!' Linda whispered.

Myron wasted no time. Whispering back, he said, 'I found the guy from the pay phone dead. Shot twice in the head. Chad's ring was in his car. But no sign of Chad.'

'Get out!'

'I just wanted to warn you. Be careful. They're playing for keeps.'

Her eyes darted about the yard. She nodded and turned away.

'When's the drop-off?' Myron tried. 'And where's Jack? Make sure you see Chad with your own eyes before you hand over anything.'

But if Linda heard him, she gave no indication. She hurried down the driveway, opened the door, and disappeared from sight.

Chapter 25

Win opened the bedroom door. 'You have visitors.'

Myron kept his head on the pillow. Friends not knocking hardly fazed him anymore. 'Who is it?'

'Law enforcement officials,' Win said.

'Cops?'

'Yes.'

'Uniformed?'

'Yes.'

'Any idea what it's about?'

'Oooo, sorry. That would be a no. Let's move on to Kitty Carlisle.'

Myron picked the sleep out of his eyes and threw on some clothes. He slipped into a pair of Top-Siders without socks. Very Win-like. A quick brush of the teeth, for the sake of breath rather than long-term dental health. He opted for a baseball cap rather than taking the time to wet his hair. The baseball cap was red and said TRIX CEREAL in the front and SILLY RABBIT on the back. Jessica had bought it for him. Myron loved her for it.

The two uniforms waited with cop-patience in the living room. They were young and healthy-looking. The taller one said, 'Mr Bolitar?'

'Yes.'

'We'd appreciate it if you would accompany us.'

'Where?'

'Detective Corbett will explain when we arrive.'

'How about a hint?'

Two faces of stone. 'We'd rather not, sir.'

Myron shrugged. 'Let's go then.'

Myron sat in the back of the squad car. The two uniforms sat in the front. They drove at a pretty good clip but kept their siren off. Myron's cell phone rang.

'Do you guys mind if I take a call?'

Taller said, 'Of course not, sir.'

'Polite of you.' Myron hit the *on* switch. 'Hello.'

'Are you alone?' It was Linda Coldren.

'Nope.'

'Don't tell anyone I'm calling. Can you please get here as soon as possible? It's urgent.'

'What do you mean you can't deliver it until Thursday?' Mr Throw Them Off Track.

'I can't talk right now either. Just get here as soon as you can. And don't say anything until you do. Please. Trust me on this.'

She hung up.

'Fine, but then I better get free bagels. You hear me?'

Myron turned off the cell phone. He looked out the window. The route the cops were taking was overly familiar. Myron had taken the same one to Merion. When they reached the club entranceway on Ardmore

244

Avenue, Myron saw a plethora of media vans and cop cars.

'Dang,' the taller cop said.

'You knew it wouldn't stay quiet for long,' Shorter added.

'Too big a story,' Taller agreed.

'You fellas want to clue me in?'

The shorter cop twisted his head toward Myron. 'No, sir.' He turned back around.

'Okeydokey,' Myron said. But he didn't have a good feeling about this.

The squad car drove steadily through the press gauntlet. Reporters pushed against the windows, peering in. Flashes popped in Myron's face. A policeman waved them through. The reporters slowly peeled off the car like dandruff flakes. They parked in the club lot. There were at least a dozen other police cars, both marked and unmarked, nearby.

'Please come along,' Taller said.

Myron did so. They walked across the eighteenth fairway. Lots of uniformed officers were walking with their heads down, picking up pieces of lord-knows-what and putting them in evidence bags.

This was definitely not good.

When they reached the top of the hill, Myron could see dozens of officers making a perfect circle in the famed stone quarry. Some were taking photos. Crime scene photos. Others were bent down. When one stood up, Myron saw him.

He felt his knees buckle. 'Oh no . . .'

In the middle of the quarry – sprawled in the famed hazard that had cost him the tournament twenty-three years ago – lay the still, lifeless body of Jack Coldren.

The uniforms watched him, gauging his reaction. Myron showed them nothing. 'What happened?' he managed.

'Please wait here, sir.'

The taller cop walked down the hill; the shorter stayed with Myron. Taller spoke briefly to a man in plainclothes Myron suspected was Detective Corbett. Corbett glanced up at Myron as the man spoke. He nodded to the shorter cop.

'Please follow me, sir.'

Still dazed, Myron trudged down the hill into the stone quarry. He kept his eye on the corpse. Coagulated blood coated Jack's head like one of those spray-on toupees. The body was twisted into a position it was never supposed to achieve. Oh, Christ. Poor, sad bastard.

The plainclothes detective greeted him with an enthusiastic handshake. 'Mr Bolitar, thank you so much for coming. I'm Detective Corbett.'

Myron nodded numbly. 'What happened?'

'A groundskeeper found him this morning at six.'

'Was he shot?'

Corbett smiled crookedly. He was around Myron's age and petite for a cop. Not just short. Plenty of cops were on the short side. But this guy was small-boned to the point of being almost sickly. Corbett covered up the small physique with a trench coat. Not a great summer look. Too many episodes of *Columbo*, Myron guessed.

'I don't want to be rude or anything,' Corbett said, 'but do you mind if I ask the questions?'

Myron glanced at the still body. He felt light-headed. Jack dead. Why? How did it happen? And why had the police decided to question him? 'Where is Mrs Coldren?' Myron asked.

Corbett glanced at the two officers, then at Myron. 'Why would you want to know that?'

'I want to make sure she's safe.'

'Well then,' Corbett began, folding his arms under his chest, 'if that's the case, you should have asked, "How is Mrs Coldren?" or "Is Mrs Coldren all right?" – not "Where is Mrs Coldren?" I mean, if you're really interested in how she is.'

Myron looked at Corbett for several seconds. 'God. You. Are. Good.'

'No reason for sarcasm, Mr Bolitar. You just seem very concerned about her.'

'I am.'

'You a friend?'

'Yes.'

'A close friend?'

'Pardon me?'

'Again, I don't want to appear rude or anything,' Corbett said, spreading his hands, 'but have you been – you know – porking her?'

'Are you out of your mind?'

'Is that a yes?'

Calm down, Myron. Corbett was trying to keep him off balance. Myron knew the game. Dumb to let it get to him. 'The answer is no. We've had no sexual contact whatsoever.'

'Really? That's odd.'

He wanted Myron to bite with a 'What's odd?' Myron did not oblige him.

'You see, a couple of witnesses saw you two together several times over the past few days. At a tent in Corporate Row, mostly. You sat alone for several hours. Very snuggly. Are you sure you weren't playing a little kissy-face?'

Myron said, 'No.'

'No, you weren't playing a little kissy-face, or no—'

'No, we weren't playing kissy-face or anything like that.'

'Uh-huh, I see.' Corbett feigned chewing over this little tidbit. 'Where were you last night, Mr Bolitar?'

'Am I a suspect, Detective?'

'We're just chatting amicably, Mr Bolitar. That's all.'

'Do you have an estimated time of death?' Myron asked.

Corbett offered up another cop-polite smile. 'Once again, far be it from me to be obtuse or rude, but I would rather concentrate on you right now.' His voice gathered a little more muster. 'Where were you last night?'

Myron remembered Linda's call on the cell phone. Undeniably the police had already questioned her. Had she told them about the kidnapping? Probably not. Either way, it was not his place to mention it. He didn't know where things stood. Speaking out of turn could jeopardize Chad's safety. Best to get out of here pronto.

'I'd like to see Mrs Coldren.'

'Why?'

'To make sure she's okay.'

'That's sweet, Mr Bolitar. And very noble. But I'd like you to answer my question.'

'I'd like to see Mrs Coldren first.'

Corbett gave him the narrow cop-eyes. 'Are you refusing to answer my questions?'

'No. But right now my priority is my potential client's welfare.'

'Client?'

'Mrs Coldren and I have been discussing the possibility of her signing on with MB SportsReps.'

'I see,' Corbett said, rubbing his chin. 'So that explains your sitting together in the tent.'

'I'll answer your questions later, Detective. Right now I'd like to check up on Mrs Coldren.'

'She's fine, Mr Bolitar.'

'I'd like to see for myself.'

'You don't trust me?'

'It's not that. But if I am going to be her agent, then I must be at her disposal first and foremost.'

Corbett shook his head and raised his eyebrows. 'That's some crock of shit you're peddling, Bolitar.'

'May I go now?'

Corbett gave the big hand spread again. 'You're not under arrest. In fact' – he turned to the two officers – 'please escort Mr Bolitar to the Coldren residence. Make sure nobody bothers him on the way.'

Myron smiled. 'Thank you, Detective.'

'Think nothing of it.' As Myron began to walk away, Corbett called out, 'Oh, one more thing.' The man had definitely watched too much *Columbo*. 'That call you got in the squad car just now. Was that from Mrs Coldren?'

Myron said nothing.

'No matter. We can check the phone records.' He gave the Columbo wave. 'Have a special day.'

Chapter 26

There were four more cop cars outside the Coldren house. Myron walked to the door on his own and knocked. A black woman Myron did not recognize opened it.

Her eyes flicked at the top of his head. 'Nice hat,' she said without inflection. 'Come on in.'

The woman was about fifty years old and wore a nicely tailored suit. Her coffee skin looked leathery and worn. Her face was kind of sleepy, her eyes half-closed, her expression perpetually bored. 'I'm Victoria Wilson,' she said.

'Myron Bolitar.'

'Yes, I know.' Bored voice too.

'Is anybody else here?'

'Just Linda.'

'Can I see her?'

Victoria Wilson nodded slowly; Myron half expected her to stifle a yawn. 'Maybe we should talk first.'

'Are you with the police?' Myron asked.

'The opposite,' she said. 'I'm Mrs Coldren's attorney.'

'That was fast.'

'Let me put this plainly,' she ho-hummed, sounding like a diner waitress reading off the specials in the last hour of a double shift. 'The police believe that Mrs Coldren killed her husband. They also think that you're involved in some way.'

Myron looked at her. 'You're kidding, right?'

The same sleepy expression. 'Do I look like a prankster, Mr Bolitar?'

Rhetorical question.

'Linda does not have a solid alibi for late last night,' she went on, still with the flat tone. 'Do you?'

'Not really.'

'Well, let me tell you what the police already know.' The woman took blasé and raised it to an art form. 'First' – raising a finger in the air seemed to take great effort – 'they have a witness, a groundskeeper, who saw Jack Coldren enter Merion at approximately one in the morning. The same witness also saw Linda Coldren do likewise thirty minutes later. He also saw Linda Coldren leave the grounds not long after that. He never saw Jack Coldren leave.'

'That doesn't mean—'

'Second' – another finger in the air, making a peace sign – 'the police received a report last night at approximately two in the morning that your car, Mr Bolitar, was parked on Golf House Road. The police will want to know what you were doing parking in such a strange spot at such a strange time.'

'How do you know all this?' Myron asked.

'I have good connections with the police,' she said. Again bored. 'May I continue?'

'Please.'

'Third' – yep, another finger – 'Jack Coldren had been seeing a divorce attorney. He had, in fact, begun the process of filing papers.'

'Did Linda know this?'

'No. But one of the allegations Mr Coldren made concerned his wife's recent infidelity.'

Myron put both hands to his chest. 'Don't look at me.'

'Mr Bolitar?'

'What?'

'I am just stating facts. And I'd appreciate it if you didn't interrupt. Fourth' – final finger – 'on Saturday, at the US Open golf tournament, several witnesses described you and Mrs Coldren as being a bit more than chummy.'

Myron waited. Victoria Wilson lowered the hand, never showing the thumb.

'Is that it?' Myron asked.

'No. But that's all we'll discuss for now.'

'I met Linda for the first time on Friday.'

'And you can prove that?'

'Bucky can testify to it. He introduced us.'

Another big sigh. 'Linda Coldren's father. What a perfect, unbiased witness.'

'I live in New York.'

'Which is less than two hours by Amtrak from Philadelphia. Go on.'

'I have a girlfriend. Jessica Culver. I live with her.'

'And no man has ever cheated on his girlfriend before. Stunning testimony.'

Myron shook his head. 'So you're suggesting—'

'Nothing,' Victoria Wilson interrupted him with the monotone. 'I am suggesting absolutely nothing. I am telling you what the police believe – that Linda killed

Jack. The reason why there are so many police officers surrounding this house is because they want to make sure that we do not remove anything before a search warrant is issued. They have made it crystal clear that they want no Kardashians on this one.'

Kardashian. As in O.J. The man had changed law lexicon forever. 'But . . .' Myron stopped. 'This is ridiculous. Where is Linda?'

'Upstairs. I've informed the police that she is too grief-stricken to speak to them at this time.'

'You don't understand. Linda shouldn't even be a suspect. Once she tells you the whole story, you'll see what I mean.'

Another near yawn. 'She has told me the whole story.'

'Even about . . . ?'

'The kidnapping,' Victoria Wilson finished for him. 'Yes.'

'Well, don't you think that kind of exonerates her?'

'No.'

Myron was confused. 'Do the police know about the kidnapping?'

'Of course not. We are saying nothing at this time.'

Myron made a face. 'But once they hear about the kidnapping, they'll focus on that. They'll know Linda couldn't be involved.'

Victoria Wilson turned away. 'Let's go upstairs.'

'You don't agree?'

She didn't respond. They began to climb the staircase. Victoria said, 'You are an attorney.'

It didn't sound like a question, but Myron still said, 'I don't practice.'

'But you passed the bar.'

'In New York.'

'Good enough. I want you to be co-counsel in this case. I can get you an immediate dispensation.'

'I don't do criminal law,' Myron said.

'You don't have to. I just want you to be an attorney of record for Mrs Coldren.'

Myron nodded. 'So I can't testify,' he said. 'So everything I hear falls under privilege.'

Still bored. 'You are a smart one.' She stopped next to a bedroom door and leaned against a wall. 'Go in. I'm going to wait out here.'

Myron knocked. Linda Coldren told him to come in. He opened the door. Linda stood by the far window looking out onto her backyard.

'Linda?'

Her back still faced him. 'I'm having a bad week, Myron.' She laughed. It was not a happy sound.

'Are you okay?' he asked.

'Me? Never better. Thanks for asking.'

He stepped toward her, unsure what to say. 'Did the kidnappers call about the ransom?'

'Last night,' Linda said. 'Jack spoke to them.'

'What did they say?'

'I don't know. He stormed out after the call. He never told me.'

Myron tried to picture this scene. A call comes in. Jack answers it. He runs out without saying anything. It didn't exactly mesh.

'Have you heard from them again?' he tried.

'No, not yet.'

Myron nodded, even though she wasn't facing him. 'So what did you do?'

'Do?'

'Last night. After Jack stormed out.'

Linda Coldren folded her arms across her chest. 'I waited a few minutes for him to calm down,' she said. 'When he didn't come back, I went out looking for him.'

'You went to Merion,' Myron said.

'Yes. Jack likes to stroll the grounds. To think and be alone.'

'Did you see him there?'

'No. I looked around for a while. Then I came back here. That's when I ran into you.'

'And Jack never came back,' Myron said.

With her back still to him, Linda Coldren shook her head. 'What tipped you off, Myron? The dead body in the stone quarry?'

'Just trying to help.'

She turned to him. Her eyes were red. Her face was drawn. She was still incredibly beautiful. 'I just need someone to take it out on.' She shrugged, tried a smile. 'You're here.'

Myron wanted to step closer. He refrained. 'You've been up all night?'

She nodded. 'I've been standing right here, waiting for Jack to come home. When the police knocked on the door, I thought it was about Chad. This is going to sound awful, but when they told me about Jack, I was almost relieved.'

The phone rang.

Linda spun around with enough speed to start up a wind tunnel. She looked at Myron. He looked at her.

'It's probably the media,' he said.

Linda shook her head. 'Not on that line.' She reached for the phone, pressed the lit-up button, picked up the receiver.

'Hello,' she said.

A voice replied. Linda gasped and bit down in mid-scream. Her hand flew to her mouth. Tears pushed their way out of her eyes. The door flew open. Victoria Wilson stepped into the room, looking like a bear stirred from a power nap.

Linda looked up at them both. 'It's Chad,' she said. 'He's free.'

Chapter 27

Victoria Wilson took control. 'We'll go pick him up,' she said. 'You stay on the line with him.'

Linda started shaking her head. 'But I want—'

'Trust me on this, honey. If you go, every cop and news reporter will follow. Myron and I can lose them if we have to. I don't want the police talking to your son until I have. You just stay here. You say nothing. If the police come in with a warrant, you let them in. You don't say a word. No matter what. Do you understand?'

Linda nodded.

'So where is he?'

'On Porter Street.'

'Okay, tell him Aunt Victoria is on the way. We'll take care of him.'

Linda grabbed her arm, her face pleading. 'Will you bring him back here?'

'Not right away, hon.' The voice was still matter-of-fact.

'The police will see. I can't have that. It'll raise too many questions. You'll see him soon enough.'

Victoria Wilson turned away. There was no debate with this woman.

In the car, Myron asked, 'How do you know Linda?'

'My mother and father were servants for the Buckwells and Lockwoods,' she replied. 'I grew up on their estates.'

'But somewhere along the line you went to law school?'

She frowned. 'You writing my biography?'

'I'm just asking.'

'Why? You surprised that a middle-aged black woman is the attorney for rich WASPs?'

'Frankly,' Myron said, 'yes.'

'Don't blame you. But we don't have time for that now. You got any important questions?'

'Yes,' Myron said. He was doing the driving. 'What aren't you telling me?'

'Nothing that you need to know.'

'I'm an attorney of record on the case. I need to know everything.'

'Later. Let's concentrate on the boy first.'

Again the no-argument monotone.

'Are you sure we're doing the right thing?' Myron continued. 'Not telling the police about the kidnapping?'

'We can always tell them later,' Victoria Wilson replied. 'That's the mistake most defendants make. They think they have to talk their way out of it right away. But that's dangerous. There is always time to talk later.'

'I'm not sure I agree.'

'Tell you what, Myron. If we need some expertise on negotiating a sneaker deal, I'll put you in charge. But while this thing is still a criminal case, let me take the lead, okay?'

'The police want to question me.'

'You say nothing. That is your right. You don't have to say a word to the police.'

'Unless they subpoena me.'

'Even then. You are Linda Coldren's attorney. You don't say anything.'

Myron shook his head. 'That only works for what was said *after* you asked me to be co-counsel. They can ask me about anything that happened before.'

'Wrong.' Victoria Wilson gave a distracted sigh. 'When Linda Coldren first asked you to help, she knew you were a bar-appointed attorney. Therefore everything she told you fell under attorney-client.'

Myron had to smile. 'That's reaching.'

'But that's the way it is.' He could feel her eyes on him now. 'No matter what you might want to do, morally and legally you are not allowed to talk to anyone.'

She was good.

Myron drove a bit faster. No one was tailing them; the police and the reporters had stuck to the house. The story was all over the radio. The anchorman kept repeating a one-line statement issued by Linda Coldren: 'We are all saddened by this tragedy. Please allow us to grieve in peace.'

'You issue that statement?' Myron asked.

'No. Linda did it before I got there.'

'Why?'

'She thought it would keep the media off her back. She knows better now.'

They pulled up on Porter Street. Myron scanned the sidewalks.

'Up there,' Victoria Wilson said.

Myron saw him. Chad Coldren was huddled on the

ground. The telephone receiver was still gripped in one hand, but he wasn't talking. The other hand was heavily bandaged. Myron felt a little queasy. He hit the gas pedal. The car jerked forward. They pulled up to the boy. Chad stared straight ahead.

Victoria Wilson's indifferent expression finally melted a bit. 'Let me handle this,' she said.

She got out of the car and walked over to the boy. She bent down and cradled him. She took the receiver away from him, talked into it, hung up. She helped Chad to his feet, stroking his hair, whispering comforts. They both got into the backseat, Chad leaned his head against her. She made soothing shushing noises. She nodded at Myron. Myron put the car in drive.

Chad did not speak during the drive. Nobody asked him to. Victoria gave Myron directions to her office building in Bryn Mawr. The Coldren family doctor – a gray-haired, old family friend named Henry Lane – had his office there too. He unwrapped Chad's bandage and examined the boy while Myron and Victoria waited in another room. Myron paced. Victoria read a magazine.

'We should take him to a hospital,' Myron said.

'Dr Lane will decide if that's necessary.' Victoria yawned and flipped a page.

Myron tried to take it all in. With all the activity surrounding the police accusation and Chad's safe recovery, he had almost forgotten about Jack Coldren. Jack was dead. It was almost impossible for Myron to comprehend. The irony did not escape him: the man finally has the chance at redemption and he ends up dead in the same hazard that altered his life twenty-three years ago.

Dr Lane appeared in the doorway. He was everything you wanted a doctor to look like – Marcus Welby without the receding hairline. 'Chad is better now. He's talking. He's alert.'

'How's his hand?' Myron asked.

'It'll need to be looked at by a specialist. But there's no infection or anything like that.'

Victoria Wilson stood. 'I'd like to talk to him.'

Lane nodded. 'I would warn you to go easy on him, Victoria, but I know you never listen.'

Her mouth almost twitched. Not a smile. Not even close. But there was a sign of life. 'You'll have to stay out here, Henry. The police may ask you what you heard.'

The doctor nodded again. 'I understand.'

Victoria looked at Myron. 'I'll do the talking.'

'Okay.'

When Myron and Victoria entered the room, Chad was staring down at his bandaged hand like he expected the missing finger to grow back.

'Chad?'

He slowly looked up. There were tears in his eyes. Myron remembered what Linda had said about the kid's love of golf. Another dream lay in ashes. The kid did not know it, but right now he and Myron were kindred spirits.

'Who are you?' Chad asked Myron.

'He's a friend,' Victoria Wilson replied. Even with the boy, the tone was completely detached. 'His name is Myron Bolitar.'

'I want to see my parents, Aunt Vee.'

Victoria sat across from him. 'A lot has happened, Chad. I don't want to go into it all now. You'll have to trust me, okay?'

Chad nodded.

'I need to know what happened to you. Everything. From the beginning.'

'A man car-jacked me,' Chad said.

'Just one man?'

'Yeah.'

'Go on. Tell me what happened.'

'I was at a traffic light, and this guy just opens the passenger door and gets in. He's wearing a ski mask and sticks this gun in my face. He told me to keep driving.'

'Okay. What day was this?'

'Thursday.'

'Where were you Wednesday night?'

'At my friend Matt's house.'

'Matthew Squires?'

'Yes.'

'Okay, fine.' Victoria Wilson's eyes did not wander from the boy's face. 'Now where were you when this man got into your car?'

'A couple of blocks from school.'

'Did this happen before or after summer school?'

'After. I was on my way home.'

Myron kept quiet. He wondered why the boy was lying.

'Where did the man take you?'

'He told me to drive around the block. We pulled into this parking lot. Then he put something over my head. A burlap bag or something. He made me lie down in the back. Then he started driving. I don't know where we went. I never saw anything. Next thing I knew I was in a room someplace. I had to keep the bag on my head all the time so I didn't see anything.'

'You never saw the man's face?'

'Never.'

'Are you sure it was a man? Could it have been a woman?'

'I heard his voice a few times. It was a man. At least, one of them was.'

'There was more than one?'

Chad nodded. 'The day he did this . . .' He lifted his bandaged hand into view. His face went totally blank. He looked straight ahead, his eyes unfocused. 'I had that burlap bag over my head. My hands were handcuffed behind my back.' His voice was as detached as Victoria's now. 'That bag was so itchy. I used to rub my chin against my shoulder. Just for relief. Anyway, the man came in and unlocked the handcuffs. Then he grabbed my hand and put it flat on the table. He didn't say anything. He didn't warn me. The whole thing took less than ten seconds. He just put my hand on the table. I never saw a thing. I just heard a whack. Then I felt this weird sensation. Not even pain at first. I didn't know what it was. Then I felt a warm wetness. From the blood, I guess. The pain came a few seconds later. I passed out. When I woke up, my hand was wrapped. The throbbing was awful. The burlap bag was back over my head. Someone came in. Gave me some pills. It dulled the pain a little. Then I heard voices. Two of them. It sounded like they were arguing.'

Chad Coldren stopped as though out of breath. Myron watched Victoria Wilson. She did not go over and comfort him.

'Were the voices both male?'

'Actually, one sounded like a female. But I was pretty out of it. I can't say for sure.'

Chad looked back down at his bandages. He moved his fingers a bit. Testing them out.

'What happened next, Chad?'

He kept his eyes on the bandages. 'There's not a lot to tell, Aunt Vee. They kept me that way for a few days. I don't know how many. They fed me mostly pizza and soda. They brought a phone in one day. Made me call Merion and ask for my dad.'

The ransom call at Merion, Myron thought. The kidnapper's second call.

'They also made me scream.'

'Made you scream?'

'The guy came in. He told me to scream and to make it scary. Otherwise, he would make me scream for real. So I tried different screams for, like, ten minutes. Until he was satisfied.'

The scream from the call at the mall, Myron thought. The one where Tito demanded a hundred grand.

'That's about it, Aunt Vee.'

'How did you escape?' Victoria asked.

'I didn't. They let me go. A little while ago someone led me to a car. I still had the burlap bag on my head. We drove a little. Then the car stopped. Someone opened the door and pulled me out. Next thing I knew, I was free.'

Victoria looked over at Myron. Myron looked back. Then she nodded slowly. Myron took that as his cue.

'He's lying.'

Chad said, 'What?'

Myron turned his attention to him. 'You're lying, Chad. And worse, the police will know you're lying.'

'What are you talking about?' His eyes sought Victoria's. 'Who is this guy?'

'You used your ATM card at 6:18 P.M. on Thursday on Porter Street,' Myron said.

Chad's eyes widened. 'That wasn't me. It was the asshole who grabbed me. He took my wallet—'

'It's on videotape, Chad.'

He opened his mouth, but nothing came out. Then: 'They made me.' But his voice was weak.

'I saw the tape, Chad. You were smiling. You were happy. You were not alone. You also spent an evening at the sleazy motel next door.'

Chad lowered his head.

'Chad?' It was Victoria. She did not sound pleased. 'Look at me, boy.'

Chad slowly raised his eyes.

'Why are you lying to me?'

'It has nothing to do with what happened, Aunt Vee.'

Her face was unyielding. 'Start talking, Chad. And now.'

He looked down again, studying the bandaged hand. 'It's just like I said – except the man didn't grab me in my car. He knocked on my door at that motel. He came in with a gun. Everything else I told you is the truth.'

'When was this?'

'Friday morning.'

'So why did you lie to me?'

'I promised,' he said. 'I just wanted to keep her out of this.'

'Who?' she asked.

Chad looked surprised. 'You don't know?'

'I have the tape,' Myron said, giving a little bluff here. 'I haven't shown it to her yet.'

'Aunt Vee, you have to keep her out of it. This could really hurt her.'

'Honey, listen to me now. I think it's sweet that you're trying to protect your girlfriend. But I don't have time for that.'

Chad looked from Myron to Victoria. 'I want to see my mom please.'

'You will, honey. Soon. But first you have to tell me about this girl.'

'I promised that I would keep her out of it.'

'If I can keep her name out of this, I will.'

'I can't, Aunt Vee.'

'Forget it, Victoria,' Myron said. 'If he won't tell, we can all just watch the tape together. Then we can call the girl on her own. Or maybe the police will find her first. They'll have a copy of the tape too. They won't be so worried about her feelings.'

'You don't understand,' Chad said, looking from Victoria Wilson to Myron, then back at Victoria again. 'I promised her. She can get in serious trouble.'

'We'll talk to her parents, if need be,' Victoria said. 'We'll do what we can.'

'Her parents?' Chad looked confused. 'I'm not worried about her parents. She's old enough . . .' His voice died away.

'Who were you with, Chad?'

'I swore I'd never say anything, Aunt Vee.'

'Fine,' Myron said. 'We can't waste time on this, Victoria. Let the police track her down.'

'No!' Chad looked down. 'She had nothing to do with it, okay? We were together. She went out for a little while and that's when they grabbed me. It wasn't her fault.'

Victoria shifted in her seat. 'Who, Chad?'

His words came out slow and grudging. But they were also quite clear. 'Her name is Esme Fong. She works for a company called Zoom.'

Chapter 28

It was all starting to make awful, horrible sense.

Myron did not wait for permission. He stormed out of the office and down the corridor. It was time to confront Esme.

A scenario was fast taking shape in Myron's mind. Esme Fong meets Chad Coldren while negotiating the Zoom deal with his mother. She seduces him. Why? Hard to say. For kicks maybe. Not important.

Anyway, Chad spends Wednesday night with his buddy Matthew. Then on Thursday he meets up with Esme for a romantic tryst at the Court Manor Inn. They pick up some cash at an ATM. They have their fun. And then things get interesting.

Esme Fong has not only signed Linda Coldren, but she has managed to land wunderkind Tad Crispin. Tad is playing wonderfully well in his first US Open. After one round, he is in second place. Amazing. Great publicity. But if Tad could somehow win – if he could catch the veteran with a gigantic lead – it would give Zoom's launch into the golf business a nuclear boost. It would be worth millions.

Millions.

And Esme had the leader's son right in front of her.

So what does the ambitious Esme Fong do? She hires Tito to grab the boy. Nothing complicated. She wants to distract Jack big-time. Make him lose that edge. What better way than kidnapping his kid?

It all kinda fit together.

Myron turned his attention to some of case's more bothersome aspects. First of all, the not demanding the ransom for so long suddenly made sense. Esme Fong is no expert at this and she doesn't want a payoff – that would just complicate manners – so the first few calls are awkward. She forgets to demand a ransom. Second, Myron remembered Tito's 'chink bitch' call. How had he known Esme was there? Simple. Esme had told him when she would be there – to scare the hell out of the Coldrens and make them think they were being watched.

Yep. It fit. Everything had been going according to Esme Fong's plan. Except for one thing.

Jack continued to play well.

He maintained his insurmountable lead through the next round. The kidnapping may have stunned him a bit, but he had regained his footing. His lead was still huge. Drastic action was necessary.

Myron got into the elevator and headed down to the ground-floor lobby. He wondered how it had happened. Maybe it had been Tito's idea. Maybe that was why Chad had heard two voices arguing. Either way, someone decided to do something that was guaranteed to throw Jack off his game.

Cut off Chad's finger.

Like it or not – Tito's idea or hers – Esme Fong took advantage. She had Linda's car keys. She knew what her car looked like. It wouldn't take much. Just a turn of the key, a quick drop on the car seat. Easy for her. Nothing suspicious. Who would notice an attractive, well-dressed woman unlocking a car with a key?

The severed finger did the trick, too. Jack's game was left in shambles. Tad Crispin stormed back. It was everything she wanted. But, alas, Jack had one more trick up his sleeve. He managed to land a big putt on the eighteenth hole, forcing a tie. This was a nightmare for Esme. She could not take the risk of Tad Crispin losing to Jack, the ultimate choker, in a one-on-one situation.

A loss would be disastrous.

A loss would cost them millions. Maybe destroy her entire campaign.

Man, did it fit.

When Myron thought about it, hadn't he heard Esme voice that very viewpoint with Norm Zuckerman? Her Buffalo Bill analogy – hadn't he been standing right there when she said it? Now that she was trapped, was it so hard to believe that she'd go the extra mile? That she would call Jack on the phone last night? That she would set up a rendezvous at the course? That she would insist he come alone – right now – if he wanted to see his son alive?

Ka-bang.

And once Jack was dead, there was no reason to hold on to the kid anymore. She let him go.

The elevator slid open. Myron stepped out. Okay, there were holes. But maybe after confronting Esme, he would be able to plug a few of them up. Myron pushed open the glass door. He headed into the parking lot. There were taxis waiting near the street. He was midway through the lot when a voice reached out and pulled him to a stop.

'Myron?'

An icy nerve-jangle punctured a hole through his heart. He had heard the voice only once before. Ten years ago. At Merion.

Chapter 29

Myron froze.

'I see you've met Victoria,' Cissy Lockwood said.

He tried a nod, but it wouldn't happen.

'I called her as soon as Bucky told me about the murder. I knew she'd be able to help. Victoria is the best lawyer I know. Ask Win about her.'

He tried the nod again. Got a little motion going this time.

Win's mother stepped closer. 'I'd like a word with you in private, Myron.'

He found his voice. 'It's not a good time, Ms Lock-wood.'

'No, I imagine not. Still, this won't take long.'

'Really, I should go.'

She was a beautiful woman. Her ash-blond hair was streaked with gray, and she had the same regal bearing as her blood niece Linda. The porcelain face, however, she had given almost verbatim to Win. The resemblance was uncanny.

She took one more step forward, her eyes never off him. Her clothes were a bit odd. She wore a man's over-size shirt, untucked, and stretch pants. Annie Hall goes maternity shopping. It was not what he'd have expected, but then again, he had bigger worries than fashion right now.

'It's about Win,' she said.

Myron shook his head. 'Then it's none of my business.'

'True enough. But that does not make you immune to responsibility, does it? Win is your friend. I count myself lucky that my son has a friend who cares like you do.'

Myron said nothing.

'I know quite a bit about you, Myron. I've had private investigators keep tabs on Win for years now. It was my way of staying close. Of course, Win knew about it. He never said anything, but you can't keep something like that from Win, now can you?'

'No,' Myron said. 'You can't.'

'You're staying at the Lockwood estate,' she said. 'In the guest cottage.'

He nodded.

'You've been there before.'

Another nod.

'Have you ever seen the horse stables?'

'Only from a distance,' Myron said.

She smiled Win's smile. 'You've never been inside?'

'No.'

'I'm not surprised. Win doesn't ride anymore. He used to love horses. More than golf even.'

'Ms Lockwood—'

'Please call me Cissy.'

273

'I really don't feel comfortable hearing this.'

Her eyes hardened a bit. 'And I do not feel comfortable telling you this. But it must be done.'

'Win wouldn't want me to hear it,' Myron said.

'That's too bad, but Win cannot always have what he wants. I should have learned that long ago. He did not want to see me as a child. I never forced it. I listened to the experts, who told me that my son would come around, that compelling him to see me would be counter-productive. But they did not know Win. By the time I stopped listening to them it was too late. Not that it mattered. I don't think ignoring them would have changed anything.'

Silence.

She stood proud and tall, her slender neck high. But something was going on. Her fingers kept flexing, as if she were fighting off the desire to make fists. Myron's stomach knotted up. He knew what was coming next. He just didn't know what to do about it.

'The story is simple,' she began, her voice almost wistful. She was no longer looking at Myron. Her gaze rose above his shoulder, but he had no idea what she was actually seeing. 'Win was eight years old. I was twenty-seven at the time. I married young. I never went to college. It was not as though I had a choice. My father told me what to do. I had only one friend – one person I could confide in. That was Victoria. She is still my dearest friend, not unlike what you are to Win.'

Cissy Lockwood winced. Her eyes closed.

'Ms Lockwood?'

She shook her head. The eyes slowly opened. 'I am getting off track,' she said, catching her breath. 'I apologize. I'm not here to tell you my life story. Just one incident in it. So let me just state it plainly.'

A deep breath. Then another.

'Jack Coldren told me that he was taking Win out for a golf lesson. But it never happened. Or perhaps they had finished far earlier than expected. Either way, Jack was not with Win. His father was. Somehow Win and his father ended up going into the stables. I was there when they entered. I was not alone. More specifically, I was with Win's riding instructor.'

She stopped. Myron waited.

'Do I need to spell this out for you?'

Myron shook his head.

'No child should see what Win saw that day,' she said. 'And worse, no child should ever see his father's face under those circumstances.'

Myron felt tears sting his eyes.

'There is more to it, of course. I won't go into it now. But Win has never spoken to me since that moment. He also never forgave his father. Yes, his father. You think he hates only me and loves Windsor the Second. But it is not so. He blames his father, too. He thinks that his father is weak. That he allowed it to happen. Utter nonsense, but that is the way it is.'

Myron shook his head. He didn't want to hear any more. He wanted to run and find Win. He wanted to hug his friend and shake him and somehow make him forget. He thought of the lost expression on Win's face as he watched the horse stables yesterday morning.

My God. Win.

When Myron spoke, his voice was sharper than he'd expected. 'Why are you telling me this?'

'Because I am dying,' she replied.

Myron slumped against a car. His heart ripped anew.

'Again, let me put this simply,' she said in too calm a voice. 'It has reached the liver. It is eleven centimeters long. My abdomen is swelling from liver and kidney failure.' That explained the wardrobe – the untucked, oversize shirt and the stretch pants. 'We are not talking months. We are talking perhaps weeks. Probably less.'

'There are treatments,' Myron tried lamely. 'Procedures.'

She simply dismissed this with a shake of her head. 'I am not a foolish woman. I do not have delusions of engaging in a moving reunion with my son. I know Win. That will not happen. But there is still unfinished business here. Once I am dead, there will be no chance for him to disentangle himself again. It will be over. I do not know what he will do with this opportunity. Probably nothing. But I want him to know. So that he can decide. It is his last chance, Myron. I do not believe he will take it. But he should.'

With that, she turned away and left. Myron watched her walk away. When she was out of sight, Myron hailed a taxi. He got in the back.

'Where to, bud?'

He gave the man the address where Esme Fong was staying. Then he settled back in the seat. His eyes stared blankly out the window. The city passed by in a misty, silent blur.

Chapter 30

When he thought that his voice would not betray him, Myron called Win on the cell phone.

After a quick hello, Win said, 'Bummer about Jack.'

'From what I hear, he used to be your friend.'

Win cleared his throat. 'Myron?'

'What?'

'You know nothing. Remember that.'

True enough. 'Can we have dinner tonight?'

Win hesitated. 'Of course.'

'At the cottage. Six-thirty.'

'Fine.'

Win hung up. Myron tried to put it out of his mind. He had other things to worry about.

Esme Fong paced the sidewalk outside the entrance to the Omni Hotel on the corner of Chestnut Street and Fourth. She wore a white suit and white stockings. Killer legs. She kept wringing her hands.

Myron got out of the taxi. 'Why are you waiting out here?' he asked.

'You insisted on talking privately,' Esme answered. 'Norm is upstairs.'

'You two live in the same room?'

'No, we have adjoining suites.'

Myron nodded. The no-tell motel was making more sense now. 'Not much privacy, huh?'

'No, not really.' She gave him a tentative smile. 'But it's okay. I like Norm.'

'I'm sure you do.'

'What's this about, Myron?'

'You heard about Jack Coldren?'

'Of course. Norm and I were shocked. Absolutely shocked.'

Myron nodded. 'Come on,' he said. 'Let's walk.'

They headed up Fourth Street. Myron was tempted to stay on Chestnut Street, but that would have meant strolling past Independence Hall and that would have been a tad too cliché for his liking. Still, Fourth Street was in the colonial section. Lots of brick. Brick sidewalk, brick walls and fence, brick buildings of tremendous historical significance that all looked the same. White ash trees lined the walk. They turned right into a park that held the Second Bank of the United States. There was a plaque with a portrait of the bank's first president. One of Win's ancestors. Myron looked for a resemblance but could not find one.

'I've tried to reach Linda,' Esme said. 'But the phone is busy.'

'Did you try Chad's line?'

Something hit her face, then fled. 'Chad's line?'

'He has his own phone in the house,' he said. 'You must have known that.'

'Why would I know that?'

Myron shrugged. 'I thought you knew Chad.'

'I do,' she said, but her voice was slow, careful. 'I mean, I've been over to the house a number of times.'

'Uh-huh. And when was the last time you saw Chad?'

She put her hand to her chin. 'I don't think he was there when I went over Friday night,' she said, the voice still slow. 'I don't really know. I guess a few weeks ago.'

Myron made a buzzing noise. 'Incorrect answer.'

'Excuse me?'

'I don't get it, Esme.'

'What?'

Myron continued walking, Esme stayed in step. 'You're what,' he said, 'twenty-four years old?'

'Twenty-five.'

'You're smart. You're successful. You're attractive. But a teenage boy – what's up with that?'

She stopped. 'What are you talking about?'

'You really don't know?'

'I don't have the slightest idea.'

His eyes bore into hers. 'You. Chad Coldren. The Court Manor Inn. That help?'

'No.'

Myron gave her skeptical. 'Please.'

'Did Chad tell you that?'

'Esme . . .'

'He's lying, Myron. My God, you know how teenage boys are. How could you believe something like that?'

'Pictures, Esme.'

Her face went slack. 'What?'

'You two stopped at an ATM machine next door to the

motel, remember? They have cameras. Your face was clear as day.' It was a bluff. But it was a damn good one. She caved a little piece at a time. She looked around and then collapsed on a bench. She turned and faced a colonial building with a lot of scaffolding. Scaffolding, Myron thought, ruined the effect – like armpit hair on a beautiful woman. It shouldn't really matter, but it did.

'Please don't tell Norm,' she said in a faraway voice. 'Please don't.'

Myron said nothing.

'It was dumb. I know that. But it shouldn't cost me my job.'

Myron sat next to her. 'Tell me what happened.'

She looked back at him. 'Why? What business is this of yours?'

'There are reasons.'

'What reasons?' Her voice was a little sharper now. 'Look, I'm not proud of myself. But who appointed you my conscience?'

'Fine. I'll go ask Norm then. Maybe he can help me.'

Her mouth dropped. 'Help you with what? I don't understand. Why are you doing this to me?'

'I need some answers. I don't have time to explain.'

'What do you want me to say? That I was dumb? I was. I could tell you that I was lonely being in a nice place. That he seemed like a sweet, handsome kid and that at his age, I figured there'd be no fear of disease or attachments. But at the end of the day, that does not change much. I was wrong. I'm sorry, okay?'

'When was the last time you saw Chad?'

'Why do you keep asking me that?' Esme insisted.

'Just answer my questions or I'll go to Norm, I swear it.'

280

She studied his face. He put on his most impermeable face, the one he'd learned from really tough cops and toll collectors on the New Jersey Turnpike. After a few seconds she said, 'At that motel.'

'The Court Manor Inn?'

'Whatever it was called. I don't remember the name.'

'What day was that?' Myron asked.

She thought a moment. 'Friday morning. Chad was still sleeping.'

'You haven't seen or spoken to him since?'

'No.'

'You didn't have any plans to rendezvous for another tryst?'

She made an unhappy face. 'No, not really. I thought he was just out for some fun, but once we were there, I could see he was developing a crush. I didn't count on that. Frankly I was worried.'

'Of what exactly?'

'That he'd tell his mother. Chad swore he wouldn't, but who knew what he'd do if I hurt him? When I didn't hear from him again, I was relieved.'

Myron searched her face and her story for lies. He couldn't find one. Didn't mean they weren't there.

Esme shifted on the bench, crossing her legs. 'I still don't understand why you're asking me all this.' She thought about it a moment and then something seemed to spark in her eyes. She squared her shoulders toward Myron. 'Does this have something to do with Jack's murder?'

Myron said nothing.

'My God.' Her voice quaked. 'You can't possibly think that Chad has something to do with it.'

Myron waited a beat. All-or-nothing time. 'No,' he said. 'But I'm not so sure about you.'

Confusion set camp on her face. 'What?'

'I think you kidnapped Chad.'

She raised both hands. 'Are you out of your mind? Kidnapped? It was completely consensual. Chad was more than willing, believe me. Okay, he was young. But do you think I took him to that motel at gunpoint?'

'That's not what I mean,' Myron said.

Confusion again. 'Then what the hell do you mean?'

'After you left the motel on Friday. Where did you go?'

'To Merion. I met you there that night, remember?'

'How about last night? Where were you?'

'Here.'

'In your suite?'

'Yes.'

'What time?'

'From eight o'clock on.'

'Anybody who can verify that?'

'Why would I need someone to verify that?' she snapped. Myron put on the impermeable face again – not even gases could get through. Esme sighed. 'I was with Norm until midnight. We were working.'

'And after that?'

'I went to bed.'

'Would the hotel's nightman be able to verify that you never left your suite after midnight?'

'I think so, yes. His name is Miguel. He's very nice.'

Miguel. He'd have Esperanza track down that one. If her alibi stuck, his neat little scenario went down the toilet. 'Who else knew about you and Chad Coldren?'

'No one,' she said. 'At least, I told no one.'

'How about Chad? Did he tell anyone?'

'It sounds to me like he told you,' she said pointedly. 'He might have told someone else, I don't know.'

Myron thought about it. The black-clad man crawling out Chad's bedroom window. Matthew Squires. Myron remembered his own teenage years. If he had somehow managed to bed an older woman who looked like Esme Fong, he would have been busting to tell someone – especially if he'd been staying at his best friend's house the night before.

Once again, things circled back to the Squires kid.

Myron asked, 'Where will you be if I need to reach you?'

She reached into her pocket and pulled out a card. 'My cell phone number is on the bottom.'

'Good-bye, Esme.'

'Myron?'

He turned to her.

'Are you going to tell Norm?'

She seemed only worried about her reputation and her job, not a murder rap. Or was this just a clever diversion? No way of knowing for sure.

'No,' he said. 'I won't tell.'

At least, not yet.

Chapter 31

Episcopal Academy. Win's high school alma mater.

Esperanza had picked him up in front of Esme Fong's and driven him here. She parked across the street. She turned off the ignition and faced him.

'Now what?' she asked.

'I don't know. Matthew Squires is in there. We can wait for a lunch break. Try to get in then.'

'Sounds like a plan,' Esperanza said with a nod. 'A really bad one.'

'You have a better idea?'

'We can go in now. Pretend we're touring parents.'

Myron thought about it. 'You think that'll work?'

'Better than hanging out here doing nothing.'

'Oh, before I forget. I want you to check out Esme's alibi. The hotel nightman named Miguel.'

'Miguel,' she repeated. 'It's because I'm Hispanic, right?'

'Pretty much, yeah.'

She had no problem with that. 'I put a call in to Peru this morning.'

'And?'

'I spoke to some local sheriff. He says Lloyd Rennart committed suicide.'

'What about the body?'

'The cliff is called *El Garganta del Diablo* – in English, Throat of the Devil. No bodies are ever located. It's actually a fairly common suicide plunge.'

'Great. Think you can do a little more background stuff on Rennart?'

'Like what?'

'How did he buy the bar in Neptune? How did he buy the house in Spring Lake Heights? Stuff like that.'

'Why would you want know that?'

'Lloyd Rennart was a caddie for a rookie golfer. That isn't exactly loads of dough.'

'So?'

'So maybe he had a windfall after Jack blew the US Open.'

Esperanza saw where he was going. 'You think somebody paid Rennart off to throw the Open?'

'No,' Myron said. 'But I think it's a possibility.'

'It's going to be hard to trace after all this time.'

'Just give it a shot. Also, Rennart got into a serious car accident twenty years ago in Narberth. It's a small town right around here. His first wife was killed in the crash. See what you can find out about it.'

Esperanza frowned. 'Like what?'

'Like was he drunk. Was he charged with anything. Were there other fatalities.'

'Why?'

'Maybe he pissed off someone. Maybe his first wife's family wants vengeance.'

Esperanza kept the frown. 'So they – what? – waited twenty years, followed Lloyd Rennart to Peru, pushed him off a cliff, came back, kidnapped Chad Coldren, killed Jack Coldren . . . Are you getting my point?'

Myron nodded. 'And you're right. But I still want you to run down everything you can on Lloyd Rennart. I think there's a connection somewhere. We just have to find what it is.'

'I don't see it,' Esperanza said. She tucked a curl of black hair behind her ear. 'Seems to me that Esme Fong is still a much better suspect.'

'Agreed. But I'd still like you to look into it. Find out what you can. There's also a son, Larry Rennart. Seventeen years old. See if we can find out what he's been up to.'

She shrugged. 'A waste of time, but okay.' She gestured toward the school. 'You want to go in now?'

'Sure.'

Before they moved, a giant set of knuckles gently tapped on Myron's window. The sound startled him. Myron looked out his window. The large black man with the Nat King Cole hair – the one from the Court Manor Inn – was smiling at him. 'Nat' made a cranking motion with his hand, signaling Myron to lower the window. Myron complied.

'Hey, I'm glad we ran into you,' Myron said. 'I never got the number of your barber.'

The black man chuckled. He made a frame with his large hands – thumbs touching, arms outstretched – and tilted it back and forth the way a movie director does.

'You with my doo,' he said with a shake of his head. 'Somehow I just don't see it.'

He leaned into the car and stuck his hand across Myron toward Esperanza. 'My name is Carl.'

'Esperanza.' She shook his hand.

'Yes, I know.'

Esperanza squinted at him. 'I know you.'

'Indeed you do.'

She snapped her fingers. 'Mosambo, the Kenyan Killer, the Safari Slasher.'

Carl smiled. 'Nice to see Little Pocahontas remembers.'

Myron said, 'The Safari Slasher?'

'Carl used to be a professional wrestler,' Esperanza explained. 'We were in the ring together once. In Boston, right?'

Carl climbed into the backseat of the car. He leaned forward so his head was between Esperanza's right shoulder and Myron's left. 'Hartford,' he said. 'At the Civic Center.'

'Mixed tag-team,' Esperanza said.

'That's right,' Carl said with his easy smile. 'Be a sweetheart, Esperanza, and start up the car. Head straight until the third traffic light.'

Myron said, 'You mind telling us what's going on?'

'Sure thing. See that car behind you?'

Myron used the passenger-side mirror. 'The one with the two goons?'

'Yep. They're with me. And they are bad men, Myron. Young. Far too violent. You know how the kids are today. *Bam, bam*, no talk. The three of us are supposed to escort you to an unknown destination. In fact, I'm supposed to be holding a gun on you now. But hell, we're all friends here, right? No need, the way I see it. So just start heading straight. The goons will follow.'

'Before we take off,' Myron said, 'do you mind if we let Esperanza go?'

Carl chuckled. 'Kinda sexist, don't you think?'

'Excuse me?'

'If Esperanza were a man – like, say, your buddy Win – would you be making this gallant gesture?'

'I might,' he said. But even Esperanza was shaking her head.

'Me thinks not, Myron. And trust me here: it would be the wrong move. The young goons back there, they'd want to know what's up. They'd see her get out of the car and they got those itchy fingers and those crazy eyes and they like hurting people. Especially women. And maybe, just maybe, Esperanza here is an insurance policy. Alone, you might try something dumb; with Esperanza right there, you might not be so inclined.'

Esperanza glanced at Myron. Myron nodded. She started the car.

'Make a left at the third light,' Carl said.

'Tell me something,' Myron said. 'Is Reginald Squires as big a nut-job as I hear?'

Still leaning forward, Carl turned to Esperanza. 'Am I supposed to be wowed by his sharp deductive reasoning skills?'

'Yes,' Esperanza replied. 'He'll be terribly disappointed if you aren't.'

'Figured that. And to answer your question, Squires is not that big a nut-job – when he stays on his medication.'

'Very comforting,' Myron said.

The young goons stayed right on their tail for the entire fifteen-minute drive. Myron was not surprised when Carl told Esperanza to turn down Green Acres Road. When they approached the ornate front entrance, the iron gates swung open like on the closing credits of *Get Smart*. They continued up a windy driveway through the heavily wooded property. After about a half mile, they hit a clearing with a building. The building was big and plain and rectangular, like a high school gym.

The only entrance Myron could see was a garage door. As if on cue, the door slid open. Carl told Esperanza to pull into it. Once far enough inside, he told her to park and kill the engine. The goon car came in behind them and did likewise.

The garage door came back down, slowly slicing out the sun. No lights were on inside; the room was submerged in total darkness.

'This is just like the haunted house at Six Flags,' Myron said.

'Give me your gun, Myron.'

Carl had his game face on. Myron handed him the gun.

'Step out of the car.'

'But I'm afraid of the dark,' Myron said.

'You too, Esperanza.'

They all stepped out the car. So did the two goons behind them. Their movements echoed off the cement floor, hinting to Myron that they were in a very large room. The interior car lights provided a modicum of illumination, but that didn't last long. Myron made out nothing before the doors were closed.

Absolute blackness.

Myron made his way around the car and found Esperanza. She took his hand in hers. They remained still and waited.

A beacon, the kind used at a lighthouse or a movie

premiere, snapped on in their faces. Myron's eyes slammed shut. He shaded them with his hand and slowly squinted them open. A man stepped in front of the bright light. His body cast a giant shadow on the wall behind Myron. The effect reminded Myron of the Bat Signal.

'No one will hear your screams,' the man said.

'Isn't that a line from a movie?' Myron asked. 'But I think the line was, "No one will hear you scream." I could be wrong about that.'

'People have died in this room,' the voice boomed. 'My name is Reginald Squires. You will tell me everything I want to know. Or you and your friend will be next.'

Oh, boy. Myron looked at Carl. Carl's face remained stoic. Myron turned back toward the light. 'You're rich, right?'

'Very rich,' Squires corrected.

'Then maybe you could afford a better scriptwriter.'

Myron glanced back at Carl. Carl slowly shook his head no. One of the two young goons stepped forward. In the harsh light, Myron could see the man's psychotic, happy smile. Myron tensed, waited.

The goon cocked a fist and threw it at Myron's head. Myron ducked, and the punch missed. As the fist flew by him, Myron grabbed the goon's wrist. He put his forearm against the back of the man's elbow and pulled the joint back in a way it was never intended to bend. The goon had no choice. He dropped to the ground. Myron added a bit more pressure. The goon tried to squirm free. Myron snapped his knee straight into the goon's nose. Something splattered. Myron could actually feel the nose cartilage give way and fan out.

The second goon took out his gun and pointed it at Myron.

'Stop,' Squires shouted.

Myron let the goon go. He slid to the floor like wet sand through a torn bag.

'You will pay for that, Mr Bolitar.' Squires liked to project his voice. 'Robert?'

The goon with the gun said, 'Yes, Mr Squires.'

'Hit the girl. Hard.'

'Yes, Mr Squires.'

Myron said, 'Hey, hit me. I'm the one who smarted off.'

'And this is your punishment,' Squires said calmly. 'Hit the girl, Robert. Now.'

Goon Robert moved toward Esperanza.

'Mr Squires?' It was Carl.

'Yes, Carl.'

Carl stepped into the light. 'Allow me to do it.'

'I did not think you were the type, Carl.'

'I'm not, Mr Squires. But Robert might do serious damage to her.'

'But that's my intent.'

'No, I mean, he'll leave bruising or break something. You want her to feel pain. That's my area of expertise.'

'I realize that, Carl. It's why I pay you what I do.'

'So then let me do my job. I can hit her without leaving a mark or permanent injury. I know control. I know the right spots.'

The shadowy Mr Squires considered this a moment. 'Will you make it painful?' he asked. 'Very painful?'

'If you insist.' Carl sounded reluctant but resolved.

'I do. Right now. I want it to hurt her a great deal.'

Carl walked up to Esperanza. Myron start to move toward him, but Robert placed the gun against his head.

There was nothing he could do. He tried fire-throwing a warning glare at Carl.

'Don't,' Myron said.

Carl ignored him. He stood in front of Esperanza now. She looked at him defiantly. Without preamble he punched her deep in the stomach.

The power of the blow lifted Esperanza off her feet. She made an oofing noise and folded at the waist like an old wallet. Her body landed on the floor. She curled up into a protective ball, her eyes wide, her chest heaving for air. Carl looked down at her without emotion. Then he looked at Myron.

'You son of a bitch,' Myron said.

'It's your fault,' Carl said.

Esperanza continued to roll on the ground in obvious agony. She still couldn't get any air into her lungs. Myron's whole body felt hot and red. He moved toward her, but Robert again stopped him by pressing the gun hard against his neck.

Reginald Squires did the big voice-projection again. 'You will listen now, won't you, Mr. Bolitar?'

Myron took deep breaths. His muscles bunched. Every part of him fumed. Every part of him craved vengeance. He watched in silence as Esperanza writhed on the floor. After a while she managed to get to all fours. Her head was down. Her body heaved. A retching noise came out of her. Then another retching noise.

The sound made Myron pause.

Something about the sound . . . Myron searched his memory banks. Something about the whole scenario, the way she doubled up, the way she rolled on the floor – it was strangely familiar. As though he'd seen it before. But that was impossible. When would he . . . ? He stopped as the answer came to him.

In the wrestling ring.

My God, Myron thought. She was faking it!

Myron looked over at Carl. There was a hint of a smile on his face.

Son of a bitch. It was an act!

Reginald Squires cleared his throat. 'You have taken an unhealthy interest in my son, Mr. Bolitar,' he continued, voice thundering. 'Are you some sort of pervert?'

Myron almost flew off another wisecrack, but he bit it back. 'No.'

'Then tell me what you want with him.'

Myron squinted into the light. He still couldn't see anything but the shadowy outline of Squires. What should he say? The guy was a major loony tune. No question about that. So how to play this . . . ?

'You've heard about Jack Coldren's murder,' Myron said.

'Of course.'

'I'm working on the case.'

'You're trying to find out who murdered Jack Coldren?'

'Yes.'

'But Jack was murdered last night,' Squires countered. 'You were asking about my son Saturday.'

'It's a long story,' Myron said.

The shadow's hands spread. 'We have all the time in the world.'

How did Myron know he was going to say that?

With nothing much to lose, Myron told Squires about the kidnapping. Most of it anyway. He emphasized several times that the actual abduction had happened at the

Court Manor Inn. There was a reason for that. It had to do with the egocentricity. Reginald Squires – the ego in question – reacted in predictable fashion.

'Are you telling me,' he shouted, 'that Chad Coldren was kidnapped at *my* motel?'

His motel. Myron had figured that out by now. It was the only explanation for why Carl had run interference for Stuart Lipwitz.

'That's right,' Myron said.

'Carl?'

'Yes, Mr Squires?'

'Did you know anything about this kidnapping?'

'No, Mr Squires.'

'Well, something has to be done,' Squires shouted. 'No one does something like that on my turf. You hear me? No one.'

This guy had seen waaaaaay too many gangster films.

'Whoever did this is dead,' he ranted on. 'Do you hear me? I want them dead. D-E-A-D. Do you understand what I'm saying, Mr Bolitar?'

'Dead,' Myron said with a nod.

The shadow pointed a long finger at Myron. 'You find him for me. You find who did this and then you call me. You let me handle it. Do you understand, Mr Bolitar?'

'Call you. You handle.'

'Go then. Find the wretched bastard.'

Myron said, 'Sure thing, Mr Squires. Sure thing.' Hey, two can play the Bad Movie Dialogue game. 'But the thing is, I need some help.'

'What sort of help?'

'With your permission, I'd like to speak with your son Matthew. Find out what he knows about all this.'

'What makes you think he knows anything?'

'He's Chad's best friend. He may have heard or seen something. I don't know, Mr Squires, but I'd like to check it out.'

There was a brief silence. Then Squires snapped, 'Do it. Carl will take you back to the school. Matthew will speak freely to you.'

'Thank you, Mr Squires.'

The light went off, bathing them again in thick darkness. Myron felt his way to the car door. The 'recovering' Esperanza managed to do likewise. So did Carl. The three of them got in.

Myron turned around and looked at Carl. Carl shrugged his shoulders and said, 'Guess he forgot to take his medication.'

Chapter 32

'Chad, like, told me he was hooking up with an older babe.'

'Did he tell you her name?' Myron asked.

'Nah, man,' Matthew Squires said. 'Just that she was take-out.'

'Take-out?'

'You know. Chinese.'

Jesus.

Myron sat facing Matthew Squires. The kid was pure Yah Dude. His long, stringy hair was parted in the middle and hung past his shoulders. The coloring and texture reminded Myron of Cousin It from the *Addams Family*. He had acne, a fair amount of it. He was over six feet and weighed maybe one hundred twenty pounds. Myron wondered what it had been like for this kid growing up with Mr Spotlight as a father.

Carl was on his right. Esperanza had taken a taxi to

check out Esme Fong's alibi and look into Lloyd Rennart's past.

'Did Chad tell you where he was meeting her?'

'Sure, dude. That hot sheet is, like, my dad's haunt, you know.'

'Did Chad know your father owned the Court Manor?'

'Nah. We don't, like, talk daddy's dinero or anything. Not righteous, you know what I'm saying?'

Myron and Carl exchanged a glance. The glance bemoaned today's youth.

'Did you go with him to the Court Manor?'

'Nah. I went later, you know. I figured the dude would want to party after getting a little, you know. Kinda celebrate and shit.'

'So what time did you go to the Court Manor?'

'Ten thirty, eleven, something like that.'

'Did you see Chad?'

'Nah. Things got, like, so weird right away. Never got the chance.'

'What do you mean, weird?'

Matthew Squires hesitated a bit. Carl leaned forward. 'It's okay, Matthew. Your father wants you to tell him the whole story.'

The kid nodded. When the chin went down, the stringy hair slid across the face. It was like a tasseled curtain opening and closing in rapid succession. 'Okay, like, here's the deal: When I pulled my Benz into the parking lot, I saw Chad's old man.'

Myron felt a queasy surge. 'Jack Coldren? You saw Jack Coldren? At the Court Manor Inn?'

Squires nodded. 'He was just, like, sitting in his car,' he said. 'Next to Chad's Honda. He looked really pissed off, man. I wanted no part of it, you know? So I took a hike.'

297

Myron tried not to look too stunned. Jack Coldren at the Court Manor Inn. His son inside a room screwing Esme Fong. The next morning Chad Coldren would be kidnapped.

What the hell was going on?

'Friday night,' Myron continued, 'I saw someone climb out the window of Chad's room. Was that you?'

'Yeah.'

'You want to tell me what you were doing?'

'Seeing if Chad was home. That's what we do. I climb through his window. Like Vinny used to do with Doogie Howser. Remember that show?'

Myron nodded. He did know. Kinda sad when you thought about it.

There was not much more to extract from young Matthew. When they finished up, Carl walked Myron to his car.

'Strange shit,' Carl said.

'Yep.'

'You'll call when you learn something?'

'Yep.' Myron didn't bother telling him that Tito was already dead. No point. 'Nice move, by the way. The fake punch with Esperanza.'

Carl smiled. 'We're professionals. I'm disappointed you spotted it.'

'If I hadn't seen Esperanza in the ring, I wouldn't have. It was very nice work. You should be proud.'

'Thanks.' Carl stuck out his hand. Myron shook it. He got in the car and drove away. Now where?

Back to the Coldren house, he guessed.

His mind still reeled from this latest revelation: Jack Coldren had been at the Court Manor Inn. He had seen his son's car there. How the heck did that fit into this?

Was Jack Coldren following Chad? Maybe. Was he just there by coincidence? Doubtful. So what other options were there? Why would Jack Coldren be following his own son? And where had he followed him from – Matthew Squires's house? Did that make sense? The man plays in the US Open, has a great opening round, and then goes parking in front of the Squires estate waiting for his kid to pull out?

Nope.

Hold the phone.

Suppose Jack Coldren had not been following his son. Suppose he had been following Esme Fong.

Something in his brain went 'click.'

Maybe Jack Coldren had been having an affair with Esme Fong too. His marriage was on the rocks. Esme Fong was probably a bit of a kinkster. She had seduced a teenage boy – what would have stopped her from seducing his father? But did this make sense either? Was Jack stalking her? Had he somehow found out about the tryst? What?

And the larger question: What does any of this have to do with Chad Coldren's kidnapping and Jack Coldren's murder?

He pulled up to the Coldren house. The media had been kept back, but there were now at least a dozen cops on hand. They were hauling out cardboard boxes. As Victoria Wilson had feared, the police had gotten a search warrant.

Myron parked around the corner and walked toward the house. Jack's caddie, Diane Hoffman, sat alone on the curb across the street. He remembered the last time he had seen her at the Coldren house: in the backyard, fighting with Jack. He also realized that she had been one

of the very few people who knew about the kidnapping –
hadn't she been standing right there when Myron first
talked about it with Jack at the driving range?

She was worth a conversation.

Diane Hoffman was smoking a cigarette. The several
stubs by her feet indicated that she had been there for
more than a few minutes. Myron approached.

'Hi,' he said. 'We met the other day.'

Diane Hoffman looked up at him, took a deep drag of
the cigarette, released it into the still air. 'I remember.'
Her hoarse voice sounded like old tires on rough pavement.

'My condolences,' Myron said. 'You and Jack must
have been very close.'

Another deep drag. 'Yeah.'

'Caddy and golfer. Must be a tight relationship.'

She looked up at him, squinting suspiciously. 'Yeah.'

'Almost like husband and wife. Or business partners.'

'Uh-huh. Something like that.'

'Did you two ever fight?'

She glared at him for a second, then she broke into a
laugh that ended in a hacking cough. When she could talk
again, she asked, 'Why the hell do you want to know
that?'

'Because I saw you two fighting.'

'What?'

'Friday night. You two were in the backyard. You
called him names. You threw down your cigarette in
disgust.'

Diane Hoffman crushed out the cigarette. There was
the smallest smile on her face. 'You some kinda Sherlock
Holmes, Mr Bolitar?'

'No. I'm just asking you a question.'

'And I can tell you to go mind your own fucking business, right?'

'Right.'

'Good. Then you go do that.' The smile became fuller now. It was not a particularly pretty smile. 'But first – to save you some time – I'll tell you who killed Jack. And also who kidnapped the kid, if you like.'

'I'm all ears.'

'The bitch in there.' She pointed to the house behind her with a thumb. 'The one you got the hots for.'

'I don't have the hots for her.'

Diane Hoffman sneered. 'Right.'

'What makes you so sure it was Linda Coldren?'

'Because I know the bitch.'

'That's not much of an answer.'

'Tough luck, cowpoke. Your girlfriend did it. You want to know why Jack and me was fighting? I'll tell you. I told him he was being an asshole for not calling the police about the kidnapping. He said he and Linda thought it best.' She sneered. 'He and Linda, my ass.'

Myron watched her. Something wasn't meshing again.

'You think it was Linda's idea not to call the police?'

'Damn straight. She's the one who grabbed the kid. The whole thing was a big setup.'

'Why would she do that?'

'Ask her.' An awful smile. 'Maybe she'll tell you.'

'I'm asking you.'

She shook her head. 'Not that easy, cowpoke. I told you who did it. That's enough, don't you think?'

Time to approach from another angle. 'How long have you been Jack's caddie?' he asked.

'A year.'

'What's your qualifications, if I may ask? Why did Jack choose you?'

She snorted a chuckle. 'Don't matter none. Jack didn't listen to caddies. Not since ol' Lloyd Rennart.'

'Did you know Lloyd Rennart?'

'Nope.'

'So why did Jack hire you?'

She did not answer.

'Were you two sleeping together?'

Diane Hoffman gave another cough-laugh. A big one. 'Not likely.' More hacking laughter. 'Not likely with ol' Jack.'

Somebody called his name. Myron turned around. It was Victoria Wilson. Her face was still sleepy, but she beckoned him with some urgency. Bucky stood next to her. The old man looked like a window draft would send him skittering.

'Better head on down there, cowpoke,' she mocked. 'I think your girlfriend is gonna need some help.'

He gave her a last look and turned toward the house. Before he moved three steps, Detective Corbett was on him. 'Need a word with you, Mr Bolitar.'

Myron brushed past him. 'In a minute.'

When he reached Victoria Wilson, she made herself very clear: 'Do not talk to the cops,' she said. 'In fact, go to Win's and stay put.'

'I'm not crazy about taking orders,' Myron said.

'Sorry if I'm bruising your male ego,' she said in a tone that made it clear she was anything but. 'But I know what I'm doing.'

'Have the police found the finger?'

Victoria Wilson crossed her arms. 'Yes.'

'And?'

'And nothing.'

Myron looked at Bucky. Bucky looked away. He turned his attention back to Victoria Wilson. 'They didn't ask you about it?'

'They asked. We refused to answer.'

'But the finger could exonerate her.'

Victoria Wilson sighed and turned away. 'Go home, Myron. I'll call you if anything new turns up.'

Chapter 33

It was time to face Win.

Myron rehearsed several possible approaches in the car. None felt right, but that really did not matter much. Win was his friend. When the time came, Myron would deliver the message and Win would adhere to it or not.

The trickier question was, of course, should the message be delivered at all? Myron knew that repression was unhealthy and all that – but did anybody really want to risk unbottling Win's suppressed rage?

The cell phone rang. Myron picked it up. It was Tad Crispin.

'I need your help,' Tad said.

'What's up?'

'The media keep hounding me for a comment. I'm not sure what to say.'

'Nothing,' Myron told him. 'Say nothing.'

'Yeah, okay, but it's not that easy. Learner Shelton – he's the Commissioner of the USGA – called me twice. He wants to have a big trophy ceremony tomorrow. Name me US Open champion. I'm not sure what to do.'

Smart kid, Myron thought. He knows that if this is handled poorly, it could seriously wound him. 'Tad?'

'Yes?'

'Are you hiring me?' Business was still business. Agenting was not charity work.

'Yeah, Myron, you're hired.'

'Okay then, listen up. There'll be details to work out first. Percentages, that kinda thing. Most of it is fairly standard.' Kidnapping, limb-severing, murder – nothing stopped the almighty agent from trying to turn a buck. 'In the meantime, say nothing. I'll have a car come by to pick you up in a couple of hours. The driver will call up to your room before he gets there. Go straight to the car and say nothing. No matter what the press yells at you, keep silent. Do not smile or wave. Look grim. A man has just been murdered. The driver will bring you to Win's estate. We'll discuss strategy then.'

'Thanks, Myron.'

'No, Tad, thank you.'

Profiting from a murder. Myron had never felt so much like a real agent in all his life.

The media had set up camp outside Win's estate.

'I've hired extra guards for the evening,' Win explained, empty brandy snifter in hand. 'If anybody approaches the gate, they've been instructed to shoot to kill.'

'I appreciate that.'

Win gave a quick head bow. He poured some Grand Marnier into the snifter. Myron grabbed a Yoo-Hoo from the fridge. The two men sat.

'Jessica called,' Win said.

'Here?'

'Yes.'

'Why didn't she call me on the cellular?'

'She wanted to speak with me,' Win said.

'Oh.' Myron shook his Yoo-Hoo, just like the side of the can said. SHAKE! IT'S GREAT! Life is poetry. 'What about?'

'She was worried about you,' Win said.

'Why?'

'For one thing, Jessica claimed that you left a cryptic message on the answering machine.'

'Did she tell you what I said?'

'No. Just that your voice sounded strained.'

'I told her that I loved her. That I'd always love her.'

Win took a sip and nodded as though that explained everything.

'What?'

'Nothing,' Win said.

'No, tell me. What?'

Win put down the snifter and steepled his fingers. 'Who were you trying to convince?' he asked. 'Her or you?'

'What the hell does that mean?'

Bouncing the fingers now instead of steepling. 'Nothing.'

'You know how much I love Jessica.'

'Indeed I do,' Win said.

'You know what I've gone through to get her back.'

'Indeed I do.'

'I still don't get it,' Myron said. 'That's why Jess called you? Because my voice sounded strained?'

'Not entirely, no. She'd heard about Jack Coldren's

murder. Naturally, she was upset. She asked me to watch your back.'

'What did you tell her?'

'No.'

Silence.

Win lifted the snifter in the air. He swirled around the liquid and inhaled deeply. 'So what did you wish to discuss with me?'

'I met your mother today.'

Win took a slow sip. He let the liquid roll over his tongue, his eyes studying the bottom of the glass. After he swallowed, he said, 'Pretend I just gasped in surprise.'

'She wanted me to give you a message.'

A small smile came to Win's lips. 'I assume that dear ma-ma told you what happened.'

'Yes.'

A bigger smile now. 'So now you know it all, eh, Myron?'

'No.'

'Oh come, come, don't make it so easy. Give me some of that pop psychology you're so fond of expounding. An eight-year-old boy witnessing his grunting mother on all fours with another man – surely that scarred me emotionally. Can we not trace back everything I've become to that one dastardly moment? Isn't this episode the reason why I treat women the way I do, why I build an emotional fortress around myself, why I choose fists where others choose words? Come now, Myron. You must have considered all this. Tell me all. I am sure it will all be oh-so-insightful.'

Myron waited a beat. 'I'm not here to analyze you, Win.'

'No?'

'No.'

Win's eyes hardened. 'Then wipe that pity off your face.'

'It's not pity,' Myron said. 'It's concern.'

'Oh please.'

'It may have happened twenty-five years ago, but it had to hurt. Maybe it didn't shape you. Maybe you would have ended up the exact same person you are today. But that doesn't mean it didn't hurt.'

Win relaxed his jaw. He picked up the snifter. It was empty. He poured himself more. 'I no longer wish to discuss this,' he said. 'You know now why I want nothing to do with Jack Coldren or my mother. Let us move on.'

'There's still the matter of her message.'

'Ah, yes, the message,' Win repeated. 'You are aware, are you not, that dear ma-ma still sends me presents on my birthday and assorted holidays?'

Myron nodded. They had never discussed it. But he knew.

'I return them unopened,' Win said. He took another sip. 'I think I will do the same with this message.'

'She's dying, Win. Cancer. She has maybe a week or two.'

'I know.'

Myron sat back. His throat felt dry.

'Is that the entire message?'

'She wanted you to know that it's your last chance to talk to her,' Myron said.

'Well, yes, that's true. It would be very difficult for us to chat after she's dead.'

Myron was flailing now. 'She's not expecting any kind of big reconciliation. But if there are any issues you want to resolve . . .' Myron stopped. He was being redundant and obvious now. Win hated that.

'That's it?' Win asked. 'That's your big message?'

Myron nodded.

'Fine, then. I'm going to order some Chinese. I hope that will be suitable with you.'

Win rose from his seat and strolled toward the kitchen.

'You claim it didn't change you,' Myron said. 'But before that day, did you love her?'

Win's face was a stone. 'Who says I don't love her now?'

Chapter 34

The driver brought Tad Crispin in through the back entrance.

Win and Myron had been watching television. A commercial came on for Scope. A married couple in bed woke up and turned their heads in disgust. Morning breath, the voice-over informed them. You need Scope. Scope cures morning breath.

Myron said, 'So would, say, brushing your teeth?'

Win nodded.

Myron opened the door and led Tad into the living room. Tad sat on a couch across from Myron and Win. He glanced about, his eyes searching for a spot to settle on but not having any luck. He smiled weakly.

'Would you care for a beverage?' Win asked. 'A croissant or a Pop Tart perhaps?' The Host with the Most.

'No, thank you.' Another weak smile.

Myron leaned forward. 'Tad, tell us about Learner Shelton's call.'

The kid dove right in. 'He said that he wanted to congratulate me on my victory. That the USGA had officially declared me the US Open champion.' For a moment, Tad stopped. His eyes hazed over, the words hitting him anew. Tad Crispin, US Open champion. The stuff of dreams.

'What else did he say?'

Crispin's eyes slowly cleared. 'He's holding a press conference tomorrow afternoon. At Merion. They'll give me the trophy and a check for $360,000.'

Myron did not waste time. 'First of all, we tell the media that you do not consider yourself the US Open champion. If they want to call you that, fine. If the USGA wants to call you that, fine. You, however, believe that the tournament ended in a tie. Death should not rob Jack Coldren of his magnificent accomplishment or his claim to the title. A tie it ended. A tie it is. From your vantage point, you two are co-winners. Do you understand?'

Tad was hesitant. 'I think so.'

'Now, about that check.' Myron strummed the end table with his fingers. 'If they insist on giving you the full winner's purse, you'll have to donate Jack's portion to charity.'

'Victims' rights,' Win said.

Myron nodded. 'That would be good. Something against violence—'

'Wait a second,' Tad interrupted. He rubbed the palms of his hands on his thighs. 'You want me to give away $180,000?'

'It'll be a tax write-off,' Win said. 'That knocks the value down to half that.'

'And it'll be chicken feed compared to the positive press you'll get,' Myron added.

'But I was charging back,' Tad insisted. 'I had the momentum. I would have won.'

Myron leaned in a little closer. 'You're an athlete, Tad. You're competitive and confident. That's good – heck, that's great. But not in this situation. This murder story is huge. It transcends sports. For most of the world's population, this will be their first look at Tad Crispin. We want them to see someone likable. Someone decent and trustworthy and modest. If we brag now about what a great golfer you are – if we dwell on your comeback rather than this tragedy – people are going to see you as cold, as another example of what's wrong with today's athletes. Do you see what I'm saying?'

Tad nodded. 'I guess so.'

'We have to present you in a certain light. We have to control the story as much as possible.'

'So we do interviews?' Tad asked.

'Very few.'

'But if we want publicity—'

'We want carefully orchestrated publicity,' Myron corrected. 'This story is so big, the last thing we need to do is create more interest. I want you to be reclusive, Tad. Thoughtful. You see, we have to maintain the right balance. If we toot our horn, it looks like we're grandstanding. If we do a lot of interviews, it looks like we're taking advantage of a man's murder.'

'Disastrous,' Win added.

'Right. What we want to do is control the flow of information. Feed the press a few tiny morsels. No more.'

'Perhaps one interview,' Win said. 'One where you will be at your most contrite.'

'With Bob Costas maybe.'

'Or even Barbara Walters.'

'And we don't announce your big donation.'

'Correct, no press conference. You are far too magnanimous for such bravado.'

That confused Tad. 'How are we supposed to get good press if we don't announce it?'

'We leak it,' Myron said. 'We get someone at the charity to tell a nosy reporter, maybe. Something like that. The key is, Tad Crispin must remain far too modest a fellow to publicize his own good deeds. Do you see what we're aiming for here?'

Tad's nod was more enthusiastic now. He was warming up. Myron felt like a heel. Spin-doctoring – just another hat today's sports representative must wear. Being an agent was not always pretty. You had to get dirty sometimes. Myron did not necessarily like it, but he was willing. The media would portray events one way; he would present them another. Still he felt like a grinning political strategist after a debate, and you cannot get much lower than that.

They discussed details for a few more minutes. Tad started to look off again. He was rubbing the famed palms against the pants again. When Win left the room for a minute, Tad whispered, 'I saw on the news that you're Linda Coldren's attorney.'

'I'm one of them.'

'Are you her agent?'

'I might be,' Myron said. 'Why?'

'Then you're a lawyer too, right? You went to law school and everything?'

Myron was not sure he liked where this was going. 'Yes.'

'So I can hire you to be my lawyer too, right? Not just my agent?'

Myron really didn't like where this was going. 'Why would you need a lawyer, Tad?'

'I'm not saying I do. But if I did—'

'Whatever you tell me is confidential,' Myron said.

Tad Crispin stood. He put his arms out straight and gripped an imaginary golf club. He took a swing. Air golf. Win played it all the time. All golfers do. Basketball players don't do that. It's not like Myron stops at every store window and checks the reflection of his shot in the mirror.

Golfers.

'I'm surprised you don't know about this already,' Tad said slowly.

But the creeping feeling in the pit of Myron's stomach told him that maybe he did. 'Don't know about what, Tad?'

Tad took another swing. He stopped his movement to check his backswing. Then his expression changed to one of panic. He dropped the imaginary club to the floor. 'It was only a couple of times,' he said, his words pouring out like silver beads. 'It was no big deal really. I mean, we met while we were filming those ads for Zoom.' He looked at Myron, his eyes pleading. 'You've seen her, Myron. I mean, I know she's twenty years older than me, but she's so good-looking and she said her marriage was dead . . .'

Myron did not hear the rest of his words; the ocean was crashing in his ears. Tad Crispin and Linda Coldren. He could not believe it, yet it made perfect sense. A young guy obviously charmed by a stunning older woman. The mature beauty trapped in a loveless marriage finding escape in young, handsome arms. Nothing really wrong with it.

Yet Myron felt his cheeks go scarlet. Something inside of him began to fume.

Tad was still droning on. Myron interrupted him.

'Did Jack find out?'

Tad stopped. 'I don't know,' he said. 'But I think maybe he did.'

'What makes you say that?'

'It was just the way he acted. We played two rounds together. I know we were competitors and that he was trying to intimidate me. But I kind of got the impression he knew.'

Myron lowered his head into his hands. He felt sick to his stomach.

Tad asked, 'Do you think it'll get out?'

Myron held back a chuckle. This would be one of the biggest news stories of the year. The media would attack like old women at a Loehmann's clearance sale. 'I don't know, Tad.'

'What do we do?'

'We hope it doesn't get out.'

Tad was scared. 'And if it does?'

Myron faced him. Tad Crispin looked so damn young – check that, he was young. Most kids his age are happily pulling fraternity pranks. And when you thought about it, what had Tad really done that was so bad? Slept with an older woman who for some odd reason remained in a dead marriage. Hardly unnatural. Myron tried to picture himself at Tad's age. If a beautiful older woman like Linda Coldren had come on to him, would he have stood a chance?

Like, duh. He probably did not stand a chance now.

But what about Linda Coldren? Why did she stay in this dead marriage? Religion? Doubtful. For the sake of her son? The kid was sixteen years old. It might not be easy, but he'd survive.

'Myron, what'll happen if the media find out?'

But Myron was suddenly no longer thinking about the media. He was thinking about the police. He was thinking about Victoria Wilson and reasonable doubt. Linda Coldren had probably told her ace attorney about her affair with Tad Crispin. Victoria would have seen it too.

Who is declared US Open champion now that Jack Coldren is dead?

Who doesn't have to worry about out-choking the choker in front of a massive audience?

Who has all the same motives to kill Jack Coldren that Myron had earlier assigned to Esme Fong?

Whose squeaky-clean image might get soiled by a Coldren divorce, especially one where Jack Coldren would name his wife's indiscretion?

Who was having an affair with the deceased's wife?

The answer to all the above was sitting in front of him.

Chapter 35

Tad Crispin left not long after that.

Myron and Win settled into the couch. They put on Woody Allen's *Broadway Danny Rose*, one of Woody's most underrated masterpieces. What a flick. Rent it sometime.

During the scene where Mia drags Woody to the fortune-teller, Esperanza arrived.

She coughed into her fist. 'I, ahem, don't want to sound didactic or fictitious in any manner,' she began, doing a great Woody impression. She had his timing, the speech delay tactics. She had the hand mannerisms. She had the New York accent. It was her best work. 'But I may have some important information.'

Myron looked up. Win kept his eyes on the screen.

'I located the man Lloyd Rennart bought the bar from twenty years ago,' Esperanza said, returning to her own voice. 'Rennart paid him in cash. Seven grand. I also checked on the house in Spring Lake Heights. Bought at the same time for $21,000. No mortgage.'

'Lots of expenses,' Myron said, 'for a washed-up caddie.'

'Sí, señor. And to make matters more interesting, I also found no indication that he worked or paid taxes from the time he was fired by Jack Coldren until he purchased the Rusty Nail bar.'

'Could be an inheritance.'

'I would doubt it,' Esperanza said. 'I managed to go back to 1971 and found no record of him paying any inheritance tax.'

Myron looked at Win. 'What do you think?'

Win's eyes were still on the screen. 'I'm not listening.'

'Right, I forgot.' He looked back at Esperanza. 'Anything else?'

'Esme Fong's alibi checks out. I spoke to Miguel. She never left the hotel.'

'Is he solid?'

'Yeah, I think so.'

Strike one. 'Anything else?'

'Not yet. But I found the office for the local paper in Narberth. They have the back editions in a storage room. I'll go through them tomorrow, see what I can dig up on the car accident.'

Esperanza grabbed a take-out container and a pair of chopsticks from the kitchen and then she plopped down on the open couch. A mafioso hit man was calling Woody a cheesehead. Woody commented that he had no idea what that meant, but he was confident it wasn't a good thing. Ah, the Woodman.

Ten minutes into *Love and Death*, not long after Woody wondered how old Nahampkin could be younger than young Nahampkin, exhaustion overtook Myron. He fell asleep on the couch. A deep sleep. No dreams. No stirring. Nothing but the long fall down the deep well.

He woke up at eight-thirty. The television was off. A clock ticked and then chimed. Someone had laid a comforter over Myron while he'd been sleeping. Win probably. He checked the other bedrooms. Win and Esperanza were both gone.

He showered and dressed and put on some coffee. The phone rang. Myron picked it up and said, 'Hello.'

It was Victoria Wilson. She still sounded bored. 'They arrested Linda.'

Myron found Victoria Wilson in an attorney waiting area.

'How is she?'

'Fine,' Victoria replied. 'I brought Chad home last night. That made her happy.'

'So where is Linda?'

'In a holding cell awaiting arraignment. We'll see her in a few minutes.'

'What do they have?'

'Quite a bit, actually,' Victoria said. She sounded almost impressed. 'First, they have the guard who saw her entering and leaving an otherwise abandoned golf course at the time of the murder. With the exception of Jack, nobody else was seen going in or out all night.'

'Doesn't mean nobody did. It's an awfully big area.'

'Very true. But from their standpoint it gives Linda opportunity. Second, they found hairs and fibers on Jack's body and around the murder scene that preliminary tests link to Linda. Naturally, this one should be no problem to discredit. Jack is her husband; of course he'd have hair and fibers from her on his body. He could have spread them around the scene.'

'Plus she told us she went to the course to look for Jack,' Myron added.

'But we're not telling them that.'

'Why not?'

'Because right now we are saying and admitting to nothing.'

Myron shrugged. Not important. 'What else?'

'Jack owned a twenty-two-caliber handgun. The police found it in a wooded area between the Coldren residence and Merion last night.'

'It was just sitting out?'

'No. It was buried in fresh dirt. A metal detector picked it up.'

'They're sure it's Jack's gun?'

She nodded. 'The serial numbers match. The police ran an immediate ballistics test. It's the murder weapon.'

Myron's veins iced up.

'Fingerprints?' he asked.

Victoria Wilson shook her head. 'Wiped clean.'

'Are they running a powder test on her?' The police run a test on the hands, see if there are any powder burns.

'It'll take a few days,' Victoria said, 'and it'll probably be negative.'

'You had her scrub her hands?'

'And treat them, yes.'

'Then you think she did it.'

Her tone remained unruffled. 'Please don't say that.'

She was right. But it was starting to look bad. 'Is there more?' he asked.

'The police found your tape machine still hooked up to

320

the phone. They were obviously curious as to why the Coldrens found it necessary to tape all incoming calls.'

'Did they find any tapes of the conversations with the kidnapper?'

'Just the one where the kidnapper refers to the Fong woman as a "chink bitch" and demands one hundred grand. And to answer your next two questions, no, we did not elaborate on the kidnapping and yes, they are pissed off.'

Myron pondered that for a moment. Something was not right. 'That was the only tape they found?'

'That's it.'

He frowned. 'But if the machine was still hooked up, it should have taped the last call the kidnapper made to Jack. The one that got him to storm out of the house and head to Merion.'

Victoria Wilson looked at him steadily. 'The police found no other tapes. Not in the house. Not on Jack's body. Nowhere.'

Again the ice in the veins. The implication was obvious: The most reasonable explanation for there being no tape was that there was no call. Linda Coldren had made it up. The lack of a tape would have been viewed as a major contradiction *if* she had said anything to the cops. Fortunately for Linda, Victoria Wilson had never let her tell her story in the first place.

The woman was good.

'Can you get me a copy of the tape the police found?' he asked.

Victoria Wilson nodded. 'There is still more,' she said.

Myron was almost afraid to hear it.

'Let's take the severed finger for a moment,' she

continued as though ordering it as an appetizer. 'You found it in Linda's car in a manila envelope.'

Myron nodded.

'The envelope is the type sold only at Staples – their brand, the number ten size. The writing was done by a red Flair pen, medium-point. Three weeks ago, Linda Coldren visited Staples. According to the receipt found at her house yesterday, she purchased numerous office supplies, including a box of Staples' number ten manila envelopes and a red Flair medium-point pen.'

Myron could not believe what he was hearing.

'On the positive side, their handwriting analyst could not tell if the writing on the envelope came from Linda.'

But something else was dawning on Myron. Linda had waited around for him at Merion. The two of them had gone to the car together. They had found the finger together. The district attorney would pounce upon that story. Why had she waited for Myron? The answer, the DA would claim, was obvious: she needed a witness. She had planted the finger in her own car – she could certainly do that without drawing suspicion – and she needed a hapless dupe to be with her when she found it.

Enter Myron Bolitar, the dupe du jour.

But of course, Victoria Wilson had neatly arranged it so that the DA would never hear that story. Myron was Linda's attorney. He could not tell. No one would ever know.

Yep, the woman was good – except for one thing.

'The severed finger,' Myron said. 'That has to be the kicker, Victoria. Who is going to believe that a mother would cut off her own son's finger?'

Victoria looked at her watch. 'Let's go talk to Linda.'

'No, hold up here. That's the second time you blew this off. What aren't you telling me?'

She slung her purse over her shoulder. 'Come on.'

'Hey, I'm getting a little tired of getting jerked around here.'

Victoria Wilson nodded slowly, but she did not speak or stop walking. Myron followed her into a holding room. Linda Coldren was already there. She was decked out in a bright orange prison jumpsuit. Her hands were still manacled. She looked up at Myron through hollow eyes. There were no hellos or hugs or even pleasantries.

Without preamble, Victoria said, 'Myron wants to know why I don't think the severed finger helps us.'

Linda faced him. There was a sad smile on her face. 'I guess that's understandable.'

'What the hell is going on here?' Myron said. 'I know you didn't cut off your own son's finger.'

The sad smile remained. 'I didn't do it,' Linda said. 'That part is true.'

'What do you mean, that part?'

'You said I didn't cut off my son's finger,' she continued. 'But Chad is not my son.'

Chapter 36

Something in Myron's head clicked again.

'I'm infertile,' Linda explained. She said the words with great ease, but the pain in her eyes was so raw and naked that Myron almost flinched. 'I have this condition where my ovaries cannot produce eggs. But Jack still wanted a biological child.'

Myron spoke softly. 'You hired a surrogate?'

Linda looked toward Victoria. 'Yes,' she said. 'Though it was not quite so aboveboard.'

'It was all done to the letter of the law,' Victoria interjected.

'You handled it for them?' Myron asked.

'I did the paperwork, yes. The adoption was completely legal.'

'We wanted to keep it a secret,' Linda said. 'That's why I took off from the tour so early. I went into seclusion. The birth mother was never even supposed to know who we were.'

Something else in his head went click. 'But she found out.'

'Yes.'

Another click. 'It's Diane Hoffman, isn't it?'

Linda was too exhausted to look surprised. 'How did you know?'

'Just an educated guess.' Why else would Jack hire Diane Hoffman as his caddie? Why else would she have gotten upset at the way they were handling the kidnapping? 'How did she find you?'

Victoria answered that one. 'As I said, it was all done legally. With all the new disclosure laws, it wasn't that hard to do.'

Another click. 'That's why you couldn't divorce Jack. He was the biological parent. He'd have the upper hand in a custody battle.'

Linda slumped her shoulders and nodded.

'Does Chad know about all this?'

'No,' Linda said.

'At least, not to your knowledge,' Myron said.

'What?'

'You don't know for sure. Maybe he found out. Maybe Jack told him. Or Diane. Maybe that's how this whole thing got started.'

Victoria crossed her arms. 'I don't see it, Myron. Suppose Chad did find out. How would that have led to his own kidnapping and his father's murder?'

Myron shook his head. It was a good question. 'I don't know yet. I need time to think it through. Do the police know all this?'

'About the adoption? Yes.'

It was beginning to make sense now. 'This gives the DA

their motive. They'll say that Jack's suing for divorce worried Linda. That she killed him to keep her son.'

Victoria Wilson nodded. 'And the fact that Linda is not the biological mother could play one of two ways: either she loved her son so much that she killed Jack to keep him – or because Chad was not her own flesh and blood, she could indeed be driven to cut off his finger.'

'Either way, finding the finger doesn't help us.'

Victoria nodded. She did not say 'I told you so,' but she might as well have.

'Can I say something?' It was Linda. They turned and looked at her.

'I didn't love Jack anymore. I told you that straight out, Myron. I doubt I would have, if I'd been planning on killing him.'

Myron nodded. Made sense.

'But I do love my son – *my* son – more than life itself. The fact that it's more believable that I'd maim him because I'm an adoptive mother rather than a biological one is sick and grotesque in the extreme. I love Chad as much as any mother could love a child.'

She stopped, her chest heaving. 'I want you both to know that.'

'We know,' Victoria said. Then: 'Let's all sit down.'

When they were settled in their seats, Victoria continued to take charge. 'I know it's early, but I want to start thinking about reasonable doubt. Their case will have holes. I'll be sure to exploit them. But I'd like to hear some alternative theories on what happened.'

'In other words,' Myron said, 'some other suspects.'

Victoria caught something in his tone. 'That's exactly what I mean.'

'Well, you already have one ace in the hole, don't you?'

Victoria nodded coolly. 'I do.'

'Tad Crispin, right?'

This time, Linda did indeed look surprised. Victoria remained unfazed. 'Yes, he's a suspect.'

'The kid hired me last night,' Myron said. 'Talking about him would be a conflict of interest.'

'Then we won't talk about him.'

'I'm not sure that's good enough.'

'Then you'll have to dump him as a client,' Victoria said. 'Linda hired you first. Your obligation must be to her. If you feel that there is a conflict, then you'll have to call Mr Crispin and tell him that you cannot represent him.'

Trapped. And she knew it.

'Let's talk about other suspects,' Myron said.

Victoria nodded. Battle won. 'Go ahead.'

'First off, Esme Fong.' Myron filled them in on all the reasons that she made a good suspect. Again Victoria looked sleepy; Linda looked semi-homicidal.

'She seduced my son?' Linda shouted. 'The bitch came into my house and seduced my son?'

'Apparently so.'

'I can't believe it. That's why Chad was at that sleazy motel?'

'Yup—'

'Okay,' Victoria interrupted. 'I like it. This Esme Fong has motive. She has means. She was one of the few people who knew where Chad was.'

'She also has an alibi for the killing,' Myron added.

'But not a great one. There must be other ways in and out of that hotel. She could have worn a disguise. She could have sneaked out when Miguel took a bathroom break. I like her. Who else?'

'Lloyd Rennart.'

'Who?'

'Jack's former caddie,' Myron explained. 'The one who helped throw the Open.'

Victoria frowned. 'Why him?'

'Look at the timing. Jack returns to the site of his greatest failure and suddenly all this happens. It can't be a coincidence. Firing Rennart ruined his life. He became a drunk. He killed his own wife in a car crash.'

'What?' It was Linda.

'Not long after the Open, Lloyd totaled his car while DWI. His wife was killed.'

Victoria asked, 'Did you know her?'

Linda shook her head. 'We never met his family. In fact, I don't think I ever saw Lloyd outside of our home or the golf course.'

Victoria crossed her arms and leaned back. 'I still do not see what makes him a viable suspect.'

'Rennart wanted vengeance. He waited twenty-three years to get it.'

Victoria frowned again.

'I admit that it's a bit of a stretch.'

'A bit? It's ridiculous. Do you know where Lloyd Rennart is now?'

'That's a little complicated.'

'Oh?'

'He may have committed suicide.'

Victoria looked at Linda, then at Myron. 'Would you please elaborate?'

'The body was never found,' Myron said. 'But everyone thinks he jumped off a cliff in Peru.'

Linda groaned. 'Oh, no . . .'

'What is it?' Victoria asked.

'We got a postcard from Peru.'

'Who did?'

'It was addressed to Jack, but it was unsigned. It arrived last fall or winter.'

Myron's pulse raced. Last fall or winter. About the time Lloyd allegedly jumped. 'What did it say?'

'It only had two words on it,' Linda said. ' "Forgive me." '

Silence.

Victoria broke it. 'That doesn't sound like the words of a man out for revenge.'

'No,' Myron agreed. He remembered what Esperanza had learned about the money Rennart had used to buy his house and bar. This postcard now confirmed what he had already suspected: Jack had been sabotaged. 'But it also means that what happened twenty-three years ago was no accident.'

'So what good does that do us?' Victoria asked.

'Someone paid Rennart off to throw the US Open. Whoever did that would have motive.'

'To kill Rennart maybe,' Victoria countered. 'But not Jack.'

Good point. Or was it? Somebody had hated Jack enough twenty-three years ago to destroy his chances of winning the Open. Maybe that hatred had not died. Or maybe Jack had learned the truth and thus had to be quieted. Either way, it was worth looking into.

'I do not want to go digging into the past,' Victoria said. 'It could make things very messy.'

'I thought you liked messy. Messy is fertile land for reasonable doubt.'

'Reasonable doubt, I like,' she said. 'But the unknown, I don't. Look into Esme Fong. Look into the Squires family. Look into whatever. But stay away from the past, Myron. You never know what you might find back there.'

Chapter 37

On the car phone: 'Mrs Rennart? This is Myron Bolitar.'

'Yes, Mr Bolitar.'

'I promised that I'd call you periodically. To keep you updated.'

'Have you learned something new?'

How to proceed? 'Not about your husband. So far, there is no evidence that suggests Lloyd's death was anything other than a suicide.'

'I see.'

Silence.

'So why are you calling me, Mr Bolitar?'

'Have you heard about Jack Coldren's murder?'

'Of course,' Francine Rennart said. 'It's on every station.' Then: 'You don't suspect Lloyd—'

'No,' Myron said quickly. 'But according to Jack's wife, Lloyd sent Jack a postcard from Peru. Right before his death.'

'I see,' she said again. 'What did it say?'

'It had only two words on it: "Forgive me." He didn't sign it.'

There was a brief pause and then she said, 'Lloyd is dead, Mr Bolitar. So is Jack Coldren. Let it lie.'

'I'm not out to damage your husband's reputation. But it is becoming clear that somebody either forced Lloyd to sabotage Jack or paid him to do it.'

'And you want me to help you prove that?'

'Whoever it was may have murdered Jack and maimed his son. Your husband sent Jack a postcard asking for forgiveness. With all due respect, Mrs Rennart, don't you think Lloyd would want you to help?'

More silence.

'What do you want from me, Mr Bolitar? I don't know anything about what happened.'

'I realize that. But do you have any old papers of Lloyd's? Did he keep a journal or a diary? Anything that might give us a clue?'

'He didn't keep a journal or a diary.'

'But there might be something else.' Gently, fair Myron. Tread gently. 'If Lloyd did receive compensation' – a nice way of saying a bribe – 'there may be bank receipts or letters or something.'

'There are boxes in the basement,' she said. 'Old photos, some papers maybe. I don't think there are any bank statements.' Francine Rennart stopped talking for a moment. Myron kept the receiver pushed against his ear. 'Lloyd always did have a lot of cash,' she said softly. 'I never really asked where it came from.'

Myron licked his lips. 'Mrs Rennart, can I look through those boxes?'

'Tonight,' she said. 'You can come by tonight.'

*

332

Esperanza was not back at the cottage yet. But Myron had barely sat down when the intercom buzzed.

'Yes?'

The guard manning the front gate spoke with perfect diction. 'Sir, a gentleman and a young lady are here to see you. They claim that they are not with the media.'

'Did they give a name?'

'The gentleman said his name is Carl.'

'Let them in.'

Myron stepped outside and watched the canary-yellow Audi climb the drive. Carl pulled to a stop and got out. His flat hair looked freshly pressed, like he'd just gotten it 'martinized,' whatever that was. A young black woman who couldn't have been twenty years old came out of the passenger door. She looked around with eyes the size of satellite dishes.

Carl turned to the stables and cupped his big hand over his eyes. A female rider decked out in full gear was steering a horse through some sort of obstacle course.

'That what they call steeplechasing?' Carl asked.

'Got me,' Myron said.

Carl continued to watch. The rider got off the horse. She unstrapped her black hat and patted the horse. Carl said, 'You don't see a lot of brothers dressed like that.'

'What about lawn jockeys?'

Carl laughed. 'Not bad,' he said. 'Not great, but not bad.'

Hard to argue. 'You here to take riding lessons?'

'Not likely,' Carl said. 'This is Kiana. I think she may be of help to us.'

'Us?'

'You and me together, bro.' Carl smiled. 'I get to play your likable black partner.'

Myron shook his head. 'No.'

'Excuse me?'

'The likable black partner always ends up dead. Usually early on, too.'

That stopped Carl a second. 'Damn, I forgot about that.'

Myron shrugged a what-can-you-do. 'So who is she?'

'Kiana works as a maid at the Court Manor Inn.'

Myron looked at her. She was still out of earshot. 'How old is she?'

'Why?'

Myron shrugged. 'Just asking. She looks young.'

'She's sixteen. And guess what, Myron? She's not an unwed mother, she's not on welfare, and she's not a junkie.'

'I never said she was.'

'Uh-huh. Guess none of that racist shit ever seeps into your color-blind cranium.'

'Hey, Carl, do me a favor. Save the racial-sensitivity seminar for a less active day. What does she know?'

Carl beckoned her forward with a tight nod. Kiana approached, all long limbs and big eyes. 'I showed her this photo' – he handed Myron a snapshot of Jack Coldren – 'and she remembered seeing him at the Court Manor.'

Myron glanced at the photograph, and then at Kiana. 'You saw this man at the motel?'

'Yes.' Her voice was firm and strong and belied her years. Sixteen. She was the same age as Chad. Hard to imagine.

'Do you remember when?'

'Last week. I saw him there twice.'

'Twice?'

'Yes.'

'Would that have been Thursday or Friday?'

'No.' Kiana kept up with the poise. No ringing hands or happy feet or darting eyes. 'It was Monday or Tuesday. Wednesday at the latest.'

Myron tried to process this tidbit. Jack had been at the Court Manor twice *before* his son. Why? The reason was fairly obvious: If the marriage was dead for Linda, it was probably dead for Jack. He, too, would be engaging in extramarital liaisons. Maybe that was what Matthew Squires witnessed. Maybe Jack had pulled in for his own affair and spotted his son's car. It kinda made sense . . .

But it was also a hell of a coincidence. Father and son end up at the same hot sheets at the same time? Stranger things have happened, but what were the odds?

Myron gestured to Jack's photograph. 'Was he alone?'

Kiana smiled. 'The Court Manor doesn't rent out a lot of single rooms.'

'Did you see who was with him?'

'Very briefly. The guy in the photograph checked them in. His partner stayed in the car.'

'But you saw her? Briefly anyway.'

Kiana glanced at Carl, then back at Myron. 'It wasn't a her.'

'Excuse me?'

'The guy in the photograph,' she said. 'He wasn't there with a woman.'

A large boulder fell from the sky and landed on Myron's head. It was his turn now to glance at Carl. Carl nodded. Another click. A big click. The loveless marriage. He had known why Linda Coldren stayed in it – she was afraid of losing custody of her son. But what about Jack? Why hadn't he left? The answer was suddenly transparent: Being married to a beautiful, constantly traveling woman was the perfect cover. He remembered Diane Hoffman's reaction when he asked her if she'd been sleeping with Jack – the way she laughed and said, 'Not likely with ol' Jack.'

Because ol' Jack was gay.

Myron turned his focus back to Kiana. 'Could you describe the man he was with?'

'Older – maybe fifty or sixty. White. He had this long dark hair and a bushy beard. That's about all I can tell you.'

But Myron did not need more.

It was starting to come together now. It wasn't there. Not yet anyway. But he was suddenly a quantum leap closer.

Chapter 38

As Carl drove out, Esperanza drove in.

'Find anything?' Myron asked her.

Esperanza handed him a photocopy of an old news-paper clipping. 'Read this.'

The headline read: CRASH FATALITY

Economy of words. He read on:

Mr Lloyd Rennart of 27 Darby Place crashed his automobile into a parked car on South Dean Street near the intersection of Coddington Terrace. Mr Rennart was taken into police custody under suspicion of driving while intoxicated. The injured were rushed to St. Elizabeth's Medical Center, where Lucille Rennart, Mr Lloyd Rennart's wife, was pronounced dead. Funeral services are to be arranged.

Myron reread the paragraph twice. ' "The injured were rushed," ' he read out loud. 'As in more than one.'

Esperanza nodded.

'So who else was hurt?'

'I don't know. There was no follow-up article.'

'Nothing on the arrest or the arraignment or the court case?'

'Nothing. At least, nothing I could find. There was no further mention of any Rennarts. I also tried to get something from St Elizabeth's, but they wouldn't help. Hospital-patient confidentiality, they claimed. I doubt their computers go back to the seventies anyway.'

Myron shook his head. 'This is too weird,' he said.

'I saw Carl heading out,' Esperanza said. 'What did he want?'

'He came by with a maid from the Court Manor. Guess who Jack Coldren was linking up with for a little afternoon delight?'

'Tonya Harding?'

'Close. Norm Zuckerman.'

Esperanza tilted her head back and forth, as though sizing up an abstract work at the Met. 'I'm not surprised. About Norm anyway. Think about it. Never married. No family. In public, he always surrounds himself with young, beautiful women.'

'For show,' Myron said.

'Right. They're beards. Camouflage. Norm is the front man for a major sports fashion business. Being a known gay could destroy him.'

'So,' Myron said, 'if it got out that he was gay . . .'

'It would hurt a lot,' Esperanza said.

'Is that a motive for murder?'

'Sure,' she said. 'It's millions of dollars and a man's reputation. People kill for a lot less.'

Myron thought about it. 'But how did it happen? Let's

say Chad and Jack meet up at the Court Manor by accident. Suppose Chad figures out what Daddy and Norm are up to. Maybe he mentions it to Esme, who works for Norm, Maybe she and Norm . . .'

'They what?' Esperanza finished. 'They kidnap the kid, cut off his finger, and then let him go?'

'Yeah, it doesn't mesh,' Myron agreed, 'Not yet anyway. But we're getting close.'

'Oh sure, we're really narrowing down the field. Let's see. It could be Esme Fong. It could be Norm Zuckerman. It could be Tad Crispin. It could be a still-alive Lloyd Rennart. It could be his wife or his kid. It could be Matthew Squires or his father or both. Or it could be a combination plan of any of the above – the Rennart family perhaps, or Norm and Esme. And it could be Linda Coldren. How does she explain the gun from her house being the murder weapon? Or the envelopes and the pen she bought?'

'I don't know,' Myron said slowly. Then: 'But you may be on to something here.'

'What?'

'Access. Whoever killed Jack and cut off Chad's finger had access to the Coldren house. Barring a break-in, who could have gotten hold of the gun and the stationery supplies?'

Esperanza barely hesitated. 'Linda Coldren, Jack Coldren, maybe the Squires kid, since he liked to crawl in through the window.' She paused. 'I guess that's it.'

'Okay, good. Now let's move on a little. Who knew that Chad Coldren was at the Court Manor Inn? I mean, whoever kidnapped him had to know where he was, right?'

'Right. Okay, Jack again, Esme Fong, Norm Zuckerman, Matthew Squires again. Boy, Myron, this is really helpful.'

'So what names show up on both lists?'

'Jack and Matthew Squires. And I think we can leave Jack's name off – his being the victim and all.'

But Myron stopped for a moment. He thought about his conversation with Win. About the naked desire to win. How far would Jack go to guarantee victory? Win had said that he would stop at nothing. Was he right?

Esperanza snapped her fingers in his face. 'Yo, Myron?'

'What?'

'I said, we can eliminate Jack Coldren. Dead people rarely bury murder weapons in nearby woods.'

That made sense. 'So that leaves Matthew Squires,' Myron said, 'and I don't think he's our boy.'

'Neither do I,' Esperanza said. 'But we're forgetting someone – someone who knew where Chad Coldren was and had complete access to the gun and stationery supplies.'

'Who?'

'Chad Coldren.'

'You think he cut off his own finger?'

Esperanza shrugged. 'What about your old theory? The one where the kidnapping was a hoax that went out of control. Think about it. Maybe he and Tito had a falling-out. Maybe it was Chad who killed Tito.'

Myron considered the possibility. He thought about Jack. He thought about Esme. He thought about Lloyd Rennart. Then he shook his head. 'This is getting us nowhere. Sherlock Holmes warned that you should never theorize without all the facts because then you twist facts to suit theories rather than theories to suit facts.'

'That never stopped us before,' Esperanza said.

'Good point.' Myron checked his watch. 'I gotta go see Francine Rennart.'

'The caddie's wife.'

'Yup.'

Esperanza went sniff, sniff.

'What?' Myron asked.

One more big sniff. 'I smell a complete waste of time,' she said.

She smelled wrong.

Chapter 39

Victoria Wilson called on the car phone. What, Myron wondered, did people do before the car phone, before the cell phone, before the beeper?

Probably had a lot more fun.

'The police found the body of your neo-Nazi friend,' she said. 'His last name is Marshall.'

'Tito Marshall?' Myron frowned. 'Please tell me you're joking.'

'I don't joke, Myron.'

Of that he had little doubt. 'Do the police have any idea he's tied into this?' Myron asked.

'None whatsoever.'

'And I assume he died of a gunshot wound.'

'That's the preliminary finding, yes. Mr Marshall was shot twice in the head at close range with a thirty-eight.'

'A thirty-eight? But Jack was killed with a twenty-two.'

'Yes, Myron, I know.'

'So different guns killed Jack Coldren and Tito Marshall.'

Victoria did the bored thing again. 'Hard to believe you're not a professional ballistics expert.'

Everyone's a smart-ass. But this new development threw a whole bunch of scenarios out of whack. If two different guns had killed Jack Coldren and Tito Marshall, did that mean there were two different killers? Or was the killer smart enough to use different weapons? Or had the killer disposed of the thirty-eight after killing Tito and was thus forced to use the twenty-two on Jack? And what kind of warped mind names a kid Tito Marshall? Bad enough to go through life with a moniker like Myron. But Tito Marshall? No wonder the kid had turned out as a neo-Nazi. Probably started out as a virulent anti-Communist.

Victoria interrupted his thoughts. 'I called for another reason, Myron.'

'Oh?'

'Did you pass on the message to Win?'

'You set that up, didn't you? You told her I'd be there.'

'Please answer the question.'

'Yes, I delivered the message.'

'What did Win say?'

'I delivered the message,' Myron said. 'But that doesn't mean I'm giving out reports on my friend's reaction.'

'She's getting worse, Myron.'

'I'm sorry.'

Silence.

'Where are you right now?' she asked.

'I just hit the New Jersey Turnpike. I'm on my way to Lloyd Rennart's house.'

'I thought I told you to leave that path alone.'

'So you did.'

More silence.

'Good-bye, Myron.'

She hung up. Myron sighed. He suddenly longed for the days before the car phone, the cell phone, the beeper. Reaching out and touching someone was getting to be a real pain in the ass.

An hour later, Myron parked again in front of the Rennarts' modest home. He knocked on the door. Mrs Rennart opened it immediately. She studied his face for a few long seconds. Neither of them spoke. Not even a greeting or salutation.

'You look tired,' she said at last.

'I am.'

'Did Lloyd really send that postcard?'

'Yes.'

The answer had been automatic. But now he wondered – had Lloyd Rennart sent a postcard? For all he knew, Linda was simply sizing him for the title role in *Big Sap: The Musical*. Take the missing taped phone call, for example. If indeed the kidnapper had called Jack before his death, where was the tape of the call? Maybe the call had never occurred. Maybe Linda had lied about it. Maybe she was lying about the postcard too. Maybe she was lying about everything. Maybe Myron was simply being semi-seduced, like the hormone-driven male in one of those cheesy, unrated, direct-to-video, *Body Heat* rip-offs co-starring women with names like Shannon or Tawny.

Not a pleasant thought.

Francine Rennart silently led him into a dark basement. When they hit bottom, she reached up and switched on one of those swinging lightbulbs like something out of

Psycho, The room was pure cement. There was a water heater, a gas heater, a washer and dryer, and storage containers of various sizes, shapes, and material. Four boxes lay on the floor in front of him.

'That's his old stuff,' Francine Rennart said without looking down.

'Thank you.'

She tried, but she could not make herself look at the boxes. 'I'll be upstairs,' she said. Myron watched her feet disappear from view. Then he turned to the boxes and squatted down. The boxes were taped shut. He took out his key-chain penknife and slit the packing tape.

The first box had golf memorabilia. There were certificates and trophies and old tees. A golf ball was mounted to a wooden base with a rusty plaque that read:

HOLE IN ONE – 15TH HOLE AT HICKORY PARK
JANUARY 17, 1972

Myron wondered what life had been like for Lloyd on that clear, crisp golf afternoon. He wondered how often Lloyd had replayed the shot in his mind, how many times he'd sat alone in that BarcaLounger and tried to recapture that pure, cold rush. Had he remembered the feel of the club's grip, the tightness in his shoulders as he began the backswing, the clean, solid stroke of the ball, the floating follow-through.

In the second box, Myron found Lloyd's high school diploma. He found a yearbook from Penn State. There was a picture of the golf team. Lloyd Rennart had been captain. Myron's finger touched upon a large, felt *P*. Lloyd's varsity letter. There was a recommendation letter from his golf coach at Penn State. The words *bright future* jumped out at Myron. Bright future. The coach may have been a great motivator, but he made a lousy soothsayer.

The third box started off with a photograph of Lloyd in Korea. It was a casual group photo, a dozen or so boys/men in unbuttoned fatigues, arms dangling loosely around neighboring necks. Lots of smiles, seemingly happy smiles. Lloyd was thinner there, but he saw nothing gaunt or drawn in the eyes.

Myron put the picture down. In the background, Betty Buckley was not singing 'Memory,' but maybe she should have been. These boxes were a life – a life that in spite of these experiences and dreams and wants and hopes had chosen to terminate itself.

From the bottom of the box Myron pulled out a wedding album. The faded gold leaf read: *Lloyd and Lucille, November 17, 1968, Now and Forever*. More irony. The fake-leather cover was crusted with what looked like drink ringlets. Lloyd's first marriage, neatly wrapped and packed away in the bottom of a box.

Myron was about to put the album to the side when his curiosity got the better of him. He sat all the way down, his legs splayed like a kid with a new pack of baseball cards. He placed the photo album on the cement floor and began to open it. The binding made a cracking noise from the years of disuse.

The first photograph almost made Myron scream out loud.

Chapter 40

Myron's accelerator foot never eased.

Chestnut Street near Fourth is a no-parking zone, but that did not even make Myron pause. He was out of the car before it had come to a complete stop, ignoring the chorus of honking horns. He hurried through the Omni's lobby and into an open elevator. When he got off on the top floor, he found the right room number and knocked hard.

Norm Zuckerman opened the door. '*Bubbe*,' he said with a big smile. 'What a nice surprise.'

'Can I come in?'

'You? Of course, sweetheart, anytime.'

But Myron had already pushed by him. The suite's outer room was – to use hotel brochure lingo – spacious and elegantly appointed. Esme Fong sat on a couch. She looked up at him with the cornered-rabbit face. Posters and blueprints and advertisements and similar para-phernalia carpeted the floor and cascaded off the coffee table. Myron spotted blown-up images of Tad Crispin and Linda Coldren. Zoom logos were everywhere, inescapable, like vengeful ghosts or telemarketers.

'We were just doing a little strategizing,' Norm said. 'But hey, we can always take a break, right, Esme?'

Esme nodded.

Norm made his way behind a wet bar. 'You want something, Myron? I don't think they have any Yoo-Hoo in here, but I'm sure—'

'Nothing,' Myron interrupted.

Norm did the mock surrender thing with his hands. 'Sheesh, Myron, relax,' he said. 'What's twisting your nipple?'

'I wanted to warn you, Norm.'

'Warn me about what?'

'I don't want to do this. As far as I'm concerned, your love life should be personal. But it's not that easy. Not anymore. It's going to get out, Norm. I'm sorry.'

Norm Zuckerman did not move. He opened his mouth as though readying to protest. Then he stopped. 'How did you find out?'

'You were with Jack. At the Court Manor Inn. A maid saw you.'

Norm looked at Esme, who kept her head high. He turned back to Myron. 'Do you know what will happen if words gets out that I'm a *faygeleh*?'

'I can't help that, Norm.'

'I am the company, Myron. Zoom is about fashion and image and sports – which just so happens to be the most blatantly homophobic entity on this planet. Perception is everything in this business. If they find out I'm an old queen, you know what happens? Zoom goes plop down the septic tank.'

'I'm not sure I agree,' Myron said, 'but either way, it can't be helped.'

'Do the police know?' Norm asked.

'No, not yet.'

Norm threw up his hands. 'So why does it have to come out? It was just a fling, for crying out loud. Okay, so I met Jack. So we were attracted to each other. So we both had a ton to lose if either of us opened our traps. No big whup. It's got nothing to do with his murder.'

Myron stole a glance at Esme. She looked back at him with eyes that urged him to keep silent. 'Unfortunately,' Myron said, 'I think it does.'

'You think? You're going to destroy me on an "I think"?'

'I'm sorry.'

'I can't talk you out of it?'

'I'm afraid not.'

Norm moved away from the bar and half-collapsed into a chair. He put his face in the palms of his hands, his fingers sliding toward the back, meeting up in the hair, interweaving. 'I've spent my entire life with lies, Myron,' he began. 'I spent my childhood in Poland pretending I wasn't a Jew. Can you believe that? Me, Norm Zuckerman, pretending I was some slack-jawed *goy*. But I survived. I came here. And then I spent my adult life pretending I was a real man, a Casanova, a guy who always had a beautiful girl on his arm. You get used to lying, Myron. It gets easier, you know what I mean? The lies become a sort of second reality.'

'I'm sorry, Norm.'

He breathed deeply and forced up a tired smile. 'Maybe it's for the best,' Norm said. 'Look at Dennis Rodman.

He cross-dresses, for crying out loud. Hasn't hurt him any, has it?'

'No. It hasn't.'

Norm Zuckerman lifted his eyes toward Myron. 'Hey, once I got to this country, I became the most in-your-face Jew you ever saw. Didn't I? Tell me the truth. Am I not the most in-your-face Jew you've ever met, or what?'

'In my face,' Myron said.

'Bet your skinny *melinka* of a butt I am. And when I first started out, everyone told me to tone it down. Stop being so Jewish, they said. So ethnic. You'll never be accepted.' His face had true hope now. 'Maybe I can do the same for us closet *faygelehs*, Myron. Be in the world's face again, you know what I'm saying?'

'Yes, I do,' Myron said softly. Then he asked, 'Who else knew about you and Jack?'

'Knew?'

'Did you tell anybody?'

'No, of course not.'

Myron gestured toward Esme. 'How about one of those beautiful girlfriends on your arm? How about someone who practically lived with you? Wouldn't it have been easy for her to find out?'

Norm shrugged. 'I suppose so. You get this close to someone, you trust them. You drop your guard. So maybe she knew. So what?'

Myron looked at Esme. 'You want to tell him?'

Esme's voice was cool. 'I don't know what you're talking about.'

'Tell me what?'

Myron kept his eyes on hers. 'I wondered why you'd seduce a sixteen-year-old boy. Don't get me wrong. You gave a bravo performance – all that talk about being lonely and Chad being sweet and disease-free. You waxed quite eloquent. But it still rang hollow.'

Norm said, 'What the hell are you talking about, Myron?'

Myron ignored him. 'And then there was the matter of the bizarre coincidence – you and Chad showing up at the same motel at the same time as Jack and Norm. Too weird. I just couldn't buy it. But of course, we both know that it wasn't a coincidence. You planned it that way, Esme.'

'What plan?' Norm interjected. 'Myron, will you tell me what the hell is going on?'

'Norm, you mentioned that Esme used to work on Nike's basketball campaign. That she quit that job to come to you.'

'So?'

'Did she take a cut in salary?'

'A little.' Norm shrugged. 'Not much.'

'When exactly did she hook up with you?'

'I don't know.'

'Within the past eight months?'

Norm thought a moment. 'Yeah, so?'

'Esme seduced Chad Coldren. She set up a liaison with him at the Court Manor Inn. But she wasn't bringing him there for sex or because she was lonely. She brought him there as part of a setup.'

'What kind of setup?'

'She wanted Chad to see his father with another man.'

'Huh?'

'She wanted to destroy Jack. It was no coincidence. Esme knew your routine. She learned about your affair with Jack. So she tried to set it up so Chad would see what his father was really about.'

Esme remained silent.

'Tell me something, Norm. Were you and Jack supposed to meet Thursday night?'

'Yeah,' Norm said.

'What happened?'

'Jack called it off. He pulled into the lot and got spooked. He said he saw a familiar car.'

'Not just familiar,' Myron said. 'His son's. That's where Esme screwed up. Jack spotted the car. He left before Chad had a chance to see him.'

Myron stood and walked toward Esme. She remained still. 'I almost had it right from the beginning,' he told her. 'Jack took the lead at the Open. His son was there, right in front of you. So you kidnapped Chad to throw Jack's game off. It was just like I thought. Except I missed your real motive. Why would you kidnap Chad? Why would you crave such vengeance against Jack Coldren? Yes, money was part of the motive. Yes, you wanted Zoom's new campaign to succeed. Yes, you knew that if Tad Crispin won the Open, you'd be heralded as the marketing genius of the world. All that played into it. But, of course, that never explained why you brought Chad to the Court Manor Inn in the first place – *before* Jack had the lead.'

Norm sighed. 'So tell us, Myron. What possible reason could she have for wanting to hurt Jack?'

Myron reached into his pocket and pulled out a grainy photograph. The first page of the wedding album. Lloyd and Lucille Rennart. Smiling. Happy. Standing side by side. Lloyd in a tux. Lucille holding a bouquet of flowers. Lucille looking stunning in a long white gown. But that wasn't what had shocked Myron to the core. What shocked him had nothing to do with what Lucille wore or held; rather, it was what she was.

Lucille Rennart was Asian.

'Lloyd Rennart was your father,' Myron said. 'You were in the car that day when he crashed into a tree. Your mother died. You were rushed to the hospital too.'

Esme's back was rod-straight, but her breathing was coming out in hitches.

'I'm not sure what happened next,' he continued. 'My guess would be that your father had hit rock bottom. He was a drunk. He had just killed his own wife. He felt washed-up, useless. So maybe he realized that he couldn't raise you. Or he didn't deserve to raise you. Or maybe an arrangement was reached with your mother's family. In return for not pressing charges, Lloyd would give Lucille's family custody of you. I don't know what happened. But you ended up being raised by your mother's family. By the time Lloyd straightened himself out, he probably felt it would be wrong to tear you out by the roots. Or maybe he was afraid that his daughter wouldn't take back the father who'd been responsible for killing her mother. Whatever, Lloyd kept quiet. He never even told his second wife about you.'

Tears were streaming down Esme's cheeks now. Myron felt like crying too.

'How close am I, Esme?'

'I don't even know what you're talking about.'

'There'll be records,' Myron said. 'Birth certificates, for certain. Probably adoption papers. It won't take the police long to trace.' He held up the photograph, his voice soft.

'The resemblance between you and your mother is almost enough.'

Tears continued to flow, but she was not crying. No sobs. No hitching. No quivering facial muscles. Just tears. 'Maybe Lloyd Rennart was my father,' Esme said. 'But you still have nothing. The rest is pure conjecture.'

'No, Esme. Once the police confirm your parentage, the rest will be easy. Chad will tell them that it was you who suggested you go to the Court Manor Inn. They'll look closely into Tito's death. There'll be a connection there. Fibers. Hairs. It'll all come together. But I have one question for you.'

She remained still.

'Why did you cut off Chad's finger?'

Without warning, Esme broke into a run. Myron was caught off guard. He jumped over the couch to block her path. But he had misjudged her. She had not been heading for an exit; she was going into a bedroom. Her bedroom. Myron hurdled back over the couch. He reached her room, but he was a little late.

Esme Fong had a gun. She pointed it at Myron's chest. He could see in her eyes that there'd be no confession, no explanations, no talk. She was ready to shoot.

'Don't bother,' Myron said.

'What?'

He pulled out his cell phone and handed it to her. 'This is for you.'

Esme did not move for a moment. Then, with her hand still on the gun, she reached out and took the phone. She pressed it against her ear, but Myron could hear just fine.

A voice said, 'This is Detective Alan Corbett from the Philadelphia Police Department. We are standing outside your door listening to every word that has been said. Put down the gun.'

Esme looked back at Myron. She still had the gun aimed at his chest. Myron felt a bead of sweat run down his back. Looking into the barrel of a gun was like staring into the cavern of death. Your eyes saw the barrel, only the barrel, as though it were growing impossibly larger, preparing to swallow you whole.

'It would be dumb,' he said.

She nodded then and lowered the gun. 'And pointless.'

The weapon dropped to the floor. Doors burst open. Police swarmed in.

Myron looked down at the gun. 'A thirty-eight,' he said to Esme. 'That the gun you killed Tito with?'

Her expression gave him the answer. The ballistics tests would be conclusive. She would be prosecutorial toast.

'Tito was a lunatic,' Esme said. 'He chopped off the boy's finger. He started making money demands. You have to believe that.'

Myron gave a noncommittal nod. She was testing out her defense, but it sort of sounded like the truth to Myron.

Corbett snapped handcuffs onto her wrists.

Her words were spilling out fast now. 'Jack Coldren destroyed my entire family. He ruined my father and killed my mother. And for what? My father did nothing wrong.'

'Yes,' Myron said, 'he did.'

'He pulled the wrong club out of a golf bag, if you

believe Jack Coldren. He made a mistake. An accident. Should it have cost him so much?'

Myron said nothing. It was no mistake, no accident. And Myron had no idea what it should have cost.

Chapter 41

The police cleaned up. Corbett had questions, but Myron was not in the mood. He left as soon as the detective was distracted. He sped to the police station where Linda Coldren was about to be released. He took the cement steps three or four at a clip, looking like a spastic Olympian timing the triple jump.

Victoria Wilson almost – the key word being *almost* – smiled at him, 'Linda will be out in a few minutes.'

'Do you have that tape I asked you to get?'

'The phone call between Jack and the kidnapper?'

'Yes.'

'I have it,' she said. 'But why—'

'Please give it to me,' Myron said.

She heard something in his tone. Without argument, she reached into her handbag and pulled it out. Myron took it. 'Do you mind if I drive Linda home?' he said.

Victoria Wilson regarded him. 'I think maybe that would be a good idea.'

A policeman came out. 'She's ready to leave,' he said.

Victoria was about to turn away, when Myron said, 'I guess you were wrong about digging into the past. The past ended up saving our client.'

Victoria held his eye. 'It's like I said before,' she began. 'You never know what you will find.'

They both waited for the other to break the eye contact. Neither did until the door behind them opened.

Linda was back in civilian clothes. She stepped out tentatively, like she'd been in a dark room and wasn't sure her eyes could handle the sudden light. Her face broke into a wide smile when she saw Victoria. They hugged. Linda dug her face into Victoria's shoulder and rocked in her arms. When they released, Linda turned and hugged Myron. Myron closed his eyes and felt his muscles unbunch. He smelted her hair and felt the wondrous skin of her cheek against his neck. They embraced for a long time, almost like a slow dance, neither wanting to let go, both perhaps a little bit afraid.

Victoria coughed into her fist and made her excuses. With the police leading the way, Myron and Linda made it to the car with a minimum of press fuss. They strapped on their seat belts in silence.

'Thank you,' she said.

Myron said nothing. He started the car. For a while neither of them spoke. Myron switched on the air-conditioning.

'We have something here, don't we?'

'I don't know,' Myron said. 'You were worried about your son. Maybe that's all it was.'

Her face said that she was not buying. 'How about you?' Linda asked. 'Did you feel anything?'

'I think so,' he said. 'But part of that might be fear, too.'

'Fear of what?'

'Of Jessica.'

She gave a weary grin. 'Don't tell me you're one of those guys who fears commitment.'

'Just the opposite. I fear how much I love her. I fear how much I want to commit.'

'So what's the problem?'

'Jessica left me once before. I don't want to be exposed like that again.'

Linda nodded. 'So you think that's what it was? Fear of abandonment?'

'I don't know.'

'I felt something,' she said. 'For the first time in a very long time. Don't get me wrong. I've had affairs. Like with Tad. But that's not the same thing.' She looked at him. 'It felt nice.'

Myron said nothing.

'You're not making this very easy,' Linda said.

'We have other things to talk about.'

'Like what?'

'Victoria filled you in on Esme Fong?'

'Yes.'

'If you remember, she had a solid alibi for Jack's murder.'

'A night clerk at a big hotel like the Omni? I doubt that will hold up on scrutiny.'

'Don't be so sure,' Myron said.

'Why do you say that?'

Myron did not answer. He turned right and said, 'You know what always bothered me, Linda?'

'No, what?'

'The ransom calls.'

'What about them?' she asked.

'The first one was made on the morning of the kidnapping. You answered. The kidnappers told you that they had your son. But they made no demands. I always found that odd, didn't you?'

She thought about it. 'I guess so.'

'Now I understand why they did that. But back then, we didn't know what the real motive for the kidnapping was.'

'I don't understand.'

'Esme Fong kidnapped Chad because she wanted revenge on Jack. She wanted to make him lose the tournament. How? Well, I'd thought that she'd kidnapped Chad to fluster Jack. Make him lose his focus. But that was too abstract. She wanted to make sure Jack lost. That was her ransom demand right from the beginning. But you see, the ransom call came in a little late. Jack was already at the course. You answered the phone.'

Linda nodded. 'I think I see what you're saying. She had to reach Jack directly.'

'She or Tito, but you're right. That's why she called Jack at Merion. Remember the second call, the one Jack got after he finished the round?'

'Of course.'

'That was when the ransom demand was made,' Myron said. 'The kidnapper told Jack plain and simple – you start losing or your son dies.'

'Hold up a second,' Linda said. 'Jack said they didn't make any demands. They told him to get some money ready and they'd call back.'

'Jack lied.'

'But . . . ?' She stopped, and then said, 'Why?'

'He didn't want us – or more specifically, you – to know the truth.'

Linda shook her head. 'I don't understand.'

Myron took out the cassette Victoria had given him. 'Maybe this will help explain.' He pushed the tape into the cassette player. There were several seconds of silence and then he heard Jack's voice like something from beyond the grave:

'Hello?'

'Who's the chink bitch?'

'I don't know what—'

'You trying to fuck with me, you dumb son of a bitch? I'll start sending you the fucking brat in little pieces.'

'Please—'

'What's the point of this, Myron?' Linda sounded a little annoyed.

'Just hold on another second. The part I'm interested in is coming up.'

'Her name is Esme Fong. She works for a clothing company. She's just here to set up an endorsement deal with my wife, that's all.'

'Bullshit.'

'It's the truth, I swear.'

'I don't know, Jack. . . .'

'I wouldn't lie to you.'

'Well, Jack, we'll just see about that. This is gonna cost you.'

'What do you mean?'

'One hundred grand. Call it a penalty price.'

'For what?'

Myron hit the STOP button. 'Did you hear that?'

'What?'

' "Call it a penalty price." Clear as day.'

361

'So?'

'It wasn't a ransom demand. It was a penalty.'

'This is a kidnapper, Myron. He's probably not all that caught up in semantics.'

' "One hundred grand," ' Myron repeated. ' "Call it a penalty price." As if a ransom demand had already been made. As if the hundred grand was something he'd just decided to tack on. And what about Jack's reaction? The kidnapper asks for one hundred grand. You would figure he would just tell him fine. But instead he says, "For what?" Again, because it's in addition to what he's already been told. Now listen to this.' Myron pushed the PLAY button.

'Never you fucking mind. You want the kid alive? It's gonna cost you one hundred grand now. That's in—'

'Now hold on a second.'

Myron hit the STOP button again. ' "It's gonna cost you one hundred grand *now*." ' Myron repeated. '*Now*. That's the key word. *Now*. Again as if it's something new. As if before this call there was another price. And then Jack interrupts him. The kidnapper says, "That's in—" when Jack jumps in. Why? Because Jack doesn't want him to finish the thought. He knew that we were listening. "That's in addition." I'd bet anything that was the next word he was about to say. "That's in addition to our original demand." Or, "that's in addition to losing the tournament." '

Linda looked at him. 'But I still don't get it. Why wouldn't Jack just tell us what they wanted?'

'Because Jack had no intention of complying with their demand.'

That stopped her. 'What?'

'He wanted to win too badly. More than that – he

needed to win. Had to. But if you learned the truth – you who had won so often and so easily – you would never understand. This was his chance at redemption, Linda. His chance of going back twenty-three years and making his life worth living. How badly did he want to win, Linda? You tell me. What would he have sacrificed?'

'Not his own son,' Linda countered. 'Yes, Jack needed to win. But not badly enough to forfeit his own son's life.'

'But Jack didn't see it that way. He was looking through his own rose-tinted prism of desire. A man sees what he wants to, Linda. What he has to. When I showed you and Jack the bank videotape, you both saw something different. You didn't want to believe your son could do something so hurtful. So you looked for explanations that would counter that evidence. Jack did just the opposite. He wanted to believe that his son was behind it. That it was only a big hoax. That way he could continue to try his hardest to win. And if by some chance he was wrong – if Chad had indeed been kidnapped – well, the kidnappers were probably bluffing anyway. They'd never really go through with it. In other words, Jack did what he had to do: he rationalized the danger away.'

'You think his desire to win clouded his thinking that much?'

'How much clouding did he need? We all had doubts after watching that bank tape. Even you. So how hard would it be for him to go the extra step?'

Linda sat back. 'Okay,' she said. 'Maybe I buy it. But I still don't see what this has to do with anything.'

'Bear with me a little while longer, okay? Let's go back to when I showed you the bank videotape. We're at your house. I show the tape. Jack storms out. He is upset, of course, but he still plays well enough to keep the big lead.

This angers Esme. He's ignoring her threat. She realizes that she has to up the ante.'

'By cutting off Chad's finger.'

'It was probably Tito, but that's not really relevant right now anyway. The key thing is, the finger is severed, and Esme wants to use it to show Jack she's serious.'

'So she plants it in my car and we find it.'

'No,' Myron said.

'What?'

'Jack finds it first.'

'In my car?'

Myron shook his head. 'Remember that Chad's key chain has Jack's car keys on it as well as yours. Esme wants to warn Jack, not you. So she puts the finger in Jack's car. He finds it. He's shocked, of course, but he's in the lie too deep now. If the truth came out, you'd never forgive him. Chad would never forgive him. And the tournament would be over for him. He has to get rid of the finger. So he puts the finger in an envelope and writes that note. Remember it? "I warned you not to seek help." Don't you see? It's the perfect distraction. It not only draws attention away from him, but it also gets rid of me.'

Linda chewed on her lower lip. 'That would explain the envelope and pen,' she said. 'I bought all the office supplies. Jack would have had some in his briefcase.'

'Exactly. But here is where things get really interesting.'

She arched an eyebrow. 'They're not interesting now?'

'Just hold on. It's Sunday morning. Jack is about to head into the final round with an insurmountable lead. Bigger than he had twenty-three years ago. If he loses now, it would be the greatest golf collapse in history. His name would forever be synonymous with choking – the one thing Jack hated more than anything else. But on the other hand, Jack was not a complete ogre. He loved his son. He knew now that the kidnapping was not a hoax. He was probably torn, not sure what to do. But in the end he made a decision. He was going to lose the tournament.'

Linda said nothing.

'Stroke by stroke, we watched him die. Win understands the destructive side of wanting to win far better than I. He also saw that Jack had the fire back, that old need to win. But despite all that, Jack still tried to lose. He didn't completely collapse. That would have looked too suspicious. But he started dropping strokes. He made it close. And then he purposely fumbled big-time in the stone quarry and lost his lead.

'But imagine what was going on in his head. Jack was fighting against everything that he was. They say a man can't drown himself. Even if it means saving his own child's life, a man cannot keep himself under water until his lungs burst. I'm not so sure that's any different than what Jack was trying to do. He was literally killing himself. His sanity was probably ripping away like divots on the course. On the eighteenth green, the survival instinct took over. Maybe he started rationalizing again – or more likely, he just couldn't help himself. But we both saw the transformation, Linda. We saw his face suddenly crystallize on eighteen. Jack stroked that putt home and tied the score.'

Linda's voice was barely audible. 'Yes,' she said. 'I saw him change.' She sat up in her seat and let loose a long breath. 'Esme Fong must have been in a panic by then.'

'Yes.'

'Jack had left her no choice. She had to kill him.'

Myron shook his head. 'No.'

She looked contused again. 'But it adds up. Esme was desperate. You said so yourself. She wanted vengeance for her father, and on top of that she was now worried about what would happen if Tad Crispin lost. She had to kill him.'

'One problem,' Myron said.

'What?'

'She called your house that night.'

'Right,' Linda said. 'To set up the meeting at the course. She probably told Jack to come alone. To not tell me anything.'

'No,' Myron said. 'That's not what happened.'

'What?'

'If that was what happened,' Myron continued, 'we'd have the call on tape.'

Linda shook her head. 'What are you talking about?'

'Esme Fong did call your house. That part is true. My bet is that she just threatened him some more. Let him know that she meant business. Jack probably begged forgiveness. I don't know. I'll probably never know. But I'd bet he ended the call by promising to lose the next day.'

'So?' Linda said. 'What does that have to do with the call being taped?'

'Jack was going through hell,' Myron went on. 'The pressure was too much. He was probably close to a breakdown. So he ran out of the house – just as you said – and ended up at his favorite place in the world. Merion. The golf course. Did he go out there just to think? I don't know. Did he bring the gun with him, maybe even contemplating suicide? Again, I don't know. But I do know that the tape machine was still hooked up to your phone.

366

The police confirmed that. So where did the tape of that last conversation go?'

Linda's tone was suddenly more measured. 'I don't know.'

'Yes, Linda, you do.'

She gave him a look.

'Jack might have forgotten the call was recorded,' Myron continued. 'But you didn't. When he ran out of the house, you went down to the basement. You played the tape. And you heard everything. What I'm telling you in this car is not new to you. You knew why the kidnappers had taken your child. You knew what Jack had done. You knew where he liked to go when he took his walks. And you knew you had to stop him.'

Myron waited. He missed the turnoff, took the next one, U-turned back onto the highway. He found the right exit and put on his blinker.

'Jack did bring the gun,' Linda said too calmly. 'I didn't even know where he kept it.'

Myron gave a slight nod, silently trying to encourage.

'You're right,' she continued. 'When I played back the tape, I realized that Jack couldn't be trusted. He knew it too. Even with the threat of his own son's death, he had nailed that putt on eighteen. I followed him out to the course. I confronted him. He started to cry. He said he would try to lose. But' – she hesitated, weighed her words – 'that drowning man example you gave. That was Jack.'

Myron tried to swallow, but his throat was too dry.

'Jack wanted to kill himself. And I knew he had to. I'd listened to the tape. I'd heard the threats. And I had no doubts: If Jack won, Chad was dead. I also knew something else.'

She stopped and looked at Myron.

'What?' he said.

'I knew Jack would win. Win was right – the fire was back in Jack's eyes. But it was a raging inferno now. One that even he couldn't control anymore.'

'So you shot him,' Myron said.

'I struggled to get the gun from him. I wanted to injure him. Seriously injure him. If there was the possibility he could play again, I was afraid the kidnapper might just hold on to Chad indefinitely. The voice on the phone sounded that desperate. But Jack wouldn't surrender the gun – nor would he pull it away from me. It was weird. He just held on and looked at me. Almost like he was waiting. So I curled my finger around the trigger and pulled.' Her voice was very clear now. 'It didn't go off accidentally. I had hoped to wound him seriously, not kill him. But I fired. I fired to save my son. And Jack ended up dead.'

More silence.

'Then you headed back to the house,' Myron said. 'You buried the gun. You saw me in the bushes. When you got inside, you erased the tape.'

'Yes.'

'And that was why you released that press announcement so early. The police wanted to keep it quiet, but you needed the story to go public. You wanted the kidnappers to know that Jack was dead, so they'd let Chad go.'

'It was my son or my husband,' Linda said. She turned her body to face him. 'What would you have done?'

'I don't know. But I don't think I would have shot him.'

' "Don't think"?' she repeated with a laugh. 'You talk about Jack being under pressure, but what about me? I hadn't slept. I was stressed and I was confused and I was more scared than I had ever been in my entire life – and yes, I was enraged that Jack had sacrificed our son's chance of playing the game we all so loved. I didn't have the luxury of an I-don't-know, Myron. My son's life was hanging in the balance. I only had time to react.'

They turned up Ardmore Avenue and drove in silence past the Merion Golf Club. They both looked out the window at the course's gently sloping sea of green broken up only by the clean, white faces of sand. It was, Myron had to admit, a magnificent sight.

'Are you going to tell?' she asked.

She already knew the answer. 'I'm your attorney,' Myron said. 'I can't tell.'

'And if you weren't my attorney?'

'It wouldn't matter. Victoria would still be able to offer up enough reasonable doubt to win the case.'

'That's not what I meant.'

'I know,' Myron said. He left it at that. She waited, but no answer was coming.

'I know you don't care,' Linda continued, 'but I meant what I said before. My feelings for you were real.'

Neither of them spoke again. Myron pulled into the driveway. The police kept the media back. Chad was outside, waiting. He smiled at his mother and ran toward her. Linda opened the car door and got out. They might have embraced, but Myron did not see it. He was already backing out the drive.

Chapter 42

Victoria opened the door.

'In the bedroom. Follow me.'

'How is she?' Myron asked.

'She's been sleeping a lot. But I don't think the pain is that bad yet. We have a nurse and a morphine drip ready if she needs it.'

The decor was far simpler and less opulent than Myron had expected. Solid-colored furniture and pillows. Uncluttered white walls. Pine bookcases with artifacts gathered from vacations to Asia and Africa. Victoria had told him that Cissy Lockwood loved to travel.

They stopped in front of a doorway. Myron looked inside. Win's mother lay in bed. Exhaustion emanated from her. Her head was back on the pillow as though it were too heavy to lift. An IV bag was attached to her arm. She looked at Myron and mustered a gentle smile. Myron smiled back. With his peripheral vision, he saw Victoria signal to the nurse. The nurse stood and moved past him. Myron stepped inside. The door closed behind him.

Myron moved closer to the bed. Her breathing was labored and constricted, as though she was being slowly strangled from inside. Myron did not know what to say. He had seen people die before, but those had been quick, violent deaths, the life force snuffed out in one big, powerful gust. This was different. He was actually watching a human being die, her vitality dripping out of her like the liquid in her IV bag, the light in her eyes almost imperceptibly dimming, the grinding whir of tissues and sinews and organs eroding under the onslaught of whatever manic beast had lain claim to her.

She lifted a hand and put it on his. Her grip was surprisingly strong. She was not bony or pale. Her muscles were still toned, her summer tan only slightly faded.

'You know,' she said.

Myron nodded.

She smiled. 'How?'

'A lot of little things,' he said. 'Victoria not wanting me to dig into the past. Jack's mischievous past. Your too-casual comment about how Win was supposed to be playing golf with Jack that day. But mostly it was Win. When I told him about our conversation, he said that I now knew why he wanted nothing to do with you and Jack. You, I could understand. But why Jack?'

Her chest heaved a bit. She closed her eyes for a moment. 'Jack destroyed my life,' she said. 'I realize that he was only a teenager pulling a prank. He apologized profusely. He told me that he had not realized that my husband was on the premises. He said that he was certain I would hear Win coming and hide. It was all a joke, he said. Nothing more. But none of that made him less liable. I lost my son forever because of what he did. He had to face the consequences.'

Myron nodded. 'So you paid off Lloyd Rennart to sabotage Jack at the Open.'

'Yes. It was an inadequate punishment for what he had done to my family, but it was the best I could do.'

The bedroom door opened, and Win stepped into the room. Myron felt the hand release his. A sob came out of Cissy Lockwood. Myron did not hesitate or say good-bye. He turned away and walked out the door.

She died three days later. Win never left her side. When the last pitiful breath was drawn, when the chest mercifully stopped rising and falling and her face froze in a final, bloodless death mask, Win appeared in the corridor.

Myron stood and waited. Win looked at him. His face was serene, untroubled.

'I did not want her to die alone,' he said.

Myron nodded. He tried to stop shaking.

'I am going to take a walk.'

'Is there anything I can do?' Myron asked.

Win stopped. 'Actually,' he said, 'there is.'

'Name it.'

They played thirty-six holes at Merion that day. And thirty-six more the next. And by the third day, Myron was starting to get it.

Don't miss
the breathtaking thriller from
HARLAN COBEN

Available now

in Orion Hardback and eBook

Read on for a preview

www.orionbooks.co.uk

Kat Donovan spun off her father's old stool, readying to leave O'Malley's pub, when Stacy said, "You're not going to like what I did."

The tone made Kat stop mid-stride. "What?"

O'Malley's used to be an old-school cop bar. Kat's grandfather had hung out here. So had her father and their fellow NYPD colleagues. Now it had been turned into a yuppie, preppy, master-of-the-universe, poser ass-hat bar, loaded up with guys who sported crisp white shirts under black suits, two-day stubble, manscaped to the max to look un-manscaped. They smirked a lot, these soft men, their hair moussed to the point of over-coif, and ordered Ketel One instead of Grey Goose because they watched some TV ad telling them that was what real men drink.

Stacy's eyes started darting around the bar. Avoidance. Kat didn't like that.

"What did you do?" Kat asked.

3

"Whoa," Stacy said.

"What?"

"A Punch-Worthy at five o'clock."

Kat swiveled to the right to take a peek.

"See him?" Stacy asked.

"Oh yeah."

Décor-wise, O'Malley's hadn't really changed much over the years. Sure, the old console TVs had been replaced by a host of flat screens showing too wide a variety of games—who cared about how the Edmonton Oilers did?—but outside of that, O'Malley's had kept the cop feel and that was what appealed to these posers, the faux authenticity, moving in and pushing out what made this place hum, turning it into some Disney Epcot version of what it had once been.

Kat was the only cop left in here. The others now went home after their shifts, or to AA meetings. Kat still came and tried to sit quietly on her father's old stool with the ghosts, especially tonight, with her father's murder haunting her anew. She just wanted to be here, to feel her father's presence, to—corny as it sounded—gather strength from it.

But the douchebags wouldn't let her be, would they?

This particular Punch-Worthy—shorthand for any guy deserving a fist to the face—had committed a classic punch-worthy sin. He was wearing sunglasses. At eleven o'clock at night. In a bar with poor lighting. Other punch-worthy indictments included wearing a chain on your wallet, do-rags, unbuttoned silk shirts, an overabundance of tattoos (special category for those sporting tribal symbols), dog tags when you didn't serve in the military, and really big white wristwatches.

4

Sunglasses smirked and lifted his glass toward Kat and Stacy.

"He likes us," Stacy said.

"Stop stalling. What won't I like?"

When Stacy turned back toward her, Kat could see over her shoulder the disappointment on Punch-Worthy's glistening-with-overpriced-lotion face. Kat had seen that look a zillion times before. Men liked Stacy. That was probably something of an understatement. Stacy was frighteningly, knee-knockingly, teeth-and-bone-and-metal-meltingly hot. Men became both weak-legged and stupid around Stacy. Mostly stupid. Really, really stupid.

This was why it was probably a mistake to hang out with someone who looked like Stacy—guys often concluded that they had no shot when a woman looked like that. She seemed unapproachable.

Kat, in comparison, did not.

Sunglasses honed in on Kat and began to make his move. He didn't so much walk toward her as glide on his own slime.

Stacy suppressed a giggle. "This is going to be good."

Hoping to discourage him, Kat gave the guy flat eyes and a disdainful frown. Sunglasses was not deterred. He bebopped over, moving to some sound track that was only playing in his own head.

"Hey, babe," Sunglasses said. "Is your name Wi-Fi?"

Kat waited.

"Because I'm feeling a connection."

Stacy burst out laughing.

Kat just stared at him. He continued.

"I love you small chicks, you know? You're kinda adorable. A spinner, am I right? You know what would look good on me? You."

5

"Do these lines ever work?" Kat asked him.

"I'm not done yet." Sunglasses coughed into his fist, took out his iPhone, and held it up to Kat. "Hey, babe, congrats—you've just moved to the top of my to-do list."

Stacy loved it.

Kat said, "What's your name?"

He arched an eyebrow. "Whatever you want it to be, babe."

"How about Ass Waffle?" Kat opened her blazer, showing the weapon on her belt. "I'm going to reach for my gun now, Ass Waffle."

"Damn, woman, are you my new boss?" He pointed to his crotch. "Because you just gave me a raise."

"Go away."

"My love for you is like diarrhea," Sunglasses said. "I just can't hold it in."

Kat stared at him, horrified.

"Too far?" he said.

"Oh man, that's just gross."

"Yeah, but I bet you never heard it before."

He'd win that bet. "Leave. Now."

"Really?"

Stacy was nearly on the floor with laughter.

Sunglasses started to turn away. "Wait. Is this a test? Is Ass Waffle, like, a compliment or something?"

"Go."

He shrugged, turned, spotted Stacy, figured why not. He looked her long body up and down and said, "The word of the day is legs. Let's go back to your place and spread the word."

Stacy was still loving it. "Take me, Ass Waffle. Right here. Right now."

6

"Really?"

"No."

Ass Waffle looked back at Kat. Kat put her hand on the butt of her gun. He held up his hands and slinked away.

Kat said, "Stacy?"

"Hmm?"

"Why do these guys keep thinking they have a chance with me?"

"Because you look cute and perky."

"I'm not perky."

"No, but you look perky."

"Seriously, do I look like that much of a loser?"

"You look damaged," Stacy said. "I hate to say it. But the damage . . . it comes off you like some kind of pheromone that douche bags can't resist."

They both took a sip of their drinks.

"So what won't I like?" Kat asked.

Stacy looked back toward Ass Waffle. "I feel bad for him now. Maybe I should throw him a quickie."

"Don't start."

"What?" Stacy crossed her show-off long legs and smiled at Ass Waffle. He made a face that reminded Kat of a dog left in a car too long. "Do you think this skirt is too short?"

"Skirt?" Kat said. "I thought it was a belt."

Stacy liked that. She loved the attention. She loved picking up men because she thought that a one-night stand with her was somehow life changing for them. It was also part of her job. Stacy owned a private investigation firm with two other gorgeous women. Their specialty? Catching (really, entrapping) cheating spouses.

"Stacy?"

"Hmm?"

"What won't I like?"

"This."

Still teasing Ass Waffle, Stacy handed Kat a piece of paper. Kat looked at the paper and frowned:

KD8115

HottestSexEvah

"What is this?"

"KD8115 is your user name."

Her initials and badge number.

"HottestSexEvah is your password. Oh, and it's case sensitive."

"And these are for?"

"A website. YouAreJustMyType.com."

"Huh?"

"It's an online dating service."

Kat made a face. "Please tell me you're joking."

"It's upscale."

"That's what they say about strip clubs."

"I bought you a subscription," Stacy said. "It's good for a year."

"You're kidding, right?"

"I don't kid. I do some work for this company. They're good. And let's not fool ourselves. You need someone. You want someone. And you aren't going to find him in here."

Kat sighed, rose, and nodded to the bartender, a guy named Pete who looked like a character actor who always played the Irish bartender—which is what, in fact, he was. Pete nodded back, indicating that he'd put the drinks on Kat's tab.

"Who knows?" Stacy said. "You could end up meeting Mr. Right."

Kat started for the door. "But more likely, Mr. Ass Waffle."

Kat typed in "YouAreJustMyType.com", hit the RETURN button, and filled in her new user name and the rather embarrassing password. She frowned when she saw the moniker at the top of the profile that Stacy had chosen for her:

"Cute and Perky!"

"She left off *damaged*," Kat muttered under her breath.

It was past midnight, but Kat wasn't much of a sleeper. She lived in an area far too upscale for her—West 67th Street off Central Park West, in the Atelier. A hundred years ago, this and its neighboring buildings, including the famed Hotel des Artistes, had housed writers, painters, intellectuals—artists. The spacious old-world apartments faced the street, the smaller artist studios in the back. Eventually the old art studios were converted into one-bedroom apartments. Kat's father, a cop who watched his friends get rich doing nothing but buying real estate, had tried to find his way in. A guy whose life Dad had saved sold him the place on the cheap.

Kat had first used it as an undergrad at Columbia University. She had paid for her Ivy League education with a NYPD scholarship. According to the life plan, she was then supposed to go to law school and join a big white-shoe firm in New York City, finally breaking away from the cursed family legacy of police work.

Alas, it hadn't worked out that way.

A glass of red wine sat next to her keyboard. Kat drank too much. She knew that was a cliché—a cop

9

who drank too much—but sometimes the clichés are there for a reason. She functioned fine. She didn't drink on the job. It didn't really affect her life in any noticeable way, but if Kat made calls or even decisions late at night, they tended to be, er, sloppy ones. She had learned over the years to turn off her mobile phone and stay away from e-mail after ten P.M.

Yet here she was, late at night, checking out random dudes on a dating website.

Stacy had uploaded four photographs to Kat's page. Kat's profile picture, a head shot, had been cropped from a bridesmaid group photo taken at a wedding last year. Kat tried to view herself objectively, but that was impossible. She hated the picture. The woman in the photograph looked unsure of herself, her smile weak, almost as though she was waiting to be slapped or something. Every photograph—now that she went through the painful ritual of viewing them—had been cropped from group pictures, and in every one, Kat looked as though she were half wincing.

Okay, enough of her own profile.

On the job, the only men she met were cops. She didn't want a cop. Cops were good men and horrible husbands. She knew that only too well. When Grandma got terminally ill, her grandfather, unable to handle it, ran off until, well, it was too late. Pops never forgave himself for that. That was Kat's theory, anyway. He was lonely and while he had been a hero to many, Pops chickened out when it counted most and he couldn't live with that and his service revolver was sitting right there, right on the same top shelf in the kitchen where he'd always kept it, and so one night, Kat's grandfather reached up and took his piece down from the shelf and sat by himself at the kitchen table and . . .

Ka-boom.

Dad, too, would go on benders and disappear for days at a time. Mom would be extra cheery when this happened—which made it all the more scary and creepy—either pretending Dad was on an undercover mission or ignoring his disappearance altogether, literally out of sight, out of mind, and then, maybe a week later, Dad would waltz in with a fresh shave and a smile and a dozen roses for Mom, and everyone would act like this was normal.

YouAreJustMyType.com. She, the cute and perky Kat Donovan, was on an internet dating site. Man oh man, talk about the best-laid plans. She lifted the wine glass, made a toasting gesture toward the computer screen, and took too big a gulp.

The world sadly was no longer conducive to meeting a life partner. Sex, sure. That was easy. That was, in fact, the expectation, the elephant in the date room, and while she loved the pleasures of the flesh as much as the next gal, the truth was, when you went to bed with someone too quickly, rightly or wrongly, the chances of a long-term relationship took a major hit. She didn't put a moral judgment on this. It was just the way it was.

Her computer dinged. A message bubble popped up:

We have matches for you! Click here to see someone who might be perfect for you!

Kat finished the glass of wine. She debated pouring another, but really, enough. She took stock of herself and realized an obvious yet unspoken truth: She wanted someone in her life. Have the courage to admit that to yourself, okay? Much as she strove to be independent,

Kat wanted a man, a partner, someone in her bed at night. She didn't pine or force it or even make much of an effort. But she wasn't really built to be alone.

She began to click through the profiles. You got to be in it to win it, right?

Pathetic.

Some men could be eliminated with a quick glance at their profile photograph. It was key, when you thought about it. The profile portrait each man had painstakingly chosen was, in pretty much every way, the first (very controlled) impression. It thus spoke volumes.

So: If you made the conscious choice to wear a fedora, that was an automatic no. If you chose not to wear a shirt, no matter how well built you were, automatic no. If you had a Bluetooth in your ear—gosh, aren't *you* important?—automatic no. If you had a soul patch or sported a vest or winked or made hand gestures or chose a tangerine-hued shirt (personal bias) or balanced your sunglasses on top of your head, automatic no, no, no. If your profile name was ManStallion, SexySmile, RichPrettyBoy, LadySatisfier—you get the gist.

Kate clicked open a few where the guy looked . . . approachable, she guessed. There was a sad, depressing sameness to all the write-ups. Every person on the website enjoyed walks on a beach and dining out and exercising and exotic travel and wine tasting and theater and museums and being active and taking chances and grand adventures—yet they were equally content with staying home and watching a movie, coffee and conversation, cooking, reading a book, the simple pleasures. Every guy claimed that the most important quality they looked for in a woman was a sense of humor—right, sure—to the point where Kat wondered whether "sense of humor" was a euphemism for "big boobs." Of course, every man also listed preferred body type as athletic, slender *and* curvy.

That seemed more accurate, if not downright wishful.

The profiles never reflected reality. Rather than being what you are, they were a wonderful if not futile exercise in what you *think* you are or what you want a potential partner to think you are—or most likely, the profiles (and man, shrinks would have a field day) simply reflect what you want to be.

The personal statements were all over the place, but if she had to use one word to sum them up, it would probably be *treacle*. The first read, "Every morning, life is a blank canvas waiting to be painted"—click. Some aimed for honesty by telling you repeatedly that they were honest. Some faked sincerity. Some were highfalutin or showboating or insecure or needy. Just like real life, when Kat thought about it. Most were simply trying too hard. The stench of desperation came off the screen in squiggly, bad-cologne waves. The constant soulmate talk was, at best, off-putting. In real life, Kat thought, none of us can find someone we want to go out with more than once, yet somehow we believe that on YouAreJustMyType.com we will instantly find a person we want to wake up next to for the rest of our lives.

Delusional—or does hope spring eternal?

That was the flip side. It was easy to be cynical and poke fun, but when she stepped back, Kat realized something that pierced her straight through the heart: Every profile was a life. Simple, yep, but behind every cliché-ridden, please-like-me profile was a fellow human being with dreams and aspirations and desires. These people hadn't signed up, paid their fee, or filled out this information idly. Think about it: Every one of these lonely people came to this website—signed in and clicked on profiles—hoping it would be different this time, hoping against hope that finally they would meet the one person who, in the end, would be the most important person in their lives.

Wow. Just let that realization roll over you for a moment.

Kat had been lost in this thought, clicking through the profiles at a constantly increasing velocity, the faces of these men—men who had come here in the hopes of finding "the one"—blurring into a fleshy mess from the speed, when she spotted his picture.

For a second, maybe two, her brain didn't quite believe what her eyes had seen. It took another second for the finger to stop clicking the mouse button, another for the profile pictures tumbling by to slow down and come to a halt. Kat sat and took a deep breath.

It couldn't be.

She had been surfing at such a rapid pace, thinking about the men behind the photographs, their lives, their wants, their hopes. Her mind—and this was both Kat's strength and weakness as a cop—had been wandering, not necessarily concentrating on what was directly in front of her yet being able to get a sense of the big picture. In law enforcement, it meant that she was able to see the possibilities, the escape routes, the alternate scenarios, the figure lurking behind the obstacles and obfuscations and hindrances and subterfuge.

But that also meant that sometimes Kat missed the obvious.

She slowly started to click the back arrow.

It couldn't be him.